LIKE
A
FLY
ON THE
WALL

SIMONE KELLY

WILLIAM MORROW
An Imprint of HarperCollins*Publishers*

HarperCollins
PUBLISHERS
Since 1817

P.S.™ is a trademark of HarperCollins Publishers.

FIRST EDITION

Designed by Diahann Sturge

Library of Congress Cataloging-in-Publication Data has been applied for.

ISBN 978-0-06-256645-4

17 18 19 20 21   LSC   10 9 8 7 6 5 4 3 2 1

Like a Fly on the Wall is dedicated to my mother, Velma Gordon-Kelly. Although she is now one of heaven's angels, I'm sure she is smiling down at me. She knew writing was my passion and always supported my creativity even as a child. I am so happy that she was alive when I first started developing this book. I read some scenes to her when it was still just a raw idea. She loved the main character, Jacques, but I left out the R-rated scenes. Ha! Mom, please don't read those. I love and miss you so much.

Rest in peace, Mommy.

Also, I would like to dedicate this book to Edna Gordon, my grandma, whom I never had the pleasure to meet, but she lives on in my smile.

LIKE

A

FLY

ON THE

WALL

Prologue

You would think that by now I would know how to choose the perfect one. Holding it in my hands, examining and slowly squeezing it. I wasn't exactly sure what the guidelines were for picking pears. I looked around for a grocery store clerk who could help. The only people in my path were busy moms rushing to get dinner and two college kids with a cart full of frozen pizza and six-packs of beer. That's when I saw her.

Her eyes were what drew me in first—gentle yet intense. Flawless olive skin, full lips, and dark, long hair. Everyone else in the aisle disappeared from my view. All I noticed was her. She wore a mid-length pencil skirt that teased, giving me a sneak preview of her shapely legs. She had only a few items in her cart, along with a briefcase. She tossed her hair over one shoulder as we made eye contact, but to my disappointment she made a sharp turn down the paper and tissue aisle instead of cruising toward me.

I had an inkling she would be headed my way soon, though. So I waited a few minutes while humming along with the Billy Joel song that played softly over the supermarket speakers, still stumped on the pears.

Then there she was. I have never seen a shopping cart pushed so seductively. She forced me to watch her. She pushed the cart slowly, stopping, then turning around to read the ingredients on a bottled salad dressing. Finally, she glanced at me. I caught a slight grin across her face. She continued to play coy and bagged some Red Delicious apples and navel oranges. When she was done, she came closer and tried to pass by me in the aisle, but my cart was inconveniently in the way. Coincidence? I wasn't going to let her get away.

"Excuse me," she said. Her eyes were large and light brown. Her eye makeup was soft and natural. The deep burgundy of her lips lying comfortably on top of her bright smile made her mouth inviting; they matched her wine trench coat perfectly. I smelled the delicate scent of flowers as she came closer.

"I'm sorry," I replied, breaking from hypnosis, moving my cart out of the way. "Oh, excuse me, miss. I'm having trouble picking out pears. I can't remember if they should be soft or firm. Do you mind telling me how I can know if it's ripe?"

Her drawl had a faint Spanish accent. "Oh, they're tricky because pears ripen from the inside out, so you can't tell by just looking at the skin. You move the stem and if it gives way, then you'll know it's ripe." She lifted one to examine it. "Ah, see, this one is good." She smiled, looking directly into my eyes. "Nice and firm, but soft on the inside." She tossed her hair again.

Was this woman flirting? I reached for the pear and purposely touched her hand as she passed it to me. "Thank you. I didn't have a clue."

"A bachelor, huh?" I caught her glance at my cart of tea, beer, veggies, and frozen dinners.

"Yes, is it that obvious?" I chuckled, noticing that her own cart, with the briefcase, was now filled with diapers, milk, beauty products, and baby food.

"A working mother, eh?"

The grating of a rattling shopping cart with a broken wheel shattered our undivided attention. "Sorry, sir, ma'am, sorry. 'Scuse me, y'all." Her Southern accent sounded more like Alabama than Florida, and she dragged her feet. I turned around and saw a sweet, young face with deep chocolate skin framed by huge rhinestone hoop earrings. About seventeen, she wore long, fake eyelashes and what looked to be a shoulder-length wavy weave. She looked like she was desperately trying to be a twenty-five-year-old stripper and not a seventeen-year-old high school student.

"I'm finna bring this broken piece of junk ta da back." She looked back and forth at us and smiled at Burgundy Lips. Intuitively she could sense something was brewing in aisle 10. She shrugged at the awkwardness of it all and kept pushing her cart, while Barry Manilow sang his little heart out to "Can't Smile Without You."

Burgundy Lips cleared her throat. "Well . . ."

"I don't mean to be forward, but you're very attractive," I said, extending my hand. "Mind telling me your name? I'm Robert."

"Ah, thank you, Robert. I'm . . . I'm Jessica." She blushed, shaking my hand. I held on as we spoke.

"Jessica, are you in a rush to go home to your husband?" I nodded, pointing with my eyes toward the diapers in the cart.

Giggling nervously, she said, "My, you are a bit forward." Ah. She knows I'm in the chase. "I'm not married, Robert . . . but I am, well, sort of involved."

"Oh . . . that's too bad for me, huh?" I teased, releasing her hand. Curiously though, she didn't move.

I noticed her intrigued expression and that single-handedly urged me on. "What did you have in mind, Robert? Like I said, I'm not married."

I raised my eyebrows in delight as she continued. "I simply came to pick up some food and fruits. Not a strange man in the supermarket." She winked.

Oh, really now? "I'm strange to you? Must not be that strange, because you are still talking to me." I licked my lips. She began to push her cart slowly past me.

Our faces were close enough to kiss and she said, almost in a whisper, "Meet me outside when you're done, Mr. Bachelor. I'm in the silver Toyota SUV parked in front of the smoothie shop."

The hairs on my arms rose at full attention. "Will do." I watched her walk smoothly away, her stiletto heels making a confident *clickety-clack* down the linoleum aisle. The heat that exuded from her body was intense. She looked back with a mischievous light in her eyes. Blood rushed throughout my entire body, and I was glad my button-down shirt was un-tucked, hiding my excitement.

I put a few more pieces of fruit in my cart and rushed to the checkout. I looked past the cashier to the huge floor-to-ceiling window that was also the length of the store. On my right, the customer service line was long with hopeful Lotto winners and nicotine addicts, all fidgeting while they waited to get their daily fixes of Newports, Virginia Slims, or a win-ning scratch-off roll.

My items seemed to be scanned slowly. It was almost un-bearable. *Beep . . . beep . . . beep . . . beep.* The cashier was the girl with the broken cart. Her name tag read CHARDONAY. I smiled gently, trying not to laugh. I could sense her ner-vousness as she moved her artificial hair behind her ears. She scanned my green tea. *Beep . . .*

"She reeeeal pretty. I like her hair. So, what's up, you get dem digits, playa?" *Beep . . .* She giggled and tried flirt-ing with her three-inch eyelashes. What man finds that at-tractive?

Beep . . . "No, no . . ." I laughed. "I'm working on it though." Chardonay high-fived me between bagging my goods.

"Shoot, if I was a little older I would go for mine right now, mister," Chardonay said, looking directly at me.

"Oh, no, you'd have to be older. And you wouldn't need those," I said, motioning toward her eyes, shaking my head in disapproval.

"Oh, no you didn't!" She laughed. "What's wrong wit dem?"

"Char-don-nay is it?"

"Yes, you said it right, mister."

"You don't need them." I winked at her.

Chardonay lowered her chin and smiled sheepishly. She covered her mouth, trying to hide two bottom gold teeth that I'd already seen.

"Have a good night, sweetie."

"You too, mister, you too." She waved.

The sky had now turned a deep midnight blue and the moon peered from behind fluffy clouds. It was drizzling and we were probably headed for a serious Florida downpour.

Finally outside in the parking lot, I saw Jessica in her SUV. I hurried to my car and put the bags in the trunk. She saw me and drove toward me, rolling down her window.

"Hi, Robert the Bachelor. I couldn't really talk freely in there; my fiancé comes in with me all the time. It just wouldn't look right if I were to take your number. . . ."

"Oh, now he's a fiancé?"

"Well, yeah, I thought you noticed my ring?" She held up her hand and wiggled her finger.

"No, I didn't, and I'm not one to break up a happy home," I said, hoping she was going to allow me to get closer to her, at least for tonight.

"Can you come in and let's talk about it?" she said, beckoning softly.

"Come in?" I was surprised at how aggressive she was. It was both ferocious and gentle, and maddening to my senses. "Don't mind if I do." I tried to remain cool, but the stupid grin on my face had a mind of its own.

I closed my still-open trunk and lightly jogged around the

back of her SUV, escaping the rain, which started to come down like bullets.

Soft jazz played from her speakers and her sweet scent intensified in the close quarters. She smiled. "You are very attractive," she said. "You have such an exotic look. What are you? I mean, where are you from?"

"Morocco. My dad is Moroccan, my mom is European, from France. Thanks for asking though. Most people down here just assume I'm Latino and start speaking to me in Spanish."

"Well, we are in Florida! You could easily pass for a Roberto. I was going to guess Egyptian, with those eyes." Jessica laughed at her own joke and reached over, rubbing her thumb beneath my eye.

"You sure you don't have on eyeliner?"

"Come on, don't start that mess," I said, pushing her hand off playfully.

"I didn't really need anything in your aisle, you know? I just wanted to get a closer view. I saw you from the back in the frozen foods section."

"Really, so you had a plan?" Devilish, I tell you. I think I'm in love.

"I guess you might say that," she replied, opening her coat slowly; to my surprise her plump, creamy breasts made a special appearance. Her pink bra was in the car's cup holder. She must have just taken it off in the car while I was still in line.

"Wow," I whispered with a crooked smile. "You aren't wasting any time, huh?" She took my hands and placed them on her warm body. She was so in charge and she knew she had me. Her nipples were at full attention as I gently caressed her.

"Damn, Viiiickyyy, oh, I mean Jessica."

She snickered. "Vicky? Your girlfriend?"

We both laughed. "No, no, not at all."

I sucked on her neck and she tilted her head backward, inviting me in. I slid my hand between her warm thighs and squeezed her smooth skin. She didn't resist, and I pushed her skirt up. Her pink lace panties were moist from her excitement. Her legs closed unexpectedly. "Rob . . . Robertooo, I have to go home soon. My fiancé is going to be worried."

I ran my fingers through her long hair. "So soon? We were just getting to know each other. You don't really care about your fiancé, do you?" My hand pushed her thighs slightly apart. "If you did, you would have never invited me in." I caressed her panties and traced my finger outside her center. I firmly moved my hand up and down, clouding her decision making.

She squirmed with excitement as she bit her bottom lip. "Can you meet me somewhere tomorrow?" she begged. Words saying one thing, body saying another, she arched her back, aroused from my fingers.

I reached over to the driver's side, bringing her face closer to mine. I sucked on her bottom lip and started kissing her deeply. I savored her. She purred like a spoiled cat. She was definitely no amateur in the art of seduction.

I wanted her and I was going to have her. I moved her panties to the side, exploring what possibilities lay ahead. She grabbed a mound of my hair in her hands. "Ohhh, we gotta, we gotta stop, papi . . . we should . . ."

Leaning closely into her ear I said slowly, "Tell me to stop again. Come on, tell me."

Nothing.

I moved my finger inside her, causing her to moan even louder. "Tell me to stop," I whispered, torturing this time. I smiled at the pleasure I created. Again, nothing.

"Let's park over there," I demanded, looking toward the back of the parking lot. "It's pouring now, no one will see us."

The roar of the rain was peaceful even with the thunder that shuddered through the sky. She drove to the spot, looking at the backseat of the car and then again at me. Without words we scurried out and into the backseat. Cramped, I climbed on top of her as she breathed hard. I felt out of my mind, about to make love with a complete, beautiful stranger from aisle 10 in a BigMart Supermarket.

When our mouths met this time, it felt supernatural, and she tasted of cherry candy. Leaving her coat on, I pulled her panties off. Damn, she looked good like that. I was bursting through my pants by this time, and she fumbled with my belt buckle, trying to release me.

As I eased into her warmth, we sighed.

"Oh, Jessica, you . . . you can't get married now. . . . I want you for me, I want you for me. . . ."

Her nails dug into my thighs as she pushed my pants farther down. We were connected; the sweat, the sounds, made it intense. The streetlights of the parking lot shone in on us as we performed. The rain looked like a light curtain shielding us from the world. I could see her face clearly, see her seductively smiling at me, like she loved me, like she had known me for years. She felt so good, so tight, and so wet.

I couldn't contain my moan. "Ohhhhhh . . . shit!" Her nails dug into my butt, making my release that much better.

We lay there for a few minutes, crunched into the backseat, and enjoyed the moment. I asked no questions. She said nothing. We grinned, knowing we'd see each other again very soon.

I ran my fingers through her hair while her head lay on my chest. "Thank you, Jessica." I kissed her softly, respectfully, on her forehead and zipped my pants. I slowly exited her SUV, and she watched me go without saying a word. I didn't look back.

Damn, that was good.

I felt incredibly alive as I drove down the quiet, dark street. Fifteen minutes later, I pulled into my condo driveway with a smile. I saw the mysterious silver Toyota parked in front. How clever that was.

I opened the door and smelled the Nag Champa incense. Ah, the comforts of home. The wine trench coat was draped across the couch, and familiar shades of jade-green and beige living room walls welcomed me back.

"Jessica, oh, Jessica?" I sang as Vicky came out of the bedroom in pink lace panties. Her dark hair flowed over her naked perky breasts.

She held up the wall with one hand and smiled a sly grin. "Jacques, you dog! I can't let you go to the supermarket alone again. You did that one just a little too well," she said with a girlish chuckle.

I embraced her and we kissed.

"Oh, and Robert? You could use some practice. I mean, really, you picked my brother's name, Jacques! I'm a freak, but not into incest."

I chuckled and started to undress down to my boxers. I removed my silver chain and ring and put them on the glass coffee table.

"It was the first name that came into my head. But I don't think it was disturbing you that much, when you were moaning, 'Aye, Roberto, aye, Roberto!' Where'd you get that Jeep from anyhow? That's what really made it feel more mysterious." I followed her into the bedroom.

"I rented it at the airport."

"And the diapers, how clever!"

She patted herself on the back. "Yeah, I thought so, too. I didn't buy them though."

"Good, we don't need those yet." She cut her eyes at me as she sat on the bed and hugged a pillow. She looked very sexy, and I was ready for more.

She paused and smiled. "But wait, what was with the exit? Thank you and then you leave? Like I'm some prostitute? What the fuck was that?"

"You were, but for free!"

She threw a pillow at me, and I shielded myself with my arms. "Oh, come on! You had a husband, fiancé, whatever. What did you want . . . for me to ask for your number? No thanks, I don't want some man trying to kill me for taking advantage of his wife in a supermarket parking lot."

We both fell silent for a moment and then cracked up.

"Okay, okay, you are taking this way too seriously, Jacques!"

That night we cuddled tightly and fell asleep. We didn't argue or talk about the future. We simply spooned into a tight ball, enjoying our little piece of heaven.

Victoria Morena was a beautiful Puerto Rican woman, born and raised in the Bronx. Her long black hair flowed to the middle of her back, and it was what drew me to her when we first met two years ago in my NYC office. Her innocent eyes were light brown and her plump lips were a seductive rose pink. We got acquainted after a few readings I had given her regarding some missing persons cases for the 42nd Precinct in the Bronx, where she worked.

After a while, I realized she wasn't just coming to help solve cases or deal with coworker problems on the force. When you "read" someone you can see into his or her soul. I saw the deeper essence of who she was and that is what I was so drawn to, her soul.

Vicky had a tough exterior like a true New Yorker, but she was deeply passionate about helping the underdog. Her job on the police force took its toll on her at times. It was so all-consuming that she needed me to clarify some of her hunches.

Vicky's deep connection with her family is also what I saw as a soft spot. They were all very close. Her family in NYC and Puerto Rico spoke frequently, had family gatherings, and had a genuine love for one another.

I wish I had the same kind of connection with my family, but mine was small and those in France and Morocco barely kept in touch. Sadly, it was very intentional, since my parents' marriage was frowned upon from the start, mainly from the French side. So seeing someone so connected with her family did show me her soft side.

For years, I made it a rule to never, ever date clients. It just gets messy, but I made an exception this time. One dinner after her last reading turned into two years of dating. After that first year, she followed me down to Miami and got a job as a detective with the Miami Police Department. So far, her insatiable appetite for lovemaking and how good she treats me is what keeps me coming back for more. Most women really can't handle my career, but Vicky embraces it and supports me. On rough days in the life of an intuitive counselor I need it. I'm still on the fence about the next steps, but it's not her . . . it's me. I am not sure if I'm ready, so we're still in the "let's figure us out" stage.

Chapter 1

Jacques

The next day after work, I went to pick up my photos from CVS. They were a few shots I had on my flash drive that I wanted printed. Call me old school, but I love real photos that you can touch and frame.

I was exhausted after meeting with three clients back-to-back: from my one o'clock's cheating bisexual husband to my two thirty's bipolar, sexually charged teenager to my four o'clock's drug-addicted brother, I was beat. I could write a whole TV series from their stories alone! I needed to take a vacation from being psychic for a minute. My brain was literally drained from all of their depressing energies, and my body was weary, like I could sleep for two days straight. I need a long day at the beach to cleanse my energy.

Thankfully though, the highlight of my day was Sugar Sinclair, the Broadway dancer who was calling from New York. Her life was actually a happy one and I always had good news to give her. When I went into my meditation, I saw visions of some exciting things unfolding for her. It was all going to happen very fast, too! From a new commercial she's going to land to a new boyfriend. I had lots of exciting news to share with her. That pick-me-up was what I needed to end my day.

I couldn't wait to get home, but I was happy I made that last stop to get my pictures. I was looking forward to shuffling through the photos from the Poconos. Me, my brother, and some of the fellas went to play paintball a few months ago on my last trip up north.

I opened the CVS envelope, but couldn't believe my eyes. Paintball this was not! The scene was of a brilliant aqua ocean and powdery white sand. The star of the photo was a twenty-something girl with her hair pulled back into a big Afro puff. Her skin was a light golden caramel and her trim body was hugged by a tightly revealing mint-green bikini.

I looked at the photo intensely to pick up a sense of who she was. Her bright eyes sparkled. Immediately I felt an abundant wave of joy within me that wasn't mine; it was her spirit, which was light and childlike. I wanted to see her. Not in a sexual way, but I had this urge to meet her. She was a good person, and charming, too.

Whenever I look at a photo, I mean really look at a photo, I can tell a lot about a person. My stomach actually squirms with excitement, and I get goose bumps that confirm my impressions of the person. This girl was going to change my life in some way. Just how, I was not sure of yet.

I looked at the next photo. It was of the same girl with a

girlfriend. They were at a party, holding margaritas. It was obvious that the imbeciles at CVS had given me the wrong pack.

The final shot was just incredible. It was of the most radiant sunset I'd ever seen. It didn't look amateurish. I flipped the package over to find the girl's name and number: Kylie Collins. I thought I'd call her to let her know about the mix-up. I wondered if she had my photos. That would be too funny. My stomach never lies. There's a good queasy feeling I get about something or someone. I looked at the clock on the wall. Vicky wouldn't be home for another three hours or so. It couldn't hurt to call. I was just being courteous. Right? Right.

I cleared my throat and dialed the number on the package. After hearing a few rings, I got her voice mail. Her young energetic voice made me smile. "Hey, it's Kylie! Leave a message and I just might get back to ya!"

"Yes, hi, Kylie, I'm Jacques Berradi. Turns out CVS thought we were the same person and gave me your photos. I will drop them back there tomorrow. Just wanted to give you a heads-up. My number is 305-555-6443 in case you'd like to call me back."

I was startled from the vibration of my phone in my hand. "Hello?" I said.

"Hello, who's this? You just called me?"

"Well, yes, I left a message. I'm Jacques. Jacques Berradi."

"Oh, I didn't check it yet." Her tone was suspicious. "I already sent in my payment though, sir. You're from Comcast, right?"

"No."

"Macy's?"

"No, not from a company at all; there was a mix-up at the CVS photo lab."

"CVS? Oh, sorry, thought you were a bill collector."

"No, far from it." I chuckled. "Well, uh, I just called to tell you I have your photos. I ended up with your pictures instead of mine."

"What? Are you kidding me?"

"Don't worry about it. I'll bring them back tomorrow morning, first thing. I was just looking forward to seeing photos of me and my brother at a paintball range and instead I got beach photos of women in bikinis. It sucks."

"Right, your lucky day, huh?" She chuckled. "This is a bit embarrassing, though. So, you saw us dancing with that Jamaican stripper? Oh my goodness!"

I thought she was teasing, but wasn't sure.

"Actually, I didn't look through them all, but hey, if you don't mind, I think—"

"No, no, that's okay! Jack?"

"Jacques."

"Oh, that's a nice name. Do you live in the area, Jhhhaaaak?" she added with a very bad Pepé Le Pew French accent. This girl was definitely a comedian.

"Yep, I'm on Bird Avenue, in the Grove. Say, you didn't happen to pick up my photos, did you?"

"No, that would've been crazy. But it was a bunch of guys in camouflage, right? Paintball. Hmmm, I might not have returned them."

She sounded relaxed, as if she knew me. "Oh no, Kylie, you would have returned them . . . I guarantee that!" I laughed. "They're of a bunch of washed-up guys trying to look tough, playing with fake guns filled with pink paint. Not sexy, trust me."

She chimed in, "Paintball sounds like loads of fun. I have always wanted to let go of some pent-up anger. I'm too cute for prison."

I laughed. "Well, paintball is the way to do it. It will save you from the girls at work." Damn, did I just slip?

"What girls at work? How did you know that is what I was thinking?"

"You were? That's crazy. I . . . I . . ."

"No, how did you know that? How the hell . . . could you know?" she exclaimed. "There are these two girls at the job I just left. I think they were behind me getting laid off. I was just picturing shooting them with a paintball gun. That is so crazy. Like you were in my head just for that split second! Maybe you're a bit psychic. . . ."

"Actually, I am," I confessed. "Sometimes things slip out. I call them 'psychic slips.' Forgive me for alarming you."

I could actually hear her standing up as a chair squeaked. "You're psychic? Are you serious? As in predicting-the-future-tarot-cards-crystal-balls psychic?"

"Well, yes." I laughed at her electric energy. "Everything except the crystal-balls part. I like to call myself an intuitive counselor or spiritual advisor."

"I can't believe it. Can I get a quick reading, please? Just one question?" She begged like a little girl; it was so adorable.

"Sure."

"Know where Annabelle's Coffee Shop is, on Grand Street?"

"No, it sounds familiar though."

"They just turned it into a cyber-lounge. It has that huge red awning and rainbow Christmas lights around the window."

"Oh yeah, they have those lights up all year round."

"Yup. If you aren't doing anything, can you meet me there? Like in two hours maybe?"

"In two hours? As in today?"

"Well, if you have time, that is, no biggie," she said, more softly.

"Wow, ummm, okay. I am done for today, after all. All right." I couldn't say no to her. Or I would have just dropped off the pictures at CVS.

"I'm sorry. I know, I know, I can be a bit direct."

My goodness, she's a bossy one. Must be an Aries, Leo, or Sagittarius.

Fire sign all the way, or maybe even a Scorpio. "Well, I'll see you there in two hours."

"But wait, I don't know what you look like!"

"Oh, I'm six one and—"

"Never mind, let me try to guess. You already know what I look like. I just won't be wearing a bikini this time. Okay, see you in a few." She paused. "And you're sure you don't mind? I'll pay for it."

"No, it's cool." My stomach squirmed with anticipation for some reason. I felt a little guilty. I never act this available, never. Innocent flirting, I guess.

"Ciao!" she said, and we both hung up.

Guess she didn't realize I could do the reading over the phone, but that was fine with me. I felt her sense of urgency and it revived me. Did she want to find out something about a man? I shook my head and smiled. Don't they all?

I warmed up some leftover broccoli and cheddar soup and decided to eat it while checking my email. More than fifteen new clients wanted appointments and I didn't have any more slots this week! Life was good. I was going to need an assistant soon.

My energy picked up a bit and I checked my watch. Time to meet this intriguing Kylie! I pulled on a blue button-down shirt over my ribbed tank top and rolled up the sleeves. I was proud of the results I'd created from doing three hundred push-ups and crunches each morning. I slipped on loose-fitting, worn-out Tommy Hilfiger jeans and put on my favorite loafers. I paused to take a look at myself in the full-length mirror, then ran my fingers though my wavy hair as I headed out the door.

Chapter 2

Jacques

Music played softly, people chattered, and a blender whirled loudly, making smoothies. When I arrived at Annabelle's, I took my laptop to the back of the shop. I figured I'd check my email and send Paypal requests to my new clients while I waited. As I surveyed the place, I didn't see a beautiful face that matched the photo. I enjoyed the sexy Latin jazz that played as I people-watched. An older balding man dined on his doughnut and coffee and a young couple in athletic wear from head to toe tossed their Rollerblades into a pile on the ground next to them before chowing down on soups and salads.

A few more stragglers, including a group of giggling teens, came inside. I ordered some water with lemon and sat in the corner with my back turned, reading my email.

Guessing when someone was coming close was a gift. I would always know just in the nick of time when my mother was nearby, so by sixteen I could hide cigarettes, a naughty girl, or porno magazines like a champ. In some cases, I had to hide all three at once. Mom would always say that she knew I was up to something, but she could never prove it. Funny thing though, I had no clue that I was psychic back then. I just thought I "knew" people . . . that I had a way with them and understood them.

The door chime jingled against the glass and I looked in the mirror to see her reflection. Kylie was wearing a flaming-red tank top and tight low-rider jeans, which hugged her hips rather nicely. The long silver earrings she had on practically touched her shoulders. She was naturally breathtaking; she wore hardly any makeup and was vibrant. Her eyes examined the room with intensity and intent. She stared at the old man with his doughnuts, then she looked in my direction. It seemed she wasn't convinced by what she saw and decided she'd wait for "me" to actually walk in. She sat down at a small table that faced the door.

I thought I'd have some fun with her, so I called her on my cell phone. "Skills are not so good, huh?"

"Jacques! I was wondering where you were." She still didn't know, so I slowly stood up. "Is that you in the back by the computers, standing up?"

I turned around and looked at her as I spoke. "It's me. Not what you expected?"

I came closer, still talking to her on the phone, and she said, "Wow, that's you, huh?" She grinned, revealing one dimple. I loved her reaction.

We hung up and laughed. I reached my hand out to hers. "Good to meet you, Kylie!"

"Same here. Thank you so much for calling me before I went to CVS and hurt somebody! I would have lost it if one of those cashiers had sold my Jamaica photos!"

"Oh, so that's where you were?"

"Yes, it was a much-needed vacation. Probably my last vacation for a long time."

We both took a seat. "Well, without further ado," I said casually, putting the pictures on the table.

With a sly glance she asked, "Where do you live, Jacques? I think I have seen you before."

"Off Bird Street, in the Hilltop Condominiums. But I've never seen you before, because I'm sure I would have remembered you."

"Oh really?" She lifted her head up. "And why is that?" she said, fishing for compliments.

"Your light shines pretty big. You have a very bright aura." I smiled.

"Damn, you can see my aura?"

"Yes, I've been seeing them since I was a child. I just didn't understand what the colors meant."

"You have got to tell me about this whole psychic life." She cupped her face with one hand, leaning in closer. Her voice got softer as she asked, "When did you know you were psychic?"

"Oh, I've been gifted since I was a kid, about six or so, but never really developed it until my late teens. My family used to say I just had a way with people. I was the guy everyone came to for advice, and I had a lot of female friends because of that skill. Still do. I used to see and feel things all the time, but people told me I had an overactive imagination. I was a kid, so I blew off a lot of visions as 'my imagination' or just colorful dreams."

"Wow, that is so interesting. Can I ask you a question?"

"Sure."

"How much do you charge?"

"I'm a hundred dollars per hour, but I'll give you a free reading this time around. I know you said you just lost your job."

"Well, I really need one. Damn, a hundred bucks, huh? I'm in the wrong career!" she joked. "So, do we do it here or do we go to your office?"

"You can ask me a couple questions now and we can schedule a real appointment in my office next week. Wednesday at eight thirty P.M.? I would do it this week, but I leave for New York this Wednesday."

"Seriously? I'm from Brooklyn! Oh, Jacques, can you please, pleeeeease bring me back a slice of pizza?"

We laughed. "Okay, I'll see what I can do. So, next week is good?" I asked.

"That's perfect." We both plugged the date into our phones. "And it will be totally free?" Kylie raised her eyebrows.

"Totally free." I nodded with a smile.

"So, my question is . . . Oh wait, do you need to know who the person is or should I just say their name?"

I waved her on to continue her question. "Just ask."

"Is True hiding something from me about my father?"

Kylie's eyes widened as I paused for a minute to hear the answer.

I took a deep breath and visions flooded in as I closed my

eyes. First, I saw a woman full of energy. Her aura was vibrant with bright yellows and pinks, kind of like Kylie, but older. I didn't see her in a 3-D sense, but more like a silhouette.

I felt her energy inside me, as if I were her. It was young, fun, and comedic even. However, I felt she used all that to cover her burden of memories, secrets, and lots of pain. Her throat and heart felt heavy and tight. She was fighting back a lot. I asked her soul if she was hiding something. She folded her arms and turned her back to me. She didn't want me to read her.

I said to Kylie, "Yes, it's a heavy burden on her. She's been, shall we say, twisting the truth, for some time, a long time. Almost all of your life." I tilted my head, waiting for more messages from my spirit guides. After a long pause, I said, "I'm so sorry. Is she your mother or sister?"

"Oh my God! How could you know that?" She stared at me in disbelief.

"Yeah, she's my mother, but I don't call her Mom. Her real name is Paulette, but she's been calling herself True since before I was born. Total oxymoron—she's a fucking liar. The only time I even see her real name is when there's a speeding ticket or an overdue credit card bill."

"Yeah, well . . ." I smiled.

"So, is my father still alive? She told me he died in Jamaica when I was a baby." She leaned in closer, hoping to urge me into saying what she wanted to hear.

I saw a flash of a graveyard as a sign that he was long gone. "No, sorry, he isn't alive. But your dad isn't the man she told you he was."

"So, my father's not Wendell Gordon?"

I pointed my finger in the air and took a deep breath to go within. "I'll be right back. Give me a moment." I closed my eyes again and saw an older black man; he had dark skin and was balding. His energy was very cold, rigid, and controlling, like that of a military officer. She might have been better off not knowing him. His dark energy gave me the chills. A very manipulative human being.

"No, Wendell doesn't exist. He's an older man. I see a uniform, but I'm not sure what kind."

"What? Are you sure? Are you sure?" She fell back in her seat, holding her head with one hand. "This bitch has been lying to me all of my life?"

"Kylie, in her own way, she thought she was protecting you. She's embarrassed. I don't know who he is, but it's obvious she wasn't supposed to be with him."

People were starting to look at our table. It almost seemed as if we were having a lovers' quarrel. I tapped her hand. "Let's finish later." I eyed the table next to us. The Rollerblade couple were obviously trying to listen in on our conversation.

A waitress came and asked to take our orders. She smiled at me and raised her eyebrows at Kylie.

"Hey, Lana! I'll just get a latte with whipped cream."

Lana looked at me and said, "Anything for you?" She pointed to the menu.

"Oh, just some green tea for me." I smiled at Lana, who gave off a devilish vibe, almost jealous. Didn't like her aura at all. Dark, cloudy—not someone I'd want to be around.

Kylie noticed me observing and whispered, "She probably

thinks I'm a slut, since I was just here yesterday on a date with some dude I met jogging. She's a bit nosy. Oh, and he was a big loser by the way, not worth my time."

"Not bad for an amateur." I laughed and fiddled with a Sweet'N Low packet as I spoke. "But I got more of a jealous vibe from her. I must be pretty hot!"

Kylie raised her eyebrows. "Shit, you're not bad . . . for a psychic." She winked. "You threw me off! I was looking for a wise old man with a gray beard and a turban."

"Ah, you see . . . stereotypes! They've made it hard for us normal everyday psychics."

"Normal everyday psychics? That doesn't even sound right!"

We laughed and I sipped more of my drink. I felt very comfortable with Kylie. But what was I doing? Vicky would be home in about an hour and I was laughing it up with a beautiful girl. Well, client, technically.

Lana put our drinks down without making eye contact. Kylie and I gave each other a knowing smirk when she walked off.

"What's her deal? Single, miserable, dead-end job?"

"Single, angry, miserable, lonely, and hard up for a man. She thinks you're taking all of them." I pointed my finger at Kylie. "Hey, you aren't going to just start using me for my powers, are you?"

She took a sip of her latte, leaving a small foam mustache on her top lip. "I just want to get an idea of what level of jealousy she has so I can figure out what's in my drink." She giggled as she looked into her cup. "Is it a little bit of saliva or a full-fledged hock and spit?"

"Kylie, you are something else." I shook my head. "Don't worry, I'm sure it's one hundred percent latte," I reassured her and we laughed.

"Okay, okay. One more question and I'll save the rest for our meeting, I promise!"

I waved my hand for her to go for it. "Do you know if I'm going to find a job soon?" I closed my eyes and took a deep breath in through my nose and out of my mouth. I knew she wasn't getting one. She was barely looking.

In my vision, I saw her goofing off a lot. "No, not at the rate you are currently going. You'll have to apply yourself more. There are opportunities around, but I don't think you have been really clear about what you want to do. Try to summon up that fire you once had. Remember what it was that made you like your last job." She leaned in more, her eyes wide. I took a deep breath. "Kylie, I'll be frank. You got too comfortable."

"Ouch," she said.

I raised my eyebrows. "Yeah, and that's why I'm called psychic." I laughed. I put my hand on her hand gently. "Hey, I'm not gonna sugarcoat it for you. You asked for my opinion, right? If you want a job, you're gonna have to get off your butt and go to agencies, read the classifieds, and join organizations. Anything you can do."

I paused and waited for more visions to come. I took a deep breath. I saw a small, balding man. He had a bright blue-and-white glow around him. Great communicator, I felt. I saw Kylie talking to him and smiling. I heard a soft voice from one of my guides say, "He will change her life, he will take her under his wing. Doors will swing open if she allows it."

"There is a man, a short man, he sees you like his daughter. He will teach you. He will help you advance. He's very short, actually. I see you looking down at him when you talk." I tried not to laugh.

"Wow, that is short. I have no idea who that is."

"Well, maybe you don't know him yet, but he's coming. Be on the lookout."

Kylie leaned in closer and asked, "Is he white, black, Spanish, Asian?" She crinkled her nose.

"I don't know, I don't see people's faces clearly all the time. Sometimes I don't get features at all, I just know how people feel. Their temperament. What stands out most about their personalities, you know?" I looked at my watch.

"You have to run?" she asked softly.

"Yeah, I'm sorry, Kylie, but we can continue when you come by. It was really great meeting you! Don't worry about your mother, I'll work with you further so we can find out more." We both stood up and I kissed her on her cheek, then went to kiss her other cheek. She didn't realize what I was about to do and our lips brushed against each other slightly.

"Oh my," she said, blushing. "You kiss like the French." She laughed, covering her mouth. "I didn't know you were going for the other cheek."

"I'm soooo sorry, it's a habit. Comes from having a French family. Parisians do that." I really wasn't sorry. Her lips were very soft.

"Wow, Paris?"

"Yes, I'm half French."

"Oh really?" She raised her eyebrows.

"Yes, I try to go at least once a year to Paris or Morocco. I like Morocco a bit more, though. I'm closer with that side of the family. I have a lot more cousins there."

Kylie's face lit up. "Wow, you have such an interesting background! I don't think I've ever met anyone like you."

"Oh, a Moroccan and French mix is pretty common, believe it or not. A lot of them were traveling back and forth for work and such. Usually you'll see a lot of Moroccans in France working. However, my parents actually met in Morocco. My mom's an artist and was there working on a project."

"You get cooler by the minute!"

"Oh, stop it!" I blushed.

When I tell people, well, women in particular, that I'm half French, their reaction always makes me laugh. They start to look at me in a different light. I could see it in Kylie, too. She suddenly found me more attractive. People think the French are either amazing lovers or snobby foreigners.

"I knew I heard some kind of slight accent."

"I was raised in New York since I was three, but my dad is Moroccan and my mom is French. We spoke both French and English at home. I tried to hide it growing up, but it never worked."

"Really? I don't see why, it's very nice."

"I got teased as a kid."

I was a little nervous and excited at the same time, but I knew I'd better get out of there before we continued. Her dynamic personality drew me in. Kylie was attractive, too, without even trying, and so much fun to be around. However, I believed there was way more to this connection. I knew she was attracted to me as well, but that road was one I felt we shouldn't venture down.

"Thanks." I nodded, bowing gratefully. "All right, Kylie, I have to run. Talk to you when I get back in town."

Chapter 3

Jacques

Silence. Pure silence was music to my ears. It was Tuesday, my last day working before I left for New York, and I needed to recharge. I absolutely enjoyed being in deep meditation, feeling my body get heavy and sink into my favorite chair. I wanted nothing but to clear my chakras and take deep slow breaths. The calming scent of sage floated in the air. I always smudge myself and the room after readings. I had to release the stress and energy of Pamela, the worrying mom; Jack, the controlling CEO; and Wanda, the neurotic woman who pushed everyone away. The kicker today was Lacey, the manipulator.

Tightness in my throat just before a client came in was a clear sign that it was going to be a tough reading. A sign that I might not enjoy what I had to share, hence the choked-throat feeling. The throat represents communication. If I feel tight or restricted in that area, I can tell I will have some tough choices to make about how I will shell out the information to a client.

Lacey walked in and I knew right away what it was. She was elegantly tall, about five nine, but with heels, about six one. She held on to an oversize soft leather bag, which probably contained her iPhone, Beamer keys, wallet, makeup, change of panties, lube, and condoms. Oh, she was always prepared, this one. Lacey was seductive in her speech; she paused and savored the syllables as they left her shimmery lips.

She pulled her strawberry-blond hair into a bun to lift it off her neck, as if the temperature was just too hot for her. She fanned herself dramatically. "I just want to know if he's sincere, Jacques. Does he really plan to be with me and me alone?" She told me her lover's name and with my eyes closed I drew him in. I saw a mini-movie in my mind and translated for her. He was tall and charming. His features were blurry. I heard my guides say, "He is a highly effective orator. Persuasive. Very persuasive. He could run for president." I saw him, behind a podium, speaking with a lot of energy.

I told Lacey, "He can talk almost anyone into anything. He's known for his voice." I thought he might be in sales.

"Yes, yes, that's right! Boy, you're good. That's him!" She leaned in with a guilty smile. "You know, he's my pastor."

I raised my eyebrows and tried not to seem too shocked. "Oh really." It made sense, though.

She shrugged. "I know, it seems bad, but we really are in love. He told me God sent us to each other." I closed my eyes again and saw a line of women waiting for him. I didn't feel she was the only one. She was one in five at least.

"He has a wife, no?" I asked.

"Yes, but he said he's going to leave her before the end of the year. He's trying to get his paperwork together so she doesn't take everything when he files for divorce." She took a sip of her water.

I ran my hand through my waves and sighed. "Well, from what I see you aren't the only one who has heard this story. Sorry to say, Lacey, but I see a few others waiting in the wings for the year to be up."

Lacey's lips tightened as her chest heaved in anger. She startled me as she banged the desk. "I knew it. I knew it! He's such a liar! I've been waiting almost a year now. He's taken me away on trips, he buys me things, he pays my rent, but that's not all that I want. I want him. I am tired of sneaking around."

I sighed as I heard her ramble on about how much she was in love with him and in the same breath brag about how he had bought her the $600 handbag she was carrying. The woman clearly didn't know what love was and it was my job to give her a reality check. Denial was Lacey's middle name.

Lacey said she was done with the pastor for good now. She cried a bit as well, but I know it wasn't the first time she'd cried over him. Sadly, I knew it wouldn't be the last. Lacey would be back asking about him in about three to four months.

This year it's the pastor, last year it was a womanizing ob-gyn. I've recommended countless books for her to read about improving her self-esteem, since that is where the real problem lies. No man, handbag, or designer shoes were going to help that. I try my hardest not to be judgmental, but it is difficult when you see self-sabotaging behavior over and over again. People continue to do it because deep down inside they really don't think they are worthy. The issue is not just going to a psychic to get answers, but what they are going to do with the information the psychic gives them.

Many times . . . the ball gets dropped. People just don't want to do the work on themselves. I can say that I've had many sessions that are mirrors of my own life, and when I give advice, I hear my guides almost laughing, saying, "Hey, you need to take that advice for yourself. It's good stuff." Doing this work definitely has matured me on many levels.

❊ ❊ ❊

Today was a long day. After Lacey, I had Jerome on the list for readings. My stomach growled as I looked at my phone for the time. I had only a fifteen-minute break to eat my leftover tuna sandwich from lunch. As I wiped mayo off my chin, I heard the buzzer ring.

"Damn," I mumbled. Jerome McMiller, my next appointment, was five minutes early.

I buzzed him in and yelled, "I'll be right with you." I lit my white candle and opened the door.

He had a strong presence . . . intimidating. Hat on backward, about five ten, stocky build, and very intense eyes that squinted as he sized me up. However, his energy lightened after he sat down and observed some of my paintings. He nervously shook his leg. I could tell his tough-guy vibe was a front.

His black T-shirt read in bold white letters BLACK LIVES MATTER! I nodded toward his chest and said, "Nice shirt."

In a scruffy voice he replied, "Yeah, you know, I gotta represent all day." Jerome gave me a fist bump. He said, "Yo, I thought this psychic stuff was all bullshit, but my ex-coworker at the bus depot, Chantell, who, mind you, don't trust nobody . . . She kept talking about you. I mean, all the time!" He playfully rolled his eyes, shook his head, and continued, "She said you helped her get a new job and you also cured her asthma." He took off his Yankees baseball cap and put it on his knee.

"Oh, Chantell Rodriguez referred you? I love her, but don't let her exaggerate!" I smiled. "I didn't actually cure her asthma. It was actually the bus driving and the depot itself that was causing her problems—all the fumes. I also did a scan of her house and told her to check it for mold. It was moving out of there that cured her as well as getting a new job!"

"A scan of her house—hold up, like in your mind?"

I smiled and tapped my temple.

"Well damnnnn . . . that's pretty dope, too, man!"

"Thank you, thank you!" I nodded gracefully. "Well, let's get down to *your* business. Would you like some water?" I pointed toward my little fridge and he shook his head no and reached into his pocket for a crinkled piece of paper.

"Nah, homie, let's just getting it poppin'. I got my questions. Chantell kept telling me to write them down, since you might tell me so much I could forget them."

"Yes, that was a wise decision."

Jerome sat up straight, cleared his throat, and said, "I

wanna know about my girlfriend, Stacey, Stacey Roberts. I wanna know if you see if she is messing around with my friend Omar. You need a picture?"

"No, no . . . the name is fine."

I took a few deep breaths and tried to pull up anything I could feel about them, but Jerome continued venting. "I just can tell something is up, but I can't seem to catch them. They act mad suspicious when together. She giggles waaaaay too much at his jokes. And he . . . man, he is constantly telling me how lucky I am to have her. He's my guy and all, but I feel like he is sending me a hint or something. They are going to a lot of the same events but not taking any photos together. They will take pictures with other friends, but most times she won't mention that she even saw Omar. I'm like, 'Y'all must take me for a fool or something!' Trying not to be suspicious looks even more suspicious." He pointed at me with anger as if I were Omar.

Suddenly, I felt a jolt go through me, and I put my hand up to tell him to be quiet.

"Oh, my bad," he apologized.

I took three deep breaths to get even more grounded and shake off his angry energy, so I could make out the vision coming through. I closed my eyes tightly. I smelled sawdust. It was overwhelming. I realized I was back in time. I was in Jerome's body and I was a servant of some kind. I felt I was in a barn or some kind of lumberyard. I looked down at my shirt, which was white with bright red polka dots. I tasted metal. Horror took over me as I realized the red dots were blood coming from my mouth and right eye.

I felt the jolt again and it was a blow to the face. I was getting severely beaten with a club . . . a piece of wood from the barn we were in. Although I didn't feel the pain as much as he had when it happened, I still got a sense of how it felt. He was in a state of shock when it occurred. It was a traumatic memory.

I asked my guides to explain to me what was going on and to take the pain away. Where was I?

A woman's voice, which belonged to one of *his* spirit guides, said softly, "In that lifetime Jerome had an affair with his boss's wife. His boss was a wealthy man who owned a factory and was a carpenter. He was finally caught and the wife denied it all. She pretended she was being raped." My stomach turned as I took another deep breath to prepare myself for what was to come.

Then, just like a preview for a movie, it all flashed before my eyes. I saw a blond woman and a young man with sandy-brown hair having sex in what looked like a storage room for furniture. When an older man with salt-and-pepper hair walked in, she let out a bloodcurdling scream and yelled for the man to get off her. She was more in fear of the husband than anything. I felt the heavy betrayal in Jerome's heart at the time.

"You all right, man?" Jerome asked, bringing me back to the present.

I didn't realize I was rubbing my jaw and my eye, where the club had socked him. I told him what his guide said and what I saw. "In this past life, you knew them both and the boss who beat you up, that was . . . that was your friend Omar in that lifetime. You betrayed him, and in this life you have an overwhelming sense of guilt and of course paranoia."

He sat back in his seat with his mouth open.

I said, "I don't sense anything going on. However, your jealously could bring them together if you continue. The chemistry you sense is because they were actually married."

"It's gotta be something, 'cause he ain't really easy on the eyes and I'm a pretty good-looking brother." He snickered. "He got money, though. He handles his business. So I can see why some broads be into him." He tilted his head to the side. "Sooooo . . . they not fuckin' at all? At all?" He waved his hands like an umpire calling safe on the baseball field.

"No, no, I don't see it." I shook my head. "I felt a genuine friendship between them, but all that Facebook posting stuff is in your head. You guys have a lot of the same circle of friends, no?"

He nodded and cracked his knuckles.

"So, they will bump into each other. It's normal. I think in her mind, if she posted photos of her and Omar every time they were at the same event together, you would be jealous, too. Don't make yourself crazy. Are you doing detective work? I see you in her stuff. Digging through digital things."

Jerome shifted his eyes, looking down and then up to the ceiling. "Yeah . . ." He started to sniffle, and his chest was heaving up and down. He tapped his leg nervously again and then out of nowhere he started to cry. It was like a volcano erupting and quite frankly took me by surprise.

Jerome had so much pain and fear. He cried like a baby.

I passed him tissues and I know he was embarrassed, but he couldn't control it. He probably hadn't cried in years.

"Jacques, I follow her, I hacked into her email. I check her text messages when she is asleep. I bugged her phone with an app. I kept feeling something was off, but never caught them. That past life shit makes so much sense. And why was you holding your face?"

"He hit me—well, hit *you*—really hard with a stick of wood right here." I pointed to my right eyebrow.

He leaned in and showed me a birthmark on his right eyebrow. "Like right here?"

"Yeah, wow, that's wild. Have you had that since you were born?"

"Yeah, and I heard about that shit, too. That you could have a scar where you were shot in a past life. Chantell got me watching all these out-there videos on YouTube since she saw you." He sniffled.

"That's amazing. It makes sense. You had to have had a ruined face after that beating. It was bad."

"When was it? Can you see that, too? Like what year?"

I closed my eyes and saw the number 1827 almost as if it were on those big squares on *Wheel of Fortune*. Then I saw a map of the United States in my mind. The map zoomed in to south of the Midwest and then I saw the letter *O*. I said slowly, "Ohhh. Oklahoma, 1827."

"So . . . hold up, I worked for him and we were friends? Was I a slave?"

"No. You were white, like a field hand, maybe a carpenter,

since it looked like a lumberyard . . . or something of that nature. You had on overalls and a white shirt. He hit you so hard it was covered in blood. Oh, and a straw hat. You seemed much younger than your boss."

"So, she musta been a cougar." He chuckled. "That's fucked up how she ratted on me."

"I know . . . but she was about the same age. You were like twenty or twenty-one and he looked around forty-something."

"Yoooo, you have no idea how much sense this makes! Omar and I are the same age. We're both thirty-four, but he's been like a mentor to me. He acts older. He knows so much shit. Really smart dude. He showed me a lot about real estate. We are actually going in on a house together as partners . . . a duplex in Kendall. I'm soooo glad I don't have to hurt homie." He laughed and put his hat back on.

"No, no . . . please don't hurt him. You did enough damage in 1827."

"Ohhhh, that's cold!" Jerome slapped his knee. "Yeah, you right though. You right. I don't wanna go to jail. Man, this karma shit is real, huh?"

"Oh, it's verrrrrry real. Just learn to trust more and chill out on the detective work. Let Stacey breathe a little. She's a good girl."

We ended up having an hour reading instead of the thirty minutes he originally wanted, so he could talk more about his career. I recommended a few books on relationships and the law of attraction. I also gave him a few videos to check out on YouTube about meditation to help him with his anxiety.

He was very pleased when he was leaving. "Yo, Jacques,

you the truth, man!" He gave me a pound and a hug. "Imma spread the word about you at the bus depot. Get ready, man. I know a loooot of people."

"Oh, send them on!"

He waved and had extra pep in his step as he walked out. It was sessions like this that made me feel so fulfilled.

My job, as rewarding as it is, can truly take its toll. Today's sessions made me need at least one hour of meditation to release all my clients' woes and cleanse my own aura. Vicky seemed to always know when it was a tough day for me. If she came home and my office door was closed, that was a sign: meditation in progress—do not disturb. Most guys had a man cave that was full of video games and a big-screen TV. Mine had a waterfall, dark curtains, incense, candles, and essential oils. She thought twice before she dumped on me all of her day, about gang fights, drug busts, or sexist and racist coworkers. Vicky knew I, too, needed to complain and I was grateful that she knew it. The day in the life of a psychic wasn't all love stories and exotic past lives. Murders, missing children, molestations, countless infidelities, abuse, relationship dramas, crossing-over ghosts, and communicating with dead loved ones were what filled many of my days. Tough days usually started off with a minor headache and ended with a pounding migraine and extreme fatigue. And yes, even though I hate to admit it, watery eyes. It comes with the territory and is something I can't control during emotional visions when I pull up a person who died but still has regrets. It is heart-wrenching to hear a spirit on the other side telling me he or she is so sorry.

We are really the same person even after we die. The same spirit, but without the shell we call a body. Life can tug at your soul when you really go through it. Being the voice for these souls was my job. Being the mediator between their personal egos and their spirit guides was my other job. But the beauty, the real joy, is when you really help someone with a breakthrough into finding their passion when they have been stuck in the wrong career or relationship all their lives. It's great when you help someone find his true love that was right under his nose. Or, most rewarding of all, helping someone fall in love with who she is deep down inside, shedding the layers of unnecessary masks.

I enjoy encouraging people to be their authentic selves and to make no apologies for their greatness . . . helping every person recognize the God-Force within them gives me life! That part of my job isn't really intuitive, but it certainly is what drives me. It's what really keeps me coming back, because I know I am making a difference.

Chapter 4

Kylie

Jacques can so get it. Damn, why did he have to be as fine as he sounded? And French to top it off! I know I'm a big flirt, but what are the chances of someone as sexy as him getting my photos by mistake? I never even usually print out photos there, but my printer was broken. Was that an act of God? Could be, since He knows the most action I've gotten in the last three months was my Brazilian bikini wax at the Hilton in Jamaica. Jacques's eyes were dangerous—alluring even. Dark eyes and long eyelashes on a man is straight dangerous for me. He needs to wear shades for our next meeting, because it was hard not melting right in front of him.

As much as I hate to admit it, I could be wrong about why I met him. Even though I know there are no coincidences, there could be another reason we met. I'm horny beyond belief, and there is only so much a trusty vibrator can do. He looked like a good prospect to take care of the release I so desperately need. But hey, even if he can't help me "get my leg over," as my British friend Olivia would say, he could help me with my career and warn me who to avoid. There is a bright side, even if he isn't "the one."

But anyway, Jacques was really good, not a cheesy ten-dollar psychic from a street fair. He seemed very professional, down to earth, and just right on the money. He confirmed what my gut was screaming at me for all these years. My father is not the man my mom said he was. I hate her for lying to me, for denying who she is, and making me a product of her secrets. But I can't say anything, not yet. A good detective doesn't confront her suspect until she has all the facts and I'm nowhere near that.

I got back to True's place—well, my place temporarily—and kicked off my sandals near the neat pile of shoes by the door. I turned on my favorite mix by The Brass King, a vintage soul mix of classic R&B instrumentals. I went for my favorite chair in the house, the big orange fur chair that looked like it was from the "Back to School" dorm section of Target. Phantom, my baby sister, almost plowed me down when she saw me beat her to her favorite chair.

"Come here, Phantom, we can share." Her bright eyes became honey-colored slits after she sat on my lap. She purred as I stroked the big brown patch over her eye. I got her when I was eighteen years old and named her Phantom because the patch over her left eye looks just like the Phantom of the Opera's mask.

I turned on the boob tube for a second and watched a re-run of *Law & Order: SVU*. The R&B music still played in the background. Noise, the comforts of home, and not feeling alone.

I started flipping through the photos that Jacques gave me, stopping at a photo of my aunt Daphne, my two cousins, and Olivia laughing over a Jamaican brunch at the hotel. *Shit, I better hide these bad boys.* What True didn't know couldn't hurt her. She didn't need to know my real reason for going on "vacation." I quickly took those photos out of the batch.

I was happy to be able to reconnect with an aunt I had seen only twice before.

True had told me that she and Daphne had had strict upbringings, though they hadn't lived together. My cousins were very well mannered, but almost to an extreme. They were about five or six years younger than me, but acted even younger. They spoke only when spoken to. Aunt Daphne spoke slowly and softly, sat up straight like a former dancer, wore hardly any makeup, and still had flawless cocoa-brown skin. She was very pretty and I was happy to say we all looked a lot alike. Same smile and eyes. Her hair was in a perfectly smoothed-back bun. She was the total opposite of her free-spirited sister.

My mother wanted no part of her island roots and the bad memories she never talked about. It was as if she didn't grow up on ackee and saltfish, dumplings and curry chicken, and mangoes from the yard. Like she didn't chase lizards, pick ticks off the family dog, or run barefoot with her friends by the river. She keeps all these stories bottled up inside, so that I have to hear them from someone else. It was as if Paulette Collins never existed and "True" is her new truth in America.

Finding out who my father really was is just a piece of the puzzle. Daphne claimed she didn't know who my father was, yet she would never look me in my eyes when I asked about him. She would start to speak, then cut herself off as if she was holding something back. I know there's more to the story than a young pregnancy and being shipped away to hide it. I know in my heart the Collinses were protecting a secret and now my session with Jacques confirmed it: my dad wasn't the man I thought he was.

Over brunch in Jamaica, Aunt Daphne sipped a mimosa. I had hoped it would loosen her tight lips but she fed me only morsels of the knowledge I craved. "We never really got on as children," she said softly, with her proper Jamaican accent. It almost had a British twist to it. "We weren't raised together. She grew up by Braes River with our aunt and uncle and I was in the city with my father. Our mother was very sickly and couldn't take care of us. My father was a bit well off, owned a trucking business, and that, well, that caused a lot of jealously from Paulette." She shook her head and frowned, as if the memories were too painful to bring back. "It was sad though, you know? She was really treated like a Cinderella. Our uncle's wife made her clean all day. She was a wicked woman. Wicked. She hated us all. When I went to visit, I never wanted to go back. So, for Paulette to have to live there, to live with that woman full time, I don't know how your mother survived."

That part of the story rang true with what I was told, but I had no idea they were half sisters. I thought all this time they had the same dad.

I must have looked surprised or embarrassed.

"Your mother never told you any of this?"

I shook my head. She hadn't. No matter how much I begged her, True would just brush me off and tell me it was better I didn't know anything about them "damn Jamaicans." It's gotta hurt living daily in denial of your authentic self. It frustrates me that I never grew up with any culture, with the good down-home cooking most Jamaican kids grew up with. True made me spaghetti and meatballs and of course my favorite ('cause I didn't know any better), franks and beans, at least until she became a vegetarian fifteen years ago.

I do try to see her side of it all, though. She was on her own and a single mom at sixteen. True told me she was shipped off to the States, in fear of the rest of the family and community learning that she'd gotten pregnant out of wedlock. There's no doubt she wears battle scars heavy on her heart. But why should I be severed from my family ties? Because she has issues getting over her past? It's my family, too. I need to know my roots!

Before I left for Jamaica, True kept asking me where I was staying, so I made sure I showed her all the brochures of the resort in Ocho Rios—three hours away from her family. She had no clue about my reconnecting with her sister. When I arrived back from my trip, True picked me up. I was excited to see her and wished I could tell her about my cousins, about how beautiful Aunt Daphne still looked, but of course . . . she would've lost it.

I walked outside the airport, looking for her car. First, I spotted her bright red '04 Mustang with thousands of bumper

stickers on the back displaying causes she supported: BURGER
KING RULES: IF YOU LIKE DINING AT THE MORGUE, SAVE THE
WHALES, SAVE THE RAINFORESTS, and WOMEN FOR PEACE.

She sat in the car with her tweezers between her fingers,
looking in her rearview mirror. True was going to town on
all those unwanted ingrown hairs she affectionately referred
to as her "girl whiskers." Great! If that's in the genes, I have
something to look forward to in my late forties. I ran my hand
across my chin, doing a quick peach-fuzz check. She still
didn't notice me coming toward her dragging my luggage as
she plucked away.

I bent down to the window and yelled, "Okay, okay, that's
just gross, True!"

She laughed, a bit startled. "What's so gross? Girl whiskers are a part of life. You still have a good fifteen years before you get them," she teased as she got out of the car and
gave me a quick hug and a pat on the back. True was not
affectionate and never had been.

I put my two small suitcases in the trunk and mumbled,
"If I'm lucky, I'll have more of my father's genes."

"Yeah . . ." She cleared her throat nervously and strapped
on her seat belt.

"What's wrong? How come whenever I bring up my father,
you get all weird?"

"Weird? You're being ridiculous. Tell me about your trip
to that third-world island with those damn Jamaicans. Did
you have fun?" She laughed, halfheartedly acknowledging
that she, too, was from that third-world island.

"Yeah, I had a blast, but you're changing the subject. It would be nice if you could share more info, just once. It's like pulling teeth to find out anything about my father!"

The rumbling sound of the muffler choking shook the car. Then George Benson singing "Turn Your Love Around" blasted over my complaints as we drove away from Miami International Airport with the tall row of palm trees lining the road leading the way out. I turned down the music, refusing to be drowned out.

"There's nothing more to share, Kylie. I've told you all this a million times. He was my boyfriend. I got pregnant from messing around way too young. They shipped me off to the States to live with my aunt to have you, so no one would know. They abandoned me, so why should I care about them? Your father didn't give a damn and never wrote me back. I heard he died in a car accident when you were five. You've asked me a thousand times, the story won't change." She reached for the volume knob and began to sing along. "Turn your love around!" Her blond 'fro swayed to the music.

I lowered the volume again. "There's nothing more to know? What about his family? How come you never at least told me about any aunts and uncles or cousins I have?"

"He was an only child, Kylie. I told you this before!" she yelled. "I don't like talking about it."

"Maybe Aunt Daphne will." I baited her to see what she would say.

"You didn't see her, did you? Did you see her?" She took her eyes off the road and stared into mine.

"No," I lied. "I don't have a number for her. Heeeeey! Look at the road!" A car almost sideswiped us going ninety miles an hour. True swerved just in the nick of time.

"Well, I don't have one, either. She wants nothing good for either of us. She's been jealous of me since the day I was born. We don't need any of them. Any of them!" She picked up speed as her pain seeped into her voice. I reached down to make sure my seat belt was on tight. True had so much anger inside. That's how I knew there had to be more to the story.

Olivia and I took a two-day trip to Kingston while in Jamaica. It was a bumpy three-hour ride from Ocho Rios with some of the worst A/C ever.

Our saving grace was the scenic route of breathtaking hills. Oh, it was beautiful! I had a sense of pride as we drove through the towns that my ancestors called home. Jamaica's rich history was part of my heritage, too, and I couldn't wait to learn more.

When we were settled into the Spanish Court Hotel in Kingston, I called the last number I had for Aunt Daphne. I had jacked it from True's cell, but it was disconnected. However, I soon found out that if you knew the last name of someone in Jamaica and the town they live in it's not hard to get more information. Professional snoop was my side job. I was able to trace Aunt Daphne to her business, Daphne's Delights, and some locals knew exactly who she was when I asked at the front desk of the hotel.

I sat on the edge of my bed and nervously dialed. It was still early afternoon, so I hoped she would be in her shop.

"Hi, may I speak to Daphne please?"

"Yes . . . Good afternoon, ah, who is calling?" She seemed intrigued by my voice.

"Kylie Collins!" I tapped my leg nervously.

Silence and then I heard something drop.

I said it again, "Kylie? Your niece. Ummm . . . Paulette's daughter?" I tried to refresh her memory.

"Oh, mi darling, I know! I know who you are! I just can't believe it. And you sound just like your mother, Paulette. And you're here? I see a Kingston number!" Her voice cracked. "You both here? Kiss mi neck!" She was overjoyed.

"Well, no, just me and a friend. I had to track you down."

"I never knew what happened to you! Your mother never stayed in touch, she always moving and never letting anyone know anything. So glad you knew to look for mi!" She laughed. "My gooooodness, I long to you see you, man! Where are you staying? You must come see your cousins."

"I know, I know! I can't wait. We're here only one more day, then we go back to Ocho Rios."

"Oh, is that where you staying in Ochi? Okay, well tomorrow it is. I will move everything around for you, mi love."

Tears were welling behind my eyelids as I listened to her excitement. My auntie! My family was happy to see me. They were not the nasty "damn Jamaicans" my mother painted a picture of.

While I was still on the phone, Olivia was coming out of the shower and looking at me for a sign of good news. I nodded my head yes and pointed to the phone. She came over and high-fived me with a damp hand. It stung and we both laughed.

Aunt Daphne planned to pick us up for brunch the following day. Thinking back now, I realized it was one of the best days of my trip.

❖ ❖ ❖

I know I'll have more than enough time to dig around and find out what is really going on. Bamboo chimes at the door began to jingle. True must be coming in. I quickly put my photos back inside my purse and got up to help her as she juggled her massage table and the mail.

"Hey, sweetie!" her soft voice cooed. She was tired, pale, and her makeup had worn off. True was very light, could almost pass for Spanish, depending on what day it was. Even though she looked out of it, her gentle smile let me know that she had made out okay today.

"Hi, True! Long day?" I kissed her on the cheek.

She ran her fingers through her blown-out bleached-blond 'fro. It was frizzy and cracklin' dry. She needed a hot-oil treatment badly.

"Oh yeah, I was working like a dog, but my last client, Mr. Wallace, was feeling generous today, so I'm not complaining." Her ear-to-ear smile transformed into a half scowl. "Are you going deaf?"

I muted the TV to silence the piercing sirens from a car chase scene. "What did he tip you this time?"

She reached inside her bright yellow halter dress and pulled a crisp $100 bill from her cleavage. She waved it in the air.

I raised my eyebrows. "A hundred-dollar tip! Aren't your massages only seventy bucks?"

"Yes, but they don't all finish with a happy ending." She let out a throaty laugh as she picked up Phantom. Lifting the cat high in the air, she talked baby talk to her. "Riiight, baby? Mommy knows how to stroke that nice tip right out of Mr. Wallace." She rubbed her face against Phantom's fur.

I picked up her massage table and placed it on the cream fur rug in the den. "Whatever floats your boat," I replied.

She sat down with Phantom on the floor in the living room. "Speaking of floating your boat, Ky . . . Wait till you hear this one! Before Mr. Wallace there was this older black woman, Theresa Kingsley—I'll never forget that name now! I've seen her only once before. I got a weird flirty vibe from her, but I thought she got the hint that I'm strictly dic—"

"Aye, True . . . please . . ." I put my hand up like a stop sign.

She laughed and continued, "Get this! I got in the room and she was butt naked with no sheet. I told her to lay on her stomach and put the sheet over her. I must admit she had a nice body for her age, she's gotta be in her late fifties. She works out a lot or something."

I shook my head, scared to know where the rest of this story was going. I started to act like I was walking away.

"Kylieeeeee, listen!" True was giggling. "Theresa goes, 'What, you don't like what you see?'

"I had to put on my sternest face and say, 'Ma'am, I'm a massage therapist. I see naked bodies daily.'

"Then she goes, 'Ohhh, well I heard you give very gooooood sensual massagezzzzzz.' She was damn near purring as she said it. Remember Lady Eloise from *Boomerang*? Eartha Kitt played her?"

"True!" I laughed. "Oh *Gawd*, that is hysterical! Did she call you Marcussssss, too?"

"She might as well have. I still did the massage and had to just wrap her hands in the sheets, since she kept leaving them in the way so I could brush by her. What a freak! I'm like 'Lady, are you for real?' She even said, 'You can do whateverrrrr you pleasssssssse. You have full rein. Full reinnnnn." True exploded with laughter now.

"What? Are you serious? True!" I laughed so loud it scared Phantom out of her lap.

"Yes, girl, fuuuuull rein." She shrugged. "Too bad I am not a lesbian. I would have been a happy camper today. I kept it professional, though. She was waaaaay too desperate—I started to think that maybe she was a cop or some shit. They have been cracking down on massage parlors doing special add-ons."

"I ain't bailing you out for that mess!"

"Don't worry. I just gave her a pretty intense glute rub-down. I kinda wanted to see if she had implants there, too. But it was all her ass. She was squirming the whole time. Maybe she wasn't a cop. She gave me a nice tip, too."

I winced. "Oh, True, gross, aye . . . enough!"

She pointed for me to take her massage table off her rug and put it near the hallway. I cringed at the thought of jerking off some fat old banker or giving a horny lesbian sensual massages for tips. I slammed down the massage table a little harder than I should have.

True could tell from my energy shift that I hated how she told me everything. Sometimes she acted like she wanted a sister, not a daughter. "Don't act so disgusted, Kylie. If it weren't for these hands, you would have never made it through college!" She held her hands up in the air and admired her palms. "If you don't get up off your ass and start looking for a new job you might have to join me."

I plopped back down on the orange chair and reached for the remote. I stared into the screen at the *Law & Order* TV detectives and tried drowning out True's complaining. "I'll pass. I just haven't found the job for me. They all pay crap."

I was lying. I've actually been sort of looking and sort of enjoying the beach and this mini-vacation.

"This isn't New York, baby. The pay is lower, so you can't be too picky. I can get a hundred and fifty dollars for a massage in New York, but can only squeeze out sixty-five to eighty-five dollars here."

I hated her choice of words just then.

She sat down on a floor pillow next to my chair and dusted Phantom's hair off the big orange flower design on her skirt.

"Look, I don't mind you living with me so that you can hold on to your cash and save for your place, but I also know how prissy you are. I want to be able to bring a friend over here sometimes, but I don't want to hear your shit."

"Yeah, I'm not really looking forward to that."

"Well, it's my house, remember that."

I looked at my mail that she'd dropped on the table. Bills, nothing but damn bills. More than twenty thousand dollars of student loans and credit card debt is what I was drowning in. At least I didn't have rent, and I had to buy only groceries and gas. Besides, it's only right. I remember when True had fallen on some hard times. A drummer she was dating broke up with her for messing around with the guitar player in his band. According to her, it was a hot night of getting high and a three-way gone horribly wrong. She ended up with the guitar player in the end. His name was Stroke—for his guitar-playing skills, that is. She should have seen that one coming with a name like that.

She bummed off me for a good six months after that. I didn't ask her for a dime, and she sure didn't offer, either. True slept on the couch in my one-bedroom in Brooklyn and at least every other night she had Stroke over. Not to mention she also had a number of other dudes, half her age, over. My Jennifer Convertibles couch was a revolving door. I couldn't even walk around in my nightgown in my own home, for fear of what strange men scratching their balls I'd find in my living room.

I don't know what kind of magic cootchie True has, but it's like a magnet that makes these grown-assed men crawl to her with their tails between their legs, wallets in hand. She still, however, has a hard time keeping a man around for longer than a year, so I'm not sure if it's their money or her magic that wears out first.

I crumpled up my last piece of junk mail offering me another consolation credit card deal and sat on the couch.

"Ky, did you do the laundry today?"

True looked at the mountain of laundry bags in the hallway and then back at me. Isn't it obvious that "no" is the answer? Why ask?

"No, I've been out most of the day. I didn't get to it yet."

She gave a long sigh. "Out all day doing what, tanning? That's the least you can do, Kylie Rain." I know she's pissed when she calls me by my first and middle name. "You aren't looking for a job like you should be and you aren't paying rent. You—"

I blew out hot air. "I haven't been home all day and please, True, I've been here for only a month and don't plan on staying for more than two. You lived like a queen in my place for more than six months and did I let you ever lift a finger?"

True's nostrils flared. She got up and put her hand on her hip and pointed the other one at me. Her Jamaican accent made a special appearance whenever she got upset. With her chin high, she said, "Listen 'ere, you 'ave some dayaaam respect. I'm your mother. I shouldn't have to do anything. You are still my child. I carried your ass for nine months. You remember dat. Don't forget who raised you." She took an exaggeratedly deep breath.

I sat back and smiled. I wanted to tell her, "Yeah, I remember who raised me! James and Florida Evans from *Good Times*, the Jeffersons, Martin and Gina from *Martin*, and my favorite father, Mr. Ingalls from *Little House on the Prairie*." When she was out and about gallivanting with her man of the month, she dumped me in front of her nanny: the twenty-five-inch TV.

"Look, I'm going to take a walk. Excuse me."

"You're excused." She walked off with her usual sashay to her room. I learned long ago to just end confrontations before they exploded. And I figured since I can't quite shack up with Jacques the sexy psychic, I have nowhere else to go.

Chapter 5

Jacques

My flight arrived last night and as soon as I got in the taxi at LaGuardia Airport, I felt good. I took in the essence of it all. I loved the bright lights, the cobblestoned streets, the loud sirens, and even the offensive smell of Broadway after it recovered from wild nights in SoHo.

I was ready for a new adventure, even though I would miss the sun and Vicky. Every three to six months or so, I set up appointments with my New York City clients. That's where I got my start, so I have to make time for my loyal clients who were the foundation of my business. Besides, I miss the energy of the city, and I get to see my little brother, Hicham, and my mother when I go back.

My mother would always say that no city in America could compare to Paris. She didn't really appreciate New York like Hicham and I did. Nothing could measure up to New York in my eyes. I love the wild personalities and many ethnicities that season New York City's diverse stew. I moved to Miami two years ago for a more relaxed lifestyle and to be in the sun. However, the fast pace, the skyline, and, let's face it, the delis, pizzas, and bagels just cannot be duplicated.

While in town, I stayed at my mom's old loft on Mercer Street, which Hicham moved into a few years back. It was definitely an experience seeing my brother on his own, fending for himself and not being babied by our mom or some ditzy model who he met on the job.

I walked around observing the changes in the loft since his most recent girlfriend, Rachel, the bikini model, left him. It had been only a month and he'd wasted no time in turning it back into a bachelor pad, full of empty beer cans and pizza boxes underneath the couch.

"So, what happened, man? I thought Rachel was 'the one.'" I asked to be polite but I'd known she would catch on to his antics sooner or later.

"Yeah, I thought so, too, but she was getting a bit too clingy. Questioning my whereabouts, searching my pockets, finding numbers." He laughed. "You know, finding red hair in the shower . . . She's a brunette."

I shook my head as I watched my brother pull a shirt over his scrawny chest. Always one in need of attention, his gray T-shirt said in bold white letters I'D FUCK ME.

Standing at six three, slim and lanky, he looked like a featherweight. But his persona gave off a cocky Muhammad Ali vibe, as if he could take on the world. He resembled our mother, with his fair skin and bone structure. No one knew where the tall lankiness came from, but we guessed it was somewhere in our genes. We didn't really look much alike at all, but we could pass for cousins.

Hicham shrugged his shoulders. "Hey, I'm getting back to my old self again, gotta build my stable of women back up. Rachel missed out, so exit stage left, biyaaaach! There are plenty of women in line, ready to take her place," he said nonchalantly. He really thought he was the man.

"Who taught you to be so damn cold? You definitely didn't learn that from me." I mushed the side of his head with my finger.

"Of course I didn't. If I looked like your Olivier Martinez, *Entourage*-niggah-looking ass, I would have bitches all over this house like Hugh Hefner. You don't even know, man. I'm a good-looking brother—this I know—but you know you the pretty one in the fam." He rubbed the top of my head and fluffed up my hair.

"Yeah, yeah. You might be right about that." I grinned. I hated when he called me pretty.

Hicham pretended to smooth back his hair as if I'd messed it up when I pushed him. He didn't have much hair, just a low buzz cut. "I was getting soft, man, all lovey-dovey and shit. I gotta get back to the real me for my column. You know I'm syndicated now in more than a hundred blogs? I'm even getting radio and TV interviews. Small stuff but still . . ."

"I know, I know, you told me." I thumped him on the back. He'd told me about twenty times since last week.

"Man, I need to have my shit tight. Stay true to the game. Remind dudes that they should stay focused."

I nodded intently. "Right, right, stay true to the game. It's a game all right!"

"Come on, Jacques, committed dudes ain't reading my stuff. My audience wants advice from a player. A man who knows the terrain." He moved his hands up and down in an hour-glass motion and pumped the air with his crotch.

I scratched my chin. "And that would be you, huh? Stop!" I couldn't hold back my laughter. "Please stop!"

He laughed at himself, too. "Man, you don't even know. Chicks keep throwing it at me now more than ever. It's like they love that I talk so much shit. The meaner I am, the more they want it. They read my column to get advice, too. I had to start adding in some love for them, so they know a little somethin'."

"You, my dear brother, are an anomaly. Still amazes me." I couldn't hold back anymore and my grin turned into a laugh.

"Whatever, man, you need to drop that cop bitch and join the game, player. It's fun on the other side."

"Hey, hey . . . watch it!" I pointed at him. "Vicky . . . her name is Vicky."

"Oh yeah, Vicky. Yo, she still a freak?"

My eyes brightened from a flashback. "Well, you know . . . we have fun. We keep it interesting."

"So, you gonna wife her now?" Hicham tilted his head from side to side.

"No, no . . . we're still calling it dating for now. But I don't have to have ten women. We spice it up. That's what you need to learn how to do, Mister Playa! You get bored too quickly.

Keep sticking that thing in everyone you meet, it might come out with something on it that you don't want."

He sat on the arm of the couch across from me. "Oh, no, no, no. I give chicks a full inspection. Bright lights and all." He pretended to smell his fingers. "Make sure it smells right, no bumps and lumps. My bitches are thoroughbred. Dimes only. Believe dat. I always wear a condom, too. So . . ."

"Right, right . . . condoms don't cover everything."

He looked agitated and waved his hand in the air. "Yo, let's change the subject."

"Hicham, just be careful. It's not all fun and games out there."

He leaned in. "What? You getting a premonition and shit about me? What, man? Don't hold back. If you see me catching something, you better fuckin' tell me!"

"Relax! No, no I don't see that, but just be careful is all."

He headed for the bedroom, walking backward and pointing. "If you see some shit, you better tell me!"

He was so dramatic. "Yeah, yeah . . ."

I really didn't see anything directly, but I know Hicham has a low vibration at times and surrounds himself with people of similar or lower energy. When you are not grounded or you're constantly partying with drugs and alcohol, it's a recipe for disaster. I lay back on the couch and looked around. I was still tired from traveling and, let's face it, Hicham was tiring. I was happy to see him, though. He always made me laugh, whether he meant to or not.

My eyes floated around the room. The parquet floors were remarkably clean, except for two pizza boxes. They were almost a yellow wood with a tarnished aged look to them. The floors were carpeted when Mom lived here. Hicham's high ceilings and minimal furniture gave his place a spacious feel, unlike most matchbox-sized apartments in New York. When Mom lived in the loft, you could barely find space on the wall, because her paintings were everywhere. It was more her studio than a home.

I lay back on the couch and was thankful that Hicham was finally getting his act together. He hadn't borrowed any rent money from me in almost six months—an astonishing record for him. I was lost in the deep burgundy photography backdrop in the far corner of his loft. All of his camera equipment was set up there.

"What are you thinking about?" Hicham broke my concentration as he handed me a cold beer.

"You." I smiled. "I'm proud of you." I nodded my head as I took a sip of my beer.

Although he towered over me, he changed into a kid right before my eyes.

"You are? Really?" He looked like he'd been waiting forever for me to say that.

I must admit it, I was never very affectionate toward my little brother. I'd wanted to toughen him up a bit. I figured he got enough coddling from Mom. He was always her favorite. I used to be really worried about how he was going to survive on his own when Mom moved to a smaller place in TriBeCa. Now that he has transformed into a womanizer in macho-man overdrive, I wonder if I was worrying about the wrong things. . . .

"Yeah, sure I'm proud of you, Hicham. You're doing really good with your job at *Maxim* magazine, getting all that press. And I love how you're getting a lot of freelance clients, too. You haven't been sticking it to me with the sob stories for some cash."

"Oh, come on, Jacques, you act like I borrowed so much. . . ."

I shot him a look. He still owed me about $2,000.

"Well, if you were really a good brother, you would hook me up with the lottery numbers for tomorrow. What's the point of having magical powers if you don't share your gift with your loved ones?" He laughed as he took a swig of beer.

"Shut up, Hicham!" I laughed with him.

I'd never given him an actual reading and definitely had never given my mother one. Not that she even believes I can give readings. She still doesn't admit it to herself that this is who I am and this is what I do for a living. I'd rather give them advice only when absolutely necessary. I try to draw the line between business and my personal relationships. They can go haywire when I get too deeply involved with someone's life if he is close to me. And, I must admit, some things I'd just rather not know. The truth is, if I could figure out the Lotto numbers or which horse would win, I'd be in a different tax bracket by now. I know only what messages are given to me. Seeing things for my own future was not always easy and clear.

Chapter 6
Kylie

I walked into the guest room, with Phantom trailing behind me like my little shadow. The sweetness of a honeydew-scented PlugIn air freshener embraced me as I entered my room, my escape from True's stank attitude.

I rubbed my hand across the wheat-colored wallpaper. It was grainy and resembled grass blades. I dropped onto the fluffy down comforter and stared blankly at the seashells and crystals on the windowsill. My eyes floated across the room to the vase of white lilies on my mahogany dresser. It was quite obvious the decorating shows on HGTV were personal favorites of True's. She was not the greatest mother, but ironically she was one heck of a good homemaker.

It was the simplicity of this room that gave me peace and helped me forget the stress I was going through. The depression from my debt gave me a sinking feeling that never went away, no matter how many minimum payments I made on my maxed-out credit cards. My entire life was jammed into a storage garage, which was just another bill to pay. I missed my own furniture, *my* home.

I took off my jeans, earrings, and beaded belly chain and put on a sports bra, tank top, and my favorite old Columbia University shorts. A nice long speed-walk around Coconut Grove listening to my music would do me some good.

I stretched on the front porch and waved to our nosy neighbor Hilda Cruz, who loved wearing housecoats all day long, even to go to the grocery store. She was picking mangoes from her tree. "There's plenty more, honey. Tell your mom to come get some!"

"Okay!" I replied, and started to speed-walk away from a long conversation about her goofy son that I should meet. I'd seen him before. Not my type, but she brings him up every time I see her.

I took in the sweet sounds of the birds chirping and wind blowing before I totally checked out of nature and plugged in to listen to Jason Mraz, my latest musical crush. He has a sexy Jamiroquai kind of voice. Jazzy, soulful, and funky. You wouldn't believe he's a white boy.

I picked up the pace to a light jog. I felt like I'd gotten sucked into a vortex from TV Land where the *Leave It to Beaver* theme music played as I jogged. A few people waved at me and smiled. Many of these people I'd never seen before in my life! They sure were friendly down here. A few cars even stopped to let me go by, just because.

I had to turn back before it got too dark, because a few blocks farther west was the shady part of Coconut Grove, where drug dealers on bikes, prostitutes, heroin addicts, and crackheads abounded. Well, that's at least what True had told me.

I made sure I stayed on the safe side of the Grove and made a quick U-turn the second it started to look sketchy: guys on bikes, fewer tourists, and more cops. I cooled down, but still walked at a fast pace, because I knew I had something to look forward to when I got home. My reward after my four-mile speed-walk was to chat it up with my new Internet friend, Chauncey. Yes, sexy-ass Chauncey. We had a "date at eight" as we liked to call them. We've chatted online for more than two weeks and so far the conversations have been good. He intrigued me with a compliment about my musical "likes" on my Match.com profile page. I had Pat Benatar's "Love Is a Battlefield" listed as one of my favorite songs of all time. I thought it was fitting for me, seeing how my love life has been sucking ever since I left New York. Truthfully, it's been the real pits for the past two years.

I've dated a few guys and of course had my old reliable from New York: my homie-lover-friend, Breeze, who was always in the picture. But still no one that I'm trying to make babies and settle down with, that's for sure. They all insisted on being exclusive, but I'm right where I wanna be. I don't even know if I want to have children. Being responsible for another life? Hoping they don't pull the same stupid tricks you did! I'm too much of a snoop, and I might read her diary and she'll hate me forever. A mother? I don't think I'm cracked up to be one. I didn't have the best example from the beginning, after all.

Even though Chauncey lives in Orlando, four hours north, Internet romance is looking like the next best thing to the face-to-face thing. I kinda enjoy the anticipation, sexual tension, and fantasy that come along with it. I get a real rush from wondering what the person on the other side of the Wi-Fi signal will be like in 3-D. I'm hoping to keep my distance at least for a while, just so that I can get to know him better. It's my first attempt at Internet dating and I have to admit I'm a bit nervous about our first real-life meeting.

After my jog and a shower, I felt like I had a second wind for the evening. Standing on the coral-colored terrace overlooking the freshly cut grass, I took in my favorite part of the day . . . sunset. I loved the pinkish cotton candy sunset glowing and the palm trees dancing in the evening breeze. It all reminded me of how peaceful it was back in Jamaica. While I was there on the white sand, I didn't battle with my thoughts or continue to beat myself up about past mistakes. I didn't compare myself to True anymore. I finally convinced myself that I was my own woman and I sure as hell wasn't going to become her. I wanted to be focused on a job that I loved, not just money. I didn't want to be a scatterbrain like her, taking any meaningless job and falling for a money-making scheme. Gullible, I'm not. And, most important, I refuse to be somebody's forty-five-year-old, unmarried booty call. She was fine with that life, but for me, it's not going to happen.

I thought long and hard about my career direction. My last job was at EarKandy, an online magazine and social network for music lovers. I was attracted to the job in the first place because I'm an avid fan of all types of music. After two years, I feel like I can answer any obscure question on any music genre, from Captain & Tennille to Kendrick Lamar.

I always knew who was on *E! True Hollywood Story* and TV One's *Unsung* and who topped the Billboard charts. Useless music statistics started swimming around in my dreams, pushing out the juicy fantasies I should've been having. My brain was starting to get overcrowded. Sure, with all the facts and stats on music, at any party I was fully armed as the hipster-intellectual on pop culture. I also knew that after a while I could bore someone to death with my knowledge, because all I lived, slept, and breathed was music.

I was damn good at my job, better than anyone else who came before me. At least that's what I was told from the higher-ups. I was well liked by my boss, which is what caused lots of jealousy among some of my coworkers.

I knew I had "the power" and I must admit, I did abuse it somewhat. I could stroll in late to a meeting and be greeted with a smile. Others would get chastised—I mean downright screamed on—in front of everyone. I got three weeks' vacation my first year and everyone else had two.

"She's fucking him."

"I heard she sucks a mean dick."

"So-and-so caught them messing around right in his office on a Saturday."

The rumors were outrageous, and yes, they always, always got back to me. People didn't realize that I was the fact-checker and the Queen of Snoop (my girl Olivia blessed me with that name). So. Don't. Fuck. With. Me. The nosy bitches who tried to ostracize me were close with their allegations, but no cigar.

True, my boss, Howie Cantanelli, and I had a fling, but it was eons ago, back in college. A hot steamy romance it was not. We never even got 100 percent naked, which was a downer for me, since I was looking forward to my first Jungle Fever experience. He couldn't even get it up the night we tried, and I'm sure he's been wanting to make up for it ever since. For my conscience's sake, I guess it's a good thing we didn't go further than a hot humpin' kiss.

We stayed friends after college and I followed his career path as he moved up the corporate ladder at Music News. When he was appointed VP of a new website under the Music News umbrella called EarKandy, he invited me to be on his team. He knew I had majored in communications and was a music fanatic. Sure, I knew his hidden agenda might be to make his way into my panties, but I put my foot down. I told him I would take the job under the condition we didn't let anyone—not anyone—know about our past affiliation. What would his wife think? But the little innocent fling we kept a secret eventually came back to haunt us.

One day, Howie and I were staring at his computer watching a YouTube interview of a new artist. I was sitting with my back to the door, but couldn't miss the bang when it was flung open.

"Howie! My man!" a familiar voice yelled.

"Julian! Holy shit, what are you doing here?" Howie shouted.

"The receptionist let me in." I turned around to match the face with the voice. "I was in the neighborhood, and . . ." Julian comically shook his head as if seeing spots. "No way!

No freakin' way. Smiley Kylie? What the hell! Get over here, beautiful!" I laughed as he came over to scoop me out of the chair and embrace me with his signature massive bear hug. He was drowning in cologne, as usual, and his dark hair was slicked back with mousse. Very *Grease*, John Travolta, 1978. Ewww.

I kissed him on the cheek. "Julian, so good to see you! I see you filled out a bit, huh?"

He patted his stomach, which was now a beer belly instead of the trim six-pack he showed off every chance he got in college.

"Oh yeah, that's good living, sweetie. You know I married rich, right?" He slapped Howie on the back and laughed obnoxiously. We laughed, but he wasn't lying. By the looks of his tailored shirt, cuff links, and slacks, I could see she dressed him as well as she fed him.

"So, wait a minute, for Christ's sake," Julian said. "Are you two still, ummm?"

"Oh, no, no!" we yelled in unison.

"Ahaaaa! Ahaaaa!" He pointed like he'd caught us doing something. The door was open and everyone had heard his big mouth.

We didn't know that Julian's little visit was the beginning of my end at EarKandy. The rumors escalated like a California wildfire, once people started putting the details together: that we were the same age and we both went to Columbia. All of a sudden, they thought they knew why I got special treatment.

The gossip by the water cooler was at an all-time high.

One of my interns was in the copy room and reported back to me that she heard two women in my department gossiping about me and how I received special treatment. They were rambling about how I got away with everything. One even mentioned they were going to HR to report it. The other mentioned she had already complained to Howie.

I was furious, and less than a week later, the shit hit the fan. Howie had to cover his ass, so I lost my job. I know it was those two jealous chicks. Budget cuts were the excuse, but of course, I'm the only one who got laid off. He gave me six months' pay as my severance and I had unemployment, too. Most of it vanished after paying off a lot of debt.

I can survive at least another two months without a job. Guilt crept in as I remembered what Jacques said in my reading—that I was being a bit lazy. Howie told me that when things died down he might send me some freelance work and I could work from home. That's definitely my last resort. I hope I don't have to go back to that business.

I didn't miss working the long hours or the alienation, and I sure didn't miss being looked at as a whore who slept her way to the top, especially since it wasn't true!

My cell phone rang; the screen said "Tulsa OK," but I didn't know anyone in Oklahoma. I answered it anyway.

A deep baritone filled my ears. "Kylie Collins, please."

"Yes, this is she."

"Hello, I'm Chris from Macy's calling about your payment, which is currently thirty days past due." His voice was kinda scary in a James Earl Jones, you're-in-trouble kinda way.

"I'll be able to pay fifty dollars on Friday."

"Great, can we use your credit card on file?"

"No, no, I'll do it online. Thanks. Good night." I rolled my eyes and hung up quickly.

It was getting a bit hard. The stress of unpaid bills tightened around my neck like a noose. The damn calls were driving me crazy! They started at 8:00 A.M., continued every couple of hours, and stopped just short of my blowing a blood vessel around 8:45 P.M. Collection calls were sending me into a deep pit of hopelessness. Seeing all my friends back in NYC driving new cars, buying homes on Long Island, investing in stocks and bonds, and building retirement funds made me feel as if they had grown up but my life was stuck in remedial mode.

I shouldn't be upset because even with a steady paycheck, I was pretty free with my money. I know I'm a grown-up and I shouldn't blame True for teaching me her spendthrift ways, but I never really believed in having a savings account. True always said to live every day as if it were your last. Planning for a rainy day was negative thinking, she'd say. "The universe will always provide. It always has." She'd laugh gaily like she hadn't a care in the world, even if she wasn't sure where the rent money was coming from. All True seemed to ask the universe to bring her was a man. She was just dandy with that.

I could just as easily use my body and charm to get Breeze to Western Union me a few hundred or juice sweet Internet Chauncey into wining and dining me, but I do have a conscience. I don't want to use someone, since as I always say, "Karma's a bitch if you are."

As the sun lowered gracefully, saying its last good-byes, I pulled out my iPad, knowing that one of the neighbors had wireless that I could hijack. Powering up, I was right on time for my "date at eight." I logged on to Chauncey's page to see if he was online. A smiley face blinked next to his name. The greatest aphrodisiac in the world to a woman is consistency. Ah, a consistent and reliable man.

I was pleasantly surprised to see new photos of Chauncey that were added to his profile page. I had been thinking he had a bubble butt and thunder thighs, since all of his photos were from the waist up, but his new photos showed him chilling at the beach on a rock, no shirt and tan trunks. He was givin' it to me with that charming smile. I sent him an instant message.

KYLIERAIN: Nice legs!

CHAUNCEBOOGIE: You like? I put it up for you, you know?

KYLIERAIN: I'm sure you tell all the girls that. LOL. When did you take it? That tattoo of the cougar is rather sexy.

CHAUNCEBOOGIE: I took it two weeks ago at Daytona Beach with some friends. When are you coming to the Orlando area to hang out?

KYLIERAIN: Not sure . . . Shouldn't we speak on the phone first? Don't you wanna make sure I don't sound like Darth Vader or something?

CHAUNCEBOOGIE: You're a riot. LOL Well, I've wanted to speak to you since last week, but I didn't want to rush you. I'm dying to hear your voice.

KYLIERAIN: Really? Me too, but I am trying to take it slow. I'm new at this Internet dating. I don't want to show up at your place and find out you're a 14-year-old kid and To Catch a Predator gets me on their next episode.

CHAUNCEBOOGIE: LMAO. Let's talk now . . . call me 407-555-3425. Hit *67 to block your number if you are still unsure. I won't stalk you, I promise.

KYLIERAIN: K, let's do it. . . . Racing to the phone!

Breeze was out of my life for now and I was ready to see if Chauncey was a winner. I'd had a few dates here and there, but all were dead ends. Speaking to Chauncey was like foreplay. His voice was slow and smooth, as if he were really thinking about what he was going to say before the words came out of his mouth. Total opposite of me.

"So, when was the last time you had a real relationship, Kylie? I never heard you mention a salty ex-boyfriend story."

"Last dating relationship or a real boyfriend? There is a difference, ya know," I said very matter-of-factly.

He laughed nervously. "Well, do tell, what's the difference?"

"Oh, come on, you know, you have your girlfriend, the one you are committed to, probably in love with. Then you have the periods of your life when you don't have anyone who actually fits into that category, but there's someone who might be fantaaaaabulous in bed and that's it." I chuckled. "It's a sad state of affairs, but sometimes we all need a little loving." We both laughed. "The sad part about those relationships is that after the fun is over, you have nothing in common besides positions."

"Damn, when you put it that way," he said, "I guess you're right. No substance to the connection. So, which one have you been with recently, a boyfriend or a booty-call friend?"

"Neither. It's been a while since I had a real boyfriend or, quite honestly, a booty call."

"All jokes aside, I admire your honesty, Kylie," Chauncey commended me.

"Hey, no need to play games, right?" I just hoped he was as honest as I was.

"Exactly."

"Well." I sighed. "The closest thing to a boyfriend I've had was someone I dated for a while, but it was just an on-again, off-again romance that lasted about ten years. The last four years were more serious. I dated others in between, but he was really the one I wanted to be—"

Chauncey interrupted, "Did you say ten years? Damn, that's a long time. What was the problem with you guys?"

"Well, I was naive and young. He wanted to treat me like his woman, but he wasn't ready to settle down. He was an absolute mind-fucker and commitment-phobe who had every excuse in the book."

He laughed. "A mind what?"

I curled up on the bed with my pillow, smiling at how captivated he was with my boldness. "I should have apologized in advance, Chauncey. I'm a lady, but sometimes, my mouth . . ."

"No need for apologies. You are soooo real and I love that about you." I could sense him smiling through the phone.

"Well, he was a mind-fucker, a master manipulator, possessive, and controlling." I laughed, a bit embarrassed. "Oh wait, I guess this is the salty ex-boyfriend story you were talking about."

"Hey, you gotta vent sometimes. I feel you."

"Yeah, I was under his spell for a while, but I got over it."

"You sure? That was not a little while—shit, ten years is a lifetime when you're our age," he said, laughing.

Just in case he was not convinced that I was over Breeze, I tried to clean up my mess. "We're cordial still, no bitterness. It's much easier now that I live here and he's in New York. He's the type to prey on you, even after you move on."

"Sounds like a stalker. Am I going to have to watch my back, Kylie?" He was teasing, but there was a slight tension in his voice.

"No, not at all." I tried to laugh it off. Breeze was in New York, but psychologically he still had a hold on me. Just talking about him stirred up anger and even the strange love that I had for him. I was still furious with myself for letting him tie me up for so long. I knew deep down if Breeze walked in the door right now and said "I'm ready, Ky," I would want to pack up and go.

Chauncey continued to push for more info. "So, let's just say this turns out to be more than an Internet fling. Are you open to a relationship, a real commitment? Or did Mr. Mind-fucker piss you off too much to even think about it?"

"I gotta be honest." I paused to gather my thoughts. "I'm not too anxious to rush into a relationship, but I do miss the comfort of one. Having someone to share my day with, comfort me when things aren't going well, and rub my feet. Do you rub feet, Chauncey?"

"Of course, especially when they are pretty. I checked yours out already in your photos from the beach."

"Okay, you get points for being observant. I do have a thing for foot massages. If you do those well, you might have me under a spell of your own." I wiggled my toes and stretched out my legs as if he could see my nice pedicure. "It would be nice, though I'm not rushing into anything, but if it happens, I'm ready for it. So, what about you, last time in a real relationship?"

"I'm going on about two years since I broke up with my ex and about seven months of celibacy, by choice."

"Wow, seven months, you really took a hiatus, huh?" I didn't believe him for shit.

"Well, I needed it. I had to clear my mind, get back to the root of things. Get rid of distractions. Running up in too many women is not my thing. I had serious doubts I could even have a real relationship again after what my ex Le-Le did. She cheated on me with a coworker."

"Ouch, sorry to hear."

"Yeah, what made it wild is that it was a woman."

"Dayummm, that's gotta be rough." Yikes! I tried not to laugh.

"Don't worry about it. The woman she was cheating with was married and never left her husband to go romp into Lesbian Land with her. It was a fantasy she took to the next level and now she's still trying to come back into my life. She regrets her little bi-curious fun, but it's too late. I'm all for experimenting, but don't do that shit on my time."

"Karma's a bitch, man," I mumbled. Red flag for me! He's going to probably be paranoid.

Chauncey began getting into his feelings. "I was so hurt, so in shock, especially since I was faithful to her. But as they say, time heals all wounds."

"Yeah, it's true, Chauncey. The next time around is always better, because we learn from our mistakes. Now we can spot the red flags. No worries with me, I'm not into chicks."

We laughed and I slowly packed away my red flags; my closet was bursting with them. I knew I could be loyal if I had to be, if the right man came along. I didn't need to let him know just how fucked up I was, not just yet. I felt like I really knew what I was talking about but I was trying to convince myself, too, since I'm horrible at catching the signs myself.

It's true that people hold back as long as they can. They hide their true colors and their inner demons. What would he think if he knew about my mom, about the way I was raised? I had to pretend my childhood was full of baking chocolate chip cookies and backyard barbecues, even though I practically raised myself and lived in a damn-near brothel. The good part about it all is that I somehow felt that I didn't have to pretend with Chauncey. I could open up and really be Kylie.

We spoke for three hours straight and it felt nice getting

to know him. I found out he was a mortgage broker for a bank. He hated his job in Orlando but liked his paycheck. He wanted to buy a condo in Miami; he had good credit and helped other people fix theirs. I think he is a winner, but with one big no-no: He has kids. I know, I know. And not one, two! A five-year-old son and fourteen-year-old daughter. *Two baby mamas!* That means I'd be baby mama number three. His son lives in California and his daughter lives in Virginia. Lucky me, but still, just the idea of him having child support payments is enough to give me huge pause. But hey, such is life. I really like him and after our long conversation, I realized, why delay meeting him? Go for it!

"I really think you're a cool guy, Chauncey."

"Oh yeah? You ain't so bad yourself, girl."

I got brave enough to ask, "Want to come down and hang out in the M-I-A this weekend?"

"Sure. *This* weekend? You sure you ready for me?"

"Might I add, of course you'd have to get a hotel room, since I live with my mom right now."

He sucked his teeth. "Who says I would be so easy? I would get my own room anyhow. The nerve!" he said with a touch of false indignation in his voice.

"A date at eight in the flesh. 'Feel-up Friday'! I can't wait!" I teased.

"Oh, I likes. Feel-up Fridays? We should make that a holiday if this works out. But hey, just be easy on me. It's been a long time. I don't need any temptation, and by the looks of your photos, you're oh, so tempting."

"Oh, fun, I can't wait to tease you."

"Hummph, I already see you're gonna be trouble!" he mumbled.

"Who meeee? Never." I laughed.

"So, what do you want to do, any activities you recommend down there? It's been a minute."

"Beach is always easy and we can eat after?"

"Oh, wow."

"Wow what? You sound surprised."

"Well, you know . . . the beach. Most women don't wanna mess up their hair or makeup."

"Chauncey, you'll soon find that I'm not 'most women.'"

"It's actually pretty refreshing. I mean, you have no idea."

"We're gonna have fun getting to know each other."

"Yes . . . Lots of fun. I already can tell." He cleared his throat. "Okay . . . I'll check out the hotels on South Beach and get back to you tomorrow and we'll take it from there."

"That's sounds good. Okay, Chauncey! Until tomorrow, *ciao*."

"All right, sweetie." Chauncey paused as if he didn't want to hang up. "Kylie . . ."

"Yes?" I said with a smile.

"I'll be thinking about you."

My heart fluttered. "Wow, same here. Good night."

"You have a good one, too, beautiful."

I jumped up like a seventeen-year-old kid about to go to prom. I have a date. Wow! A date with Chauncey. This is going to be fun. I just love how giddy I feel after speaking with him. He makes me forget all my woes.

Chapter 7
Kylie

The night before our date, I made sure I got my hair done at Natural Trendsetters, the hottest natural hair salon in South Florida. I added a few chunky blond streaks to my honey-brown 'fro for a fun, summery look. I wanted to make an irresistible first impression. If Chauncey looked as good as he did in his photos, I was definitely going to be flirting. The two of us and the beach . . . what could be better? The poor guy had no idea what I had in store for him. The clear waters, our skin pressed up against each other, and the waves thrusting into us as we kiss and touch.

"Ky, you got a call. It's Olivia!" True was in her bright red short-shorts and sports bra, getting ready to go to the gym, looking thirty-three instead of forty-three. Her voice startled me out of my soon-to-be wet dream.

I grabbed the phone. "Thanks, True. What's up, Liv!"

True left a sweet trail of shea butter and tea tree oil floating in the air as she walked toward the door.

Olivia's British accent was always music to my ears. "Hey there, how are ya? Are you ready for your hot date?"

"Yeah, got my hair did, new bathing suit, I'm all ready."

"Beauty parlor and then beach? That's smart." She always had a snide comment.

"I'll wrap it up when we go in the water. I have to look cute, okay smart-ass?"

"Nervous?" She laughed.

"A little." I stared out the window at my neighbor's dog, Aspen, playing with his ball. "Girl, I'm praying he looks as good in person. Otherwise his personality seems solid. He's really a wonderful guy."

"Well, I'm sure he's praying the same thing about you. Let's just keep it a secret about how crazy you are. Behave yourself. You know you are an open book."

"I'm hoping I can be real with him. I want to see if he can actually handle *all* of me. He might be a bit conservative, not sure yet."

"Oh well, you better make it a quick date. Don't bring the whips, chains, and leather mask out just yet."

"Girl, please, I haven't done that in ages. My equipment is in storage anyhow." With a devilish grin I said, "And for your information, I never owned a leather mask!" I laughed so hard, tears formed in the corners of my eyes. "Those stories go with you to your grave, Olivia! You hear me? Tha graaaaaave!"

"Mum's the word, you slut." She giggled.

"Ooohh, Mommy said a bad word!" her daughter squealed.

"What?" Olivia was startled. "Get from behind me. What did I tell you about sneaking up on Mommy when she's on the phone?"

"Oh shit, she already knows that's a bad word."

"Well, yeah, she's said it before and got slapped for it."

"Kids. See why I don't want any?"

"Whatever, you'll probably be the one who ends up with triplets!"

We chuckled. "Ah! Don't curse me. I don't need that jinx!"

Olivia was well aware of my former life as a fake dominatrix. It was Breeze's fault. I only did it for him. He sparked my interest in the world of S and M and my appetite for domination became voracious. I talked dirty, pulled hair, scratched, yelled, and even beat him with a whip. Usually they say high-powered men love that stuff. They want to release all control, be submissive for once. Boy, I had a good time doing it.

As manipulative and controlling as Breeze was, it seemed he got a kick out of obeying my every command when we played. I do admit that I missed seeing him squirm with his hands tied behind his back, on his knees, and sometimes blindfolded. We were wild. Revenge was such sweet victory—for all the times he controlled me outside of the bedroom.

Olivia wasn't too crazy about the Internet dating thing. "Text message me his full name and license plate number when you see him. And be careful."

"Okay, Olivia," I reassured her. "I will be sure to get his fingerprints, too. Wish me luck."

Chapter 8

Jacques

I love New York but I hate its public transportation. I can't stand crowds or the energy that flows through them.

To avoid taking the subway, I tried desperately to hail a cab one morning in front of my brother's loft. I was on my way to visit my mom in TriBeCa. Normally I'd enjoy the long walk but it was pouring rain and the wind was unbelievably powerful. My peacoat kept me warm and I pulled my dark hoodie over my head. I soon surrendered to the shelter of the subway, when the umbrella I held had become a flimsy piece of vinyl with unruly wires.

I never liked trains or buses. It's bad enough I can read people. People are not themselves on a train. They close off and go within. Their vibrations and bad energies fight to get out and be free. People are not looking at one another, not smiling, not really thinking about anything in particular. As strange as it sounds, it's frustrating. I usually feel closed in, like I'm trapped inside a cage. I want to yell at the top of my lungs and release everything they are all holding back.

I often feel a tight hold around my neck. I have to seriously meditate to avoid that feeling. My friends used to laugh at me when I got on the train, because they could literally see how uncomfortable I got. The subway is also a haven for nutcases. For some reason, no matter how much of a sardine can the train is, they always find me. After a long day working on other people's problems, the last thing I want to do is absorb more of people's crap. I've come to realize that many of the people society calls crazy are just unresolved psychics. Many of these people were given the gift to see what others can't, but they have no control over it, and they don't know how to separate the spirit world from the real world. They aren't grounded and might really see entities from other dimensions or earthbound spirits, but they get labeled crazy and become outcasts.

As a psychology major, I studied various psychological disorders. At the time, I wanted to become a therapist. While learning about disorders, my gut feeling told me that although many of those issues were very real, they might not all be truly "disorders." The "voices" in my head or the spirits that visit me at night probably would turn the average individual into a basket case if they didn't understand that they were gifted.

I looked across the train car at a mother and two daughters who seemed mesmerized by what they were working on. The older daughter had long braids down her back. She looked like eight years old or so and was writing in a book called *You*

Can Write Cursive Too! The younger one, who was about five years old, was wearing a pink Barbie ski cap. She dug into her Barbie backpack, finally fishing out a coloring book.

As I watched her color, a rush of warm memories flooded back into my thoughts. Coloring was my first love and it always reminded me of my father, since he taught me how to do it. Although my mom was a designer and painter, she was always on tour traveling for some art showing or working at the gallery. My father was the one to play with me.

It was through coloring that I realized how connected to my father I really was. The first time it happened, my first grade teacher was quite disturbed and I had no idea of the seriousness of it all. At playtime all the kids drew with crayons. In our crude masterpieces, you'd find stick figures of friends, siblings, parents, and even the bus driver whom we affectionately called Uncle Louie. I don't remember what I drew that day, but I remember when I colored, I almost felt like I was dreaming. I was relaxed. I was off in my own world. What I didn't realize then was that particular day would be the beginning of my new life.

I sat alone on the floor under a table in the playroom, drawing. My masterpiece was a man floating in the ocean. When the small bell on the teacher's desk rang, it was time to present to the class what we'd created. I raised my hand first, because I was very proud of my work. I had beautiful blues for the ocean waves, the sun was a bright yellow, and I even added a smiley face and sunglasses to it. In the water were boats and a man lying facedown. The man was my father.

"Is he swimming?" Tammy shouted. I moved my fluffy

pageboy bangs out of my face and looked at the construction paper I held so proudly.

"Nope. I bet you can't guess!" I teased.

"Is he scuba diving? My daddy scuba dives in Puerto Rico!" my friend Ricardo shouted out from the front row.

"Well, what is he doing, Jacques?" asked Mrs. Murtha.

"He's dead. He's in heaven. He was drownding, drownding in da water," I said with a serious face. All the kids gasped in unison.

Ricardo covered his mouth and pointed. "Oooh, you in trouble. Your daddy is gonna beat you good for saying that!" The kids started heckling. Some even slapped their thighs like adults, imitating their parents' outbursts.

"Okay, that's enough, be quiet. Settle down!" Mrs. Murtha stood up.

"Jacques, see me after class." She pointed her finger at me sternly. I was very scared, because I thought she was the best teacher in the whole wide world and I'd never seen her angry, at least not at me.

Well, I never made it to the end of the day for detention. My mom came and took me out of school before recess because of an emergency none of us were prepared for. My father, Olivier Berradi, at the tender age of forty-one, was found in our bathroom tub, under the water, drowned. My father had been feeling extremely sick that week. His dark olive skin tone had been turning gray and he had been breathing strangely, so he'd decided to stay home and rest.

Mom was down at her gallery when she got a call from

a neighbor about a leak in their bathroom. When she came home, she found the entire apartment flooded and my father dead in the tub. The cops came and did an investigation, but they said they couldn't understand how he could have drowned. They concluded that he'd passed out and sank under the water. There was no suspicion of foul play and no sign of a struggle. No substance was ever found in his system. That was more than twenty-six years ago. I wasn't scared when I found out because somehow I knew my dad was okay. I felt his presence. I knew he wanted me to be strong for Mommy and for Hicham.

Mrs. Murtha waited about a month before asking my mom to come in. I listened closely by the door and peeked in the glass window every time I could without being caught. I thought I was in trouble, but I didn't understand why.

My mother's dark green eyes had an unfocused gaze as she looked around the classroom at the children's projects hung up on the walls. I knew she really didn't want to be there and talk about my dad all over again.

Even in her despair she was naturally gorgeous. Her high cheekbones, button nose, and sultry glances made her resemble a young Lauren Bacall. Her green eyes were her most striking feature, although so intense at times, they did not make her very approachable. She never thought she was *that* pretty and would scoff at the compliment or comparison, but she was truly stunning.

Although a natural beauty, she loved bright eye shadows and never ever left home without lipstick. Normally, she wore flowing dresses with bright colors, lots of gold bracelets, and floral prints, but that day she was in dark gray pants and not really put together with her usual flair.

Mrs. Murtha said, "I'm really sorry to hear about your loss. How are you and the boys coping?"

My mom's dark brown hair was in a Cleopatra bob. She kept nervously pushing one side behind her ear. "I'm doing okay, I guess. It's very hard though," she said. "Jacques is a strong boy, he's handling it better than me. He keeps telling me he knows his daddy is okay. I'm really proud of him." She wiped an eye, trying to fight back a tear.

"Well, Mrs. Berradi, I brought you here to tell you about Jacques. The day your husband was found, he drew this during playtime." She handed my mom the folded yellow construction paper with my father's demise sketched playfully in bright colors.

"I was appalled and was going to punish him, but now I think your son might have a gift!"

My mother stared at the drawing, then began crying hysterically. My mom and I made eye contact as I stood by the crack in the door. *"Qu'est ce qui t'a incite a dessiner ceci?"* She reached through the crack and tugged on my shirt collar tightly. "Tell me! Speak to me now, what made you want to draw this?" I didn't understand. Why was she so angry? Why was she crying? What did I do wrong? I burst into tears.

I looked at the ground and mumbled, "I don't know, I just wanted to. I felt . . . I felt Daddy wanted me to."

Mrs. Murtha put her hand on my mom's shoulder "Please, Mrs. Berradi, get a hold of yourself, please, it's not his fault.

He has a special gift, he just doesn't know how to control it yet."

My mom never spoke about my drawing again, but I always remember what Mrs. Murtha said about me: I was gifted. I was special.

That evening, I tried to make my mother feel better. Her back was to me while she washed the spaghetti-stained dishes in the kitchen. I approached her slowly and spoke sweetly to her. "He's okay, Mommy, Daddy's with Grandpa and Chookie. He came to me today in school during break time."

A sudsy dish fell from her hands and rattled in the sink. She turned around slowly, looking down at me. "How did you know about Chookie? He was the dog your father had before you were born."

"Daddy showed me him in my dream. He let me hold him and everything, Mommy. He's so nice and fluffy, Mommy." I paused. "Oh, and Daddy said to tell you he misses you and he forgives you."

A stinging slap caught my cheek. All I could hear was ringing in my ears. I looked up at her red face in shock. Then silent tears. Hicham saw her slap me. He dropped his toy.

"Stop it, stop it! I better never, ever, hear you talk about seeing your father. He's in heaven. You hear me, he's in heaven! He's not here!"

❊ ❊ ❊

Watching the little girl on the train coloring made my heart smile. I love to see children who haven't been burdened with the cares of the world yet; their innocence is therapeutic. Her mother went into her purse and offered them both a Starburst candy. The Crayola artist–sister squealed as her writer-sister grabbed a pink candy square. "You always get strawberry, let me get it!" she huffed.

Her sister quickly unwrapped the candy and popped it into her mouth with a sinister grin.

"Ma!" yelled the Crayola artist.

"Hush up, there's another strawberry." The mom narrowed her eyes at her daughters and reached farther in the pack. "Stop acting like a big baby."

Writer-sister agreed and continued practicing her cursive handwriting. I smiled at her mother, who shrugged her shoulders at me. "I give up." She laughed and a few other passengers chuckled along with her.

Those children are fortunate. Their mother keeps them so protected that they have no idea what pressure she is under. She looked at her watch and smoothed out her fuzzy ponytail. I quickly turned away from her, because I could see a snapshot in my mind of what was to come. I didn't want to see it, because he's going to beat her for being late. He's going to beat her very hard this time, worse than usual. I flinched, because I could almost feel the powerful blow to my own mouth. He was an evil man with a hard-on for control.

I suddenly noticed her nervous reaction from me watching her. I didn't know how long I had zoned out, staring in her direction. I closed my eyes and just prayed for God's white light to protect her tonight. I prayed that maybe this time, this time, someone would call the cops on him.

Her stop came up and she frantically yelled at the girls.

"Pack your bags, Jesse is downstairs waiting for us, hurry up. Hurry! He's gonna lose it if I'm late again."

"Don't let him hit Mommy again, hurry up." Crayola artist had let the cat out of the bag. Suddenly, she realized she was the one about to get hit the second they got off the train for having a big mouth in public.

The doors of the train beeped and the mother yelled, "Hurry up, dammit!"

Damn, I'm good. Most of the time I go with my gut, and it never lies. But when I get a confirmation that is dead-on, man, I still freak myself out, like, how did I know that? How in the hell did I know that?

❊ ❊ ❊

The short train ride to TriBeCa got less painful after the train emptied out some. That helped my anxiety and I continued visualizing I was in a force field of protection, so that any negative energy I felt wouldn't get to me. It's a little trick I taught myself over the years that works like a charm.

I got off the train, walked up the stairs into the gray mist, and took a whiff of the New York City air. I smelled the sweet bread and bagels from Lenny's bakery on Canal Street. Then a few blocks up, the aroma of a street vendor's candied walnuts took over my senses. I was glad the rain had stopped, because I had a good ten-minute hike to my mom's loft.

Being away for a little while heightened my awareness of how stylish New Yorkers are, especially compared to Miami, where people don't usually have much on at all. The people I saw swiftly charging toward me really had a knack for looking sharp and trendy. Did I walk that fast when I lived here? They were important and had somewhere to go, or at least that's what they wanted the world to believe. Chic dresses, purple streaks in their hair, black suits, nose rings, sexy boots, you name it. Canal Street was the strip for a stylish mix.

Then there were the slow-moving tourists, pointing up at the sky, turning around in circles, and walking with subway maps. They gasped at the cheap prices on Canal Street, mouths dropping at the impressive knock-off Gucci bags that just "had to be real." They would even fall for the nervous-acting Asian lady who rushed them into the cellar to look at her so-called secret collection of designer bags.

The tourists were a blast to watch, their eyes open wide with seeming fascination. I looked at both "species"—the New Yorker and the Tourist—and realized that I now fell in between the two worlds. I was feeling like a tourist who still had a little bit of city sense, street smarts, and style.

I got to my mother's building and to my surprise saw a man leaving who looked slightly familiar. Tall, thin, and almost hunching over when he walked. Gray jacket and black hat. I held the door for him as he walked toward the tall glass entryway. He looked at me as if he knew me, smiled a gentle fake smile, then tilted his hat to me and put his head back down as he passed me. I heard in my head, "Watch him." I looked back at him as he walked quickly down the stairs. Not good. But I didn't know why I knew him. He was probably just a neighbor.

Today was going to be interesting, I could tell. My mom and I don't get along like we used to, but when I visit we try to make it work. As I got older, I began to understand why she was upset about my "talent." I noticed my mother treated me differently after I predicted my dad's death. It was as if she resented me for knowing before her and not telling her. I wasn't sure why. I felt guilty for not being able to articulate how I knew that Dad was okay and that she shouldn't be afraid of what I knew.

I opened the door and it smelled like home: bread, flowers, and paint. I wished I could go back in time. Back to our old place. Back to when my father was alive. Bright colorful paintings, eclectic antique furniture, and noise—noise was always there. The sounds of music and yelling are what I remember when I think of home. Édith Piaf seemed to play endlessly as my mother and father would pace around the living room shouting at each other in French and English interchangeably. Well, it was more my mother doing the shouting. The sweet smell of French bread baking mixed with my father's Marlboros would fill our SoHo loft. Hicham and I would laugh and watch them from the staircase or hide under the dining room tablecloth while they would go at it about almost anything. And that was, for us, a good day.

I remember they would argue about her being away from home so much. "You and the church, those church people! You're obsessed!" He would wave his hands frantically. "You are away from the children too much!" he'd yell. "Jacques and Hicham need you more. You're a mother and my wife. A wife should be in the home. Both of the kids need you." He would rest his head in his hands and push his thick black waves back. "It's either the church, volunteering, or your work—you can't put them first all the time, Marguerite."

"Helping others always comes first, Olivier! God's work always comes first." She would slam something down and go into her studio and start painting with wild forceful brush-strokes to create a flower, a towering tree, or, when she was really fired up, a volcano in the jungle.

God did come first, it was true, but did she have to be out volunteering at homeless shelters and nursing homes three to five nights a week? My father was not an avid churchgoer, since he was Muslim, and my mother never seemed to push him to go to church events. Sometimes, though, she would show resentment, because he wasn't setting an example for us to love God the way she expected.

To this day, my mother is on various committees, working with soup kitchens, even teaching art classes to children in after-school programs. Pretty much all her activities are related to the church or volunteering with her "church crew," as Hicham calls them. She's even had the nerve to tell me that she continues to pray for me. To her friends and family, I'm a "counselor," as though I were a social worker or guidance counselor—which, in some ways, I suppose I am. But she would never tell anyone that I'm a psychic. My gift is a curse to her.

Unlike my mother, my father was always around playing with Hicham and I. His job working for the phone company gave him flexible hours, so he was home early enough to help us with our homework. He was definitely an introvert, who enjoyed being home with us, watching football, or playing solitaire.

Hicham was too young to remember Daddy, since he was

only three when he died. I didn't realize it until my late teens, but I took over the role of father, trying to mold him into a respectable and honorable young man. That didn't really work out like I planned.

Over the years, I heard from my cousins and aunts in Morocco that my dad was much more open-minded and spiritual. He didn't mind that my mother's religion was different from his. He would always tell Mom that she could have church at home with us sometimes. That is why her obsession with religion urged me to explore all religions and embrace their commonalities more than their differences.

I couldn't explain to Mom how happy I was when Dad came to "visit." I didn't know how to articulate it at the time. Sometimes I would be with him on a football field playing with Chookie. One minute I would be sleeping in my bed and within the blink of an eye, I would see my body lying in the bed from above. I would hover over my bed, wave to my brother as he slept, and then in a flash, I'd be somewhere extremely cool with my dad. I was having out-of-body experiences and didn't know it. My mother told me I was dreaming, but I know it was much more. It was too real to be in my mind.

At times I'd be flying or floating over crowds, or rooms, and things I loved like parades, carnivals, and birthday parties. I would wake up and you couldn't tell me what I experienced was not real. I would see him, talk to him, touch him.

I would astrally project myself and travel on a spiritual plane. I would be in my room on the floor and as I drew or colored, he would swoop me away to fun places like Giants

Stadium, the Grand Canyon, a lake upstate, all sorts of cool things. Drawing would sometimes tune me out. Even though my body was there, my soul wasn't. Outrageous stuff for a kid to digest, which is why, eventually, I didn't.

One night, about a year or so after my father died, I was about to drift off to sleep. My mom tucked me into bed really tight, as if I would fall out.

The darkness of the room swallowed me up. I wanted to fall asleep, but I felt something. A presence. I looked over to Hicham, who was curled up like a ball and almost falling off the bed. It wasn't him. The light flickered. I saw our toy chest illuminated. Flicker. Flicker. The G.I. Joe dolls on the floor to the right were suddenly in the spotlight. Flicker. Flicker. I saw the tent that we'd started to make out of sheets begin half-collapsing. Flicker.

I looked over by the dresser and the Mickey Mouse lamp turned off and on by itself. I blinked.

I thought I was seeing things and turned over on my side against the wall to fall asleep. The insides of my eyelids illuminated with a bright pink glow. I opened my eyes and now the main light for the room was on. My chest sank in when I noticed the back of a young blond girl about seven years old flicking the light switch up and down.

Hicham started to open his eyes and I was trying to call him to look, but no sound came out. I couldn't move. I felt pinned to the bed. My body was totally paralyzed by fear.

The girl said, "Shhhh, don't tell him, he has a big mouth and can't keep a secret!" I couldn't understand it. Her mouth didn't move. I didn't know that spirits could send telepathic messages at the time. I agreed that I wouldn't and suddenly I could move again.

I couldn't believe my eyes and rubbed them. She didn't look directly at me. I saw a long curly ponytail in a red velvet ribbon and a big white poodle skirt that reminded me of the TV show *Happy Days*.

"Get up! Come on! Let's play, Jacques!" I heard her vibrant voice in my head. She still didn't turn around, but somehow we understood each other. I could see her profile and her mouth never opened.

I said in my head, "No, I want to go to sleep. You gotta go. My mommy is going to be mad you're here and I'm gonna get in trouble."

"Oh, come on! No one can hear me but you. Please! Let's do something fun. Let's jump on the bed."

I got annoyed, not scared anymore, and I was just plain tired. I hid under the covers hoping I would just fall asleep and she would go away. I was wishing that it was a dream and she wasn't really standing there with her back to me. I started praying, "Dear God, please make her go away. Go away, please go away!"

I felt something over me. I pulled back the covers to see if my wishing worked. She was leaning right over me, smiling. I felt her. She was cold. I screamed. I screamed as loud as I could, but still no sound came out. Hicham kept sleeping. No one heard me.

She was missing her two front teeth and she spoke telepathically. "Oh, come on. Don't be a spoilsport, you're no fun!" Her big blue eyes were pleading with me. As frightened as I was, I was happy to see she had a sweet face and chubby cheeks. Not as scary as I was anticipating.

Somehow, I heard my dad say in my head, "Don't be scared, be firm. Don't be scared. She doesn't want to hurt you."

Even though my mouth wasn't making sounds, I knew she could hear me in her mind. So I shouted firmly out loud, "No! I don't want to play. I want to sleep. NO! Go away, little girl!" Suddenly she vanished right before my eyes. Her body, which had seemed dense and three-dimensional, became transparent and then a silhouette before disappearing completely.

My mother charged into the room, her hair sticking up on one side. "What's wrong? What happened?" She rubbed her eyes.

Hicham tossed and turned on the twin bed next to me. He was still wrapped up tight in his G.I. Joe flannel sheets. I jumped up and started off whispering, then yelling, "Mommy, there was a little blond girl in here playing with the light!" I pointed to the light switch. "I told her she had to leave, I told her I had to go to sleep."

My mother shook her head in disbelief, like she couldn't believe I woke her up for that foolishness. "Oh God! Go back to bed, Jacques. I told you to stop watching those horror movies."

"But, Mommy, I wasn't dreaming! Why don't you listen to me?" I yelled. "She was right where you are standing. Right here. She was about this tall." I motioned with my hands to show she was only a little taller than me. My heart was beating fast as I recapped the story. "She was talking to me and her mouth didn't move. It didn't move! I tried to call you, but I couldn't. I was . . . I was . . ."

My mom fluffed my hair. She looked at me with sleepy eyes. "Jacques, go to bed, sweetheart, you were having a nightmare, that's all."

After that night, I had to get used to the fact that what I saw, heard, or felt was "a gift" like Mrs. Murtha said, but somehow it seemed to make me invisible. I felt like whatever happened to me was irrelevant. By the time I reached eleven years old, I didn't see visions as much and I learned to block them for fear of being called crazy. I would draw them, color them, and hide them. After blocking them for so long, I didn't have any visions for a long time, until my late teens.

It's pretty sad that my mother doesn't support what I do for a living, even though after years of being in denial, she finally admitted to Hicham that I really can see into the future. However, my gift is a curse to her. She wishes I didn't have the ability, because according to her, the Bible says it's sorcery. Pitiful. It's as though she thinks I'm really casting spells like a warlock. All I do is give advice, intuitive advice, which I feel is sent from God. She doesn't take into consideration how many people's lives I've saved. How many relationships I've improved, how many people have improved their health, and how many families I've reunited.

Chapter 9

Kylie

S weat formed on the back of my thighs as they stuck to the leather seat in the eighty-four-degree weather. I sipped a mimosa while watching tourists walk by. They seemed so excited to be on South Beach. They looked like me when I first got here.

I sat in the lobby of the National Hotel. I heard a velvet voice play over the speakers. Sounded like Sarah Vaughan doing a jazzy remake of "I Feel Pretty." I bobbed my head to the music as I sipped my drink. I smiled back at the waiter smiling at me and eyeing my crossed legs in an orange-and-white halter sundress. I was wearing my white bikini underneath it and I couldn't wait to lie on the beach with my new friend.

"Looking for me?" I heard a man's voice say. My stomach danced with anticipation. I turned around and was greeted by a charming and confident smile. Chauncey was about six feet, medium build, and his lips . . . oh, God bless him. His lips looked like they could do a lot more than kissing.

"Damn, you are so beautiful!" he said as I stood up and hugged him.

"Hey, Chauncey! Thank you." He squeezed me like a long-lost lover. He was wearing a white tank top, beige short-sleeve shirt, and long beige army shorts to match.

A thin platinum chain and one diamond earring in his left ear were a nice touch. I smiled and took him all in. His caramel skin, white smile, and almond eyes were tantalizing.

"You aren't too shabby yourself, and you smell good! Your photos don't do you justice." I squeezed his huge biceps and laughed.

His voice was deep and smooth—even better in person than on the phone. He talked with a bit of a Southern accent. It was sexy and gentle. He bit his bottom lip. "So, you wanna grab a little something from here and bring it to the beach?" He looked directly in my eyes. I liked that. It felt intense.

"For sure, I am dying to lie down under an umbrella."

"Yeah, let's get you into that bathing suit quick." He put his arm around me.

"See! You starting already Mr. Seven Months? Be easy!" I teased.

He picked up my beach bag and we walked through the lobby to the beach area.

"Oh, come on, I can't tell you nothing. Keep it up and it will be eight months!"

"Oh God, you think I can't wait?"

He shook his head and smiled. I hit him on the shoulder with my purse and we laughed.

The conversation was easygoing. It was truly as if we'd known each other for years and had simply reunited. We were naughty with our flirting from the second the date started, so there was no denying I would definitely be tested.

We picked up some chicken Caesar wraps from the poolside bar and headed straight to the beach. The seagulls playfully made their way close to our chairs, begging for scraps. The sky was clear and huge cruise ships sailed forward leaving a wake of white foam behind them. A beautiful day for a first date. Thank God there weren't any screaming babies nearby. I wasn't in the mood. There were a couple of sunbathers show-ing off more than we wanted to see; the cellulite-revealing G-strings and KFC golden-brown skin were a bit much.

I decided to take the responsibility of making sure he wasn't harmed by the sun. "Let me put some sunblock on you. You can't go unprotected." I smirked.

"Oh, if you insist, but only if you let me return the favor."

"Oh, sure you can. It's been a while since I had a nice rubdown."

"Easy there, tiger." He laughed. "You are seriously a riot." I stepped out of my sundress and folded it neatly. I enjoyed how he watched me adjusting my bikini straps and standing over him. "Damn, Kylie. You are gorgeous."

I reveled in how his eyes wanted me. I picked up the lotion. "Lie on your stomach," I commanded. He adjusted the lounge chair to go all the way down and mumbled, "Man, whose idea was this again? This is going to be one hard afternoon for a brother."

"Hard afternoon?" I poked him.

"Exactly, pun intended!" I eased the lotion onto the nape of his neck and deeply kneaded his lower back.

I started to think that this was a bit too intimate for a first date, but I thought I would have fun with it and see the goods now. I'd rather not be surprised later and have wasted my time.

"Oh damn . . . you are really good. I mean really, really good. Oh . . ." The ocean waves were strong and the sound of seagulls had a calming effect.

"A little secret I had in my back pocket." I leaned in deeper and whispered in his ear, "My mom's a massage therapist."

"Wow, like mother like daughter?"

I cringed. "Well, not exactly. If I was, we'd already be in the water doing unspeakable things." I choked on my words.

"Damn . . . guess your mom's out there, huh?"

"'Out there' is an understatement, but I've learned to live with it."

"Oh dammmmnnn . . . Kylie. Right there." His mouth was open. Somehow, even in between the sighing, he still managed to continue probing for more intel. "Do you two . . . get along? You . . . and your mom?"

"Yeah, sure. But I'd rather not talk about my mother anymore. You're jacking up the massage, Chauncey," I playfully scolded. "Let's make today about you and me, okay?"

"Whatever you want to do, Kylie. You're the boss."

I slapped his butt. "Okay, my turn." I lay on the chair and

rested my face in my hands. I was definitely turned on, but I didn't have to let him know it. I knew I would be able to control it—at least for today.

After long sensual massages and collecting some cool seashells, we lay under the umbrella getting to know each other better.

Chauncey took a sip of his soda. "I'm sorry if I keep staring at you. I feel like a stalker. I just can't believe they make them like you anymore."

"Oh please, stalk away. I am just as bad as you. I'm really happy I'm here, Chauncey." I smiled. I really could get used to his company. Smart, witty, down to earth and slap-yo-mama sexy! I definitely want to get even closer to him.

To my surprise, he said softly, "Let's get in the water, Kylie."

I grinned and rose without hesitation. We walked toward the water. He dived in ahead of me and waited. I walked in slowly behind him, and it was warm and inviting, like a soothing bath. He looked like a shark waiting for his prey.

Everything in the sky began to blur with the clouds. All I saw was him dripping with water. Not the children playing, not the cruise ships, not the sand-joggers. Everything else was fading from my view. All I heard was the joyful cooing of the seagulls. The second I got close enough, he embraced me. His sudden aggressiveness surprised me. His skin on mine, his hands on the small of my back, his face dripping with salt water.

He said low in my ear, "Kylie, what are you doing to me? I feel like you put a spell on me."

We let the waves crash against us and push us even closer together. I felt Chauncey rising in his trunks against my thighs. He looked down and shrugged, embarrassed, like he was about to apologize for being aroused. I put my arms around his neck.

He said, "I am really digging y—" I silenced him with a kiss, a deep sensual kiss that I had been craving since I saw him. His tongue danced with mine. He sighed as he kissed me. His lips were soft. He was so passionate. His hardness was unreal, and it felt good against me. It took everything in me not to reach down and go deep-sea diving. I leaned into his wet body and let his hands slide to my butt. I leaned in closer, trying to melt into him.

Fuck. This was torture. I wanted him inside me! How could he stand this if he really hadn't had it in seven months? I was going on only two months and was losing it. But, of course I was a lady. Of course it was our first date, and we had no condoms. Ewww, not going there!

He sucked my neck and playfully pecked me, ending our marathon kiss. "Mmmmm. You know we're in troubled waters right now?" He moaned as he looked down at my wet cleavage and hard nipples shouting for attention.

"Why so?" I said coyly.

"You know, because I'm going to be hard for the rest of the night."

I laughed. "Now, why should that be a problem? You can always relieve yourself in your room before we continue our date." I gave the jerk-off motion in the air. "I have some lotion you can borrow if you need it." I winked.

"True, true, because even though I know you might try to take advantage of me, I'm not that easy, Kylie." An old couple floated by on a bright orange raft, smiling at us as we embraced.

I spoke softer. "Whatever. If I wanted you right now"—I pulled the front of his trunks and playfully slapped the elastic back to his stomach—"you wouldn't be down?"

"Nope!"

"Well, that's good self-control. Good thing I have some as well, no telling what could become of this innocent date. No telling." I lifted my eyebrows and smiled ear to ear.

He shook his head and sighed, like he was feeling the same way I was. We were both full of it. He picked me up and we waded in the water, floating, touching, kissing. Talk about more torture. I was a glutton for punishment.

If he was telling the truth about being abstinent, when we finally do "go there," it's going to be *the Fantabulous Fuckfest of the Millennium*. Freaking fireworks, cheerleaders, and Broadway dancers doing the chorus line out of the closet. I was so turned on by his touch—no, just from a glance. So, there's no telling what's going to happen when he releases that present in his trunks.

Chemistry and reliability. Chauncey's got the making of a Big Mac, definitely not a French fry, as True calls her "side" men. What more can a girl ask for? Hell, who needs French fries if he keeps this up?

We had a nice relaxing afternoon in the sun, hanging in the water and kissing. Lots and lots of kissing. His lips were magical and I couldn't get enough. They were so soft and he was so passionate. My hair got a little wet, but I didn't care. I admired how even though we teased each other, he was still a perfect gentleman.

We went back to his hotel room to shower before going to dinner. He showered first. I didn't know why I felt so comfortable alone in a stranger's room. I met him on the Internet, for Christ's sake! I didn't snoop around, even though I really wanted to. As I walked around, I observed, in his open carry-on, slacks, khaki pants, jeans, a white shirt, and—*wow*—condoms. Did he think he was getting some already? Well, at least he came prepared. Gotta respect him for playing it safe.

On the dresser was facial lotion, toner, and facial scrub. A metro-sexual, are we? He also had a laptop, folder, and a book called *The 4-Hour Workweek*. So, he was gonna squeeze in work, too? A hard-working brother. I likes, I likes.

I jumped at the sound of the bathroom door opening. He shouted, "All yours!" I looked at his moist caramel body draped in only a towel around his waist.

My lady-parts fluttered between my legs. I teased, "Did you clean up in there? I don't want to slip on anything nasty."

"Oh yeah, I had a nice time in there with myself." He looked down in his towel and pretended to speak to his manhood like it was a pet. "All better? Good, I know you feel better."

I laughed loudly. "Wow, I need a shower quick. Why do you keep teasing me?" I laughed and grabbed my bag of clothes.

"What? Me teasing? Ain't that the pot calling the kettle black."

After my shower, I admired my figure in the mirror and imagined it was his hands instead of mine rubbing me with oils. I started to dress in the bathroom. I was not going to be bold and come out in a towel like he had. We'd never make it to dinner. I had a cute peach sundress that hugged my hips just right and flared at my knees. I had to slick my hair back into an Afro puff since the water had gotten to it. My 'fro had shrunk and wasn't looking right. Thank God for scrunchies and my Nefertiti's Secrets leave-in conditioner! I wasn't trying to look like a hot mess!

My skin glistened from the coconut body oil I'd rubbed in. I didn't need a bra, because the dress was a tight strapless that held "my girls" in perfectly. But where the hell were my panties? Unbelievable! I had worn my bathing suit to the hotel but I couldn't put my sandy bikini bottom on under my dress. I could not believe I'd forgotten my damn thong. It was going to be obvious. Oh, to hell with it. I'd have to keep my legs closed like a lady and hope Madame Butterfly behaved herself and didn't get too excited by being exposed to the air. At least I had a neat Brazilian wax going for me.

I reapplied my makeup, dabbed on some perfume, and opened the door. Chauncey was buttoning up his crisp white shirt and staring at me. All I could think of was him pressing up against me in the water. I walked out of the bathroom feeling hotter than when I went in.

"My, my, you clean up well," he said, slow and sexy.

"You're not so bad yourself. You smell yummy." I walked toward him. He exuded sex and was utterly magnetizing. I fixed his collar. I wanted to be close to him. He had an earthy

look, with brown leather sandals and army-green khakis. I
looked down at his open zipper and motioned him to zip it up.
It felt natural being with him, like we were a couple who had
been together for years.

"Oops." He smiled. "So, Kylie, you feel like Japanese? I
remember you said you loved it."

"Yes, there's a spot two blocks away. We can walk." He
held my hand all the way there and I caught him staring at
me, licking his lips. I hadn't been on a real date in so long.
I forgot how good it felt to not just sit on the couch every
night. Breeze's idea of a date was watching Comedy Central
all night. Well, that is after fucking my brains out. So, I didn't
complain too much.

The sexual tension, the excitement, the mystery behind
getting to know someone, had my stomach swirling. As we
walked on Collins Avenue, girls watched us and men gave
Chauncey the head nod of approval. After dinner, we went
back to his room, so I could get my bag. We rode the hotel
elevator in silence up to the eleventh floor. As the lift came to
a stop, the floor-bell rang. *Ding!* Chauncey faced me, looked
directly into my eyes, and asked, "You want to stay a while?"

Chapter 10

Jacques

My mother's apartment was dark. The energy felt low, cold, and damp. Not a good sign. I put down my backpack and went into the kitchen. She'd left a note taped to the fridge saying she'd gone to church for a meeting and to help prepare for an art show she was hosting. She also said not to eat dinner and to wait for her. I was happy that even though she was obsessed with religion she hadn't forgotten what a talented artist she is.

Also on the fridge were a calendar of church events, a magnet of Jesus's face, a photo of Hicham and me as teens, and a photo of a group of two men and another woman with my mother. They were on Forty-Second Street in front of a Broadway theater. One man had his arm around my mother. I looked closely at the photo. He actually looked like the guy I saw leave the building earlier, but no, couldn't be, unless he lived in this building, too.

If my gut was right, the photo looked like a double date. But how odd would that be? My mother never dated, at least to our knowledge. Must just be a church outing.

I was starving and needed a little something to hold me over until she came home. I saw fruits, veggies, yogurt, left-over chicken breasts, and three bottles of wine. Wow, not like her. I hoped she hadn't started drinking again. After Dad died, she began to drink wine a little bit too often. She was never out of control, but would use it to go to sleep. I now know she was most likely depressed and anxious. I remember how dark her aura was.

My stomach growled and I pulled out a carton of yogurt. I walked around to see what she'd done with the place since I was last here six months ago. The apartment wasn't half as spacious as our old place, where Hicham resides now. She needed her own space and I think, really, she was ready to let Hicham grow up. It was a modest one-bedroom duplex with small windows on the second floor. With most of her artwork hanging up, there was hardly any bare wall space.

On the mantel over the faux fireplace was a huge golden cross with a metal Jesus on it. It was rather depressing to look at. Below it were photos of us all when Dad was alive, and nerdy photos of my brother and me in argyle sweaters and ties, with our hair slicked down. Some were in Morocco before Hicham was born, where we lived until I was three. But the majority of the photos were of Hicham and Mom. Hicham skiing with some random girlfriend, Hicham as an altar boy at eleven, in Boy Scouts, and on the red carpet for a *Maxim* event. Wow, nothing of me past the age of nineteen.

Makes sense, because that's when I reclaimed my power and no longer ignored the messages I was receiving. That's when my mother and I truly started to butt heads.

I used to tease my brother that it was the Hicham shrine, because pictures of him were everywhere. He was her special baby, her favorite. He didn't talk to dead people or see the future. I still wonder if she ever read any of his extremely misogynist articles. I find it fascinating that he hasn't heard a complaint about those yet from her. It's strange to think that he was the favorite, since I was less trouble growing up. Hicham was arrested for petty crimes as a teen, cut school a lot, had and still has anger management issues, and hung with the wrong crowds, desperately trying to be accepted. Many of the kids in his circle were Latino or black and were with the "in" crowd. We weren't really seen as black, but we weren't white or Latino. Hicham hated that white part of us, Mom's part. He didn't speak French as he got older, but he understood it when Mom or I talked to him.

Hicham tried so hard to be African American. He would never really claim the French/white side. He would say he was African to seem cool and exotic and keep it at that. He wasn't even born in Morocco, as I was. It was something he struggled with, being the palest in the family. He could actually pass for 100 percent white if he wanted to.

Growing up, most of my friends were women and the few guys were artsy hipsters. They were kids who were smart in school, but were smoking cigarettes, sneaking beer, and having sex. Some were into dark Goth or grunge. We read about magicians and sci-fi comics. We listened to hip-hop, rock,

pop, and even artists such as Portishead, No Doubt, and Res.
We talked about deep subjects like past lives, ancient civiliza-
tions, government conspiracies, and even aliens from outer
space. Many of those kids in my group were outcasts at home
just like me, so we stuck together. We saw and experienced
things deeply, but we didn't really understand then that most
of us were pretty intuitive. Hicham's group and mine never
crossed paths, because our groups wanted nothing to do with
one another.

I walked into Mom's bright turquoise bathroom. It was
smaller than I remembered, and there was a lot of clutter and
no tub—just a shower—and not enough shelves or cabinets.
Ever since Dad died she had a fear of tubs and pools. She
didn't want to be near one. "What if that happened to me?" is
what she'd say.

The sink space was tight and she had a host of pill cases.
Then there were pink and blue eye shadows, which were her
favorite colors to wear, various perfumes, and a few plastic
jars with paintbrushes in water. It was a mess. I looked up
at the shower and there were a hot-pink lace bra and panties hung up over her towel rack. "Wow!" I looked at them
to make sure I wasn't seeing things. I couldn't believe they
could belong to my mother. They were sexy. Too sexy. Something was going on. A new man? Guess Mommy is getting
her groove back. I smiled and washed my face.

"Living in sin are we, *chère mère*?" I looked in the mirror
and smiled as I rubbed my five o'clock shadow. "I'll shave
tomorrow."

As I ate my yogurt I started to feel queasy and frustrated.

I sank into the sofa and closed my eyes for a minute. I felt invisible. The Hicham shrine really bothered me! It was like those old feelings of jealousy came rushing back. I didn't like that side of me, that side that needed my mother's approval.

❈ ❈ ❈

I heard music playing faintly. It was a woman singing in French to a happy upbeat tempo. I felt happy, euphoric even. Then I saw my father and my mother dancing in the living room. Daddy turned her in a graceful spin, then winked at me. I felt like a little boy again and clapped happily. I laughed as I watched. Hicham was in his playpen. He was only about two years old.

I turned around and opened my eyes as the music seemed to get louder. Then I heard a woman humming. I wasn't dreaming anymore. I had fallen asleep on my mom's couch. She was playing "La Foule" by Édith Piaf, one of our favorites. I loved Édith. She played Édith only when she and Dad were in a good mood and not fighting.

I heard her packing away things in the kitchen, trying to be quiet, but it wasn't working. The rustling of plastic grocery bags made too much noise. She was wearing a purple dress and her hair looked darker than normal. Trying to dye her grays, I'm sure. She had on bright purple eye shadow and her lipstick had worn off.

"Mom?" I rubbed my eyes.

"Hello, sleepy boy." She bent down as she grabbed my face. She kissed me on my forehead like I was still a child. It felt good. I smelled a familiar aroma from my childhood.

"I didn't want to disturb you, but I wanted to get dinner ready. I'm making your favorite! Lamb tagine. And I see you didn't listen." She picked up the yogurt carton playfully and then dropped it on the counter. "I hope you have room for dinner. Why are you so tired? It's the middle of the day!"

"Travel and work are catching up with me, that's all. I haven't been sleeping full nights."

"Ah, it must be catching. You know I haven't slept good in months? I even got a new mattress and it didn't help. I had to go to Dr. Bennigan to prescribe me something to help me sleep."

"Oh, is that what that was in the bathroom? I was going to ask you what was wrong. I got worried."

"Oh hush, nothing to worry about, but horrid dreams."

"You know I just remembered, I had a dream before I woke up. I saw you and Daddy dancing in our old house. The music that was playing just now is what you both were dancing to." She dropped one of the cans of beans she was putting away.

"Jacques, you know it's your father who I have been having nightmares about? I keep seeing him in the bedroom. I keep seeing him in the tub, in the old house . . . how I found him. He keeps talking to me and I can't stand it, because it feels so real!"

I sat up. "Mom, I hate to tell you this, but dreams aren't always our imagination. Remember how you always thought I was dreaming? It's just the spirit world trying to communicate with us."

I felt her panic. Her chest tightened and her throat was

closing in. I picked up her energy instantly. She wanted to say something, but she was afraid. She wanted to ask me something, too.

"Jacques, please don't start talking about the spiritual world. Your father wouldn't do that to me. He wouldn't haunt me. It's just some bad dreams or maybe some spirit you conjured up in that work you do. They know I'm your mother."

I was waiting for her to crack a smile. She was serious. I tried not to react as she gently rubbed the crucifix on her neck.

I put my hand up in surrender. "Okay, Mom, no worries. I'll be right back." I ran my hands through my hair and got up quickly. I had to get some air.

She was probably missing a special message from Dad, because of her fear. Now she was drugged up at night and probably couldn't dream or remember her dreams. I wanted to scream, "WAKE THE FUCK UP, MOM!" but I would never disrespect her like that. Besides, she wouldn't know what "wake up" meant, since she's been asleep for so many years pretending none of this is real.

That's just how it was with us. The smooth communication would go for only so long before she put up a roadblock. I always smashed right into it. I learned to make a quick U-turn, keep my mouth shut, and ignore her ignorance. It pained me to hear it, but at sixty-two, she wasn't changing.

I sat on the stoop outside, texting clients who wanted a session. I was grateful for the high demand, but I had to let many of them know I had a waiting list. Kylie sent me a text, too. Really sweet.

KYLIE: Hey Jacques, just wanted to thank you again and let you know it was great meeting you! See you when you get back. Safe travels!

She was adorable. Her playful energy gave my spirits a lift.

My phone rang as I held it. Dee Johnson showed up on the caller ID. "How is the sexiest psychic ever?"

"Hey, gorgeous!"

"Heeeey! I am going to be in your neck of the woods next week, got any room for me? I am overdue!"

"Wow, really? I'm actually in your town right now. You got the clients' email blast I sent out?" I asked.

"What! No! Just my luck! I'm in San Diego right now for a sales conference."

I started to walk up and down the block. I like to pace when I'm on the phone and I think Dee made me a bit anxious and excited from her high energy. I said, "Okay, well text me or email some dates and I'll check my calendar for next week and fit you in."

Dee Johnson could make any man uneasy. She carried a strong sex appeal, a New York girl confidence, and she loved flirting. She always told me she had a crush on me and joked that that's why she pays me the big bucks.

Dee possessed the kind of brazen confidence that I'm attracted to in a woman. Sadly, her experience of being molested as a child led her to treat men poorly and have serious trust issues. I've always admired her strength, but kept her out of my fantasies. Let's just say I knew way too much.

The guilt started to creep in as I thought about Dee, so I called Vicky. "Hey, mami!" I said with my horrible impersonation of a Spanish accent.

"*Hola, papi chulo*, whatchu doing? I can't wait for you to get home. I got a new outfit waiting for you. It's a Catholic school uniform."

"Oh really, you gonna turn me into a dirty old man, huh?" I smiled. "Baby, just hold tight. I'll be home soon." A taxi horn blew loudly. Someone was taking his parking spot. I put one hand over my ear and spoke louder.

"Few more days, Vicky." Damn, she was sexy.

"Good, I need some of that, papi," she said in a syrupy voice. "But, baby, on a serious note, I might need your skills. It's been crazy here. We had a double homicide and the kids were only sixteen and seventeen! Might need your help on a case. Just some ideas, leads."

"Wow, you okay?"

"No, not really. It wasn't pretty to see the bodies. They were babies. You never get used to it. I'll be better when I see you. I'm on a quick break. They are working us overtime."

"Breathe, baby, breeeeeathe it out. You know?"

"You're amazing, Jacques Berradi. You always make it better."

"Call me when you get off." I sighed. "I'm at my mother's."

"Aye, how's that working out? Did she douse you with holy water yet?" Vicky chuckled.

"No, but it's been only thirty minutes and already she's blamed me for her bad dreams. Apparently, I conjured up spirits and they went looking for her."

"What!" She started laughing. "Noooo way!"

I looked at my reflection in a parked car and ran my fingers through my hair. I heard the window above me crack open and I saw my mom's reflection in the car window.

"Jacques, come. Dinner is ready!"

"Oh, that's her," I said.

"Okay, baby, I gotta get back, too. Muwwwwah!" Vicky said.

The scent of couscous brought me back to Fridays after the mosque with Dad. Dad insisted that we should know our roots. I went to mass sometimes with Mom and Hicham, but it wasn't my favorite thing to do. After Dad died, we were 100 percent Catholic. I would still sneak off to the mosque as I got older and I still celebrated some holidays and practices such as Ramadan, when you fast for thirty days. I felt the Muslim faith was also a connection to my father.

"You and that phone," she said, shaking her head. I helped her bring the dishes to the table. I looked at the fridge and noticed a blank white spot where the Broadway double date photo had been. Weird. I smiled. I could have been right about her church friend. I had to leave for Miami in the morning, so at least I'd get some time with Mom alone and do some more digging.

Chapter 11
Kylie

I would love to hang out some more, Chauncey, but you said yourself that we are in deep water. I don't need any more temptation for the night. I want to get my bag and go home with my self-respect intact."

I caught him looking at my butt in the reflection of the elevator mirrors. "I hear you, I hear you." He seemed slightly disappointed, but I could tell he wasn't going to pressure me. He walked into his room slowly to get my bag, stalling all he could. I stood close to the door. "Kylie, you really don't make it easy on a brother. I gotta ask you something."

"What, Chauncey?" He shifted from side to side like a nervous teenager.

He furrowed his eyebrows and scratched his head nervously. "I don't mean to be out of line, but do you have any panties on?"

I blushed and bit my bottom lip. "Actually . . . umm . . .

I don't, but it wasn't intentional. I actually forgot them. I couldn't put my wet bikini bottom back on."

"Oh, please, I am not complaining at all." He pulled me in. Soft kisses were planted everywhere, his hands were all over me. Back, waist, ass, 'fro. I knew I had to put a halt to this train before Madame Butterfly started to make an appearance. We hugged and he whispered, "Kylie, I'm really, really digging you." His warm breath sent a tingling sensation down my back.

"Can I . . ." His hands pulled me in closer and cupped my butt through my dress. The thought of no panties sadly made it worse for me. I was about to lose it. He was getting more aroused than I expected and damn, it was catching.

"Can I what?" I said with a smile, already kinda knowing.

"Can I . . . see it. You don't even need to be close to me. Just want to have sweet dreams. I'm going to be dying all night. Let me."

"See it?" I grinned devilishly. Well, I guess my mind is dirtier than his, because that's no big deal. Definitely not what I was thinking he was going to ask me. "Okay sure, but to be fair, let me see it, too. You show me yours and I'll show you mine."

We cracked up at how childish we sounded. I actually got in trouble for playing that game as an eight-year-old with a little boy at school. Curiosity got the best of me then just like it was about to this night.

"But we have to promise to just do it quick and then I'm leaving."

"Sure, it's just a game. A nasty game," he mumbled, and sat down on the couch.

"But a game nonetheless," I reassured him. We gave each other one last kiss. "Okay, ready?" I said.

He laughed, but he looked so far gone, like he would attack me. His eyes concentrated on me as I slowly gave him a full-frontal view. I felt like I was onstage at a burlesque show from the 1930s as I slowly pulled my peach dress up from my thigh to my navel.

"Oh . . . it's so beautiful . . . oooh, Kylie." He leaned back on the couch. I felt like such a whore when the breeze of the A/C vent caressed my bottom.

"Okay, your turn." I pulled my dress down quickly.

Between my legs was moist and I was trying to compose myself. I couldn't believe we were teasing each other like this. He started to walk closer to me as he unzipped his pants. Oh, man, what the hell did I get myself into?

"Psych!" He zipped back up and grabbed me.

We both laughed hysterically and I pushed him. "Oh no, you are gonna show me something, dammit!" He fought me off and we fell into the love seat, playfully wrestling. I tugged on his belt and started opening his pants.

He chuckled and pretended to fight me off. "Oh . . . oh! I didn't know you liked it rough, Kylie. Damn!"

I was on top of him, my dress rising. He unzipped his pants and his dick escaped his boxers and brushed against my inner thigh. Hard, warm, pulsating. He started kissing me and I pulled away and adjusted myself. Shit, I thought, I might as well be naked. That was way too close for comfort, especially with no condom on. "I gotta get out of here. You are soooo not slick!" I said in a nervous voice.

"What?" He had his hands up and his zipper was still open. "What just happened here? I was tackled to the couch and my pants ripped open by a panty-less vixen, I might add."

"Vixen! Don't try to act so innocent, Chauncey!" I couldn't take the smirk off my face. I had so much fun with him and, well, he did have a point.

He stood up. "All right, all right. I'll take part of the blame. I couldn't keep the little guy down, he was excited."

"Little?" I chuckled, because he was far from that. Thank *Gawd* for me. He looked down and adjusted himself, zipped all the way up. "Let me walk you to the valet, before I get into any more trouble."

I grabbed my bag and adjusted my hair in the mirror by the door. "I know, it's way too dangerous up in here." We walked into the elevator with teenagers who smiled at us.

As the doors closed, Chauncey whispered in my ear. "Yeah, bring panties next time, will ya? You big tease."

I laughed so loudly I startled the unsuspecting kids.

Chapter 12
Kylie

I didn't realize how far apart Olivia and I had grown until it was time to hang out. Olivia is busy being a mommy, wife, and all. She's just becoming an old fart. Her feet are always hurting. She's always tired and only wants to hang out at Annabelle's Coffee Shop. If I'm lucky, occasionally she'll venture out to On The B-Side Entertainment events, a famous open mic night in Miami.

I'd rather get a few moments at a bar, live music, or even go to the movies, just us girls. I wasn't trying to drag her to a strip club or pick up men anywhere, but she shied away from the things we used to do. She was a perfect example of why I wasn't sure if I wanted to be a mother or get married. I love my freedom! It was time to grow up but I don't think I am quite ready.

Getting to see her was still good, though, even if it was

just at a coffee shop on a Sunday afternoon. I couldn't wait to tell her the update.

Olivia had on a beautiful bright burnt-orange tie-dyed sundress. Her long locks were wrapped up with only a few strands caressing her face. She had a regal presence, and her British accent made her sound like royalty. If people only knew her mouth was sometimes as bad as mine.

On my phone, I showed her a photo of me and Chauncey on the beach.

"Girl, Chauncey is everything and more."

She snatched the phone to get a close-up view. "Ohhh . . . nice. Chauncey . . . Chauncey . . . He looks like he has a nice one. You fucked him, didn't you? You slut. Have you learned nothing from me?"

"I know you want to live through me vicariously, but I got nothing!" I held up my hands in surrender.

"You do tell the best stories."

"Well, at least you *got* a husband, all I got is stories."

"Oh, please, he's okay!" She blushed. She still had a glow when she spoke about her husband, even though she'd been married for four years. "You'll find yours someday, when the time is right. I didn't even know who I was until I was thirty. You're only twenty-seven, so relax."

"Oh please, you're thirty-six and you act like you're sixty-six."

"Oh hush! I'm just so happy you moved down here. I was starting to miss you. Not many people I connect with here."

"Well, I'm glad, too! Who else will remind me of how exciting my life is?" I did a sarcastic eye roll.

"It is exciting! Sooo . . . you sure you didn't do it?"

"No, I didn't! And if I learned anything from you, I would have fucked him already. You Brits are loose! I remember your stories about before you were married."

"No, no . . . you Americans are just uptight. When we like someone we just do what we want, we don't play games." I smiled at her babbling. She said, "Look at that glow, you are such a liar. You got your leg over, I knew it."

"Olivia! Come on, you know I would tell you. Shit, I came pretty close to it, but I got the hell out of there. I had a fabulous time and laughed all the way home. I couldn't wait to finish off the night and this time go all the way with B.O.B."

"Who is Bob? I don't remember him. Same website you met Chauncey on?"

"No, girl, that's just my battery-operated boyfriend."

"Oh, well, for now I guess B.O.B. will have to do. I'll give you two more dates, tops!"

"I'm not even gonna bet you." I shook my head and smiled. She sipped her tea and we laughed. "But check this out, guess who's been texting me?"

"Who else? That scoundrel Breeze."

"Yes, he keeps trying to say hello. He sends me photos and I just ignore them or reply with a smiley face."

"Please, he's such a user. You should just do away with his number. Block him."

"I know, but he's still someone I love. I just hate him at the same time."

"It's complicated, eh?" Olivia said.

"Yeah, pretty much."

She pointed at me like a big sister. "Well, you know what kind of relationship it is. A bed-buddy, nothing more and nothing less. He won't give you what you want."

"It just feels so hard to get away from him! I feel like there is some crazy connection with him."

"There has got be a part of you that enjoys the bad boy side to him. It just does not make any sense."

I sipped my coffee. "I know, I know, it's a sick addiction." I shrugged.

She leaned in. "Kylie, my love, it's self-sabotaging is what it is. It's what you are used to and I think maybe a part of you thinks it's actually normal."

"Come on! I know this strange on-again, off-again shit with Breeze is far from normal."

Olivia challenged me. "So, then why do you keep accepting it? You keep putting up with it. You make it easy for him to keep coming back. You drop everything when he calls."

I grasped for anything. "I know. . . . Maybe in my past life . . . maybe we were married."

"Or maybe you were his mistress." Olivia snorted a goofy laugh. "Why don't you ask the sexy psychic? Maybe you were lovers in a past life!"

"You know, I really believe it. When it's good it's just soooooo good with him, he knows me so well, we just gel. I feel like I am fucking floating. But when it's bad . . ." My voice faded as I tried to believe my own lies. "Well, he just does a disappearing act. He becomes so busy with work."

"What he does is abandon you, Kylie, and that's just cruel."

I gave her a harsh squint. My heart crushed when she said

it. *Abandon*. YOU. *Abandon*. YOU. It echoed in my head. She was right.

"It's like he takes me on all the rides and plays all the games with me at a fun adventure park but then instead of taking me home, he dumps me on the side of a road on a dark night to hitchhike home and figure it out."

Olivia's jaws tightened and her eyes looked dark and serious. "That is emotional abuse." She took a deep breath. "You ever think not knowing your dad could be why you are so drawn to him? An older man?"

"He's not that old, only seven years older."

"Still, he acts older, and even you said the way he talks is like an older man, always calling you darling and sugah." Olivia giggled, trying to lighten the tone.

I rubbed my temples and said sternly, "You take two psychology classes in grad school and now you want to psychoanalyze me. Guuuuurl, please!"

"What? It's not that hard to figure out, you have *daddy issues*. It's not a big deal. Most of us do."

"Well, if that is the case, I have mommy issues, too. Look, when I really think about it, Breeze was like the family I never had. He was my man, my dad, my big brother, my best friend."

Olivia said, "Well, you know how I feel. You are a precious jewel. You don't need to be treated like a cubic zirconia. When you keep letting him back you're just letting the universe know . . . 'Yeah him. Gimme this guy, that's what I deserve. I will take the scraps that he offers.' The second I stopped settling I met Keith."

I chimed in, "Oh please, you know damn well Keith was stalking you for a minute, even when we met back in yoga. You treated him like shit, that is why. Men somehow love when women treat them like crap and ignore them."

"No, no, that's not how it went. I just stopped looking and focused on myself more. I really stopped looking at every guy I met as a potential husband. That's not quite treating him like shit. I just realized how worthy I was. I put myself first. Once I did, I attracted something better and he pursued me and courted me, the way it's supposed to be. He cherished who I was."

I started shaking my head. "Wait! Wait!" I held my hand up to her. "Didn't you guys fuck on the second date in the club bathroom?"

A booming laugh escaped Olivia. She had a wide-eyed look and raised her voice. "Yes, ummm, but technically, I knew him for over a year before that! Over a year!" She pointed. "And he still cherished me. He made sure I didn't fall into the toilet. That is a bloody gentleman, I'd say." She leaned in, looked both ways, and whispered, "Bathroom fucking is so much fun."

"What I say? Brits are loose!" We broke into hysterical fits of laughter. "That's some funny shit. He's a gentleman all right, as he propped you up in a dirty bathroom stall."

Olivia's laughter was contagious and we couldn't stop. Some of Annabelle's customers looked at us and smiled, hoping to catch a sliver of our joke. If they only knew!

"Yes, let's just say we had a lot of passion. Still do."

"I like Keith for you, he's a good dude and a great dad. You lucked out."

"Oh, Kylie, there are plenty of good dudes out there. I'm going to plan a get-together so you can meet—"

"Oh no, noooooo, please. I don't want to meet none of those country bumpkins from Keith's job. We went through this before, Liv."

"Please, give it a chance. Keith has some nice-looking friends. What's wrong with a nice Southern gentleman? That's what you need, to be treated like a lady."

"Yeah, I won't hold my breath. I've seen his coworkers at his accounting firm at your last barbecue. Sorry, not my style."

"Okay, keep on playing around with those Craigslist killers."

"It's Match-dot-com! Shut up!"

"I just think it's nicer to meet in person right away. It happens more organically. Not all that swiping to the side business to find a man."

"That's Tinder. . . . You don't swipe on Match."

With a quick snort she replied, "Whatever, it's all the same shit."

"We do meet in person . . . eventually."

"And you want to have a reference. A referral. Someone who can background check and make sure they're not psycho." Olivia started fixing her head wrap as she lectured me.

"Oh please, you can be referred by Obama and the pope and still be psycho!"

"Well, when you meet him, you'll know. You know how I knew Keith was really the one? We were even."

"Even?" I furrowed my eyebrows.

"Meaning, he courted me, he called me . . . but I called

him, too. I thought about him as much as he was thinking about me. I never felt smothered and I gave him his space. We got to know each other over time and we just meshed. We were even. It was balanced. It was a no-brainer to get married. We just knew. It just made sense. When you meet *your man* you shouldn't have to be hoping and praying he calls you. You'll be even. Breeze is a magician. The disappearing act gets tired."

I waved her off; I was exhausted already with the scolding. I wish I'd never told her so much. "I hear you."

"Do you? He is not even boyfriend material, much less husband. Have him show you with his actions, not all talk. Right now his smooth words always talk your panties off and you lose your senses. I've known you for five years, Kylie, and it's been the same thing every time."

"He was my first."

"Well, he doesn't have to be the last."

I took one last sip of my drink as her husband called—saved by the ring!

Even though I felt I was in a beat-up-Breeze session, she had a lot of valid points. Frankly, it was a wake-up call that I needed to hear.

❊ ❊ ❊

Moving to South Florida from New York was a reinvention for me. I wanted change. Maybe even get to know my mother on a deeper level and ask her the questions she always avoided. Get inside her mind. True was only sixteen years older than me, but I wanted to feel like a daughter for once, be treated like her child and not her buddy. I had always wanted a mother. Still did. I thought that now that I was jobless and couldn't afford my rent in Brooklyn she would come to my rescue.

True moved down to Miami two years before I did to launch her massage business with her Big Mac man—the longest she's ever had—Basim Kharabi, the Reiki master. Basim pulled her away from the seedy massage scene. Even though he met her there, it was still no place for a woman like True. She deserved her own spot, he said. True was very guarded and he helped her release a lot of that fear over the three years they were officially together. I never heard my mother talk about a man the way she did about him. She actually respected Basim.

Basim was a handsome Iranian man, slightly balding, tall, and lanky. His energy was definitely relaxing. You could tell he was good at what he did. I learned that Reiki was a healing technique that started in Japan. It's sort of like a type of energy healing. It looks like a massage, but they don't rub you, they don't even have to touch you, which I find fascinating.

I thought it was bullshit at first, until I had a session at his spa with one of his practitioners. It was mind-blowing. I felt the heat coming from the woman's hands as she opened up all of my chakras. I felt extremely relaxed, lighter and clearer afterward. I was a believer after that! I think Basim was probably doing Reiki on True a *lot* since her energy has been better since she's known him.

He was a businessman with a successful natural healing office in Fort Lauderdale called Chakra. He rented out rooms to bodywork practitioners like acupuncturists and massage therapists. He helped True gain some stability for once in her life. He really set her up. She still works at massage parlors, and sometimes for him, but they aren't as bad as they used to be. True still does things for a tip and I don't think she'll ever stop. All over the place with no focus was True in a nutshell. Jack of all trades, master of not a damn thing but the art of seduction. And she could never resist making a quick buck.

According to True, Basim fell in love with her on the massage table in Chinatown. She was the only black masseuse in the entire parlor—all the rest were Chinese or Korean. She stuck out like a sore thumb and was frequently requested for her exotic appearance and flowing wrap dresses that hugged her in all the right places. Toe rings and henna art on her arms or hands were her trademark. Her sweet caramel complexion, deep brown eyes, and big golden Afro made her memorable. Aside from her happy endings, she was also very proud of her velvet massages, during which she got on a client's back and kneaded him with her knees and eventually her wetness. Panties? True despised them. She even used to tell me, when I was a child, that a women needs to "breathe down there." She confessed that even those massages came with a special price and she got an absolute kick out of turning these men on.

Basim doesn't seem to be going anywhere anytime soon and I'm kinda happy about that. However, being the tree-hugging hippie that he is, he's on the road for six months out of the year with one of his many activist groups. Last year, it was three months in Indonesia. This time it's the Wildlife Preservation for the Rainforests of the Amazon. He's living with shamans and pretending to be a part of their indigenous culture. He'll be back in about three months, give or take a few.

I have to make it my goal to get out of here before he comes back. Although he isn't her boyfriend, Basim is her Big Mac and the reason we could afford to stay in the plush area of Coconut Grove.

"A woman needs to always have a backup plan, Ky. Men do it allll the time," True always ranted. "You need to get you a Big Mac, a man you can rely on to take care of your basic needs. Then your French fries pick up where he's lacking. The Big Mac at least has to know how to make love and how to treat you good. The others can take care of the rest." Words of wisdom from the book of True.

Chauncey definitely had more Big Mac potential than anyone I'd come in contact with since I left New York. I had my guard up, though. I would keep it up for as long as I could and see if he failed the three-month test. That's usually the time a dude's Mr. Wonderful acting skills start to conk out on them. It's when they can no longer hide their true colors. I think, as pathetic as it sounds, I might just have to accept the fact that I might be like my mom. No husband, still trying to find myself at forty-three. Hey, I know I don't want to be in her shoes, but it's sadly a possibility. I can't wait to ask Jacques what's next.

My cell phone rang at ten P.M. I didn't recognize the number. "Hello?"

"Hey, sugah, special delivery for Miss Collins."

"Breeze?"

"The one and only! What's crackin', baby? I'm gonna be in town for the American Black Film Festival. Wanna grab a bite with me when I come? How is Friday looking?"

"Are you serious?" I couldn't help but smile and wondered if he could see me cheesing, even through the phone.

"Yeah, you're not far from South Beach, are you?"

"Fifteen minutes, depending on traffic. But when did you get—"

"Let's just make it happen, sugah," he said in a slow sexy voice.

Damn damn damn! Why can't I ever say no to him?

"I have plans, Breeze, but let me call you back. I'll try." I tried to sound uninterested, but I'm sure he knew I was full of it. He just knew me, period, maybe even better than I knew myself.

"I'll be waiting, sugah. Peace."

I put the phone down and starting pacing. I walked past Phantom, who seemed annoyed I was disturbing her sleep. I was nervous, excited, and pissed all at once. Only he knew how to evoke a whirlwind of emotions inside me.

I plopped on the bed, thinking about what I was going to do. I can't see him, I can't be in his space. Not now when I'm starting to feel my own power again, when I'm starting to really feel a connection with Chauncey. Breeze was sweet and soft like his nickname, but the hold he had on me was mighty, like a hurricane. Karma is a bitch, because it was my fault for luring him into my life.

❋ ❋ ❋

Was bad karma the result of my childhood? By the age of twelve, I knew how to get a man's attention. True's French fries would revel in how cute I was, how I looked just like a mini version of my mother. But I saw how they looked at me. Perverts.

The father I never knew, I saw in all the French fries who came in and out of our door. I never realized how I craved male attention, how unhealthy it was sitting in their laps and being alone with them while my mom was working late. My mother put me at risk each and every night. Her naiveté was pathetic.

When I first met Breeze, I was only sixteen but could have fooled someone into thinking I was about twenty. One night I sat on the couch in polka-dot panties with a white tank top, no bra. My face was close to the fan, trying to manufacture that windswept hair look. It was a hot night and the air conditioner was busted once again. But what was worse was that I was hot for something and I just wanted to see if I could get it.

True wasn't home yet. She was working late at her grimy "massage" parlor spot in Chinatown. Breeze was her newest find from a nightclub where she bartended on the weekends. He was the DJ and one of the youngest guys I ever saw her with. DJ Breeze, a college kid. True was reaching a new low. He called and I told him she'd be home in a few minutes and to come over.

Deep chocolate skin, peach fuzz on his chin, and a silky black mustache. Tall, slim, chiseled. He was fine. I knew I could get him. He was closer to my age, anyway.

The doorbell rang. I put on my Wet n Wild lip gloss and

fluffed up my straight shoulder-length hair so that I looked wild and seductive, like True. I rubbed my nipples to make them hard before opening the door, something I saw her do religiously, right before I was told to go to my room and mind my business.

"Heeey, Breeze." I smiled up at him, kinda hiding behind the door.

He walked in and looked down at my panties. My legs were exposed. Shapely, caramel, and tempting my helpless victim.

"Hey, sugah. Where's your mom?" He looked past me through the darkness of the living room. I was invisible.

"She's not home yet. Oh shit, this is dope." I reached in for his navy-blue two-way pager, which had a see-through plastic cover.

"Oh, thanks, I just got it." His smile glimmered. His bedroom eyes sparkled, reminiscent of the model Tyson Beckford. He let me know I had him.

"Can I see it?" I put a little butter in my voice, dripping with a touch of seduction. I moved close to him and started unhooking the pager from his belt. I felt so hot, I wanted to get closer. I could smell the cocoa mango oil he must have just put on before meeting his old lady lover.

I took a little longer than needed to tug on his belt and unhook the pager.

He walked around me, toward the living room, trying to control his wandering eyes. "Why don't you put some pants on, Kylie? Damn!"

"Why? Am I making you uncomfortable, Breeze? The

A/C is broken again. Just pretend I have on a bathing suit. Besides, this is what I wear to bed and it's fucking hot in here."

Breeze narrowed his eyes. "Why do you have to curse? A pretty mouth like that and nothing but dirt coming out of it. . . ." He clenched his jaw.

"Oh, so sorry I've offended you, Mr. Breeze." I held his pager and walked around him, in front of the TV, slowly. Very slowly. I knew he was watching each step and the glow from the TV was the spotlight that I needed on my silhouette. I drew him closer to me with my eyes. I had a mental lasso wrapped around his dick. I sat on the couch next to him. I felt powerful and in control. Master of the universe. I didn't even really want him, but I wanted him to want me. That was the goal.

He mumbled, "I ain't trying to catch a case messing with you."

"What's that?" I snickered.

"Nothing . . ." He grunted. He sat on the edge of the couch, but couldn't pull away from me. That lasso yanked him. Yanked him good. I sat facing him, with my knees up, so he could see all of me. I wanted him to take a peek. "The power of the P . . . goes a long way," True would say. He should want me, not her old ass.

The blue glow from a *Good Times* rerun filled the room. I didn't turn on the lights. He shifted uncomfortably on the couch. "What time is she coming home?" He wrung his hands nervously and bit his bottom lip, real sexy like. It was as if he was contemplating what to do next. Would he watch me or

Florida Evans? I stared at him and smiled, so that he could make a decision.

"At two A.M.," I said softly.

"I thought you said in a few minutes when I called?"

I chuckled. "Oh, you must have heard me wrong. What, you don't mind waiting, do you?" I leaned in. "I like your hair-cut." I ran my finger down his sideburn. I couldn't believe my own boldness.

He looked at me from the corner of his eye, shook his head, and smiled. "You are something else. But I like it. Why you so hot? You don't have a little boyfriend to take care of you?"

"No, I have friends. No boyfriend. I'm too young to be tied down like that. What about you, is True your woman now? Don't you already have a mama?" I laughed. "Or is she just one of many?" I pretended to look through the numbers in his beeper.

He had his hand out. "Come on, give it back now. You wildin', looking through my stuff."

He reached for it and I playfully pulled it away. I placed his beeper in between my legs and hit the vibrating switch. The thunderbolt feeling on my spot was unknown and curiously stimulating. I always heard True talk about vibrators with her friends, but had no idea it felt that good.

"Oh my God!" I giggled like the teenager I was. "This feels good."

I pulled his hand on top of the buzzing beeper. "Feel it, Breeze." I squirmed.

He slowly joined in with the rhythmic caressing of my spot. He didn't resist. Sweat formed on his forehead.

"Yo, Kylie. Why are you making me do this?" He nervously looked at the clock on the VCR. It said 11:58 P.M. He pulled away. "We can't."

I tugged his hand harder. His hand moved our makeshift vibrator up and down on my red polka dots. He looked at me seductively. "See what you're doing to me?" He took my hand and moved it on his long smoothness. It felt like steel under denim, bursting to venture into the forbidden and the unknown. I was curious to feel him inside me. I wanted to feel the way True felt when I heard her making love with one of her many men. I wanted to know what they did to make her feel good. I wanted to be pursued, the way she was.

We stopped. He rubbed my thighs. "How old are you again, darlin'? You can't possibly be the age your mom said."

I stood up and opened the terrace sliding door to get more air. "I'm seventeen and a half," I lied. I was sixteen.

"She said you were thirteen."

"She wishes." I laughed. "She always lies about everything. You're not the only young guy who comes over here, you know?"

He stood up next to me and pinned me up against the sliding door.

"Oh yeah? But am I the only one who has fucked you?"

"You ain't fuck me, Breeze, so don't even play yourself." I rolled my eyes. He pressed his body against me and I felt his hardness on my thigh.

He spoke in a slow deep voice, sending goose bumps down my arms. "Oh, what, you just teasing me? Inviting me over early, coming to the door with your plump little titties and ass hanging out. I can see everything, sugah."

I shifted, turned on and a bit nervous at the same time. His warm breath made me tingle as he spoke low in my ear. "You want me to fuck that tight pussy? You were going for yours and I like that shit, Kylie. I'll leave before she gets here." He kissed me on my neck. I sighed from how sexy he made me feel.

"Now who has the dirty mouth?" I laughed nervously. "Breeze, I was just testing you." I got scared and now wanted out. Kissing him I didn't mind, but sex, I was calling his bluff. I was toying with the idea of actually going through with it. True thought she was the master of the game, but it looked like I could take her crown. I moved away from the glass door and back to the couch.

He followed me and pinned me to the couch with one arm, kneeling over me. He was strong and forceful. "You're so pretty, so damn young and tender." He rubbed his peach fuzz against my cheek and started to kiss my neck. I kissed him back, grinding on him, like I did to boys my age. He got worked up and wanted to take it further.

Breeze moved my panties to the side and started working his hot fingers inside me. It felt incredible to be craved like that. His hands slowly yanked my panties halfway down. He ventured between my thighs and buried his face between my legs.

"What are you doing?" I scooted away.

"Don't tell me you never had no one eat that pussy. As bold as you want to act?"

"Nah, that shit is nasty." I started to pull my panties back up. He pulled them back down and became more aggressive. The excitement of my mother walking in on us sent me over the edge. I wanted her to see just what she'd created. I wanted her to see how she couldn't trust men, because they would always want something their own age or much younger. I sighed as he took off his pants. I was shocked to see what came out. It was bigger than I'd expected. I was even more nervous for talking so much shit. I didn't know how that thing was going inside of me. He grunted like an animal trying to get it in. He pinned me down as I winced in pain.

"Talking . . . all that smack . . . and baby girl is tight as a box. . . . This shit feels so fucking good. Are you giving it up to me? You giving me this tight stuff to me, darlin'?" He put his fingers inside me again and I scooted back from how rough he was. "You have any Vaseline? You are so tight." I pointed to the bathroom. I took a moment to catch my breath.

I wanted him. My decision was made. He came back greased up and saluting me. He eased in . . . eased in slowly. . . . I yelped. His hot dick couldn't make its way in no matter how wide I spread my legs. My cringes gave him pause. He moved down my torso and began to lick and suck. A feeling I had never experienced before. I relaxed and moaned with pleasure. He returned his face to mine. My eyes squeezed tight, wincing from the initial pain. My breath was short, legs paralyzed with fear. It hurt and yet it felt so good to know I'd gotten him under my spell. I dug into his shoulders with my nails as he entered me. I moaned, I yelled, I pretended the pain felt good. I tried to simulate the movements I'd seen in my mother's dirty pornos that I snuck and watched. I tried to suck on his neck, like I practiced on my boyfriends. I was trying too hard and my acting gave it away. My moans sounded like pain and not pleasure.

I watched his mouth open as though in extreme ecstasy, the creases in his eyebrows showing me he was in heaven. Warm . . . pulsating . . . wet. I didn't know it would go so deep inside of me. I swear I could feel it in my stomach. My back arched and he tried to be more gentle. He whispered in my ear and kissed my face. I felt so loved. I wanted him to love me, to take me away from there.

"You're a virgin?" Breeze said in my ear as his sweaty body moved in a slow, steady rhythm. Innocent, I was not. I had tried many other things and definitely gotten very close, but I had never actually gone all the way.

The joy I thought I was going to feel wasn't quite what it turned out to be. I started crying and couldn't stop crying. The guilt started to take over as I realized just how desperate I'd become for attention. I gave up my virginity to one of my mother's boyfriends. This was not the way my first time was supposed to be. What was I thinking?

"What are you crying for, darlin'? Oh, sweetness . . . oh, this pussy feels so . . . Ohhhhhhh!"

He came inside me. My mother's boyfriend came inside me. That was not supposed to happen! Sweat dripped all over me. My relaxed hair was fuzzy. Love marks were all over the insides of my thighs. Wet . . . swollen . . . dripping with his juices. Is this how it felt every night to True when she had sex with one of her random men? It felt disgusting.

"I'd better go. . . . She's gonna know we was fucking. Look at us. We smell like sex." Breeze stood over me as he wiped himself down with a towel. His body was soaked and I liked how sexy he was. The TV reflected off his carved chest.

He left the towel on the couch. It had a pink streak of my blood, evidence that I had now crossed the passage into womanhood. Disgusting. Evidence. Proof that what he took I would never get back.

I kissed him at the door. I glanced at the clock. Right on time, 1:30 A.M. The real time she was coming home. "You made me feel so good, Breeze."

"Don't let no one else have that pussy. Keep it tight. Imma call you tomorrow, darlin', okay?"

I jumped into the shower feeling scared, nervous, and accomplished all at once.

The next day, he told me he bumped into True on the way out of the building. Turns out she was coming home with a dude she met that night at the parlor. A blow to his young ego, but confirmation that he shouldn't have any guilt for banging her daughter and taking her virginity.

He started coming over at night, before True got home. He would give me money or buy me nice earrings and sneakers. True never suspected a thing. She thought she'd trained me well and I was juicing some boy at school. I still don't know if he kept seeing her, but I wouldn't put it past him.

A month after our first encounter, I noticed my nipples starting to feel full and swollen. I got sick a few times at lunch. That was just one of the three pregnancies I aborted over the years with Breeze. Even though I was on the pill, I was careless sometimes and missed days and I was apparently very fertile. He never forgave me because he wanted to start a family, but that was insane. I was a still a teenager. I wanted to live my life.

Breeze has been in and out of my life for ten years. Never quite my man, but always there. That little secret we held was what brought us closer. But I always had to keep him at a distance. If he could fuck his girlfriend's teenage daughter, what else would he be willing to do?

As I got older, his appetite for sex grew. When I was around eighteen is when he introduced me to a whole new world of erotica, porn, and exhibitionism. We did it on rooftops, in parking lots, movie theaters, and subways. Breeze taught me so many tricks, so many ways to please a man. As much as I tried, I couldn't kick the habit. He had a tame-stick between his legs and he controlled me with it. Men my age seemed immature by comparison, and I was never interested in them. Breeze stayed in my speed dial, no matter what. If there was ever a rainy night and my panties were moist, he was the one I'd call.

The secret I thought I would bring with me to my grave didn't quite stay a secret. When I went away to college, I left some photos at home and True found them. They were of Breeze and me on a Valentine's Day hanging at my dorm. She barely remembered his name, but she knew he was one of her conquests. It took three years of calling me every kind of name in the book and hardly speaking before she was over it. I always denied it. I said I didn't even know he was one of her many men. She never believed me, but I guess she saw herself in me and eventually let it go.

Guilt still consumes me from all the things I did during my teens. Now I realize I was starved for attention. At the time, in my mind, taking one of her boy toys was justified. Taking one of her men proved to me I had the power of the P and I had now graduated into womanhood. I was the new master of the game. True always claimed to have what was now in my hands.

I realize now I didn't love myself enough, and I had serious issues with True. Well, I still have issues with her, but I'm working on forgiving her and yeah . . . forgiving myself.

Even after the many ups and downs in our relationship, Breeze wouldn't take no for an answer. He tried to pull me back right before I left the Big Apple.

10:15 P.M.

BREEZE: Whatcha doing, sugah?

KYLIE: Hey you. I'm chillin' at home.

BREEZE: Feel like some company?

KYLIE: What, you have something in mind?

BREEZE: Special Delivery. Open the door in ten min.

I walked to the kitchen to put a cup in the sink. I had on boxer shorts and a tank top, and my 'fro was wild and lopsided. I fluffed it up in the mirror and splashed some water on my face and brushed my teeth. Breeze would always try to surprise me. Although some thought it was romantic, I knew better. He wanted to make sure his young piece of ass was staying in line and "keeping it tight."

The last I saw him was a little different, since he could finally tell that I was, really, leaving for Miami. The sky-high boxes packed in each corner and black squares on my wall where photos and art used to hang revealed my poor house-keeping skills.

He walked in and we embraced. "You're really leaving me, darlin'?" He smelled so good. I told myself to be strong.

"I want a change and, Breeze . . . I can't wait on you any-more. I can't do it."

"I can dig it," he said nonchalantly as he stared at my lips. "I still love you even after all this time. I know I'll always love you, but for some reason, Ky . . ." He turned away and went to sit on the couch. "I think it's that . . . you were so cruel. I don't think I could ever forgive you for what you did. No way."

"Are you kidding me?" I stood over him waving my hands in anger. "How long do you think you can use that cop-out Breeze? I wasn't gonna be your baby mama and I was way too young to have a child."

"So, why didn't you take your birth control? Maybe deep down you wanted one. You were old enough with the last one. You were twenty-one." He sulked.

"I told you, I thought I did. I messed up a few times and forgot. Look, bringing up the past will do nothing. My life is just beginning and I plan on starting over with a clean slate in Miami." It didn't make it any easier that True would go fuckin' berserk if she knew Breeze was the father of her first grandchild.

He ran his hand up my leg and leaned in. "You cutting me loose, sugah?" He looked up at me with those sly eyes. His hand slid between my legs.

I shrugged my shoulders, wishing he'd just leave and not give me any more memories, good or bad.

He kissed me and I tried to resist, but I started to melt from the short pecks and sucks.

"I . . . I miss you," I mumbled weakly. *Fuck*.

"What do you miss? Tell me, sugah."

"Kissing you." It was so good, I felt vulnerable in his arms, safe, loved. But I knew it was just a temporary illusion. My phone started to ring.

I snapped out of it and pulled away. "But the problem is . . . I'm ready, you're not, and you'll never be ready," I said.

"Now hold up. You getting bipolar on me? What?"

I got up. "You're playing games and I can't anymore, Breeze." I tried to walk away and he pulled me down by the elastic in my sky-blue boxers. Ring . . . ring . . .

"Why you always gotta bring the drama, Ky. I ain't one of these young cats you can just be running your trap at like you ain't got no—"

I got away from his gentle tug and grabbed the phone on its last ring. Dial tone. I walked back to him and sat down; he took my legs and put them across his lap. "Yeah, yeah, we've established that you ain't one of these young cats. You always say that, which leads me to believe that I should find a nice young cat who wants to be with me all the time, not just come fuck me on a Friday night when he's horny. Which, by the way, we should be doing right now. Don't you have to leave soon to get back to your other woman, before you turn into a fucking pumpkin?"

He looked a bit shocked. "What other woman?" Breeze sat up. "What?" He was speechless.

"Oh, come on, Breeze, I'm younger than you, but not dumb. I know about her and it's all good because you always covered your ass by never committing to me, but Lord only knows what you're telling that poor woman." I smirked in satisfaction.

He slouched over his knees, wiping the sweat from his brow. "Darlin' . . . she's just a friend, nothing serious. She's a singer I know who's in town and needed a place to stay."

"Right, right . . . and calling me from your fucking home phone? Your lies are so tired, Breeze. And I actually thought I was still going to fuck you and I was looking forward to one last send-off." I stormed away and came back with a box full of his tank tops, T-shirts, toothbrush, and other knickknacks he left at my place over the years. I'd planned to give it to him after some toe-curling sex, but my plans changed. He looked at the box I dumped at his feet and then looked up at me.

"Breeze, I will always love you, but you ain't gonna stress me out and run me to the ground anymore. Go home to your wifey, girlfriend, singer, whatever. Even though you look good and I'm horny as shit, I'd rather spend the night with my vibrator than with you."

Touché! I walked to the door to lead him to it. His eyes

glared at me with contempt, like high beams on a dark high-way. He walked toward me holding the box in his hands.

"Why do you have to be so evil? You're not going to give me any good-bye lovin'? How you gonna do me like that? You want to go out like this, Ky. Really?"

"I'm kinda bored with your lines, Breeze. I was looking forward to really seeing you, but you keep fucking shit up with more lies. Let's keep it simple." I opened the door and he gave me a kiss on the cheek. That was the strongest I've ever been. I was proud of myself for finally standing up to him.

Chapter 13

Jacques

I was back in Miami after five days in the Big Apple. Even though New York was home, it felt good to be back in the sun and see the sight of palm trees. Today was going to be a reunion of sorts.

I was sitting across from Dee and the tarot card showed me her miraculous turnaround, just like a mini movie flashing before my eyes. I rarely use tarot cards anymore, but I have some clients who still request them. I flipped one over and smiled at her. "You've done a lot since the last time you were here for a visit." She nodded proudly.

Her relaxed vibe said it all. She needed this vacation to Miami more than anything. When I used to meet with her at my New York office, it was as if a whirlwind blew in. The woman was always fast-paced, rushing in late from a sales meeting and dressed to the nines. But now she was on vacation and leaving the stressful life back up north, where it belonged. She was revealing a bit more now, like a sexy butterfly tattoo on the small of her back. But I'm not complaining. I could use the pick-me-up after meeting with three clients back-to-back. The pink halter and low-cut jeans she wore were a perfect combination to bring out her light caramel golden tan.

Dee sighed. "Yeah, it's going to be almost eight months that I've been trying to do me." She fixed her short-cropped bangs. Her hair was swooped up in a short Mohawk style and she ran her fingers through it. "I haven't been on a date in a while, but for the first time in my life I feel good without depending on a man for security. I've been depending on me."

I leaned in close. "I am proud of you, but also sorry to burst your girl-power moment. Someone is coming into the picture very soon." She perked up. I flipped two more tarot cards and raised my eyebrows. "I mean, very soon. Are you going out tonight with that friend you visited?"

"Nah, I'm staying with a married and pregnant friend. We aren't going nowhere, but maybe Häagen-Dazs. She's so damn greedy now." She laughed. "She is seven months and looks like ten months!"

I felt confident that this guy was going to be coming soon if she didn't already know him. "Keep your eyes and ears open."

"Are we going to be a good match? Or is he going to be good for just two months and then show his ass like the rest of them?"

"Is that a full question?" I playfully looked up to the heavens. "Is he going to show his ass like the rest of them? Pick three cards."

She shook her head as she closed her eyes and went for the deck. "Damn, I'm sorry for being so crass, you know that's me."

"Don't be sorry, be yourself." I flipped over the cards she'd picked. "You'll know when you meet him. You'll know, Dee. You will both click."

She leaned over to see the card with a knight on a white horse.

"You sure it's not you, Jacques? 'Cause you're the only man I'm gonna see tonight."

I blushed; she always loved pushing my buttons. "No, you big flirt, it's not me."

"Oh yeah?"

I licked my lips and smiled to let her imagine what I was thinking. I couldn't even pretend she didn't turn me on. Everything about her exuded *fuck me now!* The way she crossed her legs, the way she leaned in to read the cards just enough for me to see that dip in her tank top, the way she looked at me. But I had to behave. And I already knew that it wouldn't be worth it. We were no match. Sexually maybe, but after that, the fires would be blown out quickly. And of course Vicky. I cared about Vicky so much—so clean thoughts, clean thoughts only.

I cleared my throat to change the subject. "How are you doing since your mom passed?"

"Better, but I still feel the guilt big-time. I wish that we had reunited sooner. We were rebuilding our relationship and then lung cancer took her."

"Don't blame yourself, Dee. Remember, it was your mother who refused to talk to you for those six years."

"Wow, how do you remember details like that?"

"It's what I do." I smiled. "Hang in there."

"Yeah, I guess." She seemed distracted, looking at the tan line of where her watch would have been. "How much time do I have?" She finger-fluffed her bangs.

I glanced at the bamboo clock above her head. "About ten more minutes."

My guides sent me a message to share with her about her health. I sat up straight and gave her a no-nonsense glare. "You really have to take better care of yourself, too, you don't want to end up like your mom."

I pulled a card and saw an illness taking over her system within ten years or so. I actually saw inside her, like an X-ray. I saw a lot of black gook; it was an exaggerated vision that sent the message loud and clear.

"You need to cleanse, detoxify, get the junk out." I felt as if I'd lost my breath, like the wind had been knocked out of me. My spirit guides wanted to emphasize the message they were sending me. "What do you eat? I see a cloud of gray smoke around you."

"Really?" She started ruffling her hands nervously. "I eat a lot of salads mostly."

I tilted my head. "Come on, what else?"

"Chinese food, well, a lot of Chinese food, and I'll admit it, the salads are fairly new. I'm trying to do better. I do smoke still, though. I beat the habit a couple years ago, but the second I get stressed, I'm back at it."

"That's it, look, I'm not going to lie to you, the way you are living could cause a serious problem later on with your health. Your eating and smoking habits aren't going to help you in about ten to fifteen years. I'm serious. Just because you have a petite frame, don't let it fool you."

I grabbed her hand, because as I said it, I saw that same gray cloud float over her chest and lungs and then swirl into the shape of a black mask over her face. My throat felt extremely dry. All I could see was her body from the neck down. Her face was completely covered by the mask. My throat tightened even more and I couldn't breathe for one second. I started to smell rotten meat.

Cancer. My stomach jumped. It was what I called the death mask. She was literally killing herself. She was possibly going to die of cancer if she didn't make improvements now. I couldn't tell her that, it would scare her too much, but I wanted to warn her.

She narrowed her eyes. "What do you see? Why are you holding my hand so tightly?"

I had gone into a short trance state and didn't realize I'd zoned out. My eyes were beginning to water when I came out of it. "I'm sorry, I'm sorry."

"Is it that bad?" She slouched in her chair. "I know, I know I just don't give a fuck about myself sometimes. I get depressed and don't care. You know I smoke two to three packs a day now?" She shook her head and wiped away a tear.

"You have to start caring about yourself, Dee, if you want someone else to care about you. Looking good on the outside is one thing, but your body will appreciate you and reward you with a long life if you take better care of yourself."

She pouted, trying to hold it in as she pointed to the tissue box behind me. As tears cascaded down her freckled button nose, she quickly wiped them away before any more could drop. I handed her the box of tissues to dry her damp eyes. She was such a beautiful person, but her low self-esteem always got the best of her. My heart began to break for her.

I rubbed her hand. "It's okay to cry, Dee. You have to let it out sometimes. You don't always have to be the strong one."

She started to cry even more and I got up to hug her. Even I was beginning to tear up, because I hoped it wasn't too late for her to change her future. I held her gently. "Please promise me that you'll take better care of Dee. You come first, love yourself. Spend more time with yourself. Honor who you are." She squeezed me tighter and pressed her body into mine. I felt my shirt get moist with her tears. Her warmth made me tingle and the soft blow of the air conditioner on my neck gave me goose bumps. My hand was across her back, then landed on the warmth of her curvy waist, exposed by her low-rider jeans.

The butterfly was right below the warmth of my hand. She looked up at me and bit her bottom lip. "All jokes aside, I wish I could find someone like you, Jacques. You are sooooo supportive."

Oh, wow, why'd she have to say that? We were so close, the soft scent of perfume teased me to hold her just a bit longer. I touched her chin and smiled. "You'll find someone soon and he'll be even better than me. Someone without a . . . situation." I laughed, trying to make light of the awkward moment and also snapping back into reality.

I looked into her eyes and saw what a tortured soul she was. I saw how much she'd been through over the years. She was just a little girl in the body of a voluptuous woman still looking for love and acceptance.

She kissed me on the cheek. "Jacques, you are such a sweetheart. Since I can't have you, do you have a brother?"

"Oh, I have a brother, but I couldn't do that to you." I finally pulled away. Her soft skin felt so good and our energies didn't want to part. I felt good comforting her.

We sat back down. "The new guy . . . he's going to help you. I don't know if you are going to hit the jackpot with a doctor or what. Maybe he's a nutritionist, but it seems like he will be your support system to get your health back to where it needs to be. Maybe you'll do a detox together."

She shifted in her seat. "How romantic." She snickered sarcastically.

"Have you been to the doctor recently?"

"No, not in like two years. I hate doctors."

"Go to one and get a full physical, so you can see exactly where you should improve. The smoking, Dee, is number one though. This I know for sure. You must stop."

"I still don't think I'm ready for anyone new." She seemed to be ignoring my recommendation. "So much happened to me in the past year. My mom passing and my closest friend moving away to Miami, then the stress from my promotion to sales manager. I can't deal with a man right now."

"Right, whatever you say, Dee. I give you a couple more weeks before your body is shouting a different tune!"

We laughed. "Come on, Jacques, I'm not that bad!"

I shuffled the cards and just started humming like I was ignoring her. We both burst into laughter.

Chapter 14

Kylie

Jacques buzzed me into the waiting room. I heard mumbles and laughter behind the door. He was wrapping up a session with a client as I sat anxiously awaiting my reading. I was nervous and excited. The fragrance of sandalwood incense created a light smoke cloud. It circled the tall Japanese paper lamps that softly lit the waiting room.

New age music, nature sounds, and melodic Native American flutes soothed my impatience. I checked my hair in the mirror across from me. I flipped through a few magazines and came across a very entertaining article called "So, She Wants to Make It Facebook Official?"

The title was hilarious, since I've heard people talk about that stage in a relationship when you actually share with your world, aka Facebook, who your main squeeze is. The author went on to say . . .

I got an email from a dude asking me if he should cave in and make his relationship "Facebook Official," so that his girl could shut the hell up. Come on fellas, how many of you have started seeing a chick, you're diggin' her, she's diggin' you. You want to make her your number one; she wants to make you her number one and only. Big difference. You see, what she doesn't know is that she has other contenders and if she says the wrong thing or trips up in any way, she will move out of the number one slot and someone else will kindly be rotated in. Demoted, stage left, dropped from the team. Ya feel me? Someone with a bigger ass, juicier lips, freakier in bed, or, better yet, a chick who knows how to keep her mouth shut and not talk back. Ha!

Ladies say, "If I'm really your girl, put it on Facebook." Get the fuck out of here with that shit! The idea of putting it on Facebook is the dumbest shit ever. Facebook is a sea of potential ass. Why would he ruin his pool of potential pussy for a girl he's not really into? Getting us to look at you, call you, and date you is easy. But getting us to want to be with your ass is the hard part.

Fellas, don't do it. You are fuckin' it up for the rest of us. It causes nothing but controversy. All the other chicks in rotation will start their bullshit. You know, begin on a quest with their detective work. Or worse, they will IM or in-box your girl with some scandalous story that, hey . . . might be true. Respect your privacy . . . respect the game. Respect the man code. Don't make it Facebook Official. Shit, delete your account and it will make your life even easier. Grab your balls to check if they are still there and be a man. I'm just sayin' . . .

And ladies, I know I can be a bit harsh. I'm your boy and I'll keep it 100 with you, but someone has to keep it real with you. I do believe that everyone will find someone for themselves. The hard truth is that no matter how good of a catch you think you are, there are many dudes who will throw your ass back in the water. Unless he says you're his girlfriend, you're not. I don't care if you met his mom, homies, sister, aunties, and granddad. I don't care how compatible your horoscopes are! Until you're official in real life and he's verbalized it, you're just a rehearsal chick. You're just a stepping stone and, truth be told, you might just be his side-chick. When you are number one, believe me, you will know it and you won't need Facebook to convince you. Dry your tears and don't be dumb.

Dude, don't ever let it get emotional. I'm sorry, but you should have never have gone there. You have to make their role clear in the beginning. Have you learned nothing from me?

Like I always say . . .

Remember, it's just a stab,

Your boy,

Hicham Berradi

I was cracking up after reading that article. I was furious at some points, but it was also clear that the writer was an asshole on purpose. I remembered him, too. He was famous for his *It's Just a Stab* blog, which is pretty much saying it's just sex. Man, he's a jerk, but he's smart. Controversy sells! He's definitely the dude you love to hate!

Jacques opened the door and said his good-byes to a shapely golden-brown lady who had a fierce pixie cut, like Halle Berry or Toni Braxton in the nineties. She was smiling ear to ear. Her silver bracelets jingled as she floated out of the room and sat down in the waiting room. "I'm gonna wait until my ride gets here."

"Oh, no worries," Jacques said gently. "There's water if you need it. Really good seeing you, Dee." He pointed to the small fridge against the wall.

She and I exchanged smiles. She seemed so happy with her reading. I couldn't wait to be next!

"Heeeeey, Kylie!"

"Jacques!" I rose to hug him like a long-lost friend. Even though he wasn't in NYC that long, mannnnnnn, he was even finer than I remembered. He wore a black skully hat and had a bit of a five o'clock shadow. Yum. He seemed to blush as I eyed him up and down. I hated that he could probably read my mind.

"Sorry for the cold, I have no control over the A/C." He pointed at his hat. Jacques stood in the doorway, waving me in. He led me into an office drenched in warm earth tones of orange, browns, and tans. He had a candle lit, a soothing waterfall, beautiful statues, and artwork that reflected all religions. Buddha, Jesus, Hindu gods, Yoruba orishas, and more. It felt like a museum of spirituality. Sacred, relaxing, and peaceful.

He pointed to a leather chair for me to sit in. Jacques saw the magazine in my hand and said, "Oh, I see you've met my brother, Hicham." He pointed to the photo of a skinny white-looking dude whose headshot was next to the article title.

I looked at the photo and then at Jacques. "Brother? Are you serious? I thought he was a regular white dude, or maybe Latino."

"Dead serious! And, yes, like most people think I am Spanish." He raised his eyebrows with a tilt of his head. "Yeah, he's a bit longer in the face. He's much taller and skinnier, but that is my flesh and blood as much as I'm embarrassed to say at times. Hope that didn't offend you too much. His big mouth is one of his money-makers, believe it or not."

"How cool that he writes that column? Didn't it start off in *Maxim* magazine?"

"No, it was his blog first, then it went viral online, then a few magazines picked it up. Now he's syndicated. He's well connected, my little brother." He smiled with pride.

"Well, I'm fascinated that this guy is your brother. You seem like total opposites."

He took a sip of water and smoothed out his thermal shirt that showed his defined pecs and biceps. "Oh, we are; that we are."

"May I keep it?" I held up the magazine.

"Sure, take it! I can't believe you like it." He shook his head.

"Well, it gives us women a different perspective on how some men think."

"Key word: some. Some. Please don't lump us all together after reading his crazy stuff."

He handed me a bottle of water. "All right. Let's get started!" He shuffled his tarot cards and I took a deep long breath and listened to the gentle waterfall behind me.

Now, this was a freebie, so I didn't want to take advantage, but I had a gazillion questions to ask. My palms were sweating and my heart was beating fast.

He looked at me intensely. His eyes were deep and sincere. It felt like he could see right through me. "Soooo . . . are you ready to get started?"

"Okay . . . and please don't talk like that. I won't be able to concentrate."

He licked his lips and smiled. I crossed my legs and tried to say focused. "Okay, but I have to ask, do you agree with Hicham's ideas about how men have to have more than one woman?"

"Well, I guess if that is what you're into. Me, I'd rather spend my energy, time, and money on one lady."

"Oh . . ."

"Yes, you know, makes life easier. Less drama, less headache."

Humph. Whatayaknow? A loyal man. A rare species! I shifted in my seat. It suddenly got hotter in the room.

I spoke softer. "Wow, I wish there were more men like you. You are taken, right?" Hey, why not ask? I gulped, awaiting his response. He paused and tilted his head with a smile.

"Well, in a way. But, Kylie . . . if I wasn't, I'm sure we'd have much more to talk about." He winked.

"Oh, Jacques, please don't play like that!" I hit his hand across the table and smiled a girlish grin.

He pointedly cleared his throat. "Okay, now let's get down to business. From what I feel, I would have too much competition, anyhow. You have a few suitors lurking in the shadows, huh?"

"Oh really? Well, they are doing a damn good job at lurking." I guess he was referring to Chauncey and Breeze.

He looked at me with deep hypnotic eyes. "Okay, ready . . ."

"Yes, but promise me you won't tell me any scary stuff." I slipped off my flip-flops to get comfortable.

"No worries, I will only tell you what they show me. They usually don't show me the doom and gloom stuff, but if you need a warning, I will let you know what to watch out for."

"They?"

"Yes, your guides, spirit guides. They're your guardians, your protectors. We have several at a time, depending on what we need in our lives."

I was fascinated and looked around him. "Wow, so you hear them talking right now? Kinda creepy, no?"

"Well, I will hear them in a minute. I still have to meditate for a few. I'll hear them and start to see pictures. It's hard to explain, but it's like mini movies in my mind. Some things are like full-out dreams, some comedic, some like cartoons. I hear songs that I know will trigger a thought. I even see TV shows or hear commercial jingles. It's rather entertaining, my job." He smiled.

"Wow, the wonderful world of being psychic. I think this shit is so cool!"

He said, "Both of the main spirit guides I hear usually come to me as one voice in my head, but I can feel their presence. Their names are Edna and Kamani." He inhaled deeply and continued, "I heard them say, 'We brought someone for you.' A man came from behind them in a uniform." He tilted his head to the side as if trying to decipher something. "He is here." Jacques opened his eyes and looked to my right, then closed his eyes slowly. I got chills.

"He said to tell you, 'You look just like her.' He's saying you look just like your mom. He has strong energy. He's smiling. But he's very stern." He took a deep breath and backed up, as if someone were talking close to his face.

"What? My dad? My dad!"

"Yes, it's him. He's sorry, he's ashamed." Jacques's demeanor changed; he started slouching and holding his eyes, as if transforming into a depressed person. "He said he lived in guilt for years after your mother left and he's sorry."

I leaned in, eyebrows raised. I couldn't believe it. "I had no idea you talked to dead people, too!"

"Sometimes. When it's a very powerful presence, I have to send on a message."

Chapter 15

Jacques

The sun had already set and the moon was beginning to make its shy appearance. Kylie's father had more messages for me to give her but that's when the tall halogen lamp in my office flickered. It startled us. Two seconds later, the water fountain, the air-conditioning, my digital clock, and the light all shut off. I got a sense of urgency, a strange feeling swirling in my stomach. I looked outside and saw there were no streetlights on and the apartments across the street were in complete darkness.

"Did my father do that?" Kylie mumbled. "Jacques, I'm scared."

I was, too, but I didn't tell her that. We weren't completely in darkness. My savior was the dim flicker of flame on the table from the white candle I light during my readings. I stood and took the candle with me to a storage closet in my office to find more candles. My neck tensed as I thought about being surrounded by blackness.

"No, no. It's not your father. It's something else." His presence had vanished as soon as the lights went out and I lost my concentration. A reassuring voice in my head said, "Stay cool, man, stay cool. The power will come back on."

After I lit a few candles, my office was easier to be in, but the tension in my back and the queasy feeling in my stomach told me the worst was not over. I pointed to Kylie to stay put and grabbed a candle. "I'll be right back."

"Oh no, I'm not staying here by myself. I'm coming." She picked up a candle and placed her hand on my shoulder to follow me out. I wished I had a flashlight. I hoped that we'd find others in the adjoining offices this late. Kylie hung on to the sleeve of my shirt as we went to open the door and hit something on the other side.

"Ouch!" Dee rubbed her forehead and held the doorknob with her other hand.

"Sorry!" I tried not to laugh. I had forgotten she was out there waiting for her ride.

"What's with the lights? What's happening?" Dee asked.

"It's a local power outage. It should come back on soon," I reassured them both, trying to convince myself as well.

"Hello," Dee said to Kylie and squeezed my arm to make the introductions.

"Oh, forgive me! Dee, my seven thirty P.M., meet Kylie, my eight thirty P.M."

"Hi, guess I'll have to reschedule, huh?" Kylie mumbled.

"Okaaaay!" Dee laughed.

Kylie walked alongside us and I pointed down the hall. The staircase entrances, thankfully, were illuminated with emergency lights, so it wasn't pitch-black in the hallway. "There's only one other person I know who might still be here. Hey! Anyone down there?" I shouted.

I heard mumbles and then the loud voice of a man. "Yeah, ova here, in the detective agency." A door cracked open and a turbo-powered flashlight almost blinded us.

"Ova here, guys." He turned inside the office, then yelled, "Wow, we got company, Antonio."

I walked down the hallway quickly, protecting the flame from blowing out. There were two men in the small office. The one who sounded like a New Yorker was a small stocky guy about five three, in a tight dark suit. I'd seen him before. He gave me head nods in the elevator.

The other guy was on his cell phone talking with his back facing us and looking out the window. He was a black dude, very tall, about six four or six five, wearing a dark overall type uniform. It said PEST CONTROL on the back. The girls went straight to the cozy couch by the entrance that served as a waiting area. I grabbed a chair from one of the two desks to sit by them.

"I'm on the phone with my wife getting the news, she's watching TV," the short guy said as he picked up the receiver.

"Damn, it's a bit warm in here already." Kylie looked at her phone and fanned herself. "I can't get any reception. You?"

I looked at my cell and didn't see any bars. "Oh, they don't work or you'll just hear that the lines are busy," the short man said. He mocked a nasal operator's voice. "Please try your call again." He paced around the desk while on the phone. "Ya gotta use a land line." His strong accent rang through. "It's a freakin' blackout, my wife is at home in Fort Lauderdale watching CNN right now. There is a blackout in Miami! The entire city!"

We all looked at one another with raised eyebrows. It was not just a neighborhood outage like I had previously hoped.

"I'm Vince, guys. Sorry for being rude." He pointed to the phone. "But ya know . . ." He cut us off before we could introduce ourselves. "That's Antonio in the back there. He's probably the only lucky bastard with reception on his cell."

Dee jumped up. "Jacques, I gotta call my girlfriend who was supposed to pick me up. She's probably stuck in traffic. She's seven months pregnant, remember?"

"Damn, that's scary," Kylie murmured.

Vince chimed in, "Oh, it's gotta be murder out there, no stoplights working. Accidents left and right. You can use our phone to try her. Hopefully her cell works."

I leaned in toward Vince. "Easy, there." Vince had no tact, just scaring the hell out of everybody. He shrugged his shoulders and continued talking to his wife.

I said softly to Dee, "She'll be fine."

Dee ignored me and got up to use the phone on the desk by Antonio.

My stomach jumped again. I felt like this was the start of a very eventful night to say the least. Antonio had a distinctive scratchiness to his voice and a slight drawl when he spoke. His confident stride around the back of the office definitely got Kylie's attention. She watched him pace back and forth and fidget with the blinds and ornaments on the windowsill. I couldn't help but notice Dee watching him, too.

He must have felt us all looking and finally gave us a quick wave as he spoke on the phone. "I'm at work lil' man, where else? You ah-ight? Good, just stay in the house and lock the door. You have your flashlight? I'm gonna call Boogah to come check on you in a few. His cell was busy when I tried him before."

He turned toward us. "Yo, Vince, what's the number on line two?" he said into the phone in a calming voice. "Get a pen, Khalik." He read off the number from a business card Vince handed him. "Ah-ight, in case my cell doesn't work, just call this number if you hear anything. They gonna fix the lights soon, lil' man, don't be a punk." He laughed. "Yeah ah-ight, show me you the man. Love you." He held the phone up to us as if we could see through it and grinned. "That's my son, he's eleven."

"Hey, man." He gave me the head nod, then turned to Dee, who had just hung up with her friend. "I'm Antonio," he said with a smooth edginess while extending his hand.

"Hey, I'm Dee, that's Jacques and Kylie," she said looking him dead in his eyes. Then like clockwork she fluffed her bangs.

"Hey, aren't you that psychic guy?" Antonio took a swig of his bottled drink and looked me up and down.

I nodded, even though I hated being called "that psychic guy." I call myself an intuitive counselor for a reason. There isn't anything wrong with the term "psychic," it's just that people automatically think of crooked fortune tellers.

"Hold on, hon," Vince mumbled as he covered the phone. "Ya know, I always wanted to come and make an appointment, but never got the chance."

"Why not?" I said.

Kylie jumped in, "Yeah, he's good, too!"

Antonio gave Vince a stern look. "You save your money, man, you need all of it to pay me on time."

Vince tucked in his shirt over his protruding beer belly. "Antonio, shut up!" Those two seemed to have a brotherly kind of relationship, even though they looked like complete opposites. I wouldn't be surprised if they were brothers or friends in a past life. Their connection was strong. Very warm auras.

Antonio laughed and sat on the edge of the desk, observing the lovely ladies I brought with me.

Kylie grabbed one of the pillows from the couch and sat Indian style on the floor. Her eyes widened. "This is kind of exciting. I mean, who knows how long this can last? All of us, trapped here, fighting over that Snickers bar on Vince's desk or the bottle of water on that other desk."

Antonio opened the top two buttons of his uniform and wiped the sweat forming on his top lip. "Shit, this better be over in, like, twenty minutes. I just came by the office to pick up a file. My son is home by himself and it's starting to get hot as hell in here."

"Speaking of hot, you got any more water, Antonio?" Kylie

said in a sugar-coated tone. He grabbed one of the many candles on the desk and put it close to his clear bottle to show Kylie the deep green murky substance floating in his bottle.

"Ewww, I'll pass." Kylie turned up her face and waved him off.

Antonio shrugged. "There's always the fountain and I think we have some spring water in the kitchen down the hall."

Dee laughed. "What the hell is that nasty shit?"

"It's a detox drink called Super Greens, full of antioxidants and grasses and veggies."

"Oh, you're one of those fanatics." Dee tapped me.

I laughed. "Oh, okay, Super Greens! That's good stuff. I did that detox last year." I tapped Dee right back. "Remember what I said earlier, you should do something like that." I winked.

Kylie now took off her flip-flops and got even more comfortable on the floor, like she was at a slumber party. She patted the space above her on the couch to invite Antonio to sit down next to her. I don't know why, but I was a bit jealous.

Kylie turned toward Antonio. "You're the exterminator for this building? I heard you say to your son that you were at work."

"Oh, nah, I'm a private detective." He tugged at his exterminator getup. "Oh, you thought that I worked for Terminix for real? Nah, love, this was a cover when I was doing surveillance today."

Kylie was eating this up. "What kind of surveillance?"

"Cheating wife. I've seen her leaving every day at two P.M. to go sex her brother-in-law. A little afternoon delight." He seemed to enjoy his job by the smile he unleashed.

"Get out!" Kylie shouted as she hit the pillow in her lap.

Dee slapped a pack of Newports in her hand. "Shit, I wish I knew you guys years ago, so you could have followed around my ex's lying ass." Dee laughed and started to light a cigarette on one of the candles.

"Oh no, love, you can't do that in here." Antonio jumped up from the couch and walked over to Dee.

"I know, I'm sorry, I was going to do it in the hallway, but my nerves are bad."

"You shouldn't do that anyhow, destroying that beautiful body you got." He reached over and gently took the cigarette from her hand. "You know how many cells you are killing with each puff, how you are jacking up your lungs, your teeth, your skin?"

Kylie chimed in. "Yeah, you really—"

Dee pointed her finger at Kylie. "Look, I'm sorry that I'm not a health nut like the rest of you. I'm just fucking scared and I need this for my nerves. My girl Storm is out there alone. And there's probably accidents and God knows what else possibly going on."

"Chill, chill out." Antonio gently rubbed her back. It was a bit more familiar than he should have been, but Dee didn't stop him.

She held her hand up. "I'm going outside to smoke my cigarette and wait for my girl to get here. Please, just let me do it."

"You can't go out there by yourself," I told her.

"She's only about ten or so blocks away, Jacques. I'm from New York, I can handle it."

I tried to reason with her. "The elevators are out and you can't walk down the stairs alone. It's pitch-black aside for some emergency lights. Look, I'll come with you." I got up and followed her. I looked back at Kylie. "You gonna be okay?" I felt a good energy around Antonio. He was playful, but harmless. He made eye contact with me and smiled. The glow of the moon and the candles showed a grin on Kylie's face as she nodded her head yes and hugged a pillow.

Antonio jutted out his chin. "Gah 'head, man, we'll take care of her."

Chapter 16

Kylie

I was happy when they left. Dee was a pretty hot number and I couldn't tell if Antonio was flirting with me, her, or both of us. So now at least I had less competition. Looks like she shot herself in the foot with that smoking, anyhow. Health nuts don't like smokers and she was so rude.

As time went by Vince gave us minute-by-minute updates. So far, no one knew exactly what had caused the power outage, nor did they have a sign of when it would be fixed. I thought about my mom, but I knew she was still at the spa, so I wasn't too worried. I attempted to call, but I didn't know her number or the spa number by heart. Ah, the downside of technology.

Antonio was definitely sexy. He had a swagger about him that wasn't quite New York but wasn't quite Miami. He must have moved and come back, because he didn't come across as 100 percent Floridian.

I sat on the floor and watched him watching me. He took a swig of his gookie-looking drink.

"So, where are you from?" I asked.

"I'm from here. Right here in Miami. Liberty City, baby."

"But you didn't live here all your life, did you? I can tell."

"Well, nah, I moved to Philly for about eight years, but came back to take care of some family business."

"I knew it! You got that . . . that . . ."

He paced around me slowly. "That what?" he said, grinning.

"That edge to you. I don't know—a bit of city swagger with a twist of Southern."

"Oh yeah, you know that much about me already?" He licked his lips.

I smiled at how sexy he was. "Well, it has been about . . . what?" I looked at the clock on the wall. "Ninety minutes or so. I'm very observant. I catch things."

"So . . . Ky, what are you doing here? You know . . . here!" He pointed to the ground. "Why you seeing Mr. Call Mi Now Cleo. You seem like you got it all together. What are you here for?"

I sighed. "The usual. I'm almost twenty-eight and still single, in serious debt, and no job. I want to figure out what I should do with the rest of my life." I stretched out my legs. I couldn't believe how relaxed I felt with him. "Well, that's why I'm here. Just getting some inside scoop as to what the heck is next."

He wiped the perspiration from his forehead with a napkin. "Why not let life happen? Don't you like surprises?"

"No, Antonio, I don't." I laughed. "I'm impatient. Don't you ever feel that way? Like you need to know now?"

"Nah, because curiosity killed the cat, Ky."

I said, "Aren't you the least bit curious about your life, your future?"

"I'm trusting in God and it will all be good. Step out on faith. You gotta believe your ancestors got your back. We are all protected. Put your faith in God."

I fluffed up my 'fro, which was shrinking from the humidity. "You say to put faith in God. Why do you think there are people on this earth who have the gift to see the future? Don't you think they have a purpose, to guide us? I believe God gave them the message for us. It's what we do with the message that counts."

"Yeah, I guess." He wasn't trying to debate me and I think it was getting too religious for him. Antonio looked at his watch. "It's almost two hours this shit has been going on. Man, I hope my son is okay."

"So, are you a single dad?"

"I have my son every other week." He wiped the sweat from his forehead with a balled-up napkin.

"Wow, that's gotta be tough. I admire that. Not many good dads around these days."

"Just doing what a dad's gotta do."

"Where's his mom?"

"Oh, she's barely a mother to him. She's in Coral Gables living with her new familiaaaa. You would think he was a stepchild." Bitterness and sarcasm trailed his voice. "She got married three years ago when she got knocked up again by some Cuban cat."

"Oh, sorry to hear that. Where's your girl?" I was hoping to catch him off guard.

"What's with the interrogation? You ain't slick. This is my job, I do this." He pointed to his chest with a prideful smirk. "I don't have a girl. Why don't you have a man?"

"I never said I didn't." I was offended.

"Oh, you got jokes."

"Nah, I'm single for now. So, tell me about your job." I needed to shift the focus off relationships. "How is it? What are the highlights?"

"Okay . . . catch your breath, Ky!" He chuckled. "I really love it. But it's a job. Some days are so sloooow. I'm just in the car on Facebook or playing Words With Friends on my cell as I wait for someone to come out of an apartment. I don't mind it though, since in this tiny-ass office," he whispered, and smiled at Vince, who was still talking on the phone, "I can only take Vince in small doses." He shook his head. "He's like an Italian Shrek. He bites his nails down to the nub. He'll burp, fart, talk loud on the phone like ain't nobody in here with him."

I exploded with laughter. Vince shot us a look and held his ear.

"Big heart, though, but maaaaan . . . he's something else." Antonio spoke even softer. "Let's go out to talk by the stairs so we won't make noise."

I followed behind him. As we left the office I said softly, "You had me at Italian Shrek."

He smiled at Vince and pointed to the hallway to let him know we'd be close.

When Antonio opened the door to the staircase it was illuminated with emergency lights, so I figured it would be okay. I felt safe with him. I sat on the stairs and asked, "So, what's been your favorite case so far?"

"Well, we had a small-time insurance company as our client. They wanted to investigate this guy who claimed he had a slipped disk and walked with a cane. In one week alone I followed him to salsa class, Zumba, jogging, and having sex behind an LA Fitness after hours with a very young college girl."

"Dayummm, that's crazy!"

"Yeah, needless to say, he dropped his claim after we sent him all the photos. I mean *alllll*."

"Holy shit, that's like blackmail."

"No, it's called wake-the-fuck-up mail. He got the memo. I got a great photo of him getting it innnnn." Antonio laughed.

"You do sound like you enjoy your job!"

"I do, I just need some more accounts."

"It's slow?"

"Nah, Vince is just trying to do it all."

"Damn, that's hard." I was startled by the door downstairs opening. Then we heard chatter at the bottom of the stairs. It was Jacques and he had more people with him.

Chapter 17

Jacques

Tonight was starting to feel like an adventure, a bad reality show, and a big joke all at once. After flagging down Dee's friend Storm, we stopped at the nearby store to pick up a few things. Outside was more like a party than the mayhem Vince was envisioning. People were sitting out on the curbs talking, barbecuing, and drinking.

The three of us walked up the muggy staircase and heard talking and laughing at the top. As we got closer, we saw it was Antonio and Kylie sitting on the stairs illuminated by the emergency lights. Boy, my man Antonio was one smooth operator! And here I thought Dee would end up with him, since I'd just told her she'd meet a health-conscious guy into detoxing. I guess destiny had another plan.

Dee looked a bit jealous, but brushed it off. "Hey, guys, this is my friend Storm. She's been through a nightmare!"

Storm waved and they pushed the staircase door open.

Kylie followed behind us and sprang into action. "Oh my God, are you okay? Let's get you some water!" She dashed to the kitchen to get her a bottle of water.

Storm fanned her face. "Wow, it's a sauna in here!" She held her back and eased herself down onto the stiff couch. The candlelight's flicker let me see more of her. She was wearing a red sundress and although pretty huge and pregnant, she was a beautiful cocoa-brown woman.

Storm seemed frazzled. "It's crazy out there! No lights . . . the cops were barely out, people driving like maniacs! What's going on? I heard someone in the street yell that it was a terrorist attack. Have you guys heard that? My poor husband must be worried sick." She rambled without pausing and wiped her forehead with a tissue.

Kylie returned with Storm's water bottle and Vince hushed the room with his hand, the other hand gripping the cordless phone.

I put a plastic bag on the table and it made a loud bang that startled me. Everyone turned to see what goodies I had brought as I uncovered three pints of ice cream.

"Well, we didn't get much, but we lucked out with ice cream. The grocer was trying to get rid of it before it melted!"

"Preggers! You want it?" Dee asked Storm. Storm didn't look very sociable. Her jet-black hair was frizzed and pushed back. She'd really had a rough night and I could tell she was out of it. She had a very gentle and free-spirited soul, but being pregnant in a blackout seemed to be getting the best of her. I could see she was a good balance for Dee as a friend.

"No thanks, ice cream makes me sick." Storm rubbed her belly.

"I thought you craaaaaaaaved it." Dee frowned.

"Dee, that was the first trimester. Keep up." She finally laughed.

"Yeah, third trimester is just what, you being a mean bitch?" Dee teased.

"Touché, Dee! Touché!" She smiled, although she didn't seem like she was up for a play fight.

Vince finally hung up with his wife. He rubbed his ear, which was probably scorching hot, since he seemed to talk endlessly. He would hang up and keep calling her back for more information. His face lit up when he saw the ice cream.

"I'll get some cups and spoons from the kitchen." He was as excited as a little kid at a birthday party.

Antonio screamed, "Ah man, come on, maaaan! No! It's close quarters up in here with you and me, now we got what . . . six people up in here? You know ice cream and you don't agree, dawg!" He pretended to wave an imaginary fart. We all snickered. I could imagine Vince turning red, but I couldn't tell in the dark.

"Whatever! This may be our last freakin' meal! I'm gonna enjoy it!" Vince said.

Antonio raised his hands and his voice. "Yes, please enjoy it, drama king. Our last meal!"

Kylie walked over to him and said, "Vince, come on, let's stay positive. There's probably some huge computer glitch. Something electrical. Why don't we all relax and get to know one another and make the most of this." Feminine touch.

"Well, Mr. Psychic, did you know this was gonna occur?" Vince asked. He waved his hands toward the moonlit room.

I shook my head. "I'm gifted but I'm not God. I merely have a stronger insight than most."

I thought about Vicky. I turned to Antonio. "Your cell phone still working?"

Chapter 18

Kylie

This was truly turning into a college dorm room. It was 12:40 A.M. Antonio was sitting on the edge of the desk calling his son. He was relieved because his friend with a weird name was there to check on him.

"Thanks, Boogah, you my niggah! I owe you one, man," Antonio said.

I was falling in love with his mouth. His walk, his overall swaggability.

"Ah, now I can relax!" He hung up the phone and wiped his forehead with the back of his sleeve.

By this time, everyone's cell phone was either dead or had no signal. The office phones were our main lifelines connecting us with friends and family. It was a shame, because most of us didn't know our loved ones' numbers by heart or they had only cell phones, so even if we knew the numbers, their lines were busy.

I rubbed my hands together and looked at Jacques. "I don't know about you guys, but I want my reading. Just a snippet! Come on, Jacques. It will be fun." I kneeled toward the desk and put a plastic cup on it. "Look, a tip jar. We can chip in!"

"Ah nah, I'm good!" Antonio waved his hands frantically.

Antonio got on the floor next to me and stretched out his long legs. I tapped one. "Jeez, what are you so scared of, Antonio? What, you don't want your truth to be revealed?"

"What truth?" He leaned in closer, about two inches away from my face. "What you see is what you get, baby." He turned to Jacques and said, "I gots nothing to hide and no disrespect, my man, but I doubt you can read me."

Dee said, "Humph. He knows you better than you know yourself, trust me."

She got up and went down the long hallway to the bathroom with Storm. Storm led the way with the flashlight. "Don't start without us, please!" Dee begged.

Jacques shrugged his shoulders and gently laughed. "Hey, I didn't say I was doing anything."

Antonio was against it, but he still seemed curious. He played with the plastic spoon in his mouth as he slowly sucked off the ice cream. He was very sensual, but was also trying to be funny by doing it on the sly when others weren't looking.

Now, I'm usually the seducer. I love flirting, but Antonio had an edge that was actually turning me on so much that I wasn't even thinking about how melt-your-panties-off hot Jacques was.

Chapter 19

Jacques

nice warm breeze floated in the room. I was on the couch and Kylie was seated on the floor near me. She and Antonio seemed to be getting along well, talking low and laughing. I heard her say, "Just ask him!" She looked up at me and smiled.

Suddenly intrigued, Antonio tilted his head back toward me. "So, how does this work?" He sprinkled imaginary fairy dust in the air. "Do you work with a special ghost or something? Call on little fairies that whisper things in your ear?"

"Ah well, noooooo." I paused, trying to ignore the urge to read him on the spot. I felt his sadness for losing his wife. His insecurity about Latin men—I am sure he thinks I'm Latin, or I remind him of a Latino. Also, I picked up his fear of not being good enough and felt he was extremely intuitive, whether he knew it or not.

I took a deep breath and continued. "Ghosts are earthbound spirits. I mainly use spirit guides for help in my sessions. They are what some people call our guardian angels." It was apparent Antonio was nervous but was trying desperately to stay in tough-guy mode. I decided to enlighten him.

"Spirits guides have crossed over already; they are on a higher plane and are sent to help us, teach us. The sad part is, we rarely make the time and space to listen to them. When we do hear messages, we shrug them off as nonsense or imagination."

"Oh Gaaaawd, what is that?" Kylie shouted as she held her nose. We heard a spray in the back of the office and the room was enveloped in the smell of rotten eggs wrapped in lilac and vanilla air freshener.

"See, man, I told you not to mess with the ice cream, Vince. Dayummm!" Antonio cracked the door open.

Vince opened another window. "Whatever! Whatever. I'm human, whattaya want from me? Sorry!" Vince looked at me. "Hey, you ever see that guy John Howard? The guy from Long Island who talks to dead people?"

I corrected him. "You mean, John Edward, the medium?"

"Yeah! Yeah! My wife used to watch him all the time. She's into that *Long Island Medium* show now. That's some spooky shit, dude. You can do that, too?"

"Well, actually we all can."

"Ah, come on. If I could, you think I'd be in this place? I'd be in Las Vegas raking it in, baby!" Vince tucked in his shirt over his protruding beer belly and laughed at his own joke.

Dee opened the door.

"What were y'all talking about?" Dee asked as she fluffed her hair in the middle to keep her funky Mohawk style.

"Oh, just how we all can be intuitive, read minds, foresee the future, talk to people who have passed on." I looked toward Antonio. "You see, there is nothing as magical about it as you think."

The room was quiet, aside from the sirens outside and the salsa music playing next door. Antonio shifted on the floor and leaned forward. "Okay, I'm gonna address the elephant in the room and just say it. Do you use your so-called powers to manipulate women during your readings?"

"Manipulate?" Dee rolled her eyes.

"Oh, come on, Antonio, really? Really?!" Kylie yelled.

"Nah, all jokes aside," Antonio began, "you know, I'm not saying I don't believe in this shit, it's just dangerous when it's in the wrong hands."

Dee rocked back and forth in a chair. "Oh, I can assure you, it's in the right hands." She sipped her bottled water and winked at me.

Antonio waved his bottle. "Come on, your powers could manipulate people, plant little seeds in their heads. I'm not saying you ain't good, but it's possible that you can be too good. I don't wanna mess with that shit."

"What? Is that what you would do, Antonio? Manipulate people? Seems like if that's your assumption then you're projecting it on me."

"Now, wait a minute, dawg!" Antonio raised his hand toward me.

"Karma's a bitch and she knows where you live, Antonio. Not good if you would do that!" Kylie responded.

"Nah, nah. You got it all wrong, Ky!"

I tried to help him clean it up. "Yes, you're probably right. You would use it to help people, just like you do every day at work as a detective, when you get a hunch about a lead. When you get that feeling to check out a location or go back just one last time. What do you think you are using when you do that, dawg?" I said sarcastically.

Antonio scratched his head, looking dumbfounded. "Well, you know I never really looked at it that way. And please don't say 'dawg' again. It sounds weird with that accent."

"Ah!" Dee laughed. "Leave Jacques alone, anything he says sounds sexy."

"Ummm-hmmm," all three ladies hummed unanimously. I smiled.

"Merci, chères mesdames!" I turned back to Antonio. "So, seriously . . . about you. I think you started following your hunches more when you were what—seven, or was it eight? You found an old lady." I closed my eyes and saw the movie before me. "It was an old lady in your building. She almost died. You heard a noise, maybe even a scream for help. They left her for dead at the bottom of the staircase. You saw it. You knew who did it. It was your first success story. You were her hero."

Antonio jumped up, backing away. "Now, come on, man! Stop fucking with me!"

"Relax. Is it true?"

"Well, yeah. But . . . how did . . . What the fuck? How did you know all of that? I was eight. Yo . . . Yoooooo!" He scratched his head and looked around. "You are good." He shook his head in disbelief. "Wow, and that was my neighbor, Miss Marie! Her cokehead son tried to kill her."

Dee pointed toward him. "You see, we told you he is the truuuufff. Don't mess with him!" A few snickers filled the room.

I hoped that in the semi-dark no one could see me gloating. How I adored my skeptics. I always found a way to shut them up nicely.

"Antonio, I saw it, because that is what I do. I can see things. If you didn't know already, that pivotal moment in your life made you a better person. It helped you want to get in the very business you are in right now. You wanted to help people. You have this immense passion for the underdog, because many times you, too, have been the underdog and have wanted help and no one was there."

"Man . . . shit, you *are* good, dawg. You're right, you're right!" He gave me a pound.

Dee chimed in to my defense again. "Good, now you can stop being a chicken. All right, Jacques. . . . Can we learn from you? Show us how we can do it! It's something to pass the time at least."

"Ohhh, good idea!" Kylie said.

"Okay. So, let's just get everyone relaxed. Let's play a quick game, so you can do what I do."

I put the big flashlight on the floor to shine on the ceiling and give a glow to the room.

I picked up a chair. "Mind helping me?" They cooperated and we moved some chairs around the couch in a circle.

"Okay, let's all sit down; close your eyes," I said softly.

"Wait a minute, no séance shit," Antonio grumbled.

"Relax, man. This is something a five-year-old can do. Totally easy. No ghosts involved."

Vince sat down in the circle with us. "I might fall asleep, guys, so wake me up when it's over," Vince said.

Dee was on my left, Storm next to her on the couch with me. They both smelled good. I loved a woman who wore just enough perfume to leave a soft tantalizing scent.

Vince sat across from us with Kylie and Antonio, who stayed on the floor. I spoke slowly and deliberately. "All right, everyone, close your eyes and welcome in the silence. Take a deep breath of white light and peace. Breathe out with a gray mist of stress, tension."

"Blackout tension," Vince mumbled.

Someone giggled. I cleared my throat.

I was shocked when Antonio whispered, "Be serious, y'all. He's trying to calm us down."

I continued. "All right, breathe in." Everyone took a deep breath in unison. "And out . . . good, good. Wow, you feel that?" I could feel the tension release with a huge sigh. "Okay, keep that slow pace and we're gonna do this for about a minute . . . in and out . . . innnn and out, innnnn and out." My head felt lighter and my hands tingled as I breathed with them. I felt more at ease, even in the darkness, which I hated. The room vibrated. I felt like waves of a peaceful ocean were coming over me.

"Okay, now we are going to do a fun exercise. We all don't really know each other enough to get these answers right, so this is a game of trust . . . trusting your own gut."

The room was still and calm. "Slowly open your eyes." The moonlight shone in and the glow of the flashlights and candles set the tone for the ultimate relaxation room, even in the heat.

I heard everyone's light breathing. A sense of serenity floated through. I saw Vince was starting to check out; his eyes were still closed. "Vince, why don't you go first?" He snorted like he was just waking up. "Okay, maybe not you." We giggled.

"Antonio, do you mind?"

"What do I have to do?"

"Just go to each person in the circle. Tell them what their favorite pastime is. You already have one up on everyone since you are a professional investigator." I whispered loudly, "No pressure."

"Yeah, thanks, Jack." He said my name wrong on purpose. "Okay, so I gotta guess a hobby?"

"Correct. Don't judge yourself or think about it, just spit it out quickly. Start here."

I pointed at Dee, his nemesis. "Oh, that's easy, smoking Newports at a party with her friend."

"Well, yeah," Dee said. "You're kind of right!"

"Okay, okay." Antonio clapped his hands together, which startled Vince. He licked his lips as he moved toward Kylie. "Next up, Miss Ky! Ummm, I'm gonna say swimming. You got those nice shoulders and that collarbone like a swimmer." He tilted his head to the side as he eyed her up and down. "Skinny-dips from time to time." He looked at me and laughed. "She's into adventure."

"Damn!" Dee said. "Wishful thinking, Antonio!"

"Well, he's half right," Kylie said. "I do love swimming, but not to get arrested! I did skinny-dip one time in college, though." She laughed. "And, Antonio, you need to behave!"

"Ah, yeah, keep your fantasies to yourself," I chimed in. Antonio moved over toward the couch. "Okay, Storm, right?"

"Watch it now!" Dee said protectively. He took a deep breath. He was really getting into it. "I don't know, but I am gonna say what I feel. I get arts, painting, drawing, even sewing."

"Wow!" Dee shouted.

"I'm impressed," Storm said as she rubbed her belly. "Antonio, I'm a fashion designer. I have my own collection at Macy's."

"What . . . get the fuck outta here! Oh, I'm sorry, ladies. I'm sorry," he stage-whispered to the unborn baby in her belly.

Dee laughed loudly.

"See, how could you have known that except for your intuition?" I queried. "Magic happens when you go within and trust. Now, what about me?" Antonio closed his eyes and took an exaggerated breath in through his nose.

With his eyes still closed he said, "I'm gonna say reading, but not just anything; you are into some out-there, next-world, heavy metaphysical stuff. Other cultures, people who were like geniuses and didn't know it. You like aliens, too. Out-there shit." He laughed. He opened one eye. "Am I right?"

"Right again!" I was actually impressed. "Wow, not bad. Not bad for a first try." I clapped and everyone joined me.

"Okay, I'll go next!" Kylie jumped up onto her knees. She smoothed out her skirt and I admired her curves from the back. Kylie looked at Antonio and dramatically took in a long deep breath, reached for his hands, and closed her eyes. "I wanna hold hands, is that okay?"

"Anytime, baby," Antonio said.

"I think she was talking to me, Antonio." I chuckled. "Sure, follow your intuition, Kylie. You probably do better with touch. Getting close to someone's energy field works wonders."

She took a moment to breathe. "I'm gonna say shooting range. I saw you with a rifle for some reason. You exuded a lot of power when you did it." I saw him hold her hands a little tighter.

"Well, actually I do own a few guns." He laughed. "I practice at the range, so I don't get rusty."

She scooted over to me on her knees and grabbed my hands. Our connection was ignited by touch. Her hands were so warm. My palms tingled.

"I just heard Broadway, off-Broadway. Like you like plays. You like new stuff though, not the corny Disney-type Broadway, you like edgy stuff." She closed her eyes and squinted hard, like she was seeing something. "The art of expression in unique ways. One-man or one-woman shows, poetry, unique topics."

"Very good, very good!" I said.

Antonio leaned up off the floor. "Wait now, hold up, hold up. Why I gotta be the niggah with the gun and Mr. Pollyvoo France is all cultured and shit?"

"Because he's all cultured and shit!" Storm said loudly.

Everyone roared with laughter. Since she'd been so quiet most of the night it took us by surprise. Dee was holding her stomach and almost crying from the irony of his comment.

"Oh Gawwwwwwd!" Kylie screamed. "That was priceless!"

Antonio realized how he sounded and laughed as well. "I'm just saying."

"This is fun," Storm added. "But I'm so out of it, guys. Let me rest my eyes for a minute. I am praying when I open them, the lights will be on. I really am getting worried. I should have been in bed hours ago."

"No need to worry, it will be over soon," I reassured her. "Okay, break time, I guess."

"Holy shit, we're psychic!" Kylie shouted and high-fived Antonio. Vince slept throughout the laughter.

"You know," Kylie said. "I'm sleepy now, too. I used up all that brain power." She leaned on Antonio's shoulder as he looked at her and smiled.

I looked at my watch. It was one thirty A.M. I sat down on the floor with my back against the wall. I closed my eyes as the mumbles and whispers turned to deep breathing. Vince was now snoring and, surprisingly, his rhythmic breathing was our lullaby.

About twenty minutes had passed by when Dee asked, "Can you walk with me to the bathroom? I'm not going alone." I looked at everyone dozing or in a deep coma.

Without hesitation, I grabbed the smaller flashlight and said, "Come on, let's go." The hairs on my arms stood up. Dee led the way with each sway of her hips. I held the flashlight on her butt as she hurried in front of me. "Wait up, Dee. I'm supposed to be in front."

"Catch me if you can." She laughed as she walked swiftly. With each step, she was dripping with sweet sensuality. She was alluring and I was beginning to doubt she had to go to the bathroom at all. I knew she wanted me to pin her to the wall. She wanted to be held again, be touched and caressed. She slowed down and walked next to me. "That was such a cool exercise, Jacques." Her breath smelled like a fresh stick of spearmint gum.

"Yes, it's actually one of my favorites. I used to do it in workshops, but I haven't taught in a while."

"You really should, you're a great teacher, Jacques."

"Why, thank you." We stopped at the bathroom door. It was dark.

I put the light up a bit, so we could see each other better. The power of a glance. It spoke volumes. I was mesmerized by her mouth. I handed her the flashlight so she could see. The door made a slow creaking sound as I watched her go in. I wanted to follow behind her, but I waited.

I heard the toilet flush and water running. She cracked the door open. "Jacques, can you come here for a second? I wanna show you something."

My stomach churned. I felt like a nervous teenager. "Dee . . . now, that might not be a good idea."

Softly she pleaded. "Just come here, pleeeeaaase." Her hand pulled me in and I followed. I was curious, aroused, excited. I wanted to live on the edge. Just for a moment. She was a temptress and she knew it. I felt uncomfortable. My mind knew it was a bad idea. A very bad idea. I heard my spirit guides coaching me with a voice in my head saying, "Now remember, there's no turning back."

"Jacques, I know you try to be professional, but can I just get a hug? A real long one. I need it."

The room was dark. "Where's the flashlight, Dee?"

"On the sink. I know where it is. I don't want to waste the batteries." She giggled.

My back was against the door and she was standing very close to me. "Oh, is that what we're doing? Saving energy? You know, you are such a tease." I could barely see her face. The small window gave off a sliver of light from the moon. *"Tues êtes un tel fait de taquiner."* I rubbed my hands down the sides of her arms.

"Whaaaat?"

"Such a tease, you are. You know that? We know a hug is nothing, but when done in the dark, it can be dangerous and so much more."

She leaned in and whispered, "You are so fucking sexy, Jacques. And your speaking in French doesn't help make it easier." She sighed and her pelvis pressed against my arousal. "Can you read my mind?"

I put my hands, now moist from perspiration, on her waist. I felt a bit guilty, but I couldn't stop myself. My fingertips pushed into the small of her back, under her jeans and right below her belt. I guided her hips closer to me.

"Yes, I can read it. It's not very nice," I said low in her ear.

"What? You don't think so?" She laughed.

"Uh-uh. It's rather dirty." I was helpless as she breathed softly on my neck. "What is it saying?"

"It's saying you're a bad girl." I rubbed my hands up and down the sides of her arms again and squeezed them. They were a little damp from the heat of the small bathroom, but so soft. I wondered if the rest of her body felt like that. I pulled her into me. I wondered if this moment would lead to much more. I could picture her getting on her knees.

She leaned into the side of my neck and kissed it, and then tugged on my ear with her teeth and nibbled softly. Our energies were intertwined now. They were ready to kiss, touch, and undress. I kept my eyes closed and my face tilted up. I told myself, *Don't kiss her, don't do it. Don't kiss. Then it will be officially cheating.* Vicky isn't my wife but . . .

The soft sounds of our breathing filled the room. Slow. Intense. Anticipating what was next. This was already crossing the line, but a kiss or a little more would be the start of something. No turning back.

"You feeling guilty, Jacques?" She spoke right on my lips. "I can tell. I bet you I know someone who isn't."

I tried to envision Vicky. Vicky roleplaying that she was in the dark bathroom with me. It took away the guilt. I didn't look at her face. I just pretended. I thought about how powerful my mind was. That I could make things happen by just thinking it at times. I think this is one of those times. Dee rubbed the crotch of my pants. I wanted her to open them.

"Answer me, is he feeling guilty?" she said in a demanding voice. I loved her take-charge attitude. She stroked me gently and I grew even more helpless. Her bracelets jingled a sinful song of seduction as her hands rose up to my cheekbone. She tilted my face down to kiss me.

I had to act. I kissed her. She sighed as she kissed me back with wet spearmint kisses. Fast, deep, intense. Her tongue was magical. A very good kisser. The playful tension we held over the last year was ready to erupt like a violent volcano. "Damn, Jacques, I want you."

"No, Dee, you know we can't. I can't believe this." I contradicted myself by stroking her breasts and then I reached under her tank top to feel them in the flesh.

"Well, believe it." She stroked me through my pants, making me even harder.

"Dee, you know . . . if things were different. If I didn't have a girlfriend . . ."

She played with my zipper, teasing me, and gently tugged on my bottom lip with her teeth. She pulled the zipper all the way down and her small warm fingers ventured into my boxers.

"You do have a girlfriend, right?"

I nodded.

"Ohhhh, that's too bad." She wrapped her hand around my hardness and stroked it at length. "You like this?" she whispered. "Oh, shhhhhh . . . don't worry, I won't tell."

I was trying to stay focused. I didn't want to explode right on her. My head fell back in surrender. *Pourquoi tu es si bon?* Why . . . why . . . are you so soooo good?" This was something I really had to get a handle on. How could I say no to her?

She slowly got on her knees and I felt her moist, warm

mouth on the tip, teasing, her tongue flickering, licking the sides and playing with it. I wanted to grab her head and shove it to the back of her throat, but I held on to my senses. What would she think of me? This was already bad enough. She finally heard my mental plea and took me in with one swoop. "Ahhhh . . . Oh . . . Dee."

"Shhhhhh," she said.

"Ahhhh . . . Deeeee." She took me in and out while using her hands to stroke me. I was weak. My knees fought to stay strong against the pleasure she sent through my entire body.

I forgot where we were for a moment. She was incredible and I should have known, since I knew she was a . . . well, a very experienced woman. We were startled by a loud roar down the hall. Dee jumped up away from me and I pulled my pants up from my knees.

The light in the bathroom flickered, then came back on, followed by another thunderous roar of yelling and clapping. It wasn't just from our building, but from outside, across the street. It was a celebration. The lights were back on.

"Wow, talk about timing, ah?" I said as I smoothed out my clothes and adjusted my hardness.

"Yeah, aaaawkwaaaard!" She looked in the mirror and fluffed up her hair. Suddenly, we were pleasantly surprised by a cool breeze and loud noise over our heads as the A/C turned back on.

"Jacques, you're such a good man. I know you are not a cheater. I know. And I didn't know Moroccans had such big dicks! I couldn't help myself." She touched my zipper with one last stroke. I had to compose myself.

I pushed my finger to my lips. "Shhhhh, that's our little secret. We're African, you know?" I teased.

"Yeah, you definitely got some Mandingo in your bloodline." She laughed as she adjusted her breasts in her bra. "We should get back before they come looking for us. But I wanna get up with you before I leave. For reaaaaaal. We can't just end it like that. Come on!"

"I . . . I don't know." I shook my head no, as much as I really agreed. "I think the lights interrupting us was a sign."

"Well, she's a lucky lady—that bitch." She laughed and I couldn't help but chuckle.

Just then, I heard very clearly the voice of my guide Edna say, "You would have regretted it. I promise you."

I opened the door and the creaky sound seemed to shoot down the hall. I stood outside the door waiting, but I wanted to act like I was in the men's bathroom instead and decided to go across the hall.

"Oh, there you are," Kylie shouted. "You see, it's back on!"

"I can see that. Finally! I need to charge my cell."

"Where's Dee?" She looked behind me and then looked down at my pants.

"Oh, she's in the bathroom. I walked her in dark." I noticed my zipper was open. "Uh—I was going to the bathroom. Been holding it all night."

"Oh, okay." She raised an eyebrow. "Well, the slumber party is over. It's been real!" Kylie said.

"Yes, and what a party it has been." I sighed.

"Yeah, I see." She smirked as she opened the bathroom door. I knew I was caught. Kylie sensed something, even though I didn't really do anything—well, not really. I went into the bathroom and splashed water on my face. I couldn't believe what had just happened. I wanted more, but I knew that Dee was someone I should leave alone. Edna my guide made sure of that.

Chapter 20

Kylie

Wow, did I just walk into the middle of something? Dee was in the bathroom adjusting her hair, but if you heard people screaming for joy, wouldn't you want to run out and see what was going on?

Dee was calmly reapplying lip gloss. "Hey, girl! It's back on! I can't wait to get the heck outta here."

"I know! Well, it was so nice getting to know you, Dee."

She said, "Oh, I'll definitely be back after this trip!" She laughed a devilish laugh that strangely reminded me of True's.

"Ummm-hmmmmm! I bet you will."

"What does that mean?" Her tone was defensive.

"Well, it's none of my business, but I saw how open Jacques was when he came out of the bathroom." I giggled.

"Oh, no no no no no. Nothing happened. He's such an angel. Trust me, I always used to hit on him and he just turned me down. He just came with me, because it was dark."

"Um-hmmm. I believe you," I said with sarcasm.

"Please, trust me. He's loyal to his woman. Whoever she is, she must have a bomb-ass cootch with diamonds and gold dust sprinkled on it, 'cause she got him on lock." We laughed.

"Yeah, he is fine." I agreed. "It's hard not to drool around him."

We started to walk back down the hall together. "And you know they say Moroccans have some big dicks?" Dee said.

"Really? Well, I never met anyone from Morocco until him."

"Well, I'm just letting you know! I heard he has a brother. I'll take Jacques. You can have the brother." She laughed.

"Nah, I'm good. I think his brother is an asshole."

"You met him?"

"No, he writes the *It's Just a Stab* blog. Really nasty, but pretty funny. And he's not as cute as Jacques. He actually looks kind of like a nerdy white dude."

"Oh," Dee said. "I just assumed he would be fine and sweet, too."

"Nope. Definitely not."

Vince was stuffing a backpack with client folders. "Any of you lovely ladies need a ride?"

Dee gave us a hug. "Nah, we're out! I'm hungry! So good hanging with you guys. Storm already left my ass." She pointed down the hall.

"I can hearrrr you!" Storm yelled back, "Come on, Dee! My car better be where I left it."

We waved to Dee and as I was holding the door open I noticed a help wanted sign posted on it. It read:

LIKE A FLY ON THE WALL
DETECTIVE AGENCY
WE'RE HIRING—INQUIRE INSIDE!

"Hey! Are you guys really hiring?" I couldn't believe it.

Vince looked thrilled. "Yes, what—you need a job? We need a receptionist!"

"Actually, yes, I've been looking!"

Vince put his backpack on one shoulder. "Can you type?"

"Yes, seventy words per minute," I said proudly.

He looked up at me. "But can you research?" He tried to stand confidently with his small five-three stature.

"Um, research is my middle name! I was a fact-checker for a music news company and I'm an excellent snoop."

Antonio was sitting on the couch charging his phone and answering texts. He mumbled, "I'll make a note of that."

"You got a résumé and some referrals?"

"When do you want them?" I said quickly.

"When can you start?" He smiled.

"Tomorrow?"

"Okay, tomorrow. Bring 'em. I trust you for some reason," Vince said.

"Never trust a big butt and a smile," Antonio sang out from his desk.

"Shut up, Antonio!" I yelled playfully. I took it as a compliment, since I didn't think I had a big butt.

"Hey, hey! You gotta have more respect. She's gonna be your coworker!" Vince said.

"Yeah, respeckkkk!" I stuck my tongue out at Antonio. He just waved back.

I think he was excited that I would be around now. I was thrilled. I didn't know how I would get any work done with Antonio in the mix, but I had a *job*, finally a job. Now, of course I still needed to find out what kind of money they were talking about. It didn't look like they could pay much, but I would work my way up. I needed something, anything, and it was better than nothing.

"What's the pay?"

"Fifteen dollars per hour, but we can talk. If you are good and can research we can probably work up to twenty dollars."

"Okay, cool." Beggers can't be choosers. It was definitely not the salary I was used to but it would be better than nothing. I smiled appreciatively.

Antonio got up off the couch and put his phone away. "Wow, just like that, huh?"

Vince led us out of the office and had his keys out to lock up. "Hey, why not, what are the odds we meet a match like Kylie?"

"Why wasn't it that easy to hire me?" he joked.

"She's a bit sweeter."

I blushed. "I love my new job already!"

"Man, Vince, you are a cool dude, dawg. But how am I gonna get any work done with this pretty young thang around?"

"Oh, please, you ain't never here. I'll make sure to send you out more on surveillance, too. You'll be fine, just behave, she's family now."

"Oh, don't worry. I will. I will." He winked at me.

"So, see you tomorrow, Kylie." Vince looked at his watch. "We start at nine thirty A.M. You won't get much sleep."

"I'll be here with bells on!"

I couldn't believe it! I had a job. A job at Like a Fly on the Wall Detective Agency!

❊ ❊ ❊

It was almost two thirty A.M. when I got home. I fed Phantom, took a shower, and slid into a cozy T-shirt and boxers. True texted me that she was okay and had gone home with one of her coworkers. I told her what had happened but she didn't respond. Probably too busy on her back with whoever she went home with. I shook my head and played my other messages. Chauncey, Breeze, Olivia, and a few other random people I hadn't heard from in months had called to see if I was okay.

Then I heard a familiar woman's voice. "It's Aunt Daphne! I saw on the news about the blackout. Call me and let me know you guys are safe. Ya hear?"

Wow! She called me all the way from Jamaica? It felt good to know that I did have family now. Family that cared. I didn't think I'd ever felt that before. The next morning, Phantom jumped on my stomach—all fourteen pounds of her. I was startled and then laughed as she bounced around the room. Bed to floor, floor to bed to window, then back under the bed. She meowed loudly as she played.

"It's too early for this shit, Phantom." I looked at the time. It was seven thirty A.M. Today was my first day at the agency, five hours after I'd left it. I pulled out a nice business-casual dress, not too short and sky blue, and some nice blue-and-green earrings to match. For shoes, some sexy three-inch wedges.

True still didn't come home and didn't bother to call. I was sure she was fine, but I did want to tell her in person about my job. I didn't want to get too excited until I knew for sure it was a good fit and Vince wasn't just pulling my chain. And as good as Antonio looked, I thought I would stick with Chauncey. Better not to mix work and play. I was excited that I'd be able to hang out with Jacques more, too, since he was down the hall from the agency.

My first day on the job was pretty interesting. I learned the basic procedures on how the office was run, and I pretty much just answered phones. Vince said he would teach me more as time went on. I'd even get to help out with surveillance eventually. How exciting! When I got home, I saw an 876 area code show up on my phone. Jamaica?

"Hello?"

"Kylie, are you okay? Oh good, you mustn't give mi such a scare. I was worried that we just found each other and I lost you."

"Wow, the news was that scary?"

"Well, they said some people were hospitalized or died from heat-related incidents."

"I haven't had a moment to really watch the news now that it's over! I was inside an office building with a few folks for those hours. We are fine."

"Well, you know your mother wouldn't call, so I know to call you."

"Well, that was so sweet of you, Aunt Daphne."

Her Jamaican accent was so comforting. I wished I could talk like that. "We're family, man," she said gently. "You're my only niece."

"Why don't you and True get along? You guys haven't spoken since I was, like, what . . . five?"

She sighed. "Oh, Kylie, I couldn't really say much in front of your cousins when you were here. It's not that we didn't get on . . . she resented me. I told you before, I was raised in a different environment than her. I also had a father who would get me things from abroad . . . the States. I was treated much better, while she was at home with our evil aunt. There were some times Paulette would visit and she'd steal the new clothes from my closet. It caused a lot of arguments."

"Wow, steal?" I repeated.

"Yes, I'd see her with a blouse or a skirt that was mine," she said sternly. "But this you cannot repeat!"

"No, no, I won't say anything."

"She was pretty fast growing up. It's like she lived to embarrass the Collins name by her behavior."

"What behavior?" I was so happy to finally be getting a glimpse of the truth, but I could still feel the resentment steaming out of Aunt Daphne.

"She was a little toooo fast. She doesn't want to acknowledge her mistakes. She blames us for her being so distant, when it's her own guilt that keeps her away."

Part of me knew True is a wild spirit and Aunt Daphne was being judgmental, but my gut told me there was more. I also knew that you don't just start off promiscuous. I wondered what caused her to be so "wild," as they say. It doesn't happen overnight. With my new assistant detective skills, I planned to investigate more. I wanted to learn how to ask the right questions.

"She was shamed, that's why she left."

"Shamed for what, having me?"

"Well, Kylie . . ." She paused. "There's a bit more. Rumor has it that your father was a married man. He was the one who had the connections to send her away. When she was pregnant with you, I asked her about the rumor. She denied it, and that was one of the reasons she doesn't speak very fondly of me, because I knew the truth."

"But who did you hear that rumor from? It could have been a lie."

"I wish it was, but I heard it right from the horse's mouth!"

"What? So you know who my father is, Aunt Daphne? You know him?" I was more than thrilled that she was finally coming clean.

"It's . . . it's really not my place. It's not my place." She took a long pause and sighed. "God forgive me, but you have the right to know. You're a grown woman now. You know this is not easy."

"Please!" I cried. "Please tell me!"

"Wait nuh man? Soooo, long story short . . . One day, I went over to Uncle Danny's to drop off some curry chicken from Mummy. Uncle's wife was abroad in Chicago working for a family as a nanny for a few months."

"My mom told me about her auntie and said that she was evil like a witch."

"Yes, she was. Just a miza-rebel woman. She's still alive, ya know? She's in a nursing home and has dementia. You see how God takes care of you when you evil?"

"Yeah, that's sad. Wow . . . So, you dropped off the food . . ." I brought her back to the story.

"Well, I went to drop off the food and I went in through the back gate and saw the door was open. I heard the shower going and then I saw Uncle in the bathroom with the door open with no shirt on. The strangest thing, ya know? Your mother was in the shower. Paulette was whimpering, like she was crying. This was unheard of. A girl-child in the shower and a man standing there shirtless!" She sucked her teeth. "You know, Kylie, I haven't spoken about this since I was a teenager."

"Well? What happened?" I urged her on.

"Well, Paulette was crying and I heard Uncle carrying on and saying mean things. Like 'Faisty gal. I heard you went down the road. You don't think word will travel? You try to kill my baby with that Obeah shit. My only baby, you think I don't know about that root tea. I know. You lucky I don't ring your durty neck.'"

"What's root tea?"

"Some tea with special herbs to make you lose a baby. It's what they used for abortion in the old days."

I was silent.

She continued. "When he was yelling at her, I gasped and Uncle heard me." She raised her voice to imitate him. "'What de bloodclot you doing in mi 'ouse?' Without even thinking about it, he took off his belt and whipped me so bad. I had welts on my legs and arms and I still have a scar on my shoulder to this day from that beating. Broke my skin. Was bleeding and everyting. There was screaming and Paulette jumped out di bathroom in her robe soaking wet, trying to pull him off of me. She scream, she scream, and screamed for him to stop. Then she took a lickin', too. Not as bad as me. The neighbors came over to stop him. He lost control like a madman!

"This incident brought the whole family in an uproar. My father came to the house to fight him after he saw what he did to me and since Uncle Danny was a policeman, my father got arrested for assaulting an officer. Eventually he dropped the charges. But my father spent a whole month in jail and our family was never the same again. I only told my mother what the real reason was for the beating and she and Uncle Danny fell out for good after that. Paulette blames me, I'm sure, for her life. She hated me for telling, but I didn't have a choice. Word got out, especially after he had the huge fight with my dad. I never understood after that how she could stay there. How could she live with him?"

I felt horrible for True. "But wasn't it abuse? When you are that young and feel you have nowhere else to go . . . maybe she was scared to leave. He was a cop! I can only imagine how he threatened her. He probably raped her. I'm sure he did." I was so disgusted. My stomach turned. I was the product of a rape.

"No, no, I never believed that, because of how he treated her so good, especially after his wife was gone for long periods of time."

Aunt Daphne was so naive. I just couldn't believe True was willfully having an affair with her uncle. Gross! "Come on, Aunt Daphne, she was like sixteen. You really think she was that conniving then?" Then I remembered how old I was when I seduced Breeze.

She paused. "By that age, you know how to get what you want. She wore perfume, dressed seductively; she would serve him not like a niece, but like a wife. It was quite disturbing. One time she even got kicked out of church for how she was dressed. Her whole bosom out and all the men in the church drooling."

"Wow! That sounds like True." I chuckled.

"You gotta realize, he was a new man when his wife left. It was such a change for Paulette, since his wife treated her so cruel. You know his wife was barren, too? Since she couldn't bear children for him, she despised us children for even being around. This is why he wanted you to be born so bad. They were probably going to pretend that Wendell was the father, the man you thought was your father. He was a neighbor that was always hanging around Paulette."

"Oh my God, this story is soooo crazy. I can't believe it!"

"I'm so sorry, Kylie. It's best you know the truth now."

"No, no, it's all good. I feel happy, and, well . . ."

I forced a laugh and tried to make her laugh. Silence.

"Well, if I were you," she said, "I'd come back again and meet the rest of your family. You have plenty more to meet. We're so happy to have you back."

"Ah, me too . . . glad to know I have family! What was Uncle's, well, my father's, full name?"

"Daniel Kenneth. He died ten years ago from a stroke." I typed it into my phone's notepad.

It's so crazy that I'd never heard about him being a cop. True talked more about the evil aunt. "Do you have any pictures of him?"

"I think I can look for something. I'm sure I have at least two, one in his uniform and one when he got older." I got goose bumps as I remembered that Jacques said in my reading he saw him in a uniform. We thought it was military, but he was very close. Damn, he was good.

I was waiting for True to come home. Chauncey and I were texting back and forth about our next date. Breeze was also letting me know he was going to be in town in a few days. Just then, True came floating in smelling like weed.

I didn't wait for her to get settled. "True, how come you never told me about Uncle Danny?"

She froze in her steps and a deep breath whooshed from her lungs.

In typical True defensive mode she raised her voice. "What? What's there to tell?" She put her pocketbook down and took off her shawl.

I kept a stern face. "Come on, True. I know!"

She moved in close and raised an eyebrow. "You know what?" She was fishing.

"Ummmm, I don't know, maybe that he's my *father*!" Her confident face turned into a devastated frown. I knew I would get her. "What happened, how could that happen?"

"Kylie! I don't know who the hell you've been talking to, but that man is *not* your dad. Are you out of your mind?"

I held my hand up to her to calm her down. My eyes

started to water. "True, I'm sick of the lies already. Once and for all, can you speak your truth and live up to your friggin' name? Tell me, is your uncle Danny *my father*? I know already, but I need to hear you say it. I need to know where I came from, Mom!"

Just then, she melted. I haven't called her Mom since I was about ten. She thought it would be cool for me to call her True and I agreed back then.

"Look, I don't know why you've been listening to those damn Jamaicans. They've done nothing but lie lie lie about me! They've done nothing but hurt me! They don't know what I had to go through. I didn't want to have a baby. I didn't know how!" she screamed. Her body seemed lifeless as she collapsed on the love seat. "Why did you have to go digging, Kylie? Leave shit where it was."

"True . . . Mom. Please, I need to know what happened. Did he hurt you?" I went over to her and grabbed her hand.

She started to talk and then nothing came out but deep sobs of regret. She started babbling, sounding like a little Jamaican girl. "I didn't have no one, Kylie. No one to take care of me. My mummy left me, because her new husband didn't want to watch no other man's kids. My half sister was treated like a queen. Mummy didn't protect me, she didn't care. She dumped me over there like a prisoner from me eight, like I asked for that. Uncle Danny showed me love. His wife was a mean bitch, but he took care of me. He told me at first he was just showing me love." She cried as she talked. "But, as I got older, as I got older . . . I knew it was wrong! I knew it."

She started to cry more. It was a huge release, she had been holding on to this secret for years. I ran to the bathroom for some tissue.

"When his wife moved to the States, he . . . he started to rape me. Almost every night. Before it was just touching from when I was eight until thirteen, but when I started to get boobies and some ass, he couldn't stop looking at me or groping me. He made me do things to him to get money for school. Other kids had chores for allowance. Me, he made me do things. Sexual things for allowance."

My mouth was open from shock. "Oh, Mom. I'm so sorry!" I was furious.

She continued, "Eventually, I gave in. It became normal. I didn't have any choice. I didn't know anything else." She blew her nose loudly. "I was teased and called a harlot when I got pregnant, but people didn't know it wasn't from the boys in the streets. It was right at home."

I felt her pain in the pit of my stomach. True sobbed deeply for a while and I cried with her. Then she rubbed her throat and coughed. "I think I opened up my throat chakra. It feels good. It feels good to release this." She wiped her eyes and sighed. She had an odd smile on her face.

I rubbed her back and watched her in awe. I had never seen True break down. "Kylie, I know I wasn't a good mother to you. I never thought I would be, but please don't judge me. Please know I had to do it to survive."

I was emotional. It felt good to hear her say that. I couldn't stop crying. "I know, Mommy, I know." I hugged her and we cried together.

Everything made sense. I saw now why she had no deep emotional connections to men. Why she used them for money without a shred of guilt. Why she fought the reality of being my mother. It was so sad that she was trained to be who she was. But it makes sense why she wanted to change her identity so bad. Why she wanted to forget that part of her past. That night was the first time I think we ever cried so deeply. It was the first time I felt True was honest with me. It was the first time I felt like I really had a mom. From that day on, I decided I would no longer call her True.

Chapter 21

Jacques

Until I was about twelve years old, almost every other night, I saw my father, but I kept it a secret. He sat across from me in my bedroom, wearing his signature black button-down linen shirt and khaki pants. That was what he always wore in my dreams, so I take it that it must have been his favorite outfit. His accessories were his "I Love the Giants" coffee mug and a pack of Marlboros in his front pocket. He looked as if he were the same age he was when he died, only forty-one. His tan olive skin was identical to mine. Deep brown eyes stared at me, but it wasn't intimidating. He had a warm expression, not quite a smile, but a look of contentment. He also held a Bible in his hand. It looked like my mother's, because it had a leather case with her initials MMB (Marguerite Marie Berradi).

He would start to speak, but I could never hear him. His lips moved slowly, but no sound ever came out. Always the

storyteller and expressive with his hands, he frustrated me because I couldn't hear the words that went along with his animated movements. He was pointing and waving the Bible as he
spoke. Every now and then, Dad would slow down and take a
sip of his coffee. My dream always ended with him trying to
hand me the Bible. I would reach out to grab it and my hands
would transform into soft, weak, six-year-old hands. Too tiny
to grasp the heavy leather-bound book. It would fall to the
ground and the loud sound would startle me out of my dream.
My dad was Muslim, so his handing me the Bible didn't make
sense to me. He never had his own. I'd recently had this same
dream at least once a week in the last month. I couldn't figure it
out. I didn't know what he was trying to tell me. It just didn't
make any sense. . . . The Bible, coffee, his talking wildly, and
my being a child. It was frustrating, because I couldn't hear a
word. He was speaking intensely, really trying to tell me something, but no sound came out. I had to try to be awake the next
time I had it. Maybe I could read his lips or something.

❋ ❋ ❋

I remember the visions came to a halt. I think I just learned
to block the messages altogether. However, when I was seventeen years old my father was back.

I was lying in my room trying to sleep. I had the radio on
low. The soft light from my nightstand lamp bounced off my
blue walls.

I was leaving for college that fall. I thought about finally
getting out of the house and getting away from my family. I
thought about finally becoming a man, the man I'd always

wanted to be, just like my dad. Just as I thought about him, I felt a warm breeze brush by me. My radio became filled with static and I lost the station. I looked at the clock and was about to fix it, then I heard, "Jacques, tell your mother." It was very faint, but I heard it. "Tell your mother I forgive her, not to worry, I forgive her." I felt his breath, as if he were sitting right next to me on the bed.

I instantly smacked my ear like I was killing a bug. "Oh shit!" I looked around, then the radio came back on, playing Hall and Oates loud and clear. I reached for the light. My hands were shaking.

There was the loud sound of slippers racing down the hallway as my mom ran in. "What happened?" Her hair was in big plastic rollers and her eyes looked puffy. I hadn't realized that I'd screamed that loud. I sat on the edge of the bed and was staring at her in shock. I looked down at my shaking hands.

I heard the voice again, the voice of my father. This time it was more urgent, a pleading in his voice. "Tell her, son. . . . You must tell her that I know. . . ." The voice wasn't in my ear, either, it was in my head now. I could hear it as if it were my voice. Surprisingly, now I didn't feel scared. A feeling of calm came over me. I hadn't heard my dad's voice in so long. It made me feel at peace hearing it. It was my dad, it really was my dad.

"What's wrong, sweetie?" she said softly.

"It's Dad! I heard him tonight, he came to me." I grabbed her hands as she sat next to me on the bed. A tear ran down my cheek. She looked scared, like she believed me this time.

"He said to tell you he forgives you, he loves you." I looked at her for answers.

She turned away, saying, "Jacques, you were having a nightmare, baby. Go have some warm milk to help you sleep."

My voice cracked. "Mom, what did you do? Did you guys have a fight? Why does he forgive you?"

She got up. "Stop this nonsense right this second!" she screamed. "You were having a nightmare. Olivier is gone, your father is gone, stop trying to bring him back. How can you do this to your own mother?" Her eyes started to water. "I know you miss him, I know you need him now, but I'm sorry, darling, he's gone, he's in heaven, he can't talk to you. He can't send messages to me." She kissed me on the cheek. "Go to bed." She started to walk out of the room, but held on to the doorknob. "Do you want me to make you some hot cocoa? It might make you fall asleep." Her motherly smile tried to cover up the glow of her guilt. I could see she was hiding something, but what it was I couldn't figure out.

I decided not to argue and let her believe what she wanted. I tried though. My father could at least see I tried.

"No, I'm okay, sorry for waking you up. Maybe it was just a dream." I shrugged.

I lay back in my bed, this time with all the lights on. Memories flowed through me that night, almost like a light switch was turned on. My gift was back.

Chapter 22
Kylie

I was doing so well until Breeze showed up again in my life. A few days after he called me, I ended up in his hotel lobby in South Beach. I caught a glimpse of Spike Lee and Robert Townsend talking by the front desk. A few celebrities and familiar faces from B movies walked by or chatted in the lounge area.

I was waiting for Breeze to come down and meet me for a late dinner. The lobby was buzzing with bikinis, dark glasses, tight dresses, men with six-packs and open shirts, and late-night business-card swapping. I would get an alluring glance every now and then from a cutie, so I thought I would flirt at least before I saw Breeze.

I felt warm hands massage my neck and I didn't have to turn around. I knew his touch. His body was close to mine as I sat on the stool.

"You look beautiful in red." He smelled so good. "Don't turn around yet."

"Why, thank you, but don't you think you should at least introduce yourself before massaging a complete stranger?" I teased as he kneaded a stress knot out of my left shoulder. I was loving it.

"Oh, I think we've met before." He traced a finger down the middle of my back. I flinched from the tickle.

"See, I remember where you're ticklish," he whispered in my ear. "Sugah, fuck dinner." I started to turn around and he squeezed me.

"Oh, okay . . . well what do you want to do?" He grabbed my hand and I got up.

"Man, you are filling out that dress so right, Ky. You're killing me living so far away. Give me some sugar." He pulled me close and I gave him a kiss.

"Are we going to dinner or what, Breeze?"

"Shit, I'm ready for dessert." He chuckled, caressing my waist.

"Does wifey know about us meeting?"

"Whoa. Whoa. I'm single . . . very single, darlin'. Easy with dat! Do you want to hang with me tonight? I have a few passes to some late-night screenings."

"Right. Sounds good." I hated to admit it, but I wasn't in the mood for dinner and movies, either. I was trying to stay focused, but I knew I needed to hear him tell me how much he missed me. I needed to have him stare at me. I needed my ego stroked and, let's face it . . . I needed to be stroked. I promised myself that this was really the last time.

"Let's order in, Breeze. I don't feel like being in this meat market environment. Everyone is here for some ass, not a film festival."

"Oh yeah?" He laughed. "Well, Kylie, I'm actually a film connoisseur and I have friends who are releasing indie films and I'm here to support them. Of course, seeing you was the icing on the cake!" He grabbed me closer. "Stop playing, Ky, you know what's up." He kissed me gently . . . a moist juicy kiss. It felt good, like no time had passed at all. I wrestled with my conscience, but I knew that my desires would soon be sitting in the driver's seat.

❖ ❖ ❖

We went upstairs to Breeze's room. The air conditioner whispered softly as Prince played on his iPod speakers. We ordered in: crab cakes as an appetizer, steak for him, shrimp scampi for me. One thing about Breeze that I had missed was his love for eating good.

We laughed and talked about the crazy blackout experience. I held back as much bitterness and resentment as I could—just taking it for what it was, an eleven-year-long (bed-buddy/booty call/homie-lover-friend) fuckship.

My phone vibrated. The phone was on the table and it lit up with Chauncey's name in bright neon glow. Breeze saw it and smiled.

"You wanna get that?"

"Nah."

"Go 'head, he's not a threat to me, whoever he is."

Oh really, Mr. Cocky? Calling my bluff, are you? I sashayed over to the phone to show him he wasn't in charge.

"Heeeey, what's up, Chauncey!" I said in a syrupy voice that I knew made Breeze listen intently.

Chauncey sounded tired. "I'm just thinking about our next date. I can't wait to see you! I wish we could push it up."

I walked farther away from Breeze and Prince playing loudly.

"Me too!" I gushed.

"Well, I've been so anxious, I'm actually already en route."

"What?"

"Yeah, I hope you don't mind. I know it's early, but I can't wait. . . . I just can't wait to see you again. Instant messages and texting don't quite cut it."

My voice cracked. "Are you serious? Where are you?"

"Damn, you can't even be happy a brother is stalking you?" He laughed.

I sighed, realizing it was just Chauncey being Chauncey. Pulling my leg.

I paced toward the bathroom to fix my hair. Breeze's eyes went with me. "I was about to run for the hills and delete my profile page!"

"Well, it was only partly a joke. I am itching to wrap my arms around you again. But I'll be gentle this time."

Breeze cleared his throat. When I came out of the bathroom, he was butt naked on the couch, stroking himself, and he was oh so excited to see me.

"What the hell?" I laughed. "Ummm, Chauncey, babe . . . Ummm, I'm sorry, let me call you back. *Ciao.*" I hung up. I was frazzled, delighted, and aroused all in the same moment. I walked in front of Breeze.

"Ky, you know listening to you speak to that cat made me want you more. I'm here with you getting ready to fuck the shit out of you and where's he at? At home playing on the Internet or watching *SportsCenter*." He bit his bottom lip and looked down at his hardness.

"What?" I stood over him, smiling.

"I heard you talking about that site, is that what you are doing now?" He leaned in and reached under my dress to cup my butt cheeks. He brought me close then lifted my dress. He admired my thong. "Daaaaamn, sugah."

He pulled down my thong slowly and pulled me in closer to his face. "I love how you keep it clean for daddy."

The hairs on my arms stood up as he put his face between my legs and talked to Madame Butterfly. He's the one who got me into bikini waxing. He sucked and licked me. He was slow and deliberate. His fingers parted me, so he could taste me. The heat from his mouth sent me soaring. I grabbed his shoulders as my knees buckled. "Damn, your stuff is tight as a box. You've been a good girl for daddy, huh?" He looked up at me as he slowly slid a finger inside me.

"Yessss, yeeeess, daddy." I ripped off my red dress that got me this far. He laid me on the couch, because it wouldn't be long before I fell on it. He was so hard I almost got a little scared of how it would feel, since it'd been a while. I knew it was a blessing and a curse. I was just starting to get over my addiction and here I was again with Breeze, the strongest drug I'd ever been addicted to.

Sweat, screams, panting, and sighs exploded in the room. We could have steamed the windows with our energy. I didn't know what the hell had gotten into him, but he was definitely laying it down like never before. I crawled to the top of the bed and grabbed the padded leather headboard.

"Where are you going, sugah? I'm not done with you." He pulled me close in doggy style and the bed jumped violently up and down. The sensation of him inside me hit all the nerve endings in my body, sending me to new heights.

"Oh my Gawd, oh my Gaaaaaawd. . . ."

"You better not come yet. . . . Wait for me." He panted as he held on to my moist back.

I moaned in delight, collapsing on the bed.

"Don't come until I say so," he said authoritatively through his teeth.

Damn that was sexy. My face was buried in the pillow, ass up.

"Oh . . . oh, sugah, you stay right there. You got that tight . . . sweet . . . pussy. Oh, that shit is so wet for daddy. Stay right there." I got chills when he talked like that. We moved together slowly to the rhythm of Raheem DeVaughn singing "Believe."

He eased off me slowly. "You still on the pill, Ky?"

"No, why?" He held up the condom that was damn near empty and torn.

"Oh fuck, oh fuck! Damnnnn!" I ran to the bathroom and sat on the toilet to allow gravity to work out the remaining sperm. I washed myself, cursing under my breath. I know I should have just stayed away. I wasn't strong enough. I was so weak for him. I looked in the mirror, ashamed of and disappointed with myself. My face was red and full of sweat.

He knocked on the door and came in. "Sugah, you okay? What's the worst that could happen? We could finally have a baby together!"

"Right, and I'll be your baby mama and screw up the rest of my life."

He reached for a towel to wipe the sweat off his naked body. "Whoa! Kylie Rain, you need to check your tone, darlin'." He put on his stern fatherly voice. "What, you don't think I would take care of mine?"

"You are not ready to be solely committed to me if I get pregnant! I couldn't keep it, it wouldn't be fair to the child or us."

"How you mean, you can't keep it? You're almost thirty! I think it would be a sin to do that. Fucking selfish is what it is, Kylie."

"Well, it's my body last time I checked and honestly I'm not ovulating now, anyhow. So let's just drop it." I leaned against the sink and took a deep breath.

"Yeah, you ain't killing my seeds anymore." His voice had a trace of anger.

I jumped in the shower and we ended up catching the last two movies of the night. I didn't sweat it anymore and what he didn't know wouldn't kill him. But a part of me did feel guilty since he was right. I'm grown. I'd always wondered if it was the same kid who came back. I will ask Jacques about that.

* * *

The yellow morning sun hit my eyes. Breeze kissed me on my forehead and hugged me as we stood in front of the hotel waiting for the valet to bring my car.

"Why do you think our love won't go away?" he asked.

I smiled. "We'll always care about each other. We put years in. It's a given."

"It's deeper than that, Ky, and you know it. I can't stay away from you. You know no one knows you better. No one can love you better. I can't live without you, Ky."

"What are you saying?"

"I'm saying you need to come back to New York, where you belong. You need to come back." He touched my chin softly and kissed me.

The connection we tried to fight never really went away. When souls are connected—I guess they just are. No matter how bad I know he might be for me, I can't stop playing shit over and over in my head. The way he held me and whispered in my ear; he knew how to get me. He knew how to do so much by saying so little.

He leaned against the wall. "Whatchu thinking about, sugah?"

"Oh . . . just how I wish that moments stayed like this."

He rubbed my back and waist gently. "Come on, everyone has their ups and downs, darlin'. You could never stick it out."

"You always want me to stick it out. Wait for what? I really get tired of being your young tenderoni."

He chuckled and brushed my chin. "Well, you ain't that young anymore."

"Whatever! I'm seven years younger than you!"

"What if I told you I was ready now? Would you come back with me?"

My heart dropped to the ground, because for just that moment, that split second, I actually believed him.

The valet pulled up with my car and Breeze slid him a tip. "Hold up, my man. Give us a minute, please. Can you move it over to the side so we're not in the way?"

The valet nodded and got back in my car to park it.

Breeze took my hand and walked me over to the fountain in front of the hotel. He held my hand tightly.

"You gonna ignore me, Ky?"

"What?" I played dumb. I really didn't think he believed I was falling for his BS. I summoned up the courage and as my heart raced I said, "Breeze, this is my life." I pointed to the ground. "Down here. Miami. You know I love you, but I also know what last night was, one of our many nights of fun." My eyes darted away, preparing for his rebuttal.

"So, you just gonna clown me, huh? That's all that was? Come on, darlin'. A good fuck?" He grabbed my chin and brought my eyes to his.

"Breeze, you know we are way more than that. But I also know *you*. If you are really serious, show me. I'm not getting my hopes up anymore."

He raised his arms. "You want a ring? You want me to get down on one knee?"

I covered my mouth. My eyes widened as my heart balled up in knots.

"Okay, be careful about calling my bluff." He pulled my waist in close.

"I gotta go, Breeze." I gulped. "Go catch your flight. It's getting late and you have to finish packing."

He mumbled, "Don't worry about what I gotta do." His eyes were damp as he looked at my lips when I spoke. He pulled me in closer by the nape of my neck and held both sides of my face. He kissed me with so much passion. It was like he knew that maybe this was the last kiss. Maybe I was finally coming to my senses. He walked me to my car, holding my hand the entire time.

"Love you, Ky. I'll be calling you soon, sugah."

"Okay, love you, too." We hugged one last time. My chest tightened as I sat in my car. He looked at me with a down-turned mouth and his shoulders pulled low. I let out a heavy sigh and started the engine, feeling like I'd finally closed that chapter for good.

Chapter 23

Jacques

My biggest celebrity client wanted me to do a group session and meditation workshop for her Broadway show's cast. It paid well, so I couldn't pass on the opportunity. Although it was a quick three-day visit, I made time to catch up with Hicham and Mom. This time I didn't mention to my New York email list that I would be in town. I didn't want to see Dee just yet.

Mom cooked a delicious dinner for us. It felt good to sit around the table together.

"How was your day?" she asked.

"It was good. Had fun hanging with Hicham."

"You see how good he's doing? I'm so happy! Soooo, how is the girlfriend, Victoria?"

"Oh, Mom, Vicky is amazing. I think she might be the one. You know, she'll be a homicide detective soon."

"Oh my. Why would a young lady want such a gruesome

job?" She shook her head and took a sip of her red wine. "What's her religion again?"

I ignored her question. "Well, she has a passion for helping solve mysteries. If people are murdered they need justice."

"Well, yes, I guess you're right." She tapped my hand and we bowed our heads as she said a short prayer. She broke off a piece of a warm baguette and offered it to me.

"So, how is your Bible study group going? Any interesting trips lately?" I smiled, waiting for her wince. She looked nervous and dipped her bread in olive oil. She took a small bite and started choking on it.

"Drink! Drink!" I got up and rubbed her back as she choked.

"Sit down. I'm fine, I'm fine. It just went down the wrong way." She took another sip of wine. "My Bible study group is fantastic. I wish you could come! We're covering Revelations now."

Something was surely off. She was way too enthusiastic about it.

"Oh, the end-of-the-world doom-and-gloom chapter? Just fascinating," I said dryly.

"No, no!" She laughed. "Not so, Jacques. You should come. You'd really get a better understanding of the Bible. You used to be such a good Catholic boy." She shook her head as she wiped her mouth. "I don't know what happened," she mumbled.

"No, Mom, your memory is all wrong. It was Hicham who was the altar boy. I preferred going to the mosque with Dad. I'm the one who got in trouble for saying Jesus didn't have blue eyes and blond hair." Resentment trailed in my tone.

Her face turned red. She laughed. "Please, you were so small. You don't remember the mosque. You just loved to embarrass me."

"No, not so. I just like to ask questions and speak my truth. I like to think." I pointed to my temple. "I remember it very clearly, too. We'd go on Fridays to pray and when we came home you'd have dinner ready."

She blushed and said, *"Tu souviens?"* as she pushed her hair behind her ears. "Well, it was probably all your father's doing. He put a lot of those things into your head. You have his rebelliousness. He never wanted you children to be Catholic. We argued all the time about it. Before we had you, we agreed that our children could experience both religions, but the second we got married, he refused to join me at mass and he would go to mosque only. It was one of the main things we argued about."

"Yes, I remember. Tit-for-tat fights."

"Yes, I guess you could call it that. Your father was so stubborn."

"I don't know." I scraped up the last portions of cassoulet into my fork. It was really good. "I don't know if asking questions is really rebellious."

"You just don't know the Bible. If you did you wouldn't have to ask questions. You would have faith and believe."

"Good point. When is your next meeting?"

"Tomorrow, but you leave, don't you?" She didn't see it coming.

"Oh, no . . . I don't have to leave yet. I'm going to join you. It would be good to see some of the old Holy Cross folks," I said sarcastically, dabbing my mouth and smiling.

"Yes, yes." She smiled brightly.

"You are really going to go?" She seemed shocked, but covered it with a plastic smile.

"Yes." I wanted to see what all the nervousness was about.

❊ ❊ ❊

I met Mom at Holy Cross in SoHo and it brought back many memories. The large entrance that led downstairs to the classrooms now seemed like a small basement. It's amazing how your view of things changes as you grow older and taller. It had the same beige and gray paint and tiles. Very cold as always and it wasn't just the air, it was the energy. As soon as I entered the glass doors of Father Jamison's hall where all the classes were held, I felt like a prisoner again.

A sixty-something lady with bright red hair greeted me. "Welcome, welcome! A new member?"

"Oh, well not really. I'm Marguerite Berradi's son."

"What? My, my, you are so very handsome. I didn't know she had a model for a son."

I blushed and smiled. "Why, thank you, madame." I kissed her hand and she melted.

"What is your name?"

"Oh, it's Jacques. So, can you tell me where the Bible study class is?"

"Oh, it's right down the hall on the right. Your mother is upstairs in the office, but her right-hand buddy, Mr. Maganelo, is there. You know him, right?"

"Yes, yes . . . sounds familiar, but it's been years." I played dumb. "Why is he her right-hand buddy?" I leaned in closer.

She didn't look me in the eyes. She got nervous. "Well, rumor has it . . . they are best friends. Inseparable even. Lucky for him, since his wife just divorced him a few years ago." She seemed to enjoy spilling the beans. I did pick up a jealousy and gossipy vibe, but she was harmless. She seemed lonely and loved attention. So much to say and no one to listen.

"Really?" I put my arm around her and we walked the hall for a bit. "Tell me more."

"Oh yeah," she whispered. "He was always here with your mother and apparently his wife was terribly jealous. She even made a scene one day." She covered her mouth and looked up the hallway. There was my mother in a beautiful pink dress, looking a bit shocked to see me so chummy with a church lady.

"Well, it was so nice chatting with you, Miss . . . ?"

"Miss Rita. You can call me Miss Rita."

I kissed her hand again and she giggled like a schoolgirl. She was going to be my new best friend.

My mother's brows raised as she watched our exchange. "Well, hello, Miss Marguerite!"

"Hi, Rita," my mother replied flatly. "And, Jacques, baby, why are you so early?" She kissed me on both cheeks and hooked onto my arm to swiftly drag me away from Miss Rita.

"What did that witch say to you?" she whispered.

"Mom, we're in God's house!" I chuckled. "You look beautiful, by the way."

She looked down at her dress as if she'd forgotten what she was wearing. "Thank you. . . . But she . . . she is the worst person I know. I don't even know how she got to be on the

Welcoming Committee. She's evil. *Une salope!* What did she say to you? Why were you so close to her, with your arm around her? You don't do that. This isn't the place for that!"

"Relax, Mom, I was just being friendly. She didn't say much. Just telling me how handsome I was." I smoothed out my hair.

We walked into the room and a man was writing a Bible verse on the chalkboard. When he turned around, my stomach dropped. Mom smiled lovingly at him. "Look who is here!"

"Oh my goodness! Oh my. Look at you! A big strapping man now!" He came over and grabbed my shoulder as he looked at me, then looked back at my mom. It was Mr. Maganelo.

I stared in disbelief. His long lanky frame. His eyes. His ears. Even his walk. He was the man from the picture . . . but it was more than that.

"What's the matter with you, son? You look like you saw a ghost."

My mother hit my arm. "Jacques!"

"I'm sorry . . . uh. Wow, I'm sorry. It's just that you look so much like . . ." I shook my head and sat down. I felt woozy.

"Jacques, say hello and stop being rude."

"Hi." I looked up at him. I felt like I was going to cry. I felt enraged. I felt sadness. I was so light-headed. How could this be? This was why Dad kept sending me visions of Bibles! This was why he hadn't stopped visiting us.

Mr. Maganelo was the spitting image of my brother, Hicham.

I looked around at about eight other women and two men who seemed fascinated with what was coming out of Mr. Maganelo's mouth. They wrote notes furiously, not missing a word. I saw his mouth moving, but then heard nothing. The room was spinning as I tried hard to remember just how often I'd seen him as a child. I held my head. My stomach was queasy. I knew what that meant. I had to find out for sure. My intuition triggers always gave me signs.

All I could think about now was how obsessed my mother became with the church after Dad died. Of course, we figured she was in mourning and needed support from her church friends, but it's possible it was much more. That was probably just her escape, her way out. She and Mr. Maganelo were having an affair. It's pretty obvious now. If my senses were right, that was probably what she and Dad fought about all the time! He probably knew or felt something, but had no proof.

If my brother was not his, then that means that the affair had been going on since we moved to America. That was a fact I couldn't digest. I had to confirm it. I had to let Hicham know, but how? How?

I excused myself from class as if I were going to the restroom. I had to ask. I couldn't wait another thirty minutes. I wiped the sweat from my brow and called Hicham.

I heard Tupac playing in the background and two girls talking and laughing. "Yo, what up."

"Hey, Hicham, where are you? Can you talk?" I spoke low.

"Yeah, yeah, I'm home. What's up?" He hushed the girls' chatter. "Shhhh, chill y'all, I can't hear." The music was turned lower. "Why you talking like you on a secret mission and shit?"

"Just listen, do you remember Mr. Maganelo?"

"What? Of course I do. That was my man! I haven't seen him in like ten or twelve years. He really used to look out for us. Mom still hangs with him I think. He's in her church crew. You don't remember?"

"Yeah, I do, but not like that. I just remember him bringing ice cream and toys. Sneakers I think, too." I scratched my head. "But I thought it was something with the church. Shit, now that I think about it . . . he was around a lot at one point. But didn't he have a lady with him most of the time? His wife?"

"Yeah, Mrs. Maganelo. I never liked her though. She always had an attitude. Used to look me up and down, and I don't think she liked how he used to spend money on me. He even bought me Air Jordans one time when Ma was like, 'Hell no!'" He laughed. Remember he was the Cub Scouts leader, too?"

"Oh no . . ."

"Nah, it's not what you think. He wasn't no homo or nothing. I think he just wanted a kid so bad, so he was treating all of us like his. He gave me special treatment, though."

It hit me. I felt as if a windstorm flew into the room. "She knew . . . his wife knew . . . that's why. Wow, why didn't we see this?" I looked back and walked through the glass doors and toward the front of the church's hall. My voice was traveling. It was now getting dark outside. I stood by the entrance just to be sure no one heard me.

"She knew what? What the fuck is going on, man?"

"Oh man, nothing. Look, Hicham, I'm gonna call you in a few. We gotta have a serious talk with Mom." I held my head and shook it. "I mean serious."

"Yo, what the hell? Did he do something to Ma? What, man? Yo, let me know! I'll be down there in a hot minute," he yelled. I gulped. "What's up, Jacques? Say the word."

"Look, I just think he and Mom have something going on."

Hicham chuckled. "Ah shit, go Mommy—go Mommy. 'Bout time she get some ass."

I cringed, didn't need that visual. "Well, it's not recent. . . . I got a hunch and, well, some insider information that it might be a twenty-seven-year-old affair or longer."

"What? Stop playing! Mom ain't that smooth and that doesn't make much sense. I'm twenty-seven, that would mean . . . wait . . . nah."

"Yeah."

"That would mean Dad was still alive. I was just born."

It still wasn't registering with him. He didn't see what I saw. I spoke low. "Look—I don't know for sure. I just think we need to talk to her."

"Yo, where the fuck are you at? Why you whispering!"

"At the hall. I'm at Holy Cross Church. I went to Bible study with Mom."

"Get the fuck outta here! This story just gets crazier and crazier."

"I know, I know. . . . Look, I gotta get back. But I wanted to see what you remembered, because I really don't remember him that much." A cool evening breeze blew by. I stared up at the moon making an appearance. I had said too much. "Look, lemme call you back."

I walked back to the classroom with my heart beating rapidly. Sweat formed on my brow. My mother looked upset, because I had left for so long. I worried about what would happen next. I hoped Hicham could wait until later. His temper would surely cause an uprising and I wasn't looking forward to dealing with that.

After Bible study, they had a gathering in the back of the classroom, around a table filled with cookies, crackers, cheese, juice, and teas.

"Thank you for coming out, everyone," Mr. Maganelo said. He clapped his hands together, then pointed to the table in the back. "Snack time."

Miss Rita was smiling at me and called me over as she handed me a cup of tea. "So, did you enjoy Bible study?"

"Well, I'll just say . . . it was interesting. I'm open to other points of view, even though I might not always embrace them."

"Oh, so what . . . you're not Catholic?"

"No, not quite. I'm spiritual. I do believe in God, a higher power, a force above us." I pointed to the ceiling. "But I don't believe religions should be so separate. It's all the same when you really look at them."

Miss Rita's eyebrows raised in shock. I felt a jab in my side. "Jacques, let me introduce you to some more people," my mother said gently, while fake-smiling at Miss Rita.

"Oh, excuse me," I said to Miss Rita as my mom locked her arm in mine.

"Tonight you're Catholic. I don't need any more gossip about me or my kids," she whispered.

"Any more? What kind of gossip?" I teased. She rolled her eyes. Mr. Maganelo came over with a plate of chocolate chip cookies and a big coffee stain on his ruby-red shirt. My mother started to wipe it and restrained herself when she saw me watching her.

He looked down at his shirt to follow our eyes. "I know, I'm such a klutz! Hey, would you like some?" He looked at us and smiled as he held the plate of cookies.

"Oh no, not me." I waved him away. "It's bad enough I've been eating New York City pizza with Hicham. You remember my brother, right?" I put my hand on his shoulder and looked into his eyes.

"Remember? Of course! I was his Cub Scout leader. I hear he's very successful now. I'm so proud. Your mother brags about him all the time."

Miss Rita called my mother to the back table. I was relieved to have a few minutes alone with this joker to see what the real story was.

Mr. Maganelo seemed up for the challenge. "So, enough about me." He sat down and pulled out a chair for me. "What is it that you're doing now? Some sort of guidance counselor for children, right?"

I smiled. Gotta love that mother of mine. I pointed my chin up in my mom's direction. "Is that what she told you?"

He frowned. "Yes. Isn't that what you do?"

I leaned forward and scratched my chin. "Well, not exactly. You see, I get messages from, well you know." I pointed up. "The spirit world. I can read people and help them get answers." I leaned back, awaiting his reaction.

"Oh, well no . . ." He cleared his throat nervously. "She didn't tell me that. Son, you know that is nothing to fool around with."

"I don't fool around. I make a pretty good living from it and I help a lot of people get answers to their questions. Speaking of which . . . do you mind telling me what's really going on with you and my mother?" I felt anger starting to bubble up. Staring into his face was like looking into Hicham's face— only thirty years into the future.

Mr. Maganelo squinted. "Marguerite is a dear friend. Watch your tone, son."

He stood up. He knew what was coming next. I stood up with him. He was about two inches taller than me, but thin as a rail, just like my brother.

"Like I said, I know things. I have a funny feeling you were way more than a Cub Scout leader."

That last part just popped out of my mouth. I don't know what got into me. I felt almost as if my dad jumped into me. Mr. Maganelo turned as red as his shirt. I tilted my head. "Am I right?" My heart sped up.

He put his hands in his pockets and deepened his tone as if it was supposed to scare me. "Son, I think you are mistaken."

An elderly Latino man with a cane shouted behind us. "Benny! Benny, is there gonna be class next week? I might need a ride again."

Mr. Maganelo excused himself with the phoniest smile I'd ever seen. He couldn't wait to get away from me. Coward. My mother finally escaped Miss Rita and practically jogged over to me. "What were you two talking about? You look upset."

"Oh nothing. Sports. Man talk." I gave Mr. Maganelo a side glance.

"Okay, okay. Well, let's get ready to go home." She put her purse on her shoulder and began saying her last good-byes.

Mr. Maganelo gave her a kiss on the cheek and looked uneasy as I approached him.

"Bye, Benny. I can call you Benny, right?"

"Oh sure, son!" He seemed relieved.

"Yeah, I feel since we're practically family and all, Mr. Maganelo is so formal." He forced out a chuckle, realizing I was just getting warmed up.

"Okay, enjoy the rest of your stay, it was good seeing you after all these years!" What he really wanted to say was *fuck you*. I nodded and waved to keep the peace. For now . . .

We walked home at a slow pace. She'd moved to the TriBeCa neighborhood to be closer to the church, only six blocks away. "So, Mom, just how close are you and Mr. Maganelo?" I asked.

Her shoes made a steady *click-click* sound on the concrete.

"What kind of question is that? We've known each other for years." She looked as if I was invading her privacy. I didn't care.

"I kinda remember him being around a lot when we were kids. Were he and Dad buddies?"

She snickered. "Absolutely not. Your father despised my church friends. To him they were the enemy taking me away from my wifely duties." Resentment lingered in her voice.

"I didn't know Dad felt like that. So, he's not your boy-friend, then? I saw, heard, and felt some things that are mak-ing me think you aren't telling us something."

"Like?" The smirk on her face told it all.

"I saw how he rubbed your back when you sat down. How you were dying to rub out his coffee stain. How he looked into your eyes."

She pushed her hair behind her ears. "Oh, please!" Mom scoffed. My throat tightened and my stomach swirled, but I knew it was her energy and not mine.

"I'm more alert than you think. Just admit it. Hicham and I are big boys now. It's okay if you have a boyfriend. We don't care. We'd actually be happy for you." I tried to soften her up to see if she'd be willing to open up the Pandora's box she'd kept shut tight for more than twenty-some years. A taxi's horn beeped loudly followed by an ambulance racing down Canal Street.

"Huh! Boyfriend? I don't have time for a booooy-friend." She blushed.

"Whatever, Mom. He's your boooooooyfriend . . . just say it!" I laughed, trying to lighten the mood.

"Oh, please, Jacques!"

I put my arm around her, yet I was furious. I wanted to shake her for lying and part of me wanted to clock Benny in the nose.

I must have grabbed her too tightly as we walked because she yanked my arm gently, letting me know I needed to loosen my grip. "You want to tell me what the problem is?" she said softly as her pace slowed down.

"You know, I don't know what's wrong. I guess that's what is so frustrating. You ever have that feeling when you're upset, you feel something is off and you can't quite put your finger on it? Or maybe you know someone is playing games." My pace got quicker and she had to keep up with me. "They take you for a fool and they won't fess up? Do you know what I mean, Mom?"

"Jacques, you are scaring me, you sound like your father." *Click, clock, click, clock.* Her shoes seemed to slam against the concrete as she walked even faster, trying to keep up.

I released her arm and continued walking in silence. I didn't want to lose my temper in the street, so I walked fast and didn't say a word.

We got closer to the building and she couldn't take it anymore.

"What happened to you, Jacques? Did Miss Rita tell you something? Just tell me! If something is bothering you, just say it."

I think she was starting to cave, but I wasn't letting her off the hook that easily. As we walked up the stairs to her apartment, I started to feel the emotions again, the energy of Mr. Maganelo, who probably came here daily.

After entering the apartment, I paced back and forth by the kitchen door.

"Tell me something, in those bad dreams you had, what was Dad saying?"

"Why? What made you ask that?"

"Just tell me," I insisted. "You never told me what was so

bad about it. I'm wondering why you couldn't sleep. Maybe we had the same dream."

"I don't remember it all. He was saying something about you and . . . and Hicham." She turned her eyes away as she put dishes in the cabinet. "He kept showing me water. I felt like I was drowning. It was a silly dream. I don't remember." I could sense that she was lying.

"Really? I think you do, Mom. You know what Dad shows me in my dreams and visions? He's drinking coffee and he is always handing me the Bible. Specifically, the one with your embossed initials. I never understood that message until to-night."

I walked over to the Bible in the hallway, her eyes following me anxiously. I smoothed out the page it was opened to and walked back to the kitchen. "You know, it's not the fact that he's your boyfriend that disturbs me. It's that you could hide something for so long. Soooo long, Mom." I started pacing back and forth. I went over to "the Hicham shrine" and picked up a photo of him in the Cub Scouts. I looked closely in the photo and there he was: a young, more buff Mr. Maganelo in the background.

"It all makes sense now! Why you've always been so on edge, so obsessed with church. So obsessed with Hicham."

She felt my anger starting to boil and her defenses rose to the challenge.

"Obsessed? What kind of nonsense are you talking about? I love the church and Hicham is my baby. You— I don't know what your problem is. Why do you love to torment me? Why do you always love to use that . . . that thing . . . you call a gift to dissect my life?" She pointed at me.

I shrugged my shoulders. "Look, I'm just going to say it." I held the Cub Scouts photo up to her. "Don't you know Hicham is the spitting image of that man! Did you think I wouldn't notice?"

She blinked, then stared blankly at the fridge where the missing Forty-Second Street photo had been. "What are you talking about?" She grabbed the photo from my hands as if she didn't know who was in it.

"Do you seriously think I'm that dumb? Come on! Mr. Maganelo! Your boyfriend! Hicham's real father! You know? Benny!" I almost laughed at how she really thought she could keep this act up.

"You take that back. You take that back! That is absurd. He looks nothing like him. Hicham is a Berradi!"

"How can you go to church and pretend that you haven't been hiding a huge sin for close to thirty years?" I looked at her with disgust. My eyes began to water.

Her face lost all color. I walked toward the hallway. I picked up her Bible, which was on the hallway foyer table and was always left open to the Psalm 23.

"I always wondered, why would my father, a devout Muslim man, want *me* to go to Bible study? Why was he sending me that message? It has always been a mystery. And I wondered why you were always in church or volunteering so much. Most of your friends aren't even that active. Church was just your cover. Your excuse!"

She pointed to the Bible in my hands. "Put that down!"

She rushed over to me and tried to snatch it out of my hand.

"I'm tired of the lies. I know the truth already. I know Hicham is not Dad's," I screamed. "Benny's your lover! You cheated on Daddy! You cheated! You couldn't wait for Dad to die, could you?"

She slapped me across my face and the sting vibrated through my jaw. I held my face in shock. Then she tried again to take the book. I blocked her hand but it immediately felt almost as if invisible hands grabbed me and shook me so hard that I dropped the Bible.

Her voice was cold and angry. "You wretched child. You have no respect and you never did!" She rushed to pick it up, but a bookmark had fallen out. I saw the terror in her eyes as she tried to reach it, but I was quicker.

The beloved bookmark was a yellowed 3 x 5 photo. Hicham's face was painted as a lion. Mom held him and behind her, with his hands on her shoulders, was Benny Maganelo. It looked as if they were at a carnival. I turned the photo around. The date was not even a month after my father died. I felt like everything was happening in slow motion. Even her yelling was drowned out.

Why wasn't I in this photo? I didn't remember the carnival. I looked at the photo again. My stomach lurched. I felt bile in the back of my throat. I thought about Dad, how he was found dead in the tub. Drowned. How no one ever really found out what caused it. I fell to my knees.

I couldn't hold it back anymore. I hunched over and sobbed. "Mommy, how could youuuuuu? How could you do this? Why lie like this? Like this!" I held up the photo.

She watched me in awe. I don't think she believed it was really happening, didn't believe that her Pandora's box was finally open.

Her legs seemed to wobble as she sat down, speechless, and then began crying.

"This was your perfect happy little family, huh? Did you wish I'd drowned, too, so you could have your perfect family? How could you keep something like this from us?"

I looked up at her from the floor.

"Jacques, it's not what you think," she said softly.

I got up and kicked the Bible clear across the dining room floor and stormed out. I needed air. We'd been lied to all our lives. Hicham was so proud of his Moroccan half. Now, to find out he didn't have one at all. He was half Italian and half French. He was going to lose it.

As I went downstairs, my phone vibrated. It was Kylie. I normally wouldn't take it at a time like this, but I needed to hear a friendly voice.

I cleared my throat, so I wouldn't sound emotional. "Hello."

"Heeeey! Jacques! Wow, I finally got you. I've been dying to tell you the update. Is now okay?"

"Hey, Kylie," I said flatly. "I could talk for a few."

"Whooooa, are you okay?"

"Yes, well, no . . . I just found out some crazy stuff. My head is sort of spinning."

"Oh no, do you wanna talk about it?"

"No, no, I don't want to stress you out. Tell me your story, please. Please. No worries."

"Well, okay, so I finally found out who my father was!"

"What! How?"

"Oh my Gawd! You were so dead-on! Remember you said he was older and you saw him in a uniform? Well, he was a cop from Jamaica. But the disgusting and embarrassing part is that he's my father and my granduncle!"

"What?"

"Yes, you heard it right!"

"Well, are you sure?"

"Yes, True finally admitted it. Now I know that it is back in Jamaica where her personality took shape. Where she got her manipulative ways, using her body to get things. It started with her uncle."

I heard my spirit guides as I walked. Their whispers took me over. "You know it wasn't by choice. She was coerced and then manipulated."

"Oh God, oh God, Jacques. My stomach is in knots. What kind of monster was he? How could he do that? And why didn't she tell on him?"

"Kylie, she was so young. He was on a power trip and knew how to control her with fear. It all makes sense why True is who she is. Don't you see?" I walked to a dark park bench. It was damp from a light drizzle from earlier on in the evening.

I felt like I was going to explode and needed to vent. I trusted Kylie, so I shared with her. "Now, you think you got family drama, listen to this!"

"Wow, you too?"

"I've been having dreams and visions that said I needed to go to Bible study. So I went with my mom tonight. Doing what I do, I decided to follow my intuition and I bumped into an old family friend. A close friend of my mom. Apparently they are now dating."

"Wow, your mom's getting it on with her church boo?"

"Oh, that's just the beginning. I haven't seen this man in fifteen to twenty years. When I saw him tonight I realized he's the spitting—and I mean *identical*—image of my brother, Hicham!"

"Wait, Hicham, *It's Just a Stab* Hicham?"

"Yes, my brother. So now I'm in a dilemma. I had a big argument with my mom."

"Wow, are you sure, Jacques? Sometimes when you are angry your eyes can play tricks on you. That's a pretty big accusation."

"Oh, I do not even need a paternity test. Without a doubt, he's his father." I took the photo out of my pocket and the streetlight shone just enough for me to make out the painted whiskers on Hicham's cute chubby cheeks.

"Look, I got an idea!" Kylie said excitedly. "Want me to do some digging? Maybe I can find out something. Hospital records? Some sort of connection? I have access to a lot of databases now that I'm working with Vince."

"There wouldn't be anything there. My father claimed Hicham all his life. I have to be smart. I want to get everything together before I tell Hicham."

"Wait a minute! How did your dad die again?"

She stirred up my own suspicions, so we made a plan to do some research. Kylie had some extra access to public and even private records that I couldn't get a hold of. Now that she worked at Like a Fly on the Wall with Vince and Antonio she was ready to put on her detective hat. I gave Kylie all the information she needed to research Benny, my mom, and Hicham. She promised to report back within twenty-four hours.

I started to walk to my mother's, not looking forward to finishing the discussion with her. It started to drizzle again. I pulled my hoodie up.

Hicham called me. "Yo, where are you? You gotta come back to Mom's!"

"I'm down the block. You're there?"

"Yo, just hurry!" he cried. "Hurry up, man." I walked faster and then started to run. Panic filled me. My heart raced, stomach churned. I'd never heard so much fear in his voice. I saw an ambulance in front of the brownstone building.

I ran past a cop on the stairs and raced to the apartment, where EMT workers were pulling my brother away from Mom as they put her on a stretcher. She was pale and her mouth hung slightly open.

"I'm sorry, Mom. . . . I'm sorry," Hicham said, sobbing.

Fear clutched at my heart. "What happened?" I screamed at Hicham.

"Nothing! I don't know! I got here and she was on the floor. . . . There was a teapot going and she was on the floor." He was sobbing wildly. Saliva dripped from his mouth.

"Okay, calm down," an EMT worker said. "We got a pulse. It looks like a concussion. We gotta move! Get her stabilized. Let's go!" she said to her partner.

I felt a sigh of relief, but when they lifted her, there was a small pool of blood behind her head. I saw a black cloud over her and then it faded away. My stomach churned as I looked at her limp body. Her life was fading. "Mommy, hang in there." We followed closely behind the stretcher.

We watched the EMTs work on her. I was still in shock. I couldn't believe all this had happened when I had been gone for just a few minutes. "When did you get there?" I said to Hicham.

"Huh?" He wiped his eyes.

"When did you get to Mom's?"

"Right after you. She said you'd just left."

"What happened?"

His eyes darted back and forth. It was like he didn't want to speak in front of the EMTs.

"I don't know. She was making tea. I went to the bathroom and I came back and she was on the floor. I don't know!" His hands were shaking.

We got to the hospital waiting room and they gave us paperwork to fill out for her. To me, though, his story wasn't making much sense. I didn't like it at all. He was saying "I'm sorry" when I first walked in. Why?

"So you went to the bathroom and did you hear her fall? What the fuck happened, man? What was there for her to fall on that hard to hurt her head like that? The floors aren't that slippery."

A policeman walked in. "Mr. Berradi?"

"Yes." We both answered and got up.

"You are both her sons, correct?"

"Yes, yes," we answered in unison.

"Can I talk to you for a minute?"

Hicham looked at me nervously. "We have to go to the precinct? Who is gonna stay to wait on Mom?"

"Oh no, you can come right down the hall." We both followed him. He held his hand up to me. "No, please—one at a time."

Hicham was gone for no more than fifteen minutes. He came back and sat down, wiping his brow. Before he could say a word, the cop followed behind him. "You're up, sir."

He was a short Latino man with a crisp white shirt and jeans and a badge around his neck. He was ultra-macho and seemed to have a bit of a chip on his shoulder. Napoleon complex, I'm sure. He sized me up, as I did him.

"Hello, I'm Detective Santos." He shook my hand. "Sorry about your mother. Now, you want to tell me what happened?"

"Well, I went to church with my mom tonight around six thirty. We came back and she started to make tea. I had to make a phone call and went outside for a quick walk. Then I got the call from my brother, Hicham, to hurry back."

"So, was your brother there with you? Or you and your brother weren't there at the same time?" He started jotting down notes in a mini notebook.

"No, no. He wasn't there when . . . when I left." I was hoping Hicham hadn't told him otherwise.

"How long were you gone?"

"Not long, like fifteen or twenty minutes."

"There were some things on the floor," Detective Santos said. "A Bible and a broken coffee cup. Do you know about that?"

I shook my head no. Of course, I knew about the Bible,

but the coffee cup? I guess when she slipped it fell and broke. I tried to seem nonchalant, but my head swirled, trying to search for what happened. I wanted to close my eyes and see what I picked up, but I didn't want to look strange.

"Do you know if your brother and mom were getting along? No altercations in the past?"

"Yes, sir. I mean no, sir, we all get along fine. This was an accident, you know? No one would do anything to harm my mother!" I was offended now.

"I hope so. We have to investigate to make sure. Her wound looks suspicious for just a slip and fall. We have to check these things out just in case. It's just procedure," he reassured me. But I could sense he didn't trust us.

"Well, I can assure you it was an accident. We love our mother."

"Okay, well thank you, Mr. Berradi. We'll be in touch if we have any further questions." He didn't look up and jotted down some more notes. "You can go now."

Asshole. I left calmly.

I had Mom's purse and I looked through her phone and found Benny's number. I told him to come down to the hospital right away and to tell her other friends. I figured the more of her friends who came to pray for her, the more it would help.

We sat nervously in the waiting room. I watched Hicham texting people and looking very uneasy.

"You want to tell me what really happened?" I whispered.

His eyes shifted back and forth. Guilt exuded from his pores. There was a heaviness in the air, almost as if he had a dark cloud around him.

"Yo, Jacques. I already told you, man. I feel bad already. I wasn't there earlier." He sighed.

"What made you come? You had company. What, because of what I told you about Mom?"

Hicham stood up quickly, mumbling, "Yo, Jacques, please tell me you didn't invite this motherfucker."

I looked up as Benny came rushing in. "What happened? Where is she?"

I got up and put my arm on Benny's shoulder. Hicham watched him and I saw the fire in his eyes as if he knew. I was sure he saw the resemblance now, too, if he'd never caught it before. "They are trying to stabilize her now," I said. "They think it's a concussion. She slipped in the kitchen."

"A concussion?" He shrugged my hand off his shoulder.

"What did you do?" he yelled. "You were starting trouble from the moment I saw you tonight, Jacques. Why couldn't you leave well enough alone?"

"Whoa, you need to lower your voice. I wasn't even there when it happened!" I said.

Hicham stepped in. "Yo, hold up, hold up. What did *he* do? What is your problem, man?" His voice was louder now. "My brother didn't do shit. How you coming up in here beefing and you have no right. No say. You ain't family!"

Scared by Hicham's angry tone, Benny softened his. "Oh, Hicham, look . . . I'm just worried about Marguerite. I just—"

"Niggah, you ain't family!" Hicham shouted in his face. His hand was balled into a fist.

I put my hand on Hicham's arm and pulled him back.

The few other people in the waiting room watched in awe

as if it were a movie. An overweight security guard wobbled in as fast as he could. "Hey! Hey! Y'all need to lower your voices or take that outside."

I tapped Hicham. "Chill, man," I said in his ear.

"No, chill. Fuck that! Answer the question, Mr. Maganelo. Uncle Benny." He turned to me. "You know Mom wanted us to call him Uncle Benny? You don't remember that shit?"

Hicham was pretty much fuming with anger at this point. He looked again at Benny, who was speechless and quite nervous. "Soooooo, what's up? What gives you the right? You fucking my mom?" Hicham leaped from my grasp and poked Benny in the chest, provoking a fight. "What's up? Are you the one that did that shit? You trying to pin it on Jacques?!"

"Okay, that's enough." The guard grabbed Hicham by the shoulder.

"Get off. I'll leave." He looked back at Benny with threatening eyes. Hicham grabbed his coat and kicked the metal garbage can on the way out.

The door slammed. "I'm so sorry, everyone. I'm really sorry." I put my coat back on to follow him. Hicham had always been a loose cannon.

The door slammed behind me as the night air greeted me. Hicham was in front of the hospital, pacing back and forth. "Are you out of your fucking mind?!" I saw a young nurse standing on the side smoking, so I lowered my voice. "A detective was just here. The guards take notes on things like that. What is wrong with you? You can't act like some gangsta in a rap video."

"Sorry, but you know who the fuck you are. You ain't just

find out some mind-blowin' shit!" He pointed toward the hospital doors. He was fuming. "This motherfucker ain't living in your veins. They lied to me! They lied all my life! When was you gonna tell me, Jacques?"

My face went blank. I couldn't even imagine the betrayal he felt. He knew. He knew everything. I wanted to take him away from there, but not too far away, in case the doctors called, so we walked around the hospital block to the parking lot.

"When was you gonna tell me?" he persisted.

"Today! I just found out today, Hicham!"

"Nah, I don't believe you. You're fucking psychic. How long you know? You never felt nothing? All this time?"

We walked farther away into the parking lot. I was afraid someone would hear him yelling. I tried to calm him down by not raising my voice.

"Look, I called you earlier to ask you about him, remember? I just got clear on everything. Dad's been sending me messages in visions. They started when I was younger but they never made sense. He wanted me to know. I guess he wanted me to let you know, too."

"Dad! Dad? Even the sound of that makes me wanna rip that niggah's head off." He pointed again to the hospital entrance. "All my life, I've been hangin' off stories about a man who ain't even my dad."

"But he was, he loved you!"

"This faggot Benny ain't never step up like a man and just tell me. Yo, Jay, I don't know." Hicham clenched his jaws and then punched his fist into his palm as he paced in a circle.

"He's like sixty-five, Hicham," I said calmly. I could tell

what he was thinking of doing. "Look, right now, we gotta worry about Mom and pray that she gets better. You gotta keep cool with detectives sniffing around already." I started to heat up and removed my hat. "What really happened, Hi-cham? Are you gonna tell me the truth?"

He looked up at the sky, fighting back tears. "I didn't mean it. It was an accident, that's my word. The second you started telling me something was up with Mr. Maganelo—I mean, Benny—I just didn't feel right. I had a knot in my stomach. I hopped in a cab and came over." He paused, waiting for my reaction. I just listened intently and didn't show my anger. "I used my key and came upstairs. I heard y'all arguing. . . ."

My chest heaved as I listened. I felt horrible.

"I heard everything. When I heard you leaving, I ran up one flight of stairs and hid. I went in right after you bounced. She was frightened at first and I just went in on her. I was yelling . . . and . . ." He broke down crying. "I was yelling . . . and she was backing away from me. She dropped her cup and then slipped on the kitchen floor."

I was furious now. "So you lied. You didn't find her on the floor, you saw it happen."

He shook his head, agreeing. "I tried to get her up, but she was out cold. I called 911 right after." He sniffed and wiped his eyes.

The story just didn't sound right. My spirit said there was something missing from the puzzle.

"How do you just slip?"

"She was trying to back away. I told you already!"

My cell phone rang and it was the hospital. "Mr. Berradi, are you still in the building? We need you to come back immediately."

❈ ❈ ❈

The bright sun peering through the hospital windows woke us up. It was eight thirty A.M.; we'd slept on squeaky cots to watch Mom all through the night. Still no change in her condition.

Hicham's cell vibrated on the table. He picked it up and looked at it. Probably one of his girls. "Yo . . . I'll be right back." He walked outside the room to use the phone. As the nurse was leaving, he came back so fast he almost knocked her down.

"My bad, my bad. Sorry."

"No worries." She laughed and closed the door behind her. "Man! Jacques . . . Mr. Maganelo is out there talking to the damn detective!"

"Wow. Really?" I said.

"He better not say shit! My name better not come out of his mouth."

"Easy." I looked at Mom. "She's out, but she can still hear you. Just relax. He can't say anything. He'll look just as guilty if he says the truth about him being mixed up with this. Don't worry. Just chill out in here for a few."

"Man, I don't want to hurt that old man. But he better not say my name out of his mouth." He cracked his knuckles.

A few moments later there was a light knock on the door.

"Hi, it's Detective Santos. Mind if I come in?"

Hicham's head fell back dramatically as he sank in the chair. He wanted to disappear—just like me.

I got up and opened the door. "Hey, there." I smiled with a fake smile. "How can we help you?"

His voice was stern this time. "Come outside, so I can chat with you for a minute. I don't want to disturb your mom."

Hicham and I both walked outside into the hallway. The fluorescent lights were bright and intrusive.

"I heard I missed a little action last night." He smiled wryly as he adjusted his badge around his shirt.

"Action?" I asked.

"Well, yes, word gets around. A little ruckus in the waiting room?"

"Well, not really. My brother is just a bit upset. We both are." Hicham stood on the side biting his bottom lip. I knew he was holding back.

Detective Santos addressed Hicham. "Oh, so . . . Benny. What's his role in all of this? Why are you upset with him?"

"Oh, he didn't tell you?" Hicham asked in the calmest voice.

"Well, no, I think he's a bit shaken up himself," Detective Santos responded. "He doesn't understand."

"He's messing with my mom. Well, actually . . . they've been having a secret affair for years . . . and I don't know, but I think he knows something."

The detective reached in his back pocket for a pad and started taking notes. "Really, knows something? Look, can we talk alone? Let me go see which room is available. I need to get the full story. Stay right there." He rushed off to the nurse's station to check on rooms.

I looked at Hicham with disgust. "What are you doing? Are you crazy?"

"Giving that niggah a taste of his own medicine. Trying to rat on me. I got something for his ass."

"Don't be a fool. You are making assumptions. You didn't do anything, so why are you so defensive?" I could feel Hicham's guilt overwhelming him, like a swirling bruise-colored cloud.

❄ ❄ ❄

Hicham stepped away with Detective Santos. I hadn't slept all night and my nerves were shot. By now it was ten thirty A.M. A text came in from Kylie, and I decided to call her. Her pleasant voice would be music to my ears.

"Hey, you . . . I saw your text last night. How is your mom?"

I spoke low and looked at my mother. "She's still out of it. It's . . . it's not looking too good."

"Oh, Jacques. I'm soooo sorry."

"Don't be sorry, just please send prayers."

"Oh, I will, Jacques. Is now a bad time? I did a little digging. Can you talk?"

"Yes, yes, tell me please." I got up and walked down the hall and into the staircase for some privacy. The strong smell of coffee by the nurse's station perked me up.

"Well, I don't know how you're going to take this, but did you know your brother has sort of a history of violence?"

My stomach jolted. "Huh? Well, I know he has a temper. He got into trouble a lot as a teenager."

"Well, 'a bit' is an understatement. He's been arrested six times in the last four years. With eleven charges in total."

"What!" My voice echoed down the staircase. "I just knew about one time a couple of years ago. I had to wire money to one of his girlfriends to bail him out. But it was for some drunk and disorderly conduct."

"Oh, that's on there, too, but three of the times were assault, nightclub brawls, battery, and he even had a couple of cannabis possession charges, resisting arrest without force . . . but it seems he gets the charges dropped most of the time. I don't know how he's never done more than a weekend in jail. No one ever pressed charges. Seems the fights were over women each time."

"Are you serious, over women?"

"Yes, the reoccurring names as witnesses on some reports are Rachelle Sanchez and Sofia Jenore, both models. I Googled them. Pretty girls."

My heart sank in my chest. Two ex-girlfriends. I sat down on the stairs. It all made sense. Hicham would be madly in love, then all of a sudden his girlfriend would vanish and he'd be on to the next one. I'd thought he just got bored quickly.

"Well, his criminal history doesn't look good," Kylie said matter-of-factly. "Do you think he did anything . . . well, was he ever violent with your mom?"

"No—well, not that I know of!" I closed my eyes and rubbed my forehead. I saw a sudden flash of him grabbing Mom by the arms, shaking her, pushing her. I shook that dreaded vision out of my head to make it go away. I hoped he wouldn't go that far.

"Benny Maganelo is clean as a whistle, besides a couple of parking tickets in the nineties. He didn't have anything in his record that jumped out at me, but did you know he was added to your mom's deed a year ago?"

"What! Are you sure? How did you get that?"

"I have ways!" She laughed. "Antonio and Vince have been showing me a lot. It's actually public record online, you just need to know what to look for. You and Hicham are on it, he was just added."

"Man, I can't believe what a secret life she was living all this time. On the deed? This is so wild. Like I'm in a movie. I don't know what to say." I felt deeply betrayed. "So, what next? How is this info going help us? I need to speak to a lawyer probably. I really need to figure out how to keep Hicham out of jail. This doesn't look good."

"That's true. For the record, his mug shot is accessible on Google, too. He looked pretty deranged and drunk in a few of them."

I was so embarrassed. "I still can't believe he didn't tell me. He tells me everything! All right . . . Kylie . . . let me meditate on this for a minute. Thank you so much. I really, really appreciate you. Can you email me all of that stuff you found?"

"Yes, sure, sure. I'll keep you posted."

"And, Kylie . . . I'll pay you for this."

"Don't worry. I'll take a reading in exchange! I need the practice. You're my first case." I couldn't believe this sinking ship was my reality. I slowly walked back to my mom's room, hoping that Hicham and the detective were done. I had a few words for my brother.

When I entered the room I saw only a nurse checking my mother's pulse. The shrill alarm from one of the machines near her bed rang loudly. The room suddenly got cold. The nurse shook her head. "I'm so sorry. She's gone."

I reached over to hug my mother, hoping to get one last feeling of life from her. I felt a sudden *whoosh*, as if an entity came into me from her chest and left through my back. I was filled with a sense of peace and calm. That was her. She really was sending me a sign. She had transitioned out of this life.

I kissed her on her cold forehead and began to sob. "She's gone! Mom's gone!"

Hicham ran into the room and stopped cold when he saw me. He fell to his knees by the bed.

"I'll come back soon. Sorry for your loss." The nurse patted him on the shoulder. She wiped a tear from her eye and slipped from the room.

"I'm so sorry, Mom! I never meant to hurt you!" Hicham choked out, groping for Mom's cold hand.

I stood up straight. "What do you mean? What do you mean?"

Hicham was crying harder and not making much sense.

"I grabbed her, I shook her. I was yelling and I think . . . I scared her. She was trying to get . . . away from me. That's how she fell. I'm so sorry, I can't stand it that she lied to me. They lied to me all my fucking life, Jacques!" He was sobbing. "Do you understand? All of my life!" He pointed toward her.

I covered Mom's face gently with the sheet. I didn't want to see her like that anymore.

"Ohhh, man. Jaaaaaay, Mommy's dead! What are we gonna do noooooow?" Hicham screamed at the top of his lungs.

We hugged each other as I tried to quiet him down.

"Why didn't you just tell me the truth?" I asked softly. "You lied, Hicham." The news Kylie had dropped on me swirled around in my head, but I didn't think now was the time. "That detective . . . is he still here?"

"Fuck." Hicham looked toward the door. "He was grilling me like he knew something." He talked in a whisper now. "I don't want to go to jail, Jacques. I didn't mean it. I loved Mom. I'm so sorry. I didn't mean it." He got up and paced in a circle. "What the hell are we going to do?" The loud bang of him punching the wall startled me. He rubbed his knuckles as if he hadn't thought it would hurt.

I was in a daze. My stomach churned. Was the detective going to talk to me next? I was worried for Hicham. I wasn't sure if anyone had overheard his confession. He was so loud.

I knew he didn't kill Mom, but his anger caused her accident. I didn't even believe all this was happening! She was here just yesterday and now she was gone. Now we had to call everyone and plan her funeral. What were we going to do? My mom was gone! I didn't want to believe this had happened because of my digging. I felt hollow inside. I would do anything to have her yell at me now. I wanted to wake up from this nightmare. It was all my fault.

Chapter 24

Jacques

Two weeks after the funeral, I could still smell the faint scent of Mom's cooking. It was as if it lived in the walls, danced throughout her vibrant paintings, sat deeply in the worn cushions of her couch. The apartment had a distinct scent, her scent.

I felt as if she were still with us. I tried not to cry as we taped up boxes and prepared yet another pile of clothing for Goodwill. Hicham stacked two boxes of Mom's albums in a corner.

The funeral took its toll on us. We had a lot of volunteers helping us early on to pack up clothes and books for the church, but even they drained us after a while with their endless questions.

Hicham rambled as he cut duct tape for the boxes. "I'm so tired of all these church people. I know they mean well, but it's like they know. Like they know about Mom, about me, about everything. That Miss Rita is very nosy, poking around. You saw how she was looking at Mom's clothes like she wanted them for herself? I think she bagged a couple of dresses in her big-ass purse."

"Really?" I laughed, knowing Miss Rita was definitely a character. "I don't think they know, though. Maybe they know about her relationship with Benny, but not about you. I highly doubt Miss Rita was stealing dresses. You're always exaggerating!"

"Nah, kid, that's my word! For real though!" We laughed.

Suddenly, we heard keys jingling. The door opened slowly. My heart jumped.

Hicham got up quickly with the scissors in his hand. "What the fuck?!"

Benny slowly cracked the door open and looked shocked to see us. "Oh! You're still here?"

"Wait, what are you doing here?" Hicham shouted. "When did you get a key?"

"Uh, I'm sorry. . . . Ahhhhh, yes, I had an extra key. Your mother gave it to me. I just came to get some of my things. Things . . . Marguerite was holding for me. It's just a few items." He proceeded to walk toward the back.

I stood in his path. "Well, you know you have my number, right, Benny? Don't you think the respectable thing to do would be to call before coming? I mean, this is crazy! You can't just walk in here like . . . like it's okay." I was furious.

Hicham came close to us, forming a triangle. His nostrils flared and his hands were in the air. "You see, Jacques, you see? And you want me to respect this man? A man who shows

us none! He's just rolling up in here. Straight disrespect!"
He pointed to Benny's hand. "And you have a fucking key?
Really, man?"

I put my hand up to quiet Hicham down.

Benny shocked us with a stern reply and finger pointing.
"I've had just about enough of your mouth, young man. I don't
think you know who you are talking to. I know you're hurting and so am I. So am I! Your mother was my . . . she was
everything to me! She was my world. Look, I'm sorry." He
turned to me. "I didn't mean to upset you. Yes, your mother
and I were good friends. Closer than friends."

"Finally! You admit that shit!" Hicham shouted.

"Yes, I loved her dearly. Please let me just get my stuff. I
don't want to argue. I'll be out of your way in five minutes."

"What is this *stuff*? I'll get it. Where is it?" Hicham was
trying hard to get a rise out of him.

The air in the room was dense. My stomach flip-flopped. I
didn't like the energy one bit.

Benny took a deep breath. I could see the rage and sadness about to explode in him. He looked down at the floor and
shuffled his feet with embarrassment. "It's in the bedroom."

"Wowww. Really?" I said with a smirk. This guy really
had a lot of balls.

"I'll get it. Where in the bedroom?" Hicham looked at
Benny with contempt, as if he couldn't believe this was really
happening.

He walked toward the back. Benny and I followed. I
paused in the hallway in front of the bedroom door. Hicham
stood by the head of the bed, waiting to see what Benny

would do. Benny slowly walked over to the right side of the bed by the window. He knelt down next to the nightstand and started packing items from the drawer into the big duffel bag he brought with him.

Hicham was loud and belligerent. "Is this really happening, Jacques?" Hicham pretended as if Benny weren't there. "Look at this." He waved his hands wildly. "The truth finally comes out. Finally!"

I moved into the room. "All right, man, enough. Just let him get his things."

Benny proceeded to clean out the top drawer of Mom's nightstand, removing some clothes and what looked like photos.

Hicham shook his head. He wanted to make a statement. "I'm just saying. Be a man already, Benny. Just keep it one hundred!" He turned to me. "You see this shit right here? It is an insult to my intelligence. Our intelligence, Jacques! Just friends? Do friends have a whole week's worth of underwear over at another friend's house?"

Benny's voice got stern and low, like a father. "Look, like I said before. We were closer than friends. I don't want to be here for very long. If you would stop taunting me, I could be out of here sooner. It's time to grow up, Hicham! This is as difficult for me as it is for you."

"Grow up? What?" Hicham yelled.

I put my hand on Hicham's chest for him to chill out, then said to Benny, "We now know the truth, Benny. I don't know why you didn't just admit it when I asked you the first time."

"I . . . I couldn't . . . It wasn't the right time." He blew out air.

I was sick of him always dancing around the issue. "Well, you have to understand why we are upset!"

"Ohhhh nooo!" Hicham chimed in. "He don't need to understand shit. This is his joint." He waved his hands around the bedroom. "This niggah probably paying the mortgage!"

Goose bumps formed on my arms as I remembered that Kylie said his name was on the deed along with ours. I hadn't told Hicham about that yet. Benny finished packing his last T-shirt and stood up.

"What else you got, Benny?" Hicham asked. "Anything else we should know about?"

Benny gave Hicham a warning with just one look. "I'd appreciate it if you lowered your voice with me, son. I've had about enough!" Fire flared in his eyes. I actually jumped at how he raised his voice. Hicham didn't flinch.

"Oh, son now? You finally admit it!" Hicham moved in like a bully in the schoolyard.

"I'm leaving." Benny slung his now fully loaded duffel bag over his arm.

Hicham blocked the door.

"Oh, don't leave now." Benny's face got tight as he clenched his jaw. It was eerie how much he reminded me of my brother when he got upset. "We're just getting to the good part."

"Hicham, what the hell?" I shouted. "Just let it go. He's obviously not going to admit anything." I shook my head, disappointed in both of them.

"It's only right! Mom died and the only man I knew as my father died." He looked into Benny's eyes. "You are the only parent I got left!"

Benny lowered his eyes. There was an awkward silence. He adjusted the bag on his shoulder and stood up tall. His voice was steady, low, and firm. "You know, Hicham, you are just about fresh out of time with the disrespect. I might be in my sixties, but I'm not a fool or a weakling. You know, I was ready to talk to you man-to-man, to tell you. Yes! I am your father, but I'm disappointed in how this turned out. I spent years and years playing it over in my head how you would react. I knew it wouldn't be good, at first, but I didn't realize just how cruel you could be."

Hicham jumped in his face. "Cruel! And you're *just* telling me this shit. Twenty-seven years later! Now that's cruel! That's fuckin' evil!"

Benny pushed him back and stood his ground. "You are a spoiled, foul-mouthed kid who has no idea. No damn idea what it took to raise you!"

"Raise me? Man, please . . . You ain't raise me!" Hicham looked at me. I stood between them like a referee, hoping it wouldn't come to blows. I was curious to know what he meant, too.

I felt the passion in Benny's heart answer us before he could say a word.

"Who do you think took care of you on weekends?" He beat his chest with one fist. "Me." His voice got even louder. "When you were in Cub Scouts and Boy Scouts, you think that was a coincidence? Who do you think bought you your first pet turtle? Me! Who the hell do you think paid for your college tuition? That's right, me!" He slapped his chest. "Fishing trips, camping, sneakers, clothes . . . me, me, me!" He started to walk away. His voice cracked as he said, "I can't take this shit anymore!"

I saw nothing but pink around his aura, which represented love, and a bit of red, since he was furious. But he was being honest. I felt him.

Hicham and I stood there in shock, speechless—especially since we'd never seen him angry before, much less curse. He didn't stop. "Your first car? Me!" He took off his bag and started to go through some of the things he'd packed. He took out a photo in a frame. He passed it to Hicham, who slowly held out a hand for it.

"Yo . . . What the hell! You never told me. How were we supposed to know?" Hicham passed it to me. It was a photo of Benny holding Hicham as a toddler. He was smiling like a proud dad.

I held the photo up. "Yeah, you gotta realize this is some crazy stuff to take in, Benny," I said. "So many secrets. It's like our childhood . . . well, Hicham's childhood was a lie!"

"You know, I can't say that I'm proud of what I did. It was dishonest to you both, to my wife, and to your father. We made bad choices, but it was because of love. Just never ever say I wasn't there, because I was always there!" He looked into Hicham's eyes. "I even saved your first magazine article. I . . . I still have it." Tears flowed down Benny's face and he wiped them away swiftly. "You must understand I loved Marguerite. She wanted this."

I shook my head and Hicham mumbled sarcastically, "Right, love . . ." He started to weaken his stance as tears dripped down his face. He was in shock, now that the truth he never really wanted to hear was finally confirmed.

"Were you ever gonna tell me?" He paced up and down the living room. "All my life I have been a Berradi. I've been proud of my Moroccan roots, I believed in my roots . . . and now I find out that I'm not that dude? I'm a fuckin' fraud." He looked at me and laughed. "A straight white boy?"

I reassured him. "Hicham, you were raised by Berradis, so you are a Berradi."

"No, no, no. Bullshit. I'm fucking one hundred percent white boy—half French, half Guido!" He laughed. "This is a joke, for real!" He looked up at the ceiling. "Thanks, God! Funny shit. You a comedian, man!" He pointed at Benny. "You did this, because you didn't *man* up! You could have told me countless times. I was old enough in Cub Scouts to understand!"

Benny broke his silence. "I wanted to tell you, believe me. You are my only child! But I only could help behind the scenes. Your mother was protecting your father's name, and yours. Call me what you want, but I loved your mom. I loved her with all my heart." Benny started choking up as he talked. Tears streamed down his face. "I would do anything for her, anything she asked. Anything! You boys were her world. Her jewels."

I felt a sharp jolt in my stomach. It was starting to come together now. I remembered that back then I always thought Hicham was the favorite and that he was spoiled. Turns out his dad was fronting the bill and financing things behind the scenes.

They started to walk to the living room slowly. "So, did my dad know about you? He didn't suspect y'all?" Hicham asked.

"Yeah, how did he feel?" I was analyzing Benny's body movements and tone.

"Oh no, no . . . he didn't." Benny scratched his head. I sensed his nervousness. He knew I was examining him.

"Did you have something to do with my dad drowning?" Hicham asked. "Did you? Did y'all set that up?"

Benny looked horrified. "Of course not! That's absurd. No, no, no . . . that's crazy. That was a tragedy."

A loud thump startled us. A photo had fallen off the mantelpiece.

"Man, listen . . . I just don't know about you," Hicham hissed. "I don't trust anything out of your mouth. You wait twenty-seven years to tell me this shit. Something is fishy!"

"Look, Hicham, let's cool down and tomorrow . . . I would like to speak with you man-to-man. I would like to talk to you more. I want us to start over." He looked at his watch. "I am late for a meeting at church. I am counseling someone. I would like to come back here and finish talking even later tonight, if that is okay."

"Yeah, okay." Hicham looked pissed and relieved at the same time.

I stepped into their space. "What you and Mom did wasn't right. Make it right, man." I looked into Benny's eyes. "That's all I ask is that you make it right." I put my hand on his shoulder.

"I will. Jacques, you've always been a good kid. Understanding and very kind. Your mom was very proud of you."

My eyes started to water. I'd never ever heard that before.

"You have my word," Benny said.

"I'll call before I come later." He smiled, cleared his throat, and dried his eyes before walking out. The door shut loudly behind him.

Hicham whispered in disbelief. "Yo, he's my father." He plopped down on the couch.

I walked over to the photo on the floor and picked it up. "Yes, he is, Hicham, but just give it a bit of time. We'll get it all sorted out. I know we have to work on healing right now. Just give it time."

The photo was of my father and us in the park. Chills ran through me. I know that was my father sending us a message. There was so much more to this story.

I poured myself a glass of water in the kitchen. "What made you ask that question, Hicham?"

"What?"

"About his having something to do with Dad dying?"

"I don't know. I can't shake the feeling that they wanted him out the way. I can't see how they could have done it, though. Wasn't there an autopsy and shit?"

"You know, I don't know. We were kids. We just believed what they told us. I hope you're wrong." But deep down inside, I felt the same way.

I sat down next to Hicham on the couch. We didn't speak. We looked toward the large windows to watch the sun set behind the New York City skyline.

A loud chime startled us, breaking the silence. There was a new text message on my cell from Kylie.

KYLIE COLLINS: Hey . . . I think I can find out more about your dad's case. I got a direct contact now. Vince is the man. He knows everyone!

JACQUES: You might be able to get the answers we need! Wow. I will call you shortly. A new development. Your timing is crazy.

KYLIE COLLINS: Sounds juicy! Can you talk?

JACQUES: Not yet. Hicham here. But I want you to research Benny some more. I am hoping I am wrong, but I think he may have been involved with my father's death. I have a hunch he at least knows something, heard something.

KYLIE COLLINS: What? If you have a hunch, I know it's serious! lol Okay, I got you, we'll get to the bottom of it all. Don't worry, Jacques, karma's a bitch. Secrets can't be hidden forever. The truth is always revealed.

Chapter 25

Kylie

As much as my mom and I have had our battles over the years, I can't imagine ever losing her. It's even worse when death is unexpected. If she was sick, you could at least prepare for it, but just dying from a sudden accident is devastating! To make matters worse, poor Jacques was getting the hint that his dad died by foul play. It was a lot to take in.

Trying to dig up intel on a death that was more than twenty-six years old wasn't going to be easy, but I was up for the challenge. Even though it wasn't an official case of Like a Fly on the Wall, I thought Vince would be up for bartering. I was sure we could use Jacques's "Spidey" senses on some of our cases.

It was a quiet evening and I was alone at the office. I was grooving to an old Zhané album while doing research for our latest case. I was reviewing some of the emails Vince had given me for a client's cheating husband. I felt like I was reading a soap opera.

I was feeling very proud of my progress, picking things up at the agency so fast. The fellas trusted me and it felt good to actually love my new job, not to mention I'd finally gotten Macy's off my back by catching up with my bill.

A loud ring shook me out of my snooping fun. Jacques's name showed on the caller ID. I was anxious to hear what he had to say about the latest on his family mystery. To think that I thought I had family drama!

"Hey, Kylie! I can speak freely now. Hicham left and he is actually out to dinner with his . . . his dad. Wow, I can't believe I just said that."

"My goodness, so it's all out. It's official! Did Benny admit it?"

"Yes, sort of, just not really like we hoped. Hicham nearly punched it out of him. Thank God I was there."

"Jacques . . . Hicham really sounds like trouble. He might need some serious therapy." I didn't think he was wrapped too tight. It's amazing how opposite he and Jacques were.

"I think we all will need therapy after this ordeal. My mom is gone and my brother's finding out more than he bargained for. I just have a good feeling about them meeting now, though. I know Hicham is probably going to grill Benny, but I saw him break down and drop his guard. He never does that. They had a big argument and it came out just how much Benny was helping him out behind the scenes all these years. It was some deep shit."

"Wow, really?"

"Yes, like paying for things—clothes, college, his car. I mean, lots of things! I just thought he was my mom's favorite and a spoiled brat. Really threw me for a loop to know just how much deceit was going on all these years. My poor dad. I really wonder if he knew when he was alive."

"Yeah, that's a lot." I sighed.

Jacques continued, "I know he definitely knew something after he passed. For years I had visions of him asking me to tell my mom that he forgives her. I never knew what he was talking about. Now I'm wondering is it for the cheating, creating Hicham, or worse?"

"That's crazy, he was sending you messages from the other side." I was fascinated.

He said dryly, "For years. I wish I knew sooner."

I could feel his anger through the phone. What's worse is, now his mother is no longer alive to explain herself. She can't defend herself and clean up the story if needed. What a mess! I guess I'm not the only one with a dysfunctional family.

He went on, "Anyway, so sorry to just start rambling about my family drama."

"Oh no . . . I need to know this stuff. It's not rambling at all. I'm on the case, remember? I got a few things actually, just a small step in the right direction. Vince knows someone in the NYPD who can help. He's retired, but well connected. My only problem is that your father's death was more than twenty years ago, so we're hoping all the records are still intact. We can get records from the hospital, the death certificate, autopsy report, any police reports, and doctors records that can show any possible medications he was on. From what

I understand, a drowning death usually means an autopsy if it was suspicious."

Jacques said, "Well, after going through my mom's things, I found his death certificate. It said drowning accident, but also kidney failure."

"Kidney failure? Maybe he was sick from that and it led to drowning?"

"I don't know. I never heard my mom mention kidney problems, which I thought was very odd. I definitely want to see if we can get any other records. And you know my girl is a cop, right? She used to work in the Bronx, so I am sure she can help us out, too, with her connections in New York."

"Well good! Can you text me her number or make the introduction? I know it's a really tough time for you, Jacques. You are already dealing with one loss and then having to relive another."

"Yes, it's definitely the hardest thing I have ever had to deal with. I'll get you Vicky's info. And it's crazy, because in my line of work, I *know* death is not the end, it's just a new beginning. However . . . it's my mom." His voice cracked. "It was so sudden, so unexpected. She was healthy, nothing was wrong with her. I just saw her. There is so much peace and happiness I feel when I talk to people who have crossed over but . . ."

"But what?"

"I'm really worried about my mom." He paused. "I haven't told anyone this. I haven't had one dream about her yet. I don't feel her presence. I haven't *heard* her yet."

I urged him on. "What does that mean?" I began to wonder if maybe she was in hell or something and he didn't want to say it.

"It could mean that her soul hasn't crossed over. I thought it had, but I keep trying to connect with her and I hear nothing, I feel nothing."

"Damn . . . so she might be stuck somewhere, you're saying? Lost?"

"Worst case, I will go see my friend Melissa. She's a high-level medium. She talks to dead people all day long."

"Aren't you a medium?"

"Well, yes and no. I just don't do it all day. If people ask me or if I see someone—a spirit, that is—trying to talk to my client then I'll let them know, but that is her specialty and I just think I need someone else to see for me. This is just too hard. I'm going to call her today." He sighed. I'd never heard Jacques like this before. My heart felt for him.

"Good, I hope she can help you," I said. I was even thinking maybe someday this Melissa could talk to my dad, too. Who knows? The idea of talking to the dead used to freak me out. Now, after meeting Jacques, not so much.

Seeming to put on a forced chipper voice, he said, "Sooooo, how are *you* doing, Miss Kylie?"

"Well, I'm glad you asked! When you come back to the M.I.A. I need a reading for sure. I am feeling so confused in the relationship department."

"Too many men, too little time?" He chuckled, sounding like his old self again.

"Oh, come on! I wouldn't put it that way. Only two . . . well, three . . . no, really two."

"Right, see, I know you too well, already! If only all my clients had your troubles. You at least have options."

"This is true. This is true." I smiled.

We booked my session for next week. He was coming home in a few days and we were going to meet up and dig deeper on his dad's case. I couldn't wait to get some clarity on Breeze and to see if he really had turned over a new leaf.

Chapter 26

Jacques

I don't know why I trust her so much, but I feel like Kylie is definitely one of my soul mates—not in a lover kind of way, but as a friend. I'm quite sure we've had a few past lives together and fate has reconnected us. Having her in my corner feels good. I'm hoping Vicky won't mind when I bring Kylie in to help with research.

My energy was completely drained. I felt like a day after five readings, which I rarely ever do. Hicham and I had been up for hours packing things in boxes, shredding important docs, and throwing out piles of papers, magazines, paint, pamphlets, and just plain junk. My mother was a "neat" pack rat with things in organized piles. She'd hid a lot in her closets or under the bed, so you couldn't see it, but she was a hoarder nonetheless.

Going through everything bit by bit was challenging, not just because it was a chore, but because everything had a memory. Everything made me remember her and miss her.

It had been only a couple of weeks and I'd been holding it together better than I thought. The sudden loss of a loved one is jarring to one's soul. I kept hoping I'd wake up from this nightmare. I kept wondering what really happened. In all this time . . . still nothing. No visions, no dreams, no messages, no visits from her, which was very odd to me.

I was in my mom's bedroom and as I made more piles of things to give away or trash, I thought about Hicham and Benny at dinner. I was a bit nervous about how Hicham was going to handle it all. A part of me knew it was going to be the beginning of a new friendship. It was the first step of healing a heavy betrayal. Benny definitely let my mom control him. I now believed he'd wanted to claim Hicham as his own all this time. There was no denying it.

I was going through the last box I planned to tackle for the night when Hicham texted me.

HICHAM: We at Benihana. He's spending bread. Drinks on Daddy. LMAO I'll see what else I can get him to tell me.

JACQUES: lol Okay, just be easy on him and don't drink too much.

HICHAM: Whatever. I know how to handle my liquor.

JACQUES: Yeah right, so you say. Okay, I'm about to take a nap. Exhausted. Talk soon.

HICHAM: I'll holla.

I lay down on the couch; it felt so good to take a break. My body sank deep into the cozy couch and before long visions started flooding in. I was in a dark room at first, until I turned around. I saw books, soooo many books. Piles and piles. Long columns of books. It was as if I had been teleported into the middle of an ancient library of an abandoned city. Only there were no shelves. Just tiny towers of dusty books. I walked gently around them in awe, looking up.

It felt as if I were inside of a Jenga puzzle that might topple over if I just sneezed. I saw books on art, plants, gardening, Paris, recipes. Some titles looked familiar and they were. It hit me! These were my mother's books. Then I saw some black-and-white composition notebooks like the ones we used in school. I started to walk down an aisle and I must have stepped too hard. One tower began to sway like a tree in the wind. It was at least twenty feet tall. I backed up and tried to turn around to make my escape before it toppled down. Then suddenly the large library shrank. I was now in a small shed. One tower fell rapidly, the books like bombs dropping. The others started to fall down in my direction like dominos; I ran to the gate and tried to lift it to escape, but that made it worse. The loud metal grating sound shattered throughout the room and then *all* of the books tumbled on top of me. *BOOM! BOOM! BOOM!* It was as if I had been hit with mini torpedoes. I screamed, hoping someone could get me out. I shielded myself as books continued to fall.

"You forgot something, son! You are not done! You're not done, Jacques." It was my father's voice. I was curled up on the floor with books on top of me. I caught a sliver of light through the pile. My father's hand reached in to pull me out. As he lifted me forward, I felt my body sit up halfway and I was back home on the couch. My eyes opened and I took a gasp of air as if I had been truly buried alive.

I was dazed for a minute and could still feel the pain from the pounding of hardcover books on my body. Then I realized why that had happened. "Books. Mom's books. I got it. I got it. Mom's storage unit!" Shit! How could we forget that? My dad was truly incredible. Although he was gone, his soul was so alive.

❊ ❊ ❊

The next morning, I felt a bit mischievous, like a little boy peeking into places he shouldn't. It was warm and stuffy inside the storage unit, like it hadn't been opened in months. I wondered how often Mom actually came here.

I'd gotten there in the nick of time, too. In ten more days everything she had in storage would have been sold in auction. The rent was already three weeks past due and they had strict rules.

After that dream, I started to look through Mom's receipts, bills, and mail. I couldn't remember where her unit was, but I vaguely remembered her complaining about how expensive it was. She'd downsized when moving into her last place, as well as closing down her gallery on Bleecker Street. Many things she couldn't throw out or donate. Being the slight hoarder that she was, she found it painful to part with things.

I planned to see what was in there before I said anything to Hicham. My intuition gave me the urge to investigate but to keep it to myself. When my dad sent me a message, I listened now more than ever. The way the hairs stood up on my arms when I put her key into the lock was my confirmation. I knew. To my surprise there was not as much junk and clutter as in the house. It was about a 5 x 10 space, not too big at all.

There were two Moroccan rugs rolled up in a corner. I remembered seeing them in her old art studio. There were a lot of vinyl albums in open boxes with a light layer of dust over them. To the right were some lamps and random office decor on the shelves, along with some gardening tools, a shovel, and then—there it was. A pile of boxes. About five of them. They were marked PERSONAL/OFFICE/BOOKS. Jackpot!

I used my key to tear through the packing tape on one box to see what was inside. It was full of journals and black-and-white composition notebooks, just like in my vision.

I opened a journal with faded blue ink and crinkled pages. I turned to a random page and read . . .

May 13th

He's starting it again. This morning Jacques said to me in soft whisper, "The people were playing with me again, Mommy." He said they are always in the house and asked me if I saw "the people" too. At first I thought it was adorable. Looking into his big brown eyes, I almost wanted to laugh. I thought he was going through that imaginary friend stage they say children go through. But now I do believe he is seeing something. I fear that there are truly ghosts in this place. A young girl who lived here before us died here, we learned from a neighbor. I wish we had known before we moved in!

Olivier mentioned the other night he felt a presence in the kitchen. He thought it was me, then realized I wasn't home from church yet. I thought he was just trying to frighten me, since he is such a prankster, but now I believe it. I will have to call Father O'Malley to come bless the house, since I don't want to risk anything happening to any of us, especially Jacques.

Even though he's only three, he speaks as if he's much older. Each day he amazes me with his observations of things. He's wise beyond his years and people constantly say he's an old soul, or he's been here before. I don't believe in that past life rubbish, but Olivier seems to agree with those who do.

Last week, Jacques was resting on my belly and rubbing it, as if he were my husband. It was very odd. He turned to me and held my face with both hands and said, "He will be my best friend again. Just like before." With his little hand, he patted my belly, kissed it, and started to walk away.

We don't even know if this baby is a boy or a girl. I asked him what he meant by "before." He said, "You know, before he got in your belly." He pointed at my stomach matter-of-factly. Then looked at me as if I was asking him a silly question. It was very strange.

He is such a strange child. I never know what to expect from him.

My knees actually softened and I had to find a seat on a crate. The memory put a lump in my throat, because I remembered saying that to her and I remembered exactly what I meant. It knocked me down like a tidal wave. How could I have forgotten? Yes, I was only three. I remembered my little brother was a girl in a past life. He was my best friend and my playmate and I was excited he was coming back in this life as my brother. It made perfect sense to me. All her doubting me forced me to doubt myself. My memories, my visions, were all my imagination—that was what she convinced me to believe.

I looked at another journal—this one bound in black leather. It was dated before Hicham was born. We'd just moved from Morocco to New York.

January 22

I can't stand the smell of him. I can't stand his touch. He always smells of cigarettes, cigars, and coffee. Not just in the morning but all of the time. He scared me the last time we made love. He knows. He said to me it felt different, that I was different. He was especially rough with me that evening. I just wanted it to be over and done with. He was holding me harder, more aggressively, and it scared me. He just looked into my eyes as if he knew, but he couldn't prove it. I want out. I can't bear the guilt for much longer. I don't know how much longer I can live this lie. I even have to hide my books in the studio so I can have some privacy.

Benny . . . I love. I adore him. I can't stand one day without speaking to him. It kills me inside knowing he touches Emily every night. That he kisses her and makes love to her. It disgusts me. I am very jealous of her, as much as I hate to admit it.

Just recently, Olivier has been talking about moving us back to Morocco for his family business. That they need him. He can go, but I am not going anywhere and I'm not letting him take Jacques.

Aug 2

I can't believe we let it happen. I'm pregnant again. I am sure who the father is. I barely let him touch me. Olivier has been so cold to me and rightfully so. I don't want him near me. His hands are clammy, his stinking breath, I hate how he keeps putting guilt on me about Jacques, since I am at work a lot. He keeps trying to make me stay home.

Last week, he locked me out of my own house! That was the last straw. I'm actually happy to be pregnant now. He locked me out because I came home too late from a church theater performance. We did lose track of time and stayed for a long while in the car after the show. I was so scared when I got home. I

was banging and banging and he finally came to the
door. He's become an asshole!

I folded the page back to save my place and picked up
another journal. I was taking it all in and I didn't want to
stop. This one almost looked like another person's writing.
The handwriting was fast, intense, and hard as if she was
pressing forcefully into the paper.

This entry was about two years after Hicham was born.

October 16th

My art is becoming dark. That's what one of my
customers told me. They seemed to love the depth of it.
Sadly, the worse I feel and the more I drink, the better my art has become. There is no permanent relief
of sadness, I'm finding. Even the time I escape with
Benny is only temporary fleeting moments. One might
say that sadness is part of human nature. Leaving
would be the solution, but I can't leave. Not yet. Having Olivier leave me would be ideal. It would be easier.
    Olivier has gone way past what I can endure. First,
he went through my bag one night, looking for God
knows what. Then, when I came home from church,
he grabbed me between my legs, asked me who I was
fucking. Right in front of the baby!
    I slapped him off of me and he slammed me across
the bed and continued to question me until he actually ripped off my clothes. He was drunk like a

madman. I told him to stop it and he didn't. I didn't want to scream and make the neighbors call the cops. I pleaded with him to calm down. He finally relaxed and begged me not to leave him. He was a tornado of emotions that he blamed on drinking.

We ended up making love even though I really did not want to. After it all, he told me he knew I was fucking someone. He could feel it. He said I felt different. I was so scared, I just lay still and let him finish. I was so scared that he really knew.

I didn't speak to him for two days, I told him I felt very disrespected and I didn't know who he was anymore. He claims he doesn't really remember what happened that night, but I will never forget it.

I am now more afraid for Benny. Olivier said more than once, he didn't like that "church fellow." He also made a comment about Hicham, saying "How come his ears are so big? No one in his family or my family looks like him." Olivier just sipped his beer and watched me for a reaction. I ignored him.

I know I have to leave soon. I am living in fear and I don't know how much longer I can keep this up. Writing and my art are the only things helping me keep my sanity.

Oct 22nd

Last night was insane!!!! He told me I could not leave. What I was wearing was inappropriate. INAP-

PROPRIATE. It was too much makeup and my dress was too short. He must think I am his damn puppet! It was something he's seen me in a million times, but now all of a sudden I was dressed like a harlot. His jealousy was out of hand. He told me, "You must be trying to impress someone. You are not going. Stay home with your kids, with your family. You are with your church friends every day of the week, volunteering for this and helping with that. You think you're Mother Teresa?"

We had it out. I didn't even care anymore that the kids could hear. He told me if I left to not come back, so I didn't leave.

Benny was waiting for me at our diner. We were going to spend time together. Just have a coffee and talk. It's been a long while since we have been together, almost a month. We missed each other. We tried to stop, but it was not easy. He is my soul mate. My heart aches for him. I see him and I just want to melt in his arms. I never felt such an undying love for anyone. Not even Olivier in the early days. His kindness is so welcoming compared to the brute I live with.

I felt horrible since I couldn't call him to tell him I wasn't coming. Benny thought I stood him up. I had to call him this morning and let him know that Olivier just held me hostage with the constant arguing. It's getting too much, living like this. Enough is enough. I'm ready. Benny is not ready to tell his *wife. He's such a coward. He doesn't want our affair to destroy his reputation. I think he is more worried about the wrath of Olivier, since we know he's not right in his head, especially when he drinks.*

We had to wait. It's been two years of our affair. The church rumors have started. No one has said anything to my face, but the stares and snickers are there. I'm sick of pretending. From smiling in Emily's face and pretending I like her when I hate her. When I love her husband and the thought of him touching her and sleeping with her every night and not with me disgusts me to no end.

She was angry, so angry with my father. I never knew my mother had been so unhappy with him or how controlling he was. I also felt sorry for her now more than ever.

The unraveling of the truth was overwhelming me. I began making a pile of journals and sketches of future paintings and just work-related notebooks.

Before I knew it, three hours had gone by and I had traveled deep into my mother's dark world of secrets. To think . . . it was all a dream that led me here. I just hope my father wasn't as much of an animal as her diaries made him out to be. Mom could be an exaggerator, but somehow I believed what she wrote. He was probably so sick of the lies and he couldn't take it anymore. I just had to look at things from both sides.

I can see now why she was living in fear. Dad sounded very controlling, but I wonder if he became that way after she started cheating on him. Maybe Dad felt her doing something wrong and his intuition just drove him mad to the point that he lashed out and drank.

I believed my father was very intuitive as well, but probably didn't know how to handle it. He seemed to have a wild temper and drinking problem similar to Hicham's . . . even though they weren't related.

Seeing the demise of my parents' love on paper was too much to take in one sitting. Even with all their arguing, I still remember love between them. I saw them make up. Kiss. Hug. I saw my mom cooking his favorite meals, knowing how much he loved them. I'm not sure why they fell out of love, but I guess "Uncle Benny" had something that Dad didn't. It was all becoming so clear . . . she was truly living in isolation once their marriage broke down. All she had was Benny and her church, and us kids to take care of.

I definitely didn't want Hicham to get even more upset by reading these diaries. The real unpleasant truth was not something he could handle. I decided to ship the box to my house. I could have Vicky and maybe even Kylie help me go through them all and see if we could find any information related to my father's death. As bad as I felt about Mom's revelations, I also felt a sense of satisfaction. I was finally getting to the bottom of what had been hidden for so long.

❊ ❊ ❊

After leaving the post office, I hopped into a cab and called Vicky.

"Baby." I was tired.

"Hi, papi. How're you doing?" A trail of pity was in her voice.

"Not so hot. Just left a storage unit my mom had. I keep finding out more and more. It's not good."

"What? What happened, Jacques?"

"I just feel so disgusted. I'm actually nauseous, I can't . . . I don't even want to really talk about it."

I saw the taxi driver look at me in the rearview mirror as if he was enjoying the conversation.

"Look, lemme call you back in a bit. I just wanted you to know to be on the lookout for the box. I just shipped some stuff. I love you."

"Oh . . . okay. I love you, too. Call me later. I'm working the night shift."

Shit . . . I'd never actually told her I loved her before. It just kinda slipped out. I guess I did love her. I needed her now more than ever.

I raised my eyebrows at the taxi driver as if to say, "Look at the road and mind your business."

"Can you take Spring Street? This way is too congested."

"Okay, if you prefer," he said in a low voice.

Even though I'd been gone for a few years, I still knew my way around. The driver turned the sports news on his radio up. I didn't even realize he had turned it down when I got on the phone. Some people are just born snoops.

I put my headphones back in and listened to my French jazz playlist. I wanted to remember my parents dancing, happy, and even playfully arguing with the music blasting. Édith was singing "La Goualante du Pauvre Jean." The song said in French, "Without love, one is nothing at all." We all need love and that's a fact. I guess love is what my mom was craving. How she got it, I'll never approve of. I wanted to wash it all away, but the truth was unfolding and love was to blame.

❖ ❖ ❖

The sun was setting when I arrived at Hicham's loft and when I opened the door I heard the TV blasting. The sweet smell of Egyptian musk incense greeted me at the door.

"Where you been, Jay?" He had the remote in his hand and was flipping channels on his sixty-inch flat-screen TV, his feet on top of the coffee table.

"Oh, just got caught up going through some things. We gotta get going. Still a few more things left to clear out of the apartment."

"Man . . . why didn't you just take it instead of us renting it? You could have a spot to stay when you visit and rent it out on Airbnb when you aren't here."

I shook my head and walked over to the kitchen to look in the fridge. I saw nothing in there but beers, a few pieces of fruit, and leftover Chinese. "No, no. Mom died there. That was where we lost her. I don't want to live there!"

Hicham raised his voice in defense. "She didn't die there. It was an accident. She was wrong, it got out of control."

I turned around. "Wow, what's with all the defensiveness? What do you mean it got out of control, Hicham?" I walked closer to him on the couch and stood over him.

He slowly put down the remote and looked nervously up at me. "She said I was evil. That I turned into a monster. I don't know, I kinda just lost it, man. She didn't want to face the shit she did, when I asked her. Even though I heard everything y'all said! Like I don't matter. My feelings don't matter. I told you before, I kinda grabbed her." He stood up to demonstrate on me. "I just shook her by the shoulders to calm her down. We were yelling and we got to tussling." He paused and sat back down, realizing he was digging a deeper hole for himself.

I leaned in over him and said, "What the fuck, Hicham! Do you hear yourself, 'we got to tussling'? How the hell do you let it get that bad? Your story keeps changing and my guides are saying you are lying. I really don't want to believe what I feel."

"Man . . . I don't even remember how . . . It happened so fast. It was an accident, Jacques! She hit the floor before I knew it. She was tryin' to get out of my grip, we both fell. I fell on top of her, I think. I . . . tried to get her up." He mumbled, "She wouldn't get up . . . she . . ." He burst into tears. "She wouldn't get up." He started to cry silently and covered his face. "I fucked up, I fucked up bad. Mommy's gone."

I was furious with him. I felt a lump in my throat. I wanted to punch him in the face. His being such a hothead caused that "accident."

"You think I'm gonna go to jail? That detective was on my ass. What are your guides saying?"

I took a deep breath. "I don't think so. Well, I hope not. Don't we get an autopsy result soon? The detective said they were ordering one."

He replied, "Yes, he was threatening us with it."

I asked, "She didn't have any bruises, did she?"

"I don't think so. I didn't hit her—that's my word. She was just running from me . . . like . . . like I was really a monster. She could have hit her head on something on the way down or maybe when I fell on top of her. I don't know." He sniffled and walked away to the bathroom. I heard him blowing his nose. He was gone for a few minutes, most likely stalling to come out.

"How was dinner with Benny?" I shouted to him, trying to change the subject.

He came back wiping his nose and waving his hand. "Yo, he was talking about nothing. He was still kinda vague about a lot of shit. I guess I was digging too deep about him and Mom. He said I was being rude." He shrugged his shoulders with a sly smile. I could only imagine what he was asking. "The one thing he did say was how miserable Mom was with Dad, but you know a side-niggah gonna say that to make himself feel good. He said how unhappy he was with his wife, too, and how him and Mom felt like they were prisoners."

"I could feel that." I agreed. Even though I'd just read it in her journals, too.

"I can't front, though, I could tell he really did love her. And that he really wanted to tell me all these years. It was real. That's what keeps fucking with me. Like, I wondered how my life would have been if he was in the house after Dad died, if he would have just been a man. He's a good dude. It's just weird . . . having my new father and shit. It's just fucking weird. We ain't got nothing in common besides our looks. He's not a bad-looking dude, just corny. I'm gonna have to teach him some swag. Just 'cause you older don't mean you can't be fly." He got up and dusted off his shoulders playfully.

Hicham walked over to a little Cuban cigar box on the top of a shelf next to the TV and got a blunt and lit it. He took a puff and passed it to me.

"No, thanks, but I'll take a beer." I walked back to the fridge.

He took a few hits of his blunt and sat back. He said slowly, "Yooo, you see his ears, though? The shape of his head?" He shook his head and laughed. "I'm tall, built just like him, too." He took a puff and blew it out slowly while talking. "Shit is crazy, man."

I chuckled. "Yes, indeed. He couldn't deny you if he tried."

We started cracking up. "Yo, you know what was wild? Did you know he worked at Rikers Island?"

"Really? Well, he did know how to stand up to your bullying antics."

"Nah, he wasn't a guard, he was the head of the mental health division. He was a psychologist. He had to deal with a lot of crazies. He said it was rough. He's retired now, though."

"Again, makes a *whole* lot of sense of how he can handle you."

"Whatever, shut up!" He laughed, but shifted his tone and got a bit serious, leaning in to say, "Yo, I got a confession, though." He rubbed the back of his head and stretched with an exaggerated yawn. "I didn't stay the whole dinner. He said some shit that pissed me off. He was talking about my temper like he was trying to school me on some father and son shit. Saying I gotta stop acting like I'm twelve and manage my energy better."

"Well . . ." I raised my hands and shook my head. Benny had been speaking the truth, but Hicham didn't want to face it.

Hicham threw the remote at me and I put my hands up to block it, but he missed. "Fuck you, Jacques!"

"I hope you didn't cause a scene."

"Nah. I just ate my good Chinese food, got my last sip of drink, and bounced."

I shook my head. "It's Japanese, Hicham."

"Yeah, same thing. Anyhow, stop cutting into my story. . . . I told him I had to go. I had work. I don't need him trying to psychoanalyze me and shit."

"Well, I'm glad you even went." I picked up the remote off the floor and started flipping through channels.

"Yeah, I'm not *that* bad. Oh, before all that, I asked him what he told the police when they interviewed him at the hospital."

"Really, what did he say?"

"Nothing about me. He said they were asking about his relationship with Mom. He did say they asked about our argument at the hospital, but he claimed he told them it was nothing."

"You got anything else the cops might be researching?" I wanted to see how honest he would be.

Hicham sat up. "Maaannn, I ain't even think about that! I got some shit on my record for sure. Tickets and shit, nothing serious really." He shrugged his shoulders nonchalantly and took another puff, as if his assault and battery cases were nothing. My stomach churned and I shook my head.

"Don't look at me like that."

"Like what?" I guess my face couldn't hide my suspicions. I realized my eyebrows were furrowed.

"Nothing, man. Mister Goody-goody. You do nothing wrong. My bad." He got up and stormed into the bathroom again, this time slamming the door.

I really prayed that when the cops find out what Kylie had found it wouldn't cause more trouble. I would hate to lose my mother and then my brother!

I went into the back room where my bed was and started to organize my suitcase and get ready to pack for tomorrow. My flight home was in the afternoon and I planned to go to Mom's place one last time in the morning to clear out everything before the painters came. Then I was headed back to Miami to start my investigation for real.

Chapter 27
Kylie

Jacques and I have really become cool. It's almost strange that I actually had a crush on him in the beginning. I've learned to take it easy with the questions and listen to my intuition. He's taught me to follow my gut more instead of relying just on him—which leads me to my latest issue: Breeze coming back into my life and me just allowing him to. Yes, it's true the sex is unbelievable and it always has been and he's still mind-fucking me just as good. I was dying to get a reading from Jacques on what to do next about the men in my life, but I figured I already knew the answer. I just didn't want to admit it to myself.

Chauncey has taken me to new heights since we've met, even though he was once just an Internet crush, but I want to know more. Then we have Antonio. I probably should keep things platonic with him, since we work together. I'm learning a lot from Antonio, and it's such an exciting job. There is never a dull moment.

From cheating pastors to social media man-sluts, my detective work is getting better each day. These cases we have are off the chain! Miami sure is one cheating city. It's not only putting my professional snooping skills to work, but I also get to act a bit, too, and even pretend to be other people.

Our client Elizabeth Moore-Vlad hired us to catch her husband, Yuri, red-handed. She had information from others, but never enough proof. I called on an old buddy of mine from Columbia who is an IT genius. He gave me some programs to use so that I could hack into people's social media accounts. I always wanted to do something like this and now I'm getting paid to be nosy. It's a girl's dream come true!

The software he sent me allows me to see messages, deleted messages, and even their key strokes when they are logged in. We even had access to the GPS on Yuri's cell to see where he was at any given moment. I'm sure it's illegal, but I didn't ask.

I even catfished one of our clients' husbands just to see how quickly he would react. I used a photo of an amateur model, created a Facebook profile, requested him as a friend, and just like that he sent me a message asking me out on a date. What an idiot! He didn't even bother to use a fake name.

When I first met Elizabeth, I thought she was beautiful. Tall, slender yet curvy, and elegant, with deep chocolate-toned skin. Dressed in designer gear from head to toe. She was like a cross between Grace Jones and Naomi Campbell. Her exotic head wrap made her look like an African doll. I couldn't understand why Yuri would want to cheat on someone so gorgeous, but sometimes beauty is not all men want.

The day she came in to hire us, Elizabeth sat up straight

like a dancer and crossed her legs. "I really hope you can help me. He denies it every time I do catch him. He'll always have some elaborate story. I need to have evidence so I can really, really prove it. Catch him in the act if you can." Her Liberian accent was very charming, she seemed to come from money. Very classy.

Vince leaned in over his desk and said, "You know, Mrs. Vlad—"

"Please, call me Elizabeth. I'm not going to be going by that anymore. Elizabeth Moore is my birth name."

"Okay, Elizabeth, just an FYI . . . before we get started, you will have to sign a waiver and contract, because once we find out what we need to find, it's on you what you do with the evidence. We won't be held liable for what happens next."

I looked at Vince and then back at Elizabeth. He handed her a folder with the documents. I was a bit shocked at how he played that.

"I understand. I am prepared for what you find. I won't be silly. I'll leave right after. I probably won't even let him know until our day in court."

She looked the papers over briefly and signed them without really reading them.

"He is extremely possessive and controlling and I need to get out," she explained.

Vince asked, "Elizabeth, have you ever tried to leave him before?"

She looked down at her neatly manicured nails and shook her head.

"I've thought about it, but he controls everything, my

phone, my car, my bank accounts. He won't let me work. A friend gave me the money to pay you." Her deep brown eyes closed for a second, as if she were holding back tears. She was truly crying out for help. "I'm hoping I can get enough money in our divorce to move back to Liberia for a while and be with my family. He's even isolated me from them, since they don't like him."

Yup, all the signs of abuse were there, even if he'd never laid a hand on her. Controlling her money and isolating her from friends and family were enough already.

Elizabeth continued, "He's very powerful. He owns a few fast-food restaurant franchises and is well known in South Beach. In the beginning, he treated me like gold. Like his prize. Five years later, I feel used and taken advantage of. He never really loved me. I was just his little trophy to show off and bring to yacht parties with his obnoxious friends. 'Look at me and my African princezzz'"—she mocked his Russian accent—"that is what he would tell people." She scoffed as she recrossed her legs.

Vince chimed in. "I'm sorry you're going through this. We're going to get right on it. Fill out this application, too, so we can gather as much info as we can on him and let us know his hangouts." He handed her all of the paperwork on a clipboard.

I was amped up. This controlling bastard was going to be a thrill to bust. I got the vibe that not only was she terrified of him, but that he possibly beat her. She didn't feel comfortable telling us that yet, but I felt it.

"You know Yuri is a professional MMA fighter from

Russia? He is not violent toward me, but he threw our TV out the window once during an argument. He's a furniture thrower."

"Ummmm, that doesn't sound good," I said. It's like she sensed that I knew.

Elizabeth shrugged her shoulders. "He's harmless. He can throw whatever the hell he wants, because by the time you give me what I need, I'll be clear across town with all of my belongings." She dusted her hands off as if she was going to be done with him for good. "He's on the road a lot, which is where he keeps meeting these sluts. He stopped me from modeling, from doing what I love, because he didn't want me around handsome men, then he goes around and does this shit? I've contracted a few STDs in the last year from him. He's putting my life in danger. I can't wait to be rid of him." She slammed down the clipboard.

Getting STDs from your man, excuse me, your husss-band . . . That's some lowdown dirty shit. I would end up in jail if some dude did that to me. I don't need *no mo'* proof. It was time for me to put my super sleuth cape on! Vince knew I was excited to work on this and he let me take control, as long as I checked in with him and Antonio daily on my findings.

❖ ❖ ❖

The next day, I hacked into Yuri's social media accounts with no problem. He was really carrying on like a single man. From selfies in the tub to mini videos of him jerking off. It was disgusting. He was so sloppy with his interactions. I think he just had a sense of entitlement since he was wealthy.

In a typical week he went on five to seven dates with different women.

I really couldn't wait to get revenge for Elizabeth! I had the perfect plan. After a little private investigator training from Vince, I knew what to do.

Last week, Vince sat me down and gave me a few lessons in surveillance.

He said, "Kylie, the best spy doesn't even have to hide. You stay in plain sight. They won't suspect a thing! Like a fly on the wall." He pointed to the logo of the agency on the wall. "You see a fly, but you don't usually care about it. If it's not buzzing in your face or in your food, you ignore it, don't ya? You, my friend . . . become the fly. When I was a rookie, my first partner Willy B. taught me everything I know. He was a big, broad, six-foot-two black dude, but he still had a talent for blending in."

"How the hell did he pull that off? I thought I was gonna get to wear disguises and stuff."

Vince laughed and started writing in a composition notebook.

"Nah, you don't have to. Unless you want to. Look, after all my years as a homicide detective, I've seen it all. I solved the hardest cases trailing some clowns who were clueless that I was on their asses."

I was intrigued. "Was it a nerve-racking job? Working in homicide?"

"Well, it had its highs and lows. It's not like the movies. You young kids watch *Law and Order* or *CSI* and think it's all fun and games and shit gets solved in one day. You need patience. Some cases take months, some years. It's never easy seeing dead bodies, and trust me, I've seen hundreds."

"Oh my God, hundreds? I would have nightmares."

"Oh, you get those, too, trust me! But the joy, I mean the reeeeeal freakin' joy, is helping those people. I like being the voice for the dead." He smiled at the memories.

"What? You talk to dead people, too?"

"No, no, not like that! I spoke for the guy who got killed. I was his mouthpiece. Solving the crime and putting those assholes behind bars. Oh and another thing . . . every day is something different, just like this job. We get all kinds of cases. Some you will love; some not so much, but they are all challenging and different." He snapped his fingers with both hands. "Keeps you on your toes."

"I see!"

"You gotta learn your craft, kiddo. Shadow us whenever you can. I'm getting up there in age, I'll be fifty-nine this year . . . so not really on the streets as much. I keep it light. I am more of the research guy, but Antonio is a master at surveillance. Study, study, study for that PI test. I'd say in a five to six months you should be good to take it, but start studying now."

"I'm ready to learn. I'll be your faithful Jedi, Yoda."

He rolled his eyes at me. "What are you trying to say, I'm Yoda 'cause I'm little and round?" The chair squeaked as he leaned back to tuck in his shirt and cracked a smile.

I laughed, relieved he was just teasing and not really offended.

"All right, we're gonna have a little school right now! Here's a pop quiz: Let's say the person you are following is a cheating husband. You find out he has a meeting at a park with his new fling. What do you do?"

"I don't know . . . wear dark glasses and hide in the bushes?"

He shook his head and folded his arms.

"Okay, okay. Go jogging? Pretend I'm a jogger and maybe hang near them and start stretching."

"That's okay, but then what? You gonna stretch and then start taking pictures?"

I shook my head eagerly. "I could with my phone."

"Too sloppy. What I would do is act like I'm a photographer. Bring a real camera, though. Take photos of the birds, turtles, spiderwebs. Just act fascinated with nature. Zoom in on leaves and butterflies and all that shit. Most guys are so stupid, they aren't even thinking. You would have snapped ten pictures of him holding hands and making out with the chick without him having a clue!"

"Ohhh, that's a good one!"

"Remember, you are a woman, so use your femininity as a cover. No one ever suspects a woman as doing anything shady. Okay, let's say the date is in a restaurant. You follow the lady to the bathroom. Start chatting with her. Mention something about her husband and see what she says. You're a charming girl. You can get her to cough up the goods. She might go, 'Oh, that's not my husband, that my boyfriend,' then *pow*. You got 'em. It opens the door to gather more evidence. You are still new and you don't know the ropes yet. This is not so complicated, but you don't wanna get messy. We have a very good rate of solving cases and our customer satisfaction is pretty high."

"I know! I saw the reviews online."

"It came with a lot of experience. I take every case with the confidence that I'm going to solve it, Kylie. If it's out of our scope I will decline it." He took a sip of his coffee and loosened his tie.

"One of the things you will get really good at is not just surveillance, but asking the right questions and listening for the right answers. I always say, everyone who comes through that door is a liar, even the clients! I don't trust anyone until they show me I should. But you can find out what you need and learn to trust your gut by asking the right questions. You ever see Antonio in action? He's a master, but I trained him." He slapped his chest proudly.

I agreed. "He sure does ask a lot of questions."

"He can't help it. It's in his blood. The job becomes a part of you. It's in your veins. And not for nothing, all that shit Jacques does, we do, just on a different level. You gotta have your intuition on. Follow your *gut*." He grabbed his stomach with two hands, mimicking Santa Claus. "It's all in here. You gotta have that sixth sense going twenty-four/seven."

Chapter 28

Kylie

After a little bit of digging, I found out that our client's husband, Yuri, had his hands in a few rough circles. There were a few arrests for bar fights and some bad press mentioned that he was tied to the Russian Mafia that owned a boxing gym.

Now it was time to show my skills. Yuri had a date planned at a Middle Eastern spot in Brickell. It was a good twenty miles from his neck of the woods in Pembroke Pines. I guess he thought he was safe. Pretty smart choice, since the restaurant was surrounded by trees and bushes. The decor included dim lighting and was very sexy. Lucky for me I knew exactly what he looked like. I had seen more of him than I wanted from the photos he'd emailed.

The restaurant had loud music playing while a sexy belly dancer shimmied and hip-rolled around the patrons dining outside. After my coaching session with Vince I was inspired with a plan to catch Yuri red-handed.

I was dressed in a sexy hot-pink dress. My hair was blown out straight, so it was super big and long, touching my shoulders—my disguise, since I rarely wear it like that. I knew he would not be able to resist and if he saw me again with my usual 'fro, he wouldn't recognize me. I walked right up to him and his date as they waited to be seated.

"Mr. Joe! Mr. Joe!" I ran right into him and hugged him like he was my long-lost father. He hugged me back and slowly pulled away.

He smiled. His date looked bewildered.

"Oh, no, no . . . sorry, mizz. You have me miz-taken." His Russian accent was undeniable. His date was lovely—about my age, deep mocha-brown skin like his wife's, yet she was less glamorous. She had a simple librarian vibe to her. Glasses, bun, small diamond stud earrings, and lip gloss.

I put on my best performance. I raised my hands in the air and my eyes were wide open with disbelief. "You are his double . . . I mean the splitting image of my dad's best friend, Mr. Joe!" I stood back, eyeing him from head to toe. "When I saw you, I was about to lose it if he was in town and didn't call me. I gotta take a picture of you to show him, pleaasseee!" I reached in my purse for my cell.

His date laughed. "Oh, that is so sweet. Yuriiiii, you should!"

His face was frozen. I'm sure he knew in his gut it wasn't a good idea. The librarian hugged up on him to pose as I had my phone out. He couldn't resist and let me take one picture.

Then I got greedy and I quickly turned around and took a selfie with them in the background. #Winning! I was a whirlwind that happened so fast I don't think he had time to really grasp it all.

"Oh thank you, thank you. Sooooooo crazy how you guys are twins! You made my day." He had no freakin' idea how much.

As I was about to walk away, he grabbed my hand softly. "Mizz, would you like to have a drink with us?"

The librarian nodded and smiled as she licked her lips. "Yes, stay for a little."

Wow, they were bold. Looking for a threesome? I. Don't. Think. So.

"Oh no, I have to get going," I insisted. "I'd hate to be a third wheel." The intensity in Yuri's eyes was chilling. I could almost see dark thoughts going on in his mind. He wasn't too happy that I'd rejected them.

I held my phone up to say, "Thanks for the picture." Wow, poor Elizabeth had it worse than I thought. I technically wasn't supposed to do this surveillance by myself, but Antonio had to pick up his son from ball practice, so he said I should be fine alone. I was supposed to just make small talk, not take a selfie. But I wanted to take it for my first souvenir—proof of my "bust." I already saw it on my desk in a nice frame. I was looking forward to writing up my report for Vince to review and to send to our client in the morning. It would be a problem if I sent her the picture tonight. She would have come down here and I wasn't in the mood or in the right shoes to break up a fight.

Chapter 29

Jacques

I got to the airport and saw a text from Hicham as I was about to board the plane.

HICHAM: Autopsy came in. Call me ASAP!

I called him immediately but before I could speak he chimed in, "Yo, you get the message, too?"

"No, well . . . I haven't checked yet," I said.

"They emailed it to us. Detective Santos called and said they ruled it as an accident due to heart failure. Mom had a heart problem?"

I felt a pain in my heart when he said it, but it felt more like shock. It could have been the jolt from being frightened when Hicham came charging in on her.

"No, not that I know of. She was taking a few medications, but she said it was for sleep. We can check the bottles. They might still be in the bathroom."

"Man, I still can't believe this all happened. I didn't mean for this to happen, Jay, I mean really . . ."

"It was an accident." I tried to reassure him. I hoped this would teach him how to control his temper. We can't bring Mom back with an "I'm sorry."

As I sat down, the flight attendant gave me "the look."

"Well, that was good news, I guess. I gotta turn off my phone, though."

"Hell yeah, it's good news, niggah!"

"Okay, later." I really felt disgusted. Hicham cared more about himself getting off the hook than about what really happened with Mom. All the more reason I'm glad I haven't told him about the journals yet.

I took one last glimpse of the sun setting out the plane's window. I was getting ready for my two-and-a-half-hour flight and I couldn't wait to get a little nap in. The flight attendant was very nice. Long legs, and her short dark hair reminded me of Dee's. She had perfectly straight Cleopatra bangs and she was a dark chocolate tone. By the looks of her calves and curves, she must have been an avid gym goer or runner.

Our eyes met as she passed by, slamming shut the overhead compartments.

"If you need anything, you let me know, okay?" Nice lips. Plump. She smiled and had a Colgate grin. I smiled back and nodded gently. I tried not to gawk when she walked down the aisle, but she caught me anyway when she looked back.

Human nature is so interesting. It's as if the opposite sex can always tell when you have someone else. They seem to crave you more when you are involved. I think it's because we all enjoy a challenge. These last two years had been great, but I worried about my future with Vicky. I might have already tainted it with what happened during the blackout. What if there are more Dee-like encounters? What if karma was right around the corner, ready to take its toll on me? The outcomes are endless, which is why I should practice what I preach and just remain present. Remain in the *now* with the woman I love. I had never really been a player or manipulator. I left that for Hicham. It was just not my style.

The captain said over the speakers, "We're glad to have you on board. We'll give you an update on the weather in about an hour, but we might hit a few rough patches."

I put in my headphones as the plane took off and turned on my old-school hip-hop mix. A Tribe Called Quest came on. I was happy that it was a pretty empty flight overall. Just like the subway, planes aren't very easy for me due to the nervous energy I pick up from some folks. Those who hate to fly, babies, and even animals who suffer from anxiety. I usually do a deep meditation the second I lock in my seat belt.

I closed my eyes and tried to meditate. We still hit a few bumps of turbulence. A few people gasped and I opened my eyes as I felt someone grab my hand. I looked to my left and saw it was Chocolate Legs, the sexy flight attendant.

"Hi."

"Hello." I licked my lips and then tried to think clean thoughts.

I looked down and saw all thighs. Her skirt was up way high—almost to her hips. As if she'd sat down next to me without adjusting herself. Her thighs were thick and looked smooth. She could have done it by mistake, but it's highly unlikely she didn't feel the draft.

I whispered, "What are you trying to do, get fired?"

Chocolate Legs spoke softly, "No, not at all. I wanted to get your attention. I have a message for you."

I looked confused, so she cupped her hand around my ear. "Marguerite sent me."

My heart sank as goose bumps sprang up all over my arms and scalp. I pulled away quickly and looked into her eyes to see if I recognized her. "What? How?"

She smiled and reached over to check my seat belt.

We felt a strong jolt to the left and then up. The plane rocked violently. People screamed.

"This is your captain speaking! We are going to make an emergency water landing. Flight attendants, please prepare for landing. Please prepare for landing!" Everyone continued screaming, fumbling under their seats, wishing they'd paid attention to the emergency instructions.

The plane made a big thump and shook everyone. *Bang, bang.* Another flight attendant said over the speakers, "Ladies and gentlemen, please return to your seats. Fasten your seat belts."

Just then, we were shaken again, as if we were in a giant saltshaker. *Bang, bang, bang.* Oxygen masks came down, overhead bags slammed hard above, and some even fell out of the compartments. There were high-pitched yelps and screams from terrified passengers. I grabbed the arms of my chair and hung on tight.

The flight attendant was calm as she put on her oxygen mask and then helped me adjust mine.

She asked, "Can you swim?"

I nodded my head and grabbed on tight to my seat as the plane started to drop. My heart was beating fast. Gravity's pull sucked us in. I was surprisingly calm . . . until I fainted.

❈ ❈ ❈

The next memory I had was waking up to my chest heaving and my feet soaked in water. Cold water. The plane was floating, but seemed to be sinking in the water slowly. Outside a window, I saw a piece of the plane's wing floating in the water with flames around it. There were heads bobbing up and down in the water, people scattered like fish—some with life jackets, some dog-paddling in a panic. I looked around and inside it was complete turmoil! Only a few people remained and some looked badly injured. The cabin was starting to fill up with water. I had to get out. Water was up to my knees now.

I rushed to the doorway and heard splashing. I had to help a woman who seemed like she couldn't swim. The exit door was beginning to fill up fast with water, so I dragged her to the door so we could both escape before we went down with the plane. She was a small woman. She started choking and flailing her arms and screaming. She drifted away from me. I saw only the back of her, so I grabbed a floatation device and dived in to get her.

"Don't panic, don't panic. I'm right here, reach . . . reach for this."

Her hair was soaked and she turned around quickly.

I screamed, "Mommy! How could you be here?"

Her face was dripping wet, her makeup was running from her eyes, and she looked so lost and full of fear. "Save me, Jacques! Please save me."

My body jolted and I woke up in a sweat.

The plane had just landed in Miami. "Mom?" I mumbled softly. I closed my eyes quickly, hoping I could fall back into my dream.

I wanted just one more glimpse of her. It didn't work. False hope. Though I did get what I'd wanted. I'd wanted her to come to me in a dream, but I should have been careful what I wished for since this sign was not good. The second we landed, I pulled out my phone to call Melissa the medium.

Dreams tell stories that many of us ignore. Some say they are doors to other dimensions, past lives, or just our souls trying to alert us to something. The key to decoding them could unlock many mysteries.

I'd been studying dreams since I was a teenager. Since my dad always came to me in dreams, I was always fascinated by them. I owned several dream dictionaries, from Islamic to Native American interpretations. There were so many ways to decipher dreams. I knew many of the symbols and along with my sixth sense guiding me, I knew the message of this dream was not good. My mother was not in a good place.

To dream of planes, cars, trains . . . usually any form of transportation represented your life or the direction your life was going. A car going up a winding road in San Francisco might symbolize an uphill battle in your life and some obstacles you were facing. Water, too, could also represent your life. Clear, flowing water was usually a good omen. Dark murky water could be a sign of trouble ahead.

Now this dream, if I had to decipher it all, it had the true makings of a nightmare. A plane crashing in dark murky water with people screaming and then seeing my mom asking for help was clearly a sign. The universe was on a mission to wake me up! She was crying out for my help. The pain in her eyes, the fear. It tugged at my heart. I woke up before I could help her. I couldn't connect with her in my normal meditation trance, so I was going to have to go to another psychic-medium to help me. It was as if my subconsciousness was afraid to hear what she had to tell me. Maybe I didn't really want to know what happened.

Chapter 30
Kylie

I refused to call Chauncey. Yes . . . I know he and I went on only one date so far, and it seemed we had something nice brewing. He canceled our second date since he had had to leave town for work at the last minute. But I couldn't shake the anger when I checked his profile page today. My throat and chest tightened when I saw him tagged in a Facebook picture. A girl was wrapped around him in this photo. He was sweating and laughing. It seemed as if they were dancing.

He had told me he couldn't get together this weekend because he was going to watch football with the fellas. Seems he had other plans. Again, he wasn't my man, but we did speak about four to five times a week, sharing our days, and I really enjoyed his company.

True was home and I had to tell somebody. "You ain't gonna believe this shit, Mom!" She was in the kitchen cutting up veggies for her lunch tomorrow.

"Oh no, what?"

"Remember the cute guy I met online?"

"Chauncey?"

"Yes, Chauncey. This negro told me he was staying in on Sunday with the fellas or something, but instead it looks like he was hugging up on this fake Beyoncé chick at a party."

"Oh boy, see how they do? Facebook will get a fool busted." She came over with a knife and carrot in her hand. "Lemme see this."

"Mom, I will bring the computer over there. You are dripping water." I shooed her back to the kitchen. I got up and set the laptop on the counter.

She squinted at the screen. "Oh nooo, this child has no edges! That long-ass ugly weave. It's so tacky. You are way more classy, baby."

"You see her big J. Lo ass! It's huge!" I scoffed with jealousy.

"Please, that ain't nothing but those nasty butt injections. You know how many of those I rub in a day at the spa? I can tell. She looks like a retired stripper. Look at the bags under her eyes. Isn't it a white party? Why is she the only bitch in black?" She pointed to the screen. "It's says white party in the album."

True knew how to make me feel better in her own way. She was the queen of shade. "Kylie, his loss. Don't worry about it. Also, it's just a picture, he's not your man, so don't stress. Get some more French fries. Why do you think I tell you to do that? This picture wouldn't faze you if you had three other dudes. Looks like she tagged him. What's her name, Le-Le

'Boss Lady' Robinson?" She snorted and went back to rinsing off her veggies.

"Wait a minute. I think he might have had an ex with that name. I remember him talking about a Le-Le on one of our Skype dates."

·"Click her page and see!"

"I don't feel like getting pissed off. It's not really that he is dating other people, Mom, it's that he lied."

True reached over and clicked her page. "Oops!"

Her finger slipped and she liked a picture! I could die! "Mom, back up. Shit! Now this girl is going to know I looked at it." I clicked it again and unliked it.

Most of the photos were blocked, but two of them weren't. They were of her and Chauncey lying in a hammock. It was two years ago, but my stomach took a violent punch, confirming what I dreaded. He was probably getting back with her.

"Wait, ain't he the one with the lesbian girlfriend?" Mom asked.

"Well, he said she had a lesbian affair, but then wanted him back. But you know some of these chicks don't be real lesbians. They just want to do what's in."

"It's interesting, I'll say. I've had my share of threesomes and, well, foursomes and fivesomes." She laughed. "But I could never do that full time. Dining on cootchie isn't for me."

I held my hand up like a stop sign. "Really? Really? We said you would chill on the sex talk, remember? Act like my *mom*! You've traumatized me enough."

"Oh yeah, I forgot." She continued packing away her lunch into Tupperware, giggling to herself. "Well, just lay low and see if he brings it up," she advised. "He's gonna know you saw it since you'll be making love on chat in a few anyway. Why are you worried? Next! You can get someone else who lives closer!"

I walked to the fridge and poured myself some guava punch.

I thought about Breeze and how I really couldn't talk to True about him. As much as I hated to admit it, he really was my fallback guy, my Big Mac. She knew Breeze was still in the picture, I'm sure, but we just never touched that subject.

She continued, "I know what will make you feel better. Go on Match and find some new dudes to flirt with. I'll help you, I need to practice."

"Practice? Your man Basim is coming back soon."

"You see a ring on this finger?" She wiggled an empty hand.

I raised my eyebrows.

"Okaaaaay, then!" True shouted.

That's all I needed now was True . . . I mean my mom, online bringing men home. I'd rather find a new place before I helped her get into more trouble.

Twenty minutes later I heard a *ding!* It was alerting me of an in-box message from Le-Le.

I saw you liked my picture and it's all good. Pretty bold move, I'd say. I knew about you already so not surprised. Let's cut to the chase. I know you don't know me and you probably only heard lies about me. But I think telling you the truth is the only way to stop Chauncey before he hurts anyone else.

I have never been so disgusted by his lies until now. Chauncey forgetting to log off has always been his downfall. Yes, that is how I found out about you. I read all of your emails and chats to each other. Yes—all of them. I saw the pictures . . . and yes from many other women, not just you. I am assuming that when I left him is when he went searching online for my replacement.

We did break up for a few months, but we recently got back together. He left that update out for you. Just letting you know that Chauncey and I have been having unprotected sex for years and I do not want to find out that I caught some shit from one of his chicks, so from one woman to another, you should cut him off. I assume you know he can't keep it up with a condom on so you know he never uses them.

I see he told you he was gonna be with the fellas in his last message. Lies. He was between my legs the entire time.

I already know the rundown . . . He's going to play the victim and call me the crazy ex, but facts are the facts. He keeps coming back. Although he's done me dirty, I still love him. I know I sound stupid but it's the truth. Deep down he is a good man, just emotionally fucked up. I've been here this long and I am his ride or die, his other half, and I'm not going anywhere. So take your chances. Leaving is your best option.

Le-Le

What the fuck?! Are you kidding me? My stomach was swirling. I know Chauncey told me she was a bit crazy and obsessive, but this shit was insane. I didn't respond and immediately blocked her.

I didn't want to get my mom hyped up because she would make matters worse, so I went into my room and called Olivia. "Girl!"

"Hey there, what's up?"

"I just got a damn email from Chauncey's ex!"

"What? Stop kidding? What did she say?" I heard plastic bags rattling in my ear. "Sorry for the noise. Just came in from Publix."

I read the entire email to her. Olivia said, "Wait, no condoms. Wow, that's scary."

"You believe this bitch? I don't know. Just seems like a bit much. If he was that much of a dog, why would her dumb ass stay with him?"

"Because of exactly that. I have one word for you. Breeze!"

"Whatever. Breeze can't compare to this stuff. And for the record, Chauncey and I didn't have sex, but shit . . . he was rubbing up on me. We came close."

"You know you can get herpes like that?"

"Great, thanks, Liv." I rolled my eyes as if she could see me.

"What? You know one in five people have it? It's really not the end of the world if you have it. About three of my mates back in London have had it for years."

"OLIVIA! I DON'T HAVE HERPES. Stop being such

an alarmist." I was between screaming and laughing at her paranoia.

"Okay, okay . . . So what are you going to do, Kylie? Call him and let him know about his psycho woman?"

"I want to see his face, I'll probably do it via Facetime or Skype, since I want to see if I can tell if he's lying."

"Why not just call Jacques? Helloooo! How many women can say they have a personal psychic in their circle? Use him! He can probably read that girl and find out if she is telling the truth in five minutes."

"Good idea, I will try to remember."

A few hours later, before I had the nerve to reach out, Chauncey texted me.

CHAUNCEY: This is your late afternoon drive-by! Peeking in on you.

KYLIE: Keep on driving. Wrong exit.

CHAUNCEY: Huh? WTH does that mean?

KYLIE: Oh, Skype me. We need to talk about it. Your boo Le-Le emailed me.

Long pause . . .
The phone rang.
"Yes," I said flatly.
"What are you talking about, Kylie? My boo?"

"Oh, Le-Le hit me up. I feel like I'm in the freaking eighth grade. I had to block her ass."

"What, Le-Le? How did she? Wait . . . she posted that photo today! I already took it down. It was an old photo. I forgot to block her."

"That wasn't this weekend?"

"Nooo, that wasn't even this year, Kylie. Listen, she is full of drama, why do you think I have been lying low for a while and not dating? She can't take rejection and just keeps coming for me. I needed to decompress from all of her shit. I'm really sorry that she contacted you. Please do not entertain her. It's so beneath us. We're building something special and I'm loving your vibe, you know that. Don't let her mess with your mind," he pleaded.

"But wait. . . . She knew things that she shouldn't have known. About us, things you told me."

"Fuck, I already know. She is always hacking into shit. Well, it was partly my fault. I changed my password, but I didn't change my hints and she knew all of them. Fuck!" He slammed something down hard. "I know she did all of this shit yesterday. She called me tripping, trying to get back together again, and she said 'no problem,' she had something planned for me and I would have no choice. I had no idea it was this shit!"

Made me think of all of the spy programs I had access to. Le-Le probably used something similar to hack into his accounts. I had to ask, "She kept talking about you not using condoms. Like you were some ho out there screwing everything. Is that true?"

"What! Hell no, of course I do. Use condoms, that is. Come on! With her I didn't for a while, but we were exclusive. Trust me, I'm gooood. When you are ready we can get tested together for everything. You don't have to worry, Kylie. I'm so sorry. This is so childish."

I actually believed him, even though I would rather have seen his body language for confirmation, like Vince's been teaching me. . . . I felt he was just caught up with a crazy bitch.

It always troubled me to know a solid and seemingly grounded guy could pick a crazy chicken-head like that. I mean . . . how could you miss those signs? I've seen it one too many times, a good-looking, educated, and well-rounded brother pulling out his hair for a crazy gold-digging chick who is "in love with him." Well, they think it's love.

I figured as long as he put that chick in check and she was now blocked, it wouldn't happen again. I decided to let it slide for now, but my radar was up.

Chauncey tried to get off the Le-Le topic. "I want to see you this weekend. Want to meet in Naples? I found a really nice dinner cruise. That way we both only have to drive two hours."

Only two hours? Humph! But . . . I did want to see him again, too.

"Okay, cool." Even though his past was full of drama, I felt Chauncey had a good heart. He must be doing something right since Madame Butterfly couldn't stop thinking about our little peekaboo game. Breeze was still a possibility, but until I had a true Big Mac step up to the plate, French fries it would be.

Chapter 31

Jacques

When I got home to warm Coconut Grove, the box of journals were waiting for me in my home office. To save time, I figured Kylie and Vicky could help put more of the pieces together. It would take me days to go through them all by myself. Besides, I thought it would be a great way for Vicky and Kylie to meet and connect. Vicky might end up being a good mentor to Kylie since she was new to the investigative world.

It was a Friday night and Kylie headed over to my place right over after work. When I opened the door, she hugged me and smiled gently. She smelled very good—earthy, like a mix of essential oils.

"How are you, Jacques?"

"I'm as good as I could be under the circumstances."

She bobbed her head to the side, trying to look past me. "Is your girl here?"

"No, not yet, she should be here any minute. Come in, have a seat." I led her to the couch.

"Mmmmmm." She took an exaggerated whiff of the air. "What kind of incense is *that*? It's delicious." She took her sandals off without my asking her to and had a seat on the couch. Vicky can't stand shoes in the house, so they will get along just fine. I smiled to myself.

"It's sandalwood."

"I need to get that brand. I think I smelled this in your office that day. I need that in my life! Soooo . . . where are these journals? What's the game plan?" Kylie asked.

"Well, I figure we try to organize them chronologically. I want to see if I can find any clues as to what was going on with my parents. I found out a lot so far, like I told you, but no concrete proof."

"Are they all dated?"

"Pretty much, but some are just ramblings and some are not dated. But if we can at least organize by year that would help."

She grabbed a pillow from the couch and sat on the floor, leaning against it. "May I?"

"Sure, get comfortable. Come on, you're doing *me* a favor, this could take a while." I pointed toward the kitchen. "Want some tea? We have green, mango, and mint."

"Mint, please," she said in a cute little-girl voice. I shook my head at her and smiled.

I went into the kitchen and suddenly it hit me. A wave of appreciation. I realized how grateful I was to have such cool friends. Friends who were genuine and really wanted to help.

The teapot whistled loudly. "Honey or agave?" I shouted.

"Agave. So, should I just start?" she said.

"Yeah, start flipping through and skim. There are some Post-it notes on the coffee table you can use to mark any pages we might need to go back to."

"Soooo . . . I gotta ask you a question, not really as a psychic, but just as a man. One of the guys I'm dating—he's new, met him online. He's in Orlando." She walked over to the kitchen and leaned against the wall, watching me make the tea. "Well, his crazy ex contacted me and it kinda threw me for a loop. I'm like, drammaaa. I don't need it. But I really like him."

"No one really needs drama. There is always someone better out there, it's just being open to it. God is just preparing you for the right one. You have to look at what is going on within you to attract the drama. Maybe now is the time to take it slow. Maybe that is why you attracted a man in Orlando rather than someone around the corner."

"Wow, good point."

"Let him show you how serious he is. Sounds like it's still early, so just give it a chance and see. I don't think the ex is harmful." I tilted my head and took a deep breath. I saw someone who had low self-esteem but was nonconfrontational. It was a vision I had to confirm the same energy of his ex-girlfriend. "Very insecure. But harmless."

"Wow, just like"—she snapped her fingers—"I feel better! You're amazing." Kylie walked back to the living room and spoke a little louder. "Okay, I'll give him a chance and I guess work on my own drama. I really don't need any more. Can I put on some music?"

"Sure, whatever you want." I poked my head out of the kitchen and pointed to the iPod player. Kylie put her cell into the dock and some R&B started playing.

She yelled to me, "I feel so bad, like we are invading your mom's privacy."

I walked back into the living room with our teacups on a tray. "Yes, it's very weird. Man, the things I've read so far . . . things you never want to picture. I mean, never."

"Now, see if that was my mom, I wouldn't have been surprised at all. I guess your mom was pretending to be a nun."

"Yes, she was like our local Mother Teresa." I smiled, thinking about my dad teasing her and calling her that in the journal.

❋ ❋ ❋

My mom was a bit extreme with all that she did to give back, trying to save the world. It stemmed from her feeling guilty because people thought she had it all. The big family secret was that she was raised in an eleventh-century castle in France. It was an extravagant home, but even though from the outside her family looked rich, they barely had the funds to maintain it. Mom rarely told us much about it until one day Hicham, acting like a spoiled brat, brought it out of her.

He'd just gotten fired from his job at Wendy's for showing up late. He rarely got scolded, so I remember it like it happened yesterday.

Her green eyes glowed with anger as she said, "Fired for being late? Please tell me that is a mistake."

Hicham sulked. "Maaaa. I'm sorry all right? I was tired. I overslept. I had a long night!"

"A long night? A long night of what? Hanging outside on the steps with your deadbeat friends who don't have jobs? You have no idea what hard work is."

"Oh man, your castle, all that land, you had it soooo hard. Ma, you know y'all had a maid and gardeners, so stop playin'. . . ."

Mom slapped his Wendy's hat off of his head.

"Ouch!" He giggled, pretending it didn't hurt. I heard the loud smack, so I know it did.

Her eyebrows clenched together as she continued her speech: "We all chipped in. We sacrificed. That job you had helped us and now you have to find another one. Don't look at me for a dime!"

I chimed in to calm her down. "Mom, I'll talk to him."

"Yes, you do that."

Hicham's hand went up, surrendering. "Okay, I'll find something quick. Jeez."

She turned and walked away. "I'm done talking, get out of my face."

Hicham and I walked out of the living room and into the bedroom. He plopped down on his twin bed. I stood by the desk.

"Hicham. What are you doing? You can't be so careless. What happened to the alarm?"

"It came on, but I just kept pressing the snooze button."

I shook my head. "You know Mom is stressing out over bills."

"I don't know why. She acts like our family in France ain't filthy. Like she can't call Grandma for a loan."

"First of all, you know they have not been close since she became a Berradi. They didn't want her marrying a Muslim. And second, all that money is no longer. They sold that house more than fifteen years ago and that money was spread out among a bunch of aunts, uncles, and cousins. Mom saw only a fraction of that."

Mom flung the door open. She had been listening.

"Hicham, let me be clear. Even if there was money, it would be *my money*, not yours. You work on contributing to this household." She pointed to the ground. A vein popped out of her forehead. She was furious. "You are old enough at seventeen. I had to work hard! That is why I was going to college to study architecture. To make a living."

My phone rang, snapping me out of that memory, and I saw Vicky's picture show up on the screen. "Excuse me, Kylie." I walked back into the kitchen because the music was distracting.

"We got a new lead on the case with the young boys who were murdered! We think it's gang related. Gonna be home just a little later. We have to question a few neighbors. There's salmon, veggies, and sweet potatoes in the fridge."

"And a helloooo to you, too!" I laughed.

"Oh, papi! I'm so sorry, I'm in the zone. You know how I get?"

"No worries, babe, and no, I'm not hungry yet." I did love how passionate she was about her work.

"Is your friend there?" I paced back and forth down the hallway and to the kitchen. It was hard for me to keep still when on the phone sometimes.

"Yes, yes, she is. She's going through some of the journals now in the living room." I walked back to Kylie and she waved to me as if Vicky could see her.

"She says hi!"

"Okay, tell her I said hello," Vicky said flatly. "All right, well, good luck with finding out whatever you can. I'll try to be home soon." She paused and I felt it coming. The Bronx–Puerto Rican came out in her stern voice as she said, "You know I don't like no bitches in the house without me there."

I quickly moved away from Kylie. Even though the music was on, I didn't want to chance it. "Whatever, Vicky. Cut it out. She's good people," I said softly.

"Ummmhhhh. Okaaaaay, I'll be the judge of that. They're calling me. Gotta run."

"Okay, good luck with the investigation. See you soon."

I smiled to myself. Vicky was a little jealous, even though she was pretending to be teasing. She'd heard me rave about Kylie a bit too much. I went back into the living room to watch Kylie, who was engrossed in one of the composition notebooks like it was a juicy romance novel.

She looked up. "Wow, your mom was pretty deep. Intense. She seemed to be so conflicted. She is going on and on about embracing the silence, escaping it all. It almost sounds like she was on the edge of suicide. This journal was from when you were still small."

"She was kind of dark at times. Not an optimist at all. But it worked in her favor. She always bragged that her darkest work sold the most. I guess people enjoy feeling depressed."

"It's our society. We love feeling sad for some reason.

Think about it. . . . Look at Mary J. Blige. Her biggest hits were when she was the saddest. Like her *What's the 411?* album. Any happy songs, people would complain they miss the old depressed Mary. Or like country music—please, most of country music can be depressing. You ever heard Carrie Underwood's 'Before He Cheats'? Classic revenge song. Really depressing song, but women eat that shit up. And don't get me started on Beyoncé's *Lemonade* album. Women identify with it. They just feel powerful singing it. So I can totally see why your mom's darkness was a selling point."

I didn't really know much about any of the singers and just smiled and nodded. Kylie really knew a lot about music. Still, I knew where she was coming from. Some people just enjoy being in pity parties and not getting themselves out of them.

"Oh, wow, your mom talks about her first love here!" Kylie said. "Lemme read this."

Today I had a madeleine from a supermarket. Tasted nothing like a French madeleine, but it made me think of my first crush, Christian Renier, and the early days with Olivier. Christian lived down the road and worked in a bakery. He would sneak me pastries and sweets all the time. We dated for a while in our late teens, and when I went to Marrakesh, Christian thought I would come back and marry him.

My girlfriend Inez and I would go to a café in the medina and the waiter was strikingly handsome. It was Olivier. His big brown eyes were hypnotic. He had long lashes and dark brows. His features were beautiful. I wanted to paint him. In those early days I would follow him anywhere.

I now wonder how different my life would have been if I had just married Christian. How would it have been if I had stayed in France and been a rich man's wife? Would I be in this mess that I am in now?

My family was so upset when I married Olivier. They had their hearts set on my becoming a Renier. A family of lawyers and doctors. They never made a big announcement that I was married. They didn't want anyone in our town to know I'd married a Muslim, so I stayed in Morocco and then we moved to America. What would my life have been like if I'd listened to my family? But I can't change the past now.

"Wow, she followed her heart."

"I never knew that story." I smiled at hearing her talk nicely about Dad for a change.

"Wait, you gotta hear this." She began reading from another one of the journals. "'I've contemplated if I should do it. End it all. It's not worth it. It will be a waste of time.' I'm not sure if she is talking about killing herself or him."

"Probably him," I said dryly.

"Ugh. I'm so sorry. You may want to read this part." Kylie passed me the journal.

I read out loud:

April 17th

Olivier is beginning to look sick. He's not eating as much. He looks pale and tired. He doesn't like doctors, but says he's planning on going. I wouldn't hold my breath on that.

What's good is he wants less from me, he wants to sleep more and drink less. I'm happy finally. He's keeping to himself and leaving me to my art.

Kylie touched her heart and looked up at me. "Wow, she sounds pretty . . ."

"Cold-blooded," I said dryly. My stomach hurt, my throat tightened. I was furious. "This reads almost as if she was waiting for him to die. Like she didn't even care. No sadness."

"But, Jacques, it also seems like your dad was abusive in some ways. Have you taken that into consideration?"

"Yes . . . I never knew how bad things had gotten. He knew she was cheating. But she could have left him. She didn't have to stay." My stomach started to churn.

Kylie gently took the journal from me and marked that page with a sticky note. "I didn't want to say it. But yeah, cold-blooded. So, was your dad sick a long time?"

"Apparently he had kidney failure. That was on the death certificate along with the drowning. My mother never mentioned that when she talked about his dying. She always said he drowned. Even in my family . . . never have they said he had kidney failure. I remember there was speculation that he was drunk, but they said it wasn't the case. When you told me to look at the death certificate that was the first time I even knew about his kidneys."

I opened up another journal and started scanning. "Yes, this is bizarre. She doesn't seem worried about him. She was almost relieved that he was sick. Like she planned it."

I sat on the couch with the journal but hesitated to open it. This was harder than I thought it was going to be. We were uncovering the truth about who my mother really was. It was like an avalanche coming down slowly one pebble at a time.

Chapter 32

Kylie

Jacques's apartment was very soothing and earthy, like his office. The energy felt cozy. I saw a pair of black stilettos and rhinestone flip-flops by the door next to Jacques's leather loafers and Nikes. I glanced into the living room and saw *Cosmo* and a few *Latina* magazines on the coffee table. Green decor and loads of plants. Everywhere. By the door, hanging by windows. It had a Garden of Eden feel. His girl was most likely the designer.

Jacques made me feel right at home and even though the task at hand was pretty morbid, he still made me feel comfortable.

"So, how are you enjoying the new gig at Like a Fly on the Wall?"

"Oh, Jacques! So far, I love it. I am that chick who gets excited when *Law and Order* has a marathon on TV!" We laughed.

"Antonio and Vince treat me like family already. That blackout was a blessing in disguise. So was our chance meeting with the whole CVS fiasco that started it all."

"Funny how things work out, eh?" Jacques smiled. I caught him take a quick glance at my feet. I had on a long sundress and my toes were bare. He quickly shifted his eyes to a journal to go through.

I was embarrassed. "Oh, sorry. . . . Don't look, I need a pedicure."

"Oh no, no you have very . . . nice feet, actually." He nervously cleared his throat.

I got chills. I was probably blushing, too. Maybe he has a thing for unpolished toes. Was he flirting? I hope not. I can't deal with a love triangle, especially with a cop girlfriend. A chick with a gun? No thanks.

"What music is that?" He bobbed his head. "I really like that beat. Is that on your playlist?"

"Yes, it's just from my phone. That's Dwele. He's a soul singer from Detroit. Came out early two thousands. Pretty talented brother and he's kinda cute. He plays piano, trumpet, bass, and guitar."

"Okay, Kylie. Why do you sound like a reporter when you talk about music?"

"Oh sorry, that's me—useless music facts. I used to write and do fact-checking for a music site, remember? The one that laid me off, those fuckers." We laughed.

I started to sing along. "But truth be told, I think I love yoooooou." I was humming the rest. The song gave me good memories about Breeze. He used to sing it to me, even though saying those three words was never easy for him. I guess the song was his way of expressing himself.

Jacques and I were quietly reading until the song finished. He broke the silence.

"I just told Vicky I loved her," he confessed.

"I would hope so, you *are* living together." I was actually shocked he hadn't already. He's so grounded and seems in touch with his emotions, unlike most men. "You're like practically married already!"

"Exactly—we started off as lovers and roommates. But you tell a woman you love her and overnight she's picking out the wedding dress and setting up a Pinterest site with wedding themes and colors."

"Whatever! Not me. I'm gonna enjoy my single years for as long as I can. Ride it until the wheels fall off."

He raised his brows. "Sure, so you say . . . we'll see when we do your reading."

"Don't jinx me!" I laughed. I wondered if he'd already seen something in my future. "How long have you been with her?"

"About two years."

"Two years and you never said I love you? Damn! Sorry to tell you but ummm . . . that's your woman. That's wifey. Well, Jacques, what the hell are you waiting for?"

"Well, I show her more than tell her. Actions are better, no?" He blushed.

"Nooooo, we like to hear it, too, Jacques! I know your spirit guides are kicking you right now. They know!"

"Hey, relax. I just made a small step. That song was nice. Can you send it me so I don't forget it? Maybe I will play it for her."

"Oh see, now that is sweeeeeet. Text it to her one day when she's at work. She's gonna freakin' melt! She will be bragging to all of her lady cop friends about her man. Girls love that thoughtful shit!"

"Lady cop friends?" Jacques grinned. "More like her sister, mother, *abuela*, and all of her cousins in Puerto Rico on Skype." He waved me off and kicked his feet up across from the couch.

I realized that the journal we were reading from had some loose magazine articles in the back of it, folded neatly in four. They seemed pretty withered and had some things underlined in pen and some in fluorescent yellow highlighter. The ink had faded after more than twenty years.

One headline read, THE HEALTHY GUIDE TO A TOXIC-FREE STUDIO. She'd highlighted various chemicals. Seemed normal. She had an art studio and children. Maybe she didn't want to breathe in the dangerous fumes daily.

The next one . . . well, disturbed me. My throat actually got tight and my mouth got dry. I was a bit taken aback. I figured I'd read it all before I made any assumptions. I kept my mouth shut and tried to read through it without blurting something out to Jacques, but deep down I already felt his mom was evil. The article said . . .

The Top 10 Undetectable Poisons

There were a few things on the list that I knew for a fact were detectable now by medical examiners, but it was an old article, so that made sense. Science might not have been up to speed yet. What startled me most was what she was high-lighting.

On the list of ten poisons, she'd underlined number three.

No. #3: Antifreeze

Antifreeze poisoning is a fairly common occurrence with regards to poisoning—both accidental and intentional. Ingestion is the main path of entry into the body. Due to its sweet taste, antifreeze from leaking radiators or spilled bottles are quickly consumed by household pets (like dogs and cats). When mixed with alcoholic drinks it can easily be missed.

Signs and Symptoms of Antifreeze Poisoning

Nausea

Vomiting

Abdominal pain

Frequent and/or painful urination

Kidney pain and eventually kidney failure

Dizziness

Stupor similar to intoxication (drunkenness)

Shortness of breath (dyspnea)

Rapid breathing (tachypnea)

Diminished reflexes

Muscle spasms (cramps) and twitching

Partial or complete paralysis of certain body parts

Pancreatitis

Metabolic acidosis

Blindness

Seizures

Low levels of calcium

The article discussed how antifreeze poisoning was one of the worst ways to be murdered because, though many poisonings were slow, even a cupful could take a person out in a few days and the victim wouldn't see it coming.

In addition to antifreeze, the article covered rat poison, arsenic, and potassium chloride. I mean, wow . . . What. The. Fuck. This couldn't be real. It felt like an episode of *Snapped*, which features women who lose it and start killing off husbands and everyone in their way.

I wondered if they exhumed the body, after twenty-something years, could a toxicologist check it for poison to confirm and let Jacques know for sure? I didn't even think we needed to go any further. The cause of death seemed obvious to me, but it couldn't hurt to ask.

I broke the silence, startling him. "Jacques, was your dad buried in New York or Morocco?"

"He was cremated in New York City. It was a big deal, too. Muslims don't normally cremate. I found out as a teen that my aunts on my dad's side were very upset about that. They went off on my mother from what I heard."

"Oh noooo!" My fears were probably correct.

"What? What did you find?"

I handed him the antifreeze article first. He took a minute to review it. "This . . . this does not look good." He sat back down on the couch and took a sip of his tea while reading it. "First off, she didn't have a car, so there was no reason for her to have antifreeze."

"No, it doesn't sit right with me, either. That underlining

shit is what does it for me. What do you *feel*? Your *peeps* aren't saying anything to you?"

He closed his eyes, tilted his head to the left, and took a deep breath. A tear came out of his eye and he quickly wiped it away.

"They said it was a well-thought-out plan."

"They?"

"My spirit guides, or my peeps, as you say." He managed to crack a smile. "I knew, but I guess I didn't want to believe she could do something that cold. That calculated. I mean, he wasn't hurting her, beating her. He wasn't cruel to her. Maybe a bit controlling, but to have been poisoning him? Maybe for weeks or months? She fed him, made his coffee, poured his wine and beer. To think someone you love, the mother of your kids—well, kid—who you trust, could turn around and do that shit."

Suddenly he jumped up like he had springs. "Oh my goodness, my goodness! It was there all along. I can't believe it. I can't believe it. He was trying to tell me all this time!"

I was so confused by his excitement. "What? Who?"

"My dad. For years, I mean *years*, I had recurring visions and dreams. He always came with the same things. His coffee cup—it was his favorite New York Giants mug—and my mother's monogrammed Bible. How could I miss this? This is incredible!" He grabbed his head.

"So, what does that mean? The dreams? I'm sorry, but I'm lost."

He was very excited. "The Bible is what led me to Benny and how we learned that Hicham is his son. My dad didn't have a Bible, the Bible he was holding was symbolic. It just was a small clue to this big puzzle."

"This coffee cup was how she poisoned him maybe?"

"Yes, yes! It just makes sense. I can't believe all this time . . . all this time she chastised me for living my life as a psychic and she had all these secrets but this . . . this is so fucked up!" He ran his hands through his hair and sighed. "I know she must have been scared of what I knew or what I would find out as a kid. It's no wonder she always shamed me out of expanding my gift of intuition. I want to speak to Benny. If anyone knows anything he does."

"You think he helped her?"

"I did before but not now. His spirit is pretty clear, he's very genuine. I can see how unhappy he is and how remorseful he is for everything we're going through."

"I'm sorry, I know that was your mom, but to poison someone and see them every day. That's pretty fucked up. How diabolical."

His voice cracked and tears started to slowly stream out of his eyes. "She took my father's life. He was only forty-one years old. How could someone do that to another human being? Divorce him, leave him, but kill him? Why?" He sniffled and wiped his eyes with the back of his hand. "Excuse me." He rushed to the bedroom.

I felt a bit shaken up. The air was thick. I took a deep breath and said a quick prayer for him. It was almost ten P.M. when I heard a key jiggling and the front door opened slowly.

A beautiful Latina walked in. She reminded me of Rosario Dawson, but she was taller—about five nine or five ten—and a little bit browner. Gray pants suit, light makeup, and her hair in a bun. She looked tired.

She attempted a smile. Almost as if she'd forgotten I was here. "Hi there, you must be Kylie."

I got up to greet her. "Yes, that's me. Nice to meet you, Vicky." She reached out her hand and I hugged her.

"Okay, a hugger," she said, a bit shocked, and raised her eyebrows. She took off her jacket. Her gun was still on her hip.

"Yes, handshakes are for business meetings, girl." More softly, I said, "Jacques is in the back. A bit shaken up."

She leaned in, creases of concern forming on her forehead. "Why? What happened?"

I sighed. "Not sure if it's my place. We just found out some mind-blowing shit. He'll tell you." I didn't want to be the bearer of bad news.

She dropped her bag and raced to the back, calling, "Papiiiii, I'm home."

I heard the bedroom door squeak open and then close. Ten minutes later they both came out slowly. Jacques had a blank look on his face. Vicky had changed into cream leggings and a dark loose sweatshirt that fell off one shoulder. Okay, she was really, really pretty. I gotta give her props. She released her bun and her hair was flowing and shiny down her back, like she was in a shampoo commercial.

Jacques sat down across from me. "Kylie, I really want to thank you. Sorry I kinda lost it."

"Oh nooo. You are under a lot of stress. No problem. I hope you got some closure."

Vicky chimed in, rubbing his shoulders. "You should probably talk to Benny for some more confirmation on things your mom wrote about. Maybe he knows something. Heard something? You never know."

I said, "We can still see if there are any medical records."

Vicky said, "Yes, maybe the medical examiner's report?"

Jacques replied, "No. I know what I need to do. I need to talk to her myself."

I raised my eyebrows and said, "Huh? You mean your friend the medium will help you talk to her?"

"Yes. I already know the answer, though. Come on, it's pretty obvious. It's right here in black-and-white." He pointed to the journals. Vicky placed her hand on the back of his neck and rubbed it lovingly.

"Kylie, are you hungry?" Vicky inquired. "I'm about to warm up some salmon."

"No, no, I better go." I was starting to feel like a third wheel. I was itching to talk to Vince and ask him about what we should do. "We didn't finish, though. There are two journals left." I put them on the love seat.

"Oh, don't worry about it. I'll scan through them. I'm sure you both had enough for the night."

"So nice to finally meet you and thanks for helping my baby," Vicky said. "We are celebrating his birthday with a small group of friends this weekend. I'd love for you to join us."

"Your birthday?" I said to Jacques.

"Ahhh, come on, Vicky, I told you I don't want to make a big deal about it. It's just another day."

"Whatever! You do so much for everyone. Let us do something nice for you for a change," she said sweetly.

I stood up and slipped on my sandals by the door. "Of course, I'll be there. Thanks for inviting me!"

Vicky squeezed his face to hers like he was a kid and kissed him on the mouth playfully. I had to admit I was a bit jealous. Not really that she was kissing fine-assed Jacques, but that she had someone to love like that. I dreamed of Chauncey or Breeze and me being like that at one point, but who knows what the future will bring.

It was time to go. They both walked me to the door and we said our last good-byes. *"Ciao!"* I waved happily, but felt a lump in my throat as I walked off. I hoped Jacques wouldn't fall apart, and I wondered how Hicham was going to take the news. I was glad Jacques had Vicky; he would need a serious support system now facing his new dark reality.

Chapter 33

Jacques

We were finishing up dinner when Vicky got really quiet and smiled mischievously at me. "Kylie is a cutie. I like her."

"Yes, she's a nice girl." I tried to play it off.

"A nice girl? She's hoooooot. That big hair, long legs, bubbly personality. You wouldn't be interested in trying it out?" She tilted her head to the side and licked her lips.

Was this some sort of trick question? Was she saying she wanted a threesome? A nontraditional relationship? Oh, that couldn't be true. I tried to stay in a safe zone.

"Trying it out? I have you already. I'm okay in that department. You keep doing what *you* do." I pointed down to my crotch and took a sip of juice.

She kicked me under the table and started laughing. "I think she likes you."

"Nah, she has enough men to deal with. I look at her like

a little sister. You think I would really have her over here if I thought she had the hots for me? I don't need any problems. You are a temperamental Latina with a license to kill."

She laughed extra loud and said, "As long as you know, papi. As long as you knooooooow!" She held up her glass to me.

Vicky thinks she so slick trying to trap me. Like I don't know her already! "See what I mean, threats. Subtle threats. So terrible." I shook my head. "I might have to work on my will now."

I took up the dishes and started filling the dishwasher.

"Thanks, baby." Vicky pinched me on the butt as I came near her to get the rest of the dishes.

"It's been a long day. Gonna hit the shower and I'll see you in the bedroom," I said with a wide smile.

Vicky sighed. "Give me an hour or so. I want to go through these last two journals for you, so we can be done with it." She put her hair up in a ponytail. That meant she was about to get to work.

"Knock yourself out. I've had enough. I don't know how I am going to sleep tonight. My chest is physically hurting from all this shit. My heart chakra."

"Don't worry about any of that." She rubbed my chest gently. "I'll help you get to sleep." She laughed and blew a kiss as she headed to the living room.

* * *

After my shower, Vicky was in the bedroom waiting for me, but she was still reading the journals. She said, "Jacques, you

have to read this. This was the last journal. The other one
didn't have much in there but church notes and design ideas
sketched out."

"Is it bad?"

"Just read it." She reached for the nightstand light, turned
it on, and pulled down the comforter for me.

I took a deep breath and got under the covers with her and
began to read it.

April 29th

His health is declining rapidly. I didn't really want
to see him go like this. Not like this. He has been
so nice to me, so kind, loving . . . like the Olivier I
knew over eight years ago when we first fell in love. I
know he realized that I don't love him anymore. He
is sick and I am all he has. He went to the doctor's
and they can't seem to pinpoint what was wrong.
It all happened so fast. But thank goodness, I don't
want him to suffer too much. I can't turn back the
hands of time now.

I wonder if it's too late to just leave peacefully?
Still, I know Olivier would never let me leave without a fight. He would want to battle me for the kids.
Even though he has hinted that Hicham doesn't look
like him and jokes that I got pregnant from an old
Paris boyfriend who came to town. He doesn't really
know, but he does joke about it a lot.

Just yesterday made it worse. Jacques was playing

with a puzzle on the living room floor while Olivier was watching football. Jacques yelled out, "Mommy, why doesn't my brother look like me? I look like Daddy and Hicham looks more like you. Is that so you can share? God made it like that so you can share?"

I just agreed with him and told him it was God's way of sharing like he said. MY LORD! The look on Olivier's face sent chills down my back. And just weeks ago Benny and I had the scare of our lives. For a few weeks I thought I might be pregnant again. I haven't been intimate with Olivier in over three months, so there would have been no hiding it. We have to be more careful.

May 1st

My Olivier is gone. He's gone. I am starting over. It's not at all how I imagined.

"That's it? She doesn't write any more after that. That's it. How priceless, now he is 'my Olivier.' This just disgusts me. That is the day he died. May first."

Vicky rubbed my hair. "I know, papi."

"I am ashamed to even be her son." I threw the journal to the ground.

Chapter 34
Kylie

I called Vince the second I got in the car.

"What's up? You okay?" Vince said in a raspy voice, like he had been asleep.

"Yes, oh, sorry I didn't realize it was so late!"

"Oh, don't sweat it, Kylie. Keeps my wife on her toes. Makes her think I have a little girlfriend."

"Ewww, Vince! Stop it!"

"What? Not *youuuu*. She's asleep anyhow. She is out like a light by nine thirty! So what's up, kiddo?"

"Okay, so I think I just solved a case. But I need to know what to do next! Remember the whole Jacques story?" I was excited.

"Yeah, yeah, did you go through the mom's diaries already?"

"Yes, and get this, we found sooooo much stuff. From how unhappy she was, to how she was having an affair. But this . . . this was icing on the cake, I found! She had articles on chemicals and poisons. . . . Undetectable poisons, like anti-freeze!"

"Now, that's priceless. Why would you save that shit?"

"She had them in an old storage unit. She probably forgot!"

"Well, most murderers who are that calculating don't give a fuck. They think they are invincible . . . untouchable. And she was, she escaped prison all those years."

"Yeah, only to die young anyway."

"Well, that's karma. The law of give and take. It always come back to ya," Vince said sternly.

"That's what I always say, karma is a bitch and she knows where you live! It's just wild! She was so innocent-looking. Jacques showed me her photos and she was so sweet. She lived her life like a devout Catholic woman. Wholesome, even if she had an eccentric artist side to her."

Vince shouted, "Never judge a book!"

"True, so true. Soooo, we know, or at least we feel in our heart of hearts, that she pulled this off on her own. His death certificate said kidney failure in addition to drowning."

"Oh yeah, antifreeze will eat up your organs in weeks if not days. What a fucked-up way to die!" Vince said. "If he's open to it, you can go back to the precinct that did the initial investigation and present your new evidence and they can re-open the case with a new detective. This was over ten years ago or what?"

"No, twenty-six years!"

"Oh yeah, I highly doubt you can get much. If a detective

reopens the case maybe they can exhume the body and do all the testing to look for traces of poison."

"Nope. No can do. He was cremated!"

"Son of a bitch! She was really covering her tracks. You gotta give it to her. She was kinda smart. But wait, not so fast. If he was going to the doctor they might still have his blood test results on file."

"What? Really? That long."

"Yes! They wouldn't have the blood anymore, obviously, but the results might show something consistent with antifreeze poisoning. Okay, well those are your next steps, kiddo. But you know I say follow your gut. So, what's it saying?"

I paused and felt it in my stomach. "I have a feeling she actually did it. She killed him."

"Yeah, I feel it, too. Well, consider this like your internship project. I think you did great on that Elizabeth Moore case. She emailed me tonight saying her lawyers were pleased with the evidence you submitted. The social media and photos. They were loving it."

"Really?" I was glowing.

"All right, see you when I see you. This old man has to hit the hay."

"Good night, Vince! *Ciao!*"

Only about an hour later, when I'd just walked in my door, Antonio called me on three-way with Vince.

Vince said, "Ahhh, hate to break the news, but wanted to tell you both now since we're not in the office tomorrow. Bad news."

"What!" I gasped.

"Well, Elizabeth is in the hospital. Yuri is now in jail for smashing her head against the wall in their apartment. Turns out he went into a rage when she confronted him. Bad move. Women never listen. I told her just give the evidence to her lawyer and not confront him personally. Hop on a plane to Africa and get the fuck out of here. Well, you know what? Now her jaw is wired shut!"

"Get the fuck outta here!" Antonio said.

"That's terrible," I shouted.

Vince continued, "You wanna know what's terrible? They know we did it. Stupid chick either told him or he checked her phone and traced it—not sure, but got a prank call today with a Russian dude telling me to mind my fucking business! I didn't even do that math until she texted me."

Suddenly, it came back to me. The pictures. I was in one of them. I couldn't remember if I'd sent them both.

"Did he see the pictures we took?"

"Not sure, she just texted me, but didn't respond when I texted her back. Maybe she ditched her phone. She is terrified for her life. Her attorney is on it and they are working on getting her out of Miami. The guy is a fucking monster. He thinks he's invincible."

"Yes, I saw it in his eyes. He has serial killer eyes." I got chills.

Vince chimed in, "So, why were you not there with Kylie, Antonio?"

"I know, man . . . I should've been. I had a family emergency, I didn't think it was a big job."

Vince said, "Well, Kylie over here likes to take selfies, which was not good. Never ever put yourself in the picture, Kylie! You need to remain invisible. Stealth mode, you hear me? Just keep your eyes open around the office and never be alone. Kylie . . . you hear me?"

"Yeeees, Vince." I felt like the father I never had was scolding me. I was shaking.

"Now you know why we have people sign a waiver. No one can sue us because we are covered. Unfortunately, this jerk is probably only going to do the weekend in jail. He has the bread to get out on bail. I checked his record and he gets into brawls frequently but never stays more than a night in jail."

Antonio said sternly, "Well, homie better not even think about coming for us."

"Nah, I don't think he will, but it's better to play it safe. No one close up the office alone. I'm more concerned for Elizabeth and that she makes it out of America alive."

I hung up and my hands were shaking. I hated that I got overexcited and took a damn selfie. I don't want them to ever recognize me. I'm glad at least my hair was straight that day. I guess I won't be flat ironing my hair anytime soon until this dies down. I resolved to just follow the rules and work on playing it safe. After all, flies on the wall are silent and go unnoticed. They don't take selfies. Lesson learned.

Chapter 35

Jacques

It's my birthday. I'm thirty-two today and in my prime! Hicham is in town for my birthday, which is part of the surprise Vicky planned. He also is such a hustler that he made it a business trip, so he won't have to pay for his hotel. He is doing a photo shoot on South Beach for the magazine. His favorite place to be is South Beach. I'm happy he's coming, yet a bit nervous to finally have the talk about what I found in the journals.

I brought some of the journals with me to his hotel so I could show him what I found. I knew I couldn't keep it a secret for much longer. He had the right to know. At the very least, he should know that he was made from love. Even if Mom lied and cheated to make him, she and Benny loved each other—and loved Hicham.

I was also excited to speak with Melissa, the medium. We had a meeting set up for tomorrow to do a reading and speak

to my mom. I know she has to cross her over. Even though
what Mom did was not right, I still loved her and wanted her
soul to rest in peace.

I got to the Blue Oasis Hotel, a very sexy spot. Looked expensive. I heard spa music and smelled essential oils the second I got off the elevator on Hicham's floor. I thought that was
strange. I looked at my phone again to check the text. Room
1544. I knocked on the door and this beautiful brown Indian
girl opened the door. Long hair down to her butt. Wow, she
had Vicky beat with the hair. Gold bikini. Black stilettos.

"Jacques?" She giggled at the blank look on my face.

"Ah yes, I thought . . . I thought I had the wrong room." I
passed my hand through my waves.

She slowly opened the door and the music got louder and
the scent of lavender took over me. "No, you are in the right
room. I'm here for your surprise birthday gift. Happy birthday! I'm Aanya. Your brother was very generous and gave
you access to the full menu. Please . . ." She showed me to the
office area of the suite. "Have a seat and review the menu." I
looked to the back and didn't see anyone else. The place was
massive. Looked like four hotel rooms in one. I guess he was
going to be shooting some pictures here, too, on their dime,
since I knew he couldn't afford all of this.

I hesitantly sat down and tried not to stare as she pranced
around in front of me in a bikini as if this was an everyday
occurrence. She had such a nice walk. Elegant, regal . . . yes
even half-naked in stilettos.

"Please, review the menu, Jacques." I was staring again,
holding the brochure.

"Whoa, I think this is all really nice. I mean, *you* are very nice." I pointed to her body. "But it's just not my thing. I don't want to go there."

"What? A massage? That's all it is. It's VIP service, that's all." She reassured me as she handed me a glass of water from the minibar.

"Oh, okay!" I felt relieved, although a little suspicious, too.

I picked up the menu and I had to smile to myself. Part of me did think this was some prank.

"Well, I have to ask, what did you *think* this was going to be?" She laughed. "You know I normally wear blue baggy scrubs, but we just finished doing a photo shoot for Mr. Hicham and he asked that we stay like this." I tried not to laugh at her calling him Mr. Hicham. Did he pay her to say that, too?"

"We?"

"Oh yes, it's two-on-one massage. My assistant, Sky, is going to help me."

"Wow." I shifted my legs as I glanced at Aanya's smooth abs, her thighs, her curves, her white smile. Damn, that little jerk of a brother really loves me if this isn't a prank. Then I smelled the faint scent of marijuana and heard a door bang open and hissing, like someone trying to hold in laughter.

"Baaaah haha hahaha. Oh mannn! Stop being a punk and take it. It's a gift, don't disrespect me and reject it."

I got up and Hicham ran over to me, hugging me and yelling, "We won't tell your girl. Happy birthday, motherfucker!" He slapped me hard on the back. I laughed and sat back down, relieved there weren't cameras rolling anywhere.

Aanya stood behind me in my chair and started to massage one of my shoulders. I pointed at him. "I'm gonna get you for this!"

Aanya whispered in my ear, "Just relax. Please go into the next room and disrobe. Get under the sheet and ring the bell when you are ready. The massage table is all set up and heated. I think you will enjoy it. Sky and I will take care of you." I raised my eyebrows at Hicham.

Hicham was smiling and rubbing his hands together. "Don't say little bro ain't never hook you up. This is some *Coming to America* shit, right? 'What-teva youuuu like'?" He cackled, impersonating a scene from the movie.

My legs got weak, because I knew I was going to enjoy this more than I should. Aanya reached under my collar and kneaded a knot on the left side of my neck. My goodness, I wasn't even in the room yet and it was feeling like heaven.

"Jacques, it's so good you are here, my love. You have a lot of tension! Did you pick from the menu?"

Hicham pointed to it. "Yo, son, get the 'Indulge Me'! I had it earlier, you won't be sorry. You already got the 'Double Your Pleasure,' but you can add on. How do they say . . . à la carte and shit." His eyes were slits. He was definitely smoking a lot today. He was always extra animated when he was high. I thought it was supposed to calm you down.

I fumbled with the menu and noticed my hands were actually shaking. I couldn't believe what a punk I was really turning into. I mean . . . am I really in love now? I guess I was feeling conflicted.

Hicham had the wildest Jack Nicholson–esque smirk on

his face. He was enjoying my shock a bit too much. "You want a puff?" He passed me his blunt. "Looks like you need one to loosen up."

I waved him off. "Nah, you know I don't smoke anymore. I need to have my wits about me right now."

"Fuck wits, it's your birthday, niggah!" He walked up closer to me and spoke lower. "Yo, you know what I was thinking? Is it wrong for me to say that now? Being that I'm like all gringo and shit." He laughed extra loud. His whispers were never whispers. I saw Aanya crack a smile. I couldn't help but laugh with him. He was too funny when he smoked.

"Yeah, you might want to go easy on the N word," I said.

"Fuck that, ain't nobody gotta know. You think I'm telling people? Shit . . ." He put his finger to his lips to hush me, as if I were the one blabbing. Aanya walked to the bathroom and was fixing her hair and reapplying lip gloss with the door open. Leaning over the sink and pushing her bottom out. She was so nice to observe from afar.

Then the other girl, Sky, finally poked her head out of another room in the back.

"What up, Sky." Hicham smiled at her. She came out slowly to see what was going on. I didn't even realize she was here already. A head full of curls—big fluffy auburn and blond curls. Maaaan, she was hot! She could be black, Spanish, or mixed. I wasn't sure. Bronzed skin as if she just finished tanning this morning. Her powder-pink bikini was very, very tiny and she was even bustier than Aanya. Her hour-glass figure almost looked unreal. But she definitely didn't look surgically enhanced like a lot of these women down here. Hips so wide and waist so tiny. My heart sank. I was speechless as she stood there in the hallway, teasing me with her eyes. She had deep brown eyes and she used them to her advantage as she looked coyly at me. "'Appy berthday." Her Spanish accent was very thick. "Ju almost ready for massage?"

Hicham leaned up against the minibar and was getting a real kick out of all of this. He poured a drink for himself. "Uh-huh . . . uh-huh. I know you, big bro. I knooow you! I knew you would like this bonus gift."

I was smiling waaaaay too hard; I could feel my face hurting. My heart racing. He knows I have a thing for exotic women. "Man, this better be legit. Just a massage? No funny business." I pointed at him.

"Yo, maaaann the *fuck* up!" He put up his glass as if to toast me, even though I was drinking water. "*Salut!*"

Aanya took my hand, led me to the back room, and showed me the massage table to sit on. Incense was burning now and music was playing on an iPad. It was the sound of a gentle rain shower with light piano. Very relaxing.

I was pretty nervous. "Wow, I never had a massage with two women before."

"Ah, no worries. We'll be gentle, unless you like deep tissue," Aanya said.

Sky asked gently, "Ju pick?" as she pointed to the menu. I wondered if she could even read it. Her accent sounded like she barely spoke English, but I don't know why I loved that even more. Gave me the feeling of being on an exotic island.

I reviewed the menu one more time and said, "Oh, I don't want this, but was just curious . . . what is the Bad Boy Special?" I directed my question to Aanya because I figured she could explain it better.

Sky and Aanya looked at each other and smiled. Aanya answered, "Well, that is if you like a little dirty talk and some spanking."

Sky chimed in, "Ju like a bad boy! Pao-Pao." And pretended to hit my bottom.

"Oh no no no. That's okay. I'll stick with a regular deep tissue. I guess this is really the Double Your Pleasure package?"

Aanya's voice was sultry and slightly deep . . . she sounded mature, experienced. "Yes, we both work on you at the same time, so it truly intensifies the pleasure." She closed the door to block the distant game sounds from the TV. "Trust me, you will be thoroughly satisfied." She licked her lips and kept intense eye contact with me. Was I being seduced? Yes. I knew . . . I really knew she wanted to do more than a massage and my will would be tested. I figured I could handle it. I was thirty-two . . . I'd have to handle it like a man.

Sky tapped the massage table I was sitting on. "Okay, ju undress now, okay?"

She had a tattoo of Tinker Bell on her right hip that was half hidden by her bikini. I couldn't help but stare. She saw me gawking, but ignored my eyes. She said, "Put clothes there, ring bell, we will be back for ju, okay?" I watched them walk out and all I could think was that I was going to wake up soon. I was sure of it.

I hoped I would start off facedown, because I felt like I would be pitching a tent with the sheet. My excitement grew as I undressed. I got on the heated table, which seemed to hug me like a giant electric blanket. This *is* really happening. These *two* beautiful girls. Exotic. Sexy. Bodies out of this world. They looked classy, too. Not your typical South Beach gold diggers full of silicone. I know you only live once, so to hell with it. It's my birthday! I rang the bell gleefully.

❊ ❊ ❊

It was more than thirty minutes in and so far I was extremely proud of my behavior. They both had magical hands and every minute felt like I was being touched everywhere at the same time. I'd never experienced anything so exhilarating. It was so pleasurable. I think I might have drooled a few times.

It was all good when I was facedown, but then they had me turn over onto my back. They put a lavender-scented eye pillow on me to block out the light and so I couldn't see. Aanya was working on my thighs and I'd just had leg day at the gym, so it was pretty intense. It hurt so good. Her hands moved to my inner thighs, a bit too close to turn this into more than a massage. I moved the eye pillow and saw she was smiling as she rubbed oils up and down my leg. Only now she was *topless*. I didn't know how long she'd been without her bikini top. I instantly started to rise under the sheets she had tucked in between my legs to get to my thighs.

"Ummm, do you mind? Aanya, can you put your top back on? I can't take that." She kept rubbing as if she didn't hear me.

My neck was being rubbed by Sky, who asked, "Uh-oh, y el psychic? Ju brudder say you can . . . *Como se dice?* Ehhhh . . . read the mind? Hmmmm?"

She stood up from the chair. I glanced up. The view of her face was upside down since she was behind me and her breasts almost touched my face as she leaned over me. She'd removed her top, too! "Whoa, you too?" I chuckled nervously.

"Oh, Jacques, we were told to give you the fuuuull service. Since you're psychic we thought you got the message. Remember, Mr. Hicham said to give you the VIP treatment?" Aanya moved up closer and grabbed my hand and put it on one breast. "You can touch. Feels good, huh?" She whispered, "Niiiice and soft."

I closed my eyes and just slid my hand off her hard nipple. The battle in my mind was torturous. "No, no. I just want the massage." I laughed nervously.

Sky giggled as they switched places. Tag-teaming me, they were getting a kick out of teasing me. What was the point of the darn menu? They didn't listen to my choices. Aanya went toward my head and sat down on the stool. She pulled both arms back and started to pull them gently toward her, then proceeded to rub them. Felt so good, but it was actually to restrain me.

Sky—oh, my weakness—started on my thighs and then moved her hands under the sheet. She stroked my balls softly and I sighed. She was about to give me a hand job and I knew I had to go. I was going to fuck both of them if I didn't. I saw my life flash before my eyes—visions of Vicky finding out and moving out!

My body tensed up. "Hey . . . ladies. I think I better go. This was nice. I mean, really nice." I sat up and covered my hardness with the sheet.

Sky went from sweet and alluring to angry and bitter. "Wha are you a gay? Ju like man?" I had offended her and her beautiful, beautiful breasts.

"What? No! No! I have a woman. A beautiful woman! A girlfriend. I just can't do this."

Both of them topless. Standing in front of me. Me naked. In a sheet.

"It's no sex, just looky looky, little touch," Sky argued.

"Look, I know you ladies got paid a lot to do that and I reaaaaally appreciate it. But I gotta go. This isn't my thing." The background music got intense along with the mood of the room. The sounds of a soothing rain shower now sounded like a raving thunderstorm with lightning.

Aanya put her top back on, shrugged, and walked out to the bathroom. Sky shook her head, baffled. She looked at me as if I were crazy. She was probably right. She left the room topless and then came back for the rest of her bikini, which was draped across the stool. "Okay, Jacques. It was nice meeting you. Maybe one day I will call you for a reading. I heard you were really good." She pointed at me. "Your girlfriend is very lucky. Very lucky. Not many men can turn us down." Strangely, her Spanish accent sounded like perfect English now. Really?

She closed the door and I went totally limp from their scowls of disappointment. I wondered what they had in store for me. If this was just a job and they were in character, they sure played it well. I slid on my pants and T-shirt quickly before the devil got the best of me.

I walked out the door behind them and Hicham looked

back from his football game and said, "Yo, where y'all going? Jay! Yo, Jacques where you going?"

"I gotta run. Thanks for the gift. Really! I will call you later. We gotta talk, too, about other important stuff. See you later tonight."

He yelled, "Yo, you are fucking crazy!" The door slammed before he could finish.

Chapter 36

Jacques

I hopped into my car and called Vicky, overwhelmed with guilt.

"Heeeeeey, baby, you home yet?" I asked her.

"I'm on the way, not yet, what's up?" I heard the highway wind blowing into the car.

Anxiety penetrated my tone. "Nothing, I'll see you when I get home. Be ready for me."

She giggled. "Ooooh, okay, birthday boy!"

Forty-five minutes later I walked in and she was already in the kitchen, still in her pants suit with her badge around her neck.

"Hey, papi!" She was washing lettuce for a salad. The food in the oven smelled good. I charged in fast. Eyes glazed. My breathing thick. I pushed the strainer out of her hand and turned her around. I started kissing her. Ravishing her. Her tongue danced with mine. Her wet hands grabbed my back, then my neck. She was overwhelmed by affection. The water kept running.

"Oh my God, Jacques, what's gotten into you?" She felt my hardness through my jeans as I pressed against her and stared into her eyes. I didn't answer her and started unbuttoning her blouse; she helped by taking off her pants. The fire grew inside me.

She pushed the faucet down and instinctively turned off the oven. She knew. "Jacques. I'm all sweaty from a long day. Lemme take a shower." She panted in between kisses. I had her pinned up against the sink, not giving her a minute to escape. "I don't care. You think I care?" I slid my hand between her thighs. "I love it sweaty. This is mine. Mine." I bit her bottom lip.

"Oh shit, I don't know what's gotten into you, but I like it." She slid her panties off and I played with her, sticking my fingers in deep and rubbing her until she shouted with pleasure. Gentle moans escaped her. She said so slowly, so seductively, "Oooooooh, Jacques . . . you see how wet it is already?" Her voice sent chills down my back. She knew just how to talk to me. Then I put my finger in my mouth and licked it, smiling at her. "Oh, you are such a nasty birthday boy. I got something for you, though."

She dropped down to her knees and pulled my pants all the way down to my ankles. We were trying to make room in the cramped kitchen, so I shook off one foot of my jeans and brought her to the living room instead. She turned the tables on me and became the aggressor, pushing me against the wall. Then going down and sucking me the way I loved it. I yanked her long hair around my wrist and tugged it lightly. She loved it when I was rough with her. Vicky was reckless. Intense. The loud sucking noises and moans were intensified. I pulled her off for a second.

"Not yet. Come here." I led her back to the dining room, where we had chairs. I was fast, passionate, and impatient to enter her. I tugged on her shirt. "Take that off." It was open, teasing me. She had on nothing else, but I wanted to see it all. I kicked off my jeans completely, along with my boxers; by now our clothes made a scandalous trail to the dining room.

"Kneel." She turned her back to me and did as I commanded. She was kneeling on the soft dining room chair as I took her from the back and entered her. She surrendered with a long sigh as I dug into her walls with deep long thrusts. I saw flashes of Aanya and Sky. I thought about being able to actually go through with it. How would it have felt? Those two gorgeous women. Beautiful from head to toe. Massaging me, topless, letting me touch them, fuck them, do what I wanted with no drama, no strings. I looked at Vicky's round ass and pictured her there, too. All four of us. I pictured them fighting for me, which one would I enter next? I went deeper, harder, I felt her wetness. She was so warm. I was pulsating inside her, thrusting harder and harder.

Vicky's screams brought me back to the dining room. "*Papi, cojelo con el*, take it easy. . . . *Aye, que rico, asi* . . . yes, papi . . . *dame tu leche*, papi come for me. I wanna feel all of it."

She drove me wild when she talked like that. Her long hair was everywhere; I pulled it into a ponytail and yanked it. She grunted like a wild animal. "Grab my titties," she commanded. I followed instructions and hit all of the angles I knew her body craved. But I felt Sky's titties, I wanted to grab them. I got a small feel of Aanya's, but I wanted to suck them. Both of them I wanted. I remembered Sky standing over me, them hanging in my face. Shit! How could I have not gone through with it? I know . . . Karma. I grabbed onto Vicky's waist, rubbing the sweat down to her butt and thighs. My hands dug into her thighs as she thrusted back. We were connected, going at a steady groove. Vicky moaned and it vibrated throughout my body . . . caused an eruption. My legs vibrated. I felt it. "Oh shit. Oh my *God*. Ohhhh . . . I'm coooooooming. That was, that was . . ."

"Incredible," we said simultaneously. Panting. The joys of ecstasy. I collapsed on her and kissed her back. We were dripping with sweat. She could barely stand and just surrendered back to doggy-style position, dropping her head down. I was light-headed, but felt amazing. Accomplished. I slapped her on her fat ass and said, "I'm going to the shower, come let me wash you down."

She was panting heavily and smiling. "Wait, wait . . . I think I'm disabled. My ovaries have been rearranged." She laughed as she held her stomach.

"Oh yeah?" I rubbed my hands through her damp hair. "You seemed to like it. I didn't hear you complaining much." I rubbed her moist back. The room smelled of sex.

"Shut up." She had a smile plastered across her face. She turned around and sat down. I went to get us a glass of water. Suddenly the guilt of what had happened earlier was overwhelming. I might tell her what Hicham set up. Just not today.

I said, "Ready?" She took my hand and followed me to the shower.

I was lucky to have this woman. Even though a part of me wished I'd had the balls to go through with it, when Aanya and Sky gave me the chance. But somehow, I knew I would have regretted it later. And truth be told, if the tables were turned I would be devastated if Vicky did that to me. I couldn't do that ever again.

❋ ❋ ❋

After a thirty-minute nap Vicky jumped up frantically. "Oh shit. I have to go to the office. I forgot a folder I need in the morning. I have to be in court early and won't have time to get it."

"Okay, so go."

"But your party!?"

"We have time, baby, it's not even nine P.M. yet. Didn't you tell people ten o'clock?"

"Aye, that means I have to get dressed now or bring the clothes." She jumped in the bathroom and starting putting on her makeup and styling her hair. I watched her get ready for a while. I really adored her. I fell asleep with a smile on my face. I was delighted to get an hour more before my celebration.

❋ ❋ ❋

Later that night, though, I was racing through traffic, thirty minutes late to my own birthday party.

"Where are you?" Vicky asked. I could tell she was irritated, holding the phone close to her ear so no one else could hear her.

"I'm coming, I'm coming, babe. I'm sorry, I thought you set the alarm for me before you left. I fell asleep. I'm on my way!"

"Oh, blame me! Really? Just a few folks are here, please drive safe. I'll see you when you get here."

When I got to Sugarcane there was a crowd mingling in front. Reggae music was playing loudly. There was a sexy after-work crowd mingling by the bar outside. People were in line waiting to be seated. I couldn't make out any familiar faces. I was about to call Vicky again when Kylie grabbed my arm.

"Hey, you! Happy birthdaaaay!" Kylie hugged me and she smelled delicious. She had on a cute black dress and short jean jacket. All legs. I never really knew they were that long.

"Thank you! You look amazing." I had to remember to make eye contact.

"Thanks, I was just coming from the ladies' room. Follow me, we're right over here." She pointed to a seating area in the corner. She shook my shoulder as we walked. "Soooo, I met Hicham!"

"Oh boy, how'd that go?"

"He's interesting. Very confident, I must say." She walked slower to tell me more before we got to the group. "His pickup line was, 'What do I have to do to get you to be my emergency contact?'" She laughed. "I mean funny and yet, very stalker-ish. Let's just say he's been pretty persistent so far. He's a trip. He must have got that from the other side of the fam."

"Yes, he is a trip. So glad you made it, Kylie. The other guys coming?"

"Yes, Antonio for sure, Vince maybe. If he isn't stuck working, he said he would pass by. He's an older dude, not really into this life."

Vicky was watching us as we came closer and I got a weird vibe. The energy in the room was uncomfortable . . . tense. I couldn't put my finger on it.

"Hey, papi!" She reached up and hugged me extra hard. Very territorial, but I loved it. Her hair was up in a high bun and she had on a very low-cut cream jumpsuit that accentuated every curve of her body.

"What are you doing out here without me, in thiiiiis?" I brought her in, kissed her, and planted more on her neck. I grabbed her waist tight. She liked when I let everyone know she was mine. She laughed and I could see whatever jealousy she might have felt about me subsided. From the stares of the fellas by the bar, I could tell they weren't too happy with my arrival. We sat down at a booth for about six. It was going to be intimate because I didn't really want a lot of people. Vicky and Kylie continued talking about whatever girls talk about. They seemed to be getting along better than I'd hoped.

Hicham stood up. "Our waiter is taking too fucking long. Gonna go to the bar, whatchu drinking, Jay? I got you."

"Just some Hennessy, no ice."

Hicham said, "Say word? Okay, okaaaay, you trying to get fucked up tonight? It's about time!"

Vicky shot me a concerned look. "Papi, you know you don't drink like that!"

"I know, come on, I was just kidding. Okay, let me go with you over there so I can see what kind of wines they have."

I got up and started to walk over with him. Vicky looked toward the door to my left. Her face turned into a frown. I didn't understand why. I followed her eyes and there she was, just gliding into the room. It was Sky! She had on a sparkly silver tube top and short jean shorts. I mean short. Half of her cheeks were coming out. Her stomach was exposed, showing a belly ring with a hanging diamond on it. Big hoop earrings and bright pink lipstick. I gulped and I think my hands started shaking.

Everyone was turning their heads to get a peek, even the women. Sky's auburn and blond curls seemed to need a room of their own. They were definitely an attention grabber. We made eye contact.

"There you go, birthday boooooooy!" Her heels were clicking fast in my direction, then she reached in and gave me a long hug and kiss on the cheek, even though we'd just met this afternoon. I was hesitant to hug back.

Hicham seemed to stand in the way of Vicky's view and she was staring intensely. I felt her glare penetrating the back of my neck.

I tilted my head to the side and said, "Oh wow, you . . . ah . . . invited her? That was nice of you." I fake-smiled and Hicham knew I was going to kill him.

"Yeah, she was asking if you had a party and I figured she could meet some new people. I'm trying to help her get out there more with her modeling career and all." He winked at me.

Sky's accent was very slight, definitely not like earlier. "You left some things in the room." She started to go in her purse. I remembered it was my silver jewelry. I forgot I had taken it off before the massage!

"Oh, thank you." My heart was pounding, because Vicky had stood up and, leaving Kylie at the table, was walking briskly over to us. Before I knew it she was right behind us.

Hicham obnoxiously cleared his throat. It was so obvious something was off.

He chimed in, "Oh, oh, this is Sky. Meet Vicky, Jacques's girlfriend."

I attempted a charming smile and nodded. "Yes! Vicky, let's get something to drink." I was trying to get her away from Sky.

Vicky extended her hand into our circle, smiled, and said, "Nice to meet you, Sky. Nice name. Are you in entertainment?"

"Oh, yes. I model, dance . . . I also have a private massage practice. And you are a verrrrry lucky woman." She looked at me with her pink glossy lips puckered up playfully. Was this woman trying to set me up? She really needed to take up acting, since she was speaking like a college graduate now and not someone who'd just come to America last week.

"I'm lucky, huh?" Vicky's eyes narrowed. Her eyes hissed at Hicham and me suspiciously. Sweat formed on my brow. I wanted to separate those two immediately. I started to put my arm around Vicky to walk her to the bar. Vicky grabbed my face and with her thumb quickly wiped off Sky's lipstick from my cheek—a little rougher than necessary.

"Wait! Your jewelry." Sky handed my ring and chain to me. "Where's the bathroom?" I pointed quickly so she would hurry and leave. Vicky looked into my hand and then looked

Sky up and down as she glided to the bathroom. Everyone watched with a smile. She had a tiny waist and her voluptuous butt cheeks were spilling from her shorts. Vicky was not amused.

"Why does she have your jewelry, Jacques? What the fuck is going on?"

My throat tightened. This wasn't going to be good. "Weeeell, um, Hicham sort of surprised me earlier. She's a massage therapist and she gave me a—"

"Wait, really . . . a massage therapist? That's the best you got? She looks like a fucking escort-service ho off of Craigslist. We bust chicks like this every week. No, maybe she's a dancer-stripper ho with a name like Sky . . . and she has your fucking jewelry? Really, Jacques? Really? And earlier when? When you went to see Hicham?" She wasn't coming up for air or letting me get a word in.

"Relax, she was professional." I couldn't even look her in the eyes when I said it.

"Oh, professional?" She pointed to the bar with authority. "Go get your drink, Jacques." She walked off back to the booth, fuming.

Hicham stood there smiling with a goofy look on his face. I went off. "What the hell is wrong with you? Why would you invite her?" I pointed my hand in the direction of the bathroom. "You trying to get me killed tonight . . . on my damn birthday?" I was furious.

"Yo, Vicky is a baaaad bitch. You see what she got on, son? You got both of them feeling you like that? You should be happy, man!"

"Fool, this is not high school. I gotta *live* with this woman. Then this ditzy girl is going to bring my jewelry and give it to me in *front* of Vicky. Is she trying to get me back for rejecting her?"

"Nah, she's just not thinking. She's a little slow and truth be told, I had to hit that. She was soooo horny after you left, so I had to handle that. She got some gooooood pussy, Jay. You stupid. She will do anything, I mean anything. She is trying to get a deal at a modeling agency. One of my boys is an agent and I'm connecting her." He slapped me on the back. "She deserves it. . . . I'm just sa—"

Cutting him off, I said, "Selling these young girls dreams." I shook my head. "How many other photographers, video directors, and agents you think she has done? She's a user, Hicham."

"Use me, baby, use me!" He did a little playful shimmy. "Yo, don't be mad you just missed out." He slapped my shoulder and leaned on it. We stood by the bar and he reached his other hand out. "Yo . . . homie. We need some drinks over here." He turned to me. "I think she really likes you, though. She wants to feel up on that body again." I felt a tap on my shoulder. I looked behind me. It was Vicky.

She said low in my ear, "Oh really, she wants to feel that booooody again? What the fuck is going on, Jacques? Did you fuck this bitch or what? Did you do it right before you fucked me today? Why would you invite her to a party I planned? Why would you disrespect me like that?"

Hicham tried to save me by saying, "Yo, chill, Vicky, I invited her, I invited her! Relaaaax, ma. She's just a massage therapist. Nothing to get all emotional about and shit."

Vicky's eyes narrowed and I could tell she had been drinking before I got there. "Oooooh, emotional and shit? Hicham, you are nothing but a fucking troublemaker! You know he has a girl, why would you get him a massage with a . . . You know what? You know what?" She waved him off like he was a waste of her time.

"Vicky, calm down and lower your voice. Please!" I grabbed her arm and pulled slightly.

She just shook my hand off her and started to walk out of the restaurant. I knew Vicky had a jealous streak, but I'd never seen her react like this before! Granted, I'd never given her a reason to until now. She left and I followed behind her. All eyes were on us. I was extremely embarrassed—and I hadn't even cheated! If Vicky only knew just how much I avoided today. If she only knew how much I could have done! Now I was being punished for it!

"Go to your little party with all of your bitches, Jacques!"

I lightly jogged behind her, trying to explain. Her stilettos slammed into the ground with each forceful step. "Listen to me. Stop walking and listen to me!" Passersby stopped in their tracks. She turned around and finally stopped. "How many, Jacques?" She stared up at the sky and a tear rolled down her cheek.

"There hasn't been anyone but you, Vicky, stop this nonsense." I grabbed her hands. She snatched them away. "Come on, Vic, it was a massage. That's it, a fucking massage. I didn't do anything, I promise you. As a matter of fact, I left early and came home."

"Oh, is that why you were so fucking worked up today? That's why you fucked the shit out of me today?"

I felt like I was being attacked for doing the right thing. "Well, yes, you said the key words, Vicky. Fucked you." I lowered my voice and said, "I fucked you. No one else. *You*. I didn't disrespect you. I didn't cross the line. It was just a massage. I came home to *you*!" I grabbed her hand. "Come on back to the party. Stop acting like this. You're better than this. This isn't you, Vicky. You had too much to drink, baby. Come on."

It was like what I said meant nothing. "Don't 'baby' me. And oh, I'm better than this? Am I better than Kylie? Am I better than Dee?" My stomach churned. My heart sank. I was paralyzed. I felt sick and slightly dizzy.

She went into her purse. "Here's your phone, Jacques." I extended my hand and took the phone from her. "I figured you might be looking for it. You left it on the table. Dumb move. Dumb fuckin' move! Your hoes left you some reaaaally nice messages." Her nostrils flared. "You gonna fuck that *sucia* and then come home to me with a dirty dick on top of that? Then you gonna have this bitch Kylie in our *house*, smiling up in my motherfucking face like it's all good when I knew she wanted you. I KNEW IT! When you get home I won't be there. Trust me on that one!" Vicky's voice was cracking like she was about to cry. "I'm out. DO. NOT. FOLLOW ME!"

She kept walking fast and I followed. "I can explain. Stop it. I love you!" I yelled like a lunatic. I couldn't even believe myself. Everything was crumbling so fast.

"Stop following me!" Her pace was slower, but still hard.

She was crying and talking, and it was tearing me up to see her in pain. "I don't love *you*. I love that other guy you pretended to be. Fuck *you*, Jacques! I'm not going to be taken for a fool. Fuck that!" She pointed her finger at me to stop. I stopped in my tracks and stood there. I made sure she got in her car safely and then turned back in defeat.

Nausea took me over. I opened my phone to see what she had seen.

DEE: Hey, handsome. Happy birthday in advance! I wanted to come to town and escape this cold. I hope you have a good one.

JACQUES: Thanks, Dee. I really appreciate it.

DEE: I would have loved to see you and finish what we started. I can't stop thinking about that night. You are so fucking passionate.

Fuck. My knees weakened as I remembered the conversation. I'd forgotten to delete it.

JACQUES: Yeah, but you know. That was something that shouldn't have happened. It was nice, but it shouldn't have happened.

DEE: Well, when you are ready for me. Just know, I am soooo ready for you. I've wanted you for a long time.

I never replied. But that was enough for Vicky, I'm sure. No denying that. I couldn't get out of that one. Then I scrolled to see what she was talking about with Kylie. It was a text she sent earlier that I hadn't even seen yet.

KYLIE: Hey you . . . here's that special dedication for you! Youtube.com/dweleloveyouvideo

I clicked the link and it was for the song "I Think I Love You" by Dwele. I slapped my head. Are you kidding me? I'm going down for *this*, too? This was for Vicky, a song I was going to play for *her*!

I was so embarrassed. Everyone had watched us having a shouting match. I hate people in my business. Now I look like the asshole boyfriend to everyone and I can't claim to be 100 percent innocent, since I'd never disclosed the whole Dee encounter. I'm sure if I had told Vicky about that, she would have left then, too. I really didn't even want to go back inside, but I knew I had to. Following Vicky now wouldn't be good. She was emotional and I knew whatever I said would just sound like a lie. Those damn text messages! Vicky wasn't the kind to break or burn up my stuff. She's a cop, she's not that stupid. I figured she would probably go over to one of her girlfriend's houses for the weekend and then cool down. That's what I hoped for, at least.

I went back into Sugarcane and everyone was listening intently to Hicham telling a story, as if nothing happened.

"Hey, I just wanted to thank you guys for coming and

sorry for all the drama, just a little misunderstanding. I think I'm gonna go. I just want to go home."

Hicham raised his hands in the air. "Come on, man. It's your birthday! Don't ruin it. Vicky will cool down. You know how Latina women are, all melodramatic and shit!"

"Watch it!" Sky shouted with a smile. I swear she seemed almost thrilled Vicky was gone.

I heard a deep scratchy voice from behind me. "Ayoooo. Happy birthday, Mr. Cleo!" I turned around; it was Antonio. He gave me a pound and slap on the back. I had to laugh. He shook hands with everyone and hugged Kylie. I sat down next to her.

I slouched in my seat, holding my head. I couldn't believe what had just happened. I hoped Vicky would at least wait until I got home to talk. I decided to stay and not destroy everyone's night. We all ordered food and I tried to enjoy myself and not think about how I would get myself out of the doghouse. This was the worst birthday I'd ever had in my life.

Everyone was eating their appetizers and chatting. Antonio seemed fascinated by Sky's modeling career and she continually groped his biceps as she laughed. Hicham was a bit jealous and decided to flirt with Kylie. Kylie would try to include me in the conversation to have a buffer from Hicham's intense stare.

Hicham said, "You good, Jay?"

"It's all your fault, you know? Vicky was in my phone, too! Why'd you—" I caught Sky staring at me. "Let's move for a minute." I grabbed his arm to walk away from the table.

"How is it *my* fault? You are the one with bitches calling you."

"First off, they're not bitches, they're friends and clients. Second of all, it was a pure misunderstanding. Vicky never goes in my stuff! Kylie sent me a song that I was going to play for Vicky. She took it as if it were a love song Kylie was sending to me. The other text was from a client who flirts with me all of the time." I left out the details, since when Hicham drinks he tells your business. "My point is, if you thought with your brain and not your dick you would have known it wasn't a smart move to invite Sky. Vicky trusts me, she never went through my phone before tonight."

"Yo, Jay, if you really think tonight was the first time she went through your phone, you trippin'—annnnnd she's a cop? Niggah, please. She probably got a GPS tracker on your ride." He put both hands on my shoulders as if he were my mentor. "Player rule number one, never eva evaaaa leave your phone around your girl. Rule number two, always have a password to lock yo' shit."

"I'm not a player, I have nothing to hide."

"Apparently you did!" Hicham laughed. "Yo, let's get back to your party. Let her cool off before she fuck around and put a boot on your car."

We walked back to the table, but he grabbed my arm and said in my ear, "Why you ain't tell me Kylie was that fine, yo? You know I got a thing for them natural sisters."

"Stay in your lane, little bro. Not Kylie."

"You hit that? She smells like she puts juices and berries in her 'fro. . . . She looks so sexy."

"Come on, no! She's a friend, so noooo. Don't even try it." I knew Kylie already wasn't into him, so thank God for that.

The party ended up not being as horrible as I anticipated. I still tried to make contact with Vicky and got sent to voice mail twice. Sky and Antonio ended up leaving together and that was no surprise. A few more friends and clients popped in during the night and it was really good to see everyone. Sugarcane closed by two A.M. and we all went to another lounge on the same strip that had really good live jazz. By five A.M. the kitchen was closed and we were all starving. I really didn't want to go home and I think Kylie and Hicham sensed it. I also knew Hicham was trying to keep her around for as long as he could. So home was not the next stop.

We were starting to walk to our cars when Hicham said, "Yo, let's go to IHOP! You wanna roll with us, Kylie?"

"I don't know. I don't like eating this late." Her lipstick was worn off and her eyes looked tired.

Hicham's energy was high, as if he'd just woken up. "It's not late, it's morning. The sun is about to come up. Let's go! Jacques? You down?"

I yawned. "Well, I think I deserve some pancakes with a lot of syrup on my birthday." I rubbed my abs.

"Yeah, it's not like you will get fat with that six-pack." Kylie rolled her eyes. "You men lose weight in like two days."

❀ ❀ ❀

When we got to IHOP, we were lucky there was no wait and we were seated immediately in a small booth. Kylie slid in first next to me and Hicham sat across from her. Our food arrived quickly and we all were eating like we were starving.

I had a few bites of my blueberry pancakes and the wine started to wear off. Then it hit me. Hicham still didn't know what we found out about Mom.

"Hicham, I didn't get a chance to tell you earlier, you are not going to believe this, but I found some of Mom's journals and what was in them was so not good."

He took a sip of his coffee. "What? Get out of here, what was in them? I want to see them!"

"I had some of them in the car earlier, before I was ambushed by your massage team."

"What?" Kylie laughed, confused.

I tapped her hand. "I'll tell you later. Anyhow, she had all kinds of stuff in there about how sad she was, how Dad treated her bad. How she couldn't stand the sight of him. It was pretty hurtful stuff."

Kylie chimed in. "How she fell in love with him but then was in love with Benny."

"Wait, hold up, hold up! Did *you* see them?" He looked at Kylie, then back at me as if he were watching a tennis match.

"Oh, yeah . . . she was helping me go through them. It was a lot to go through, before you got to Miami." He folded his arms, listening intently. His jaw tightened and a vein popped out from his forehead. "Well, she had articles on poisons that were undetectable. She was highlighting the symptoms of antifreeze poisoning."

Hicham leaned back dramatically. "What! What the fuck kinda evil shit is that?"

"It was disturbing to know she really planned it. I mean,

she was really researching. I'm convinced she did it alone. But you think Benny could have heard her maybe talk about it? I don't think Benny did it. You?"

"Man, I wouldn't put it past anyone. We would never think Mom could pull off something as planned out as that. Don't sleep on anyone!" Hicham barked.

Kylie said, "Yes, he might remember something. Ask him."

Hicham said, "It's almost seven A.M., he's up. Let's call him right now."

"So early?"

"He told me he gets up at five A.M. to jog. He's up, man." Hicham threw a crumpled-up napkin onto his empty plate.

I shook my head and put my fork down after my last bite. "I don't want to do it in here. Everyone can hear. And you know you're too loud." I waved him to follow me outside. "We'll be right back, Kylie." She nodded and went back to enjoying the rest of her omelet.

We went around the back of IHOP, where it was quiet.

"Yo, even Kylie saw it before me? Really, Jay?"

"Come on, don't start, it wasn't intentional. Remember, she is a detective in training and a fast reader. She has a good eye for things. She's been helping us thus far. I brought them today, but you never gave me a chance to tell you."

Hicham hit the speed dial and I was surprised to see he had Benny in his phone as "Da NEW Pops." Benny answered the phone on the first ring, a bit shocked I guess to get a call at 6:45 A.M.

"Hey, Benny, it's Jacques and Hicham, sorry to call so early," I said on speaker phone.

"Oh helloooo there, is everything okay?" The TV was going in the background pretty loud. He sounded wide awake.

"Oh well, yes and no. We got some heavy news about Mom and were wondering if you had any insight on it."

He cleared his throat. "Oh sure, what is it? How can I help?"

"We found some of her journals. She had a storage unit, did you know about it?"

"No, no, I didn't. What journals?" He was intrigued.

"Well, in the journals she paints the picture of being madly in love with you and hating my father, but the most startling thing is that we found an article on poisoning and she had antifreeze highlighted like crazy."

"Come again? Did you say antifreeze?"

Hicham said, "Yeah, did Mom ever talk about getting rid of our dad, well I mean . . . Olivier?"

I corrected Hicham. "He's still your dad, too. You can have two."

"Well, not in a serious way. Antifreeze is making me wonder now. Wow." Benny released a deep breath. "I used to tell Marguerite about some of the inmates I knew at Rikers and she would grill me for details. She loved hearing about how they got arrested.

"But this one particular case, I'll never forget it. He was a heavyweight amateur boxer who was mentally disturbed, had six women and ten children. He was only thirty. He wanted out of all the responsibility. He was being weighed down with child support and lost a lot for not paying.

"He slowly started to poison the kids one household at a

time. Everyone got extremely sick within a few weeks. He said he put it in their juice. He ended up poisoning and killing seven out of the ten children. One of the children actually saw him putting something in their drinks and that is how he got caught. He ended up going to a maximum-security prison, where he eventually was murdered by an inmate." He paused as if trying to remember.

"Dear Lord. Marguerite was obsessed with that story, and I remember she even joked around about getting rid of Olivier that way. I just thought she was joking. I could never imagine her doing that! I mean, she would have had to really plan that out."

"Well, that's the thing. Looks like she did, Benny." I looked at Hicham, whose face was blank from shock.

"It's just so unbelievable. I know she loved me, but to kill Olivier? She was a good Catholic woman. Why?"

There was an awkward silence and Benny sniffled as if he were trying to pull himself together. It was a lot to take in.

Benny said, "Truth be told, I do feel Marguerite suffered from some type of depression and she drank a lot at times. When she wasn't submerged in her art . . . Marguerite was angry and she could be dark. She did say how Olivier would hold her captive, was very controlling, and things of that nature. I'm not justifying what she did in any way. But I know he was abusive to her in some ways."

"Shit, he probably knew she was doing something. She hid all her life from us, so I don't know why y'all are so shocked. She didn't care about anyone but herself!" Hicham yelled, then took a deep breath. "I got my confirmation, Jay. Benny, we good. Thanks for that."

"I'm so, so sorry." Benny sighed.

I said, "Don't be sorry, if she didn't get it from you, she could have gotten it from anywhere. She seemed pretty determined to be rid of my dad. Sad that we can't hear her side. Well, let's talk some more tomorrow."

"Cool. Let's do that." Hicham hung up and put his arm around me. "Come on, Jay, we got a birthday to celebrate and need to forget about how fucked up our family is!" He put his arm around me and we walked back into IHOP.

❄ ❄ ❄

I got home around nine A.M. to a half-empty closet. I was convinced Vicky was never going to talk to me. I'd texted and called her more than ten times since the fight. She must have blocked me. My heart hurt but I tried to push the mess with Vicky aside in my mind so I could focus on gaining some clarity today with Melissa. I needed to feel my mom's presence. I needed to know that she was okay.

After only a few hours of sleep, I pulled myself together and headed out the door for my appointment. Melissa lived with her girlfriend in North Miami Beach. Her home was very welcoming. A beautiful cottage-style house in a very quaint area on the water. Gated community. Serene. Surrounded by trees for privacy. Bright white and pale yellow walls. High ceilings and huge windows. We'd been friends for years and she was one of the first to really welcome me to Florida's holistic community with open arms. We met at a Reiki circle meditation and became fast friends from there. She showed me the ropes and introduced me to many workshops and local groups. She also told me who the weirdos were and how to stay clear of them.

Melissa was one of the most powerful mediums I'd met and she was only twenty-six. We bartered at least once a month and did little check-ins for each other. Truth be told, even psychics like to get readings. Even when you see the future for others so accurately, it can sometimes be difficult to see things for yourself with the same certainty. My intuition is clearer than most, but I like to get a reading from time to time to get confirmation.

We vibe off each other, because like me, Melissa was a very old soul. She carried herself as an experienced shaman, African priestess, Native American healer, and cool around-the-way Miami girl all wrapped into one.

Because she had narrow eyes that sparkled, defined cheekbones, and straight dark hair, I'd given her the nickname Pocahontas. Although she was 100 percent Cuban American with a little hood in her, she could totally pull it off as a Native American. In one of the readings I did for her last year, she was a Native American chief who saved his village from smallpox brought by the white man, I would say to her, "It's your past life fighting to come back!" In that lifetime she was the medicine man of the village as well and helped heal the tribe. It was no coincidence that in this life, along with doing mind-blowing readings, she also did hands-on healing work and developed her own herbal healing teas.

Melissa was one of the friendliest people I knew, but was a homebody for the most part. Most psychics I knew were. Limiting exposure to all the crazy energy out there helps us keep our sanity. We tend to form close-knit circles for that reason.

"Well, hello, Mr. Berradi! So nice to see you, my friend!"

"And a good day to you, Ms. Vasquez!" I bowed graciously and kissed her hand. She laughed and took me in for a big bear hug.

Standing at five nine, she was very elegant today. Normally in yoga gear, Melissa was dressed in a lavishly beaded purple-and-gold Indian tunic, wearing no shoes and adorned with lots of gold bangles. She was a beautiful full-figured woman and her magnetic energy drew people wherever she went.

"You look good, birthday boy!" She grabbed my chin gently. "I like this five o'clock shadow thing. Looks rugged. Makes you look like a thug."

"Me—a thug? Never! This is just pure neglect. Been a rough, loooong night. Haven't bothered to shave. We'll get into it, I'm sure. I'll save it for the reading."

"We will figure it out, Jacques, don't you worry. Come." She waved me to follow her. We passed a long hallway full of books on everything from healing, natural herbs, acupuncture, and reflexology to astrology, tarot cards, and pretty much anything metaphysical. Her library was top-notch and I felt like I could hang out in her home for hours.

Melissa led me to her den, which doubled as her spa room. It was where she did healings and readings. I walked closely behind her down the long hall.

"So, we're talking to your mom today?"

"Yes, and I had some other things happen. Vicky left me last night." I sulked.

She stopped in her tracks. "What? On your birthday? Why?"

"There was a misunderstanding. I feel like shit."

"Oh no. Well, we'll figure it out in the reading, but we'll do your mom first, right?"

"Yes, definitely."

There were a few floor pillows in the corner and she motioned for me to sit. Melissa lit a few white candles and closed the curtains even though there was no one in the house with us. She burned some palo santo, which I loved the smell of. Palo santo is a tree that grows on the coast of South America and is related to frankincense, myrrh, and copal. In Spanish, the name literally means "holy wood." It clears the energy of a space, similar to the way sage does. On the floor in between us, she put a few crystals down in the shape of three circles, two circles inside one big one—what some might call a crystal grid. Melissa then closed her eyes for a moment, setting her intentions. She crossed her legs and lifted her palms to the sky, took in a deep breath, and then was quiet. Her preparation was a bit more elaborate than what I do, but whatever rituals she performs before her sessions she gets from her guides. She hadn't steered me wrong yet.

Melissa opened one eye as she was getting deeper in grounding herself and said softly, "Do you want to record it?"

"Yes, actually, that's a great idea." I took my phone out and got it ready.

She closed her eyes again. "What's your mom's name again?"

"Marguerite Berradi."

I suddenly felt a strong sensation on the back of my neck, like someone had just walked by me.

"She's here," Melissa said, her eyes still closed. "She's right behind you." I looked, and although I couldn't see her I felt a presence. It felt cold.

"Mom, where are you?" I was worried.

Melissa answered in a serious flat tone, "She said she's in a river. She's lost and keeps wandering around. She's been in and out of the house. But then she ends up in the water. She doesn't understand what's going on. She's very confused. I don't think she even knows she's dead."

I asked, "Why are you wandering around? Go to the light, Mom."

Melissa was speaking for her. "Your father is there, I can't face him! I can't go there, they won't let me in. Do you know what I did? I don't deserve the light of God. I've sinned. For years, I sinned."

Melissa spoke as herself. "Slow down. Oh shit, she is talking so fast. I'm trying to catch it all. She's panicking. She is happy to see you and glad you can hear her because she feels so alone. She keeps talking about what she did. Hold up, What *did* you do, Marguerite?" Melissa was quiet for a minute. "No, no, where are you going?" She slapped her thighs. "Dammit! She is walking away from me. It's dark wherever she is. Water is flowing everywhere. It's so dark." I started to fear that Melissa was going to lose her.

"What did you do, Mom?" I pleaded, looking at Melissa.

I wanted her to say it already. I hadn't told Melissa about the journals or the poisoning, because I wanted to make sure she would be 100 percent objective.

Melissa was channeling my mother even stronger now and her eyes were open as she stared blankly at the crystals. She said slowly, in a sad voice, "I did the best I could as a mother. I couldn't love him anymore. I couldn't love him for who he became. You were right. All those years, my sweet baby. You were right. Your father saw your gift. I shunned it. But I can't face him now, not ever. I have sinned. I was so selfish."

Melissa came back as herself and sounded alarmed. "Wait, hold up, did you . . . Oh man, did she murder him? I can feel it. The fear and guilt in her soul is unbearable." She grabbed her stomach. "I feel it in the pit of my stomach. She won't say it, but I feel it. I can't see how. Not with her own hands, I'm feeling. Whatever she did, it wasn't direct. She looks wet, soaked, from her shoulders down, she is so depressed. She is surrounded by shadows," she said sadly. "My guides are saying it's her hell. She made her own hell!" The hairs rose on my arms. I watched in disbelief, but I knew Melissa was on the money. I felt the same thing. The irony was that Mom was in dark, cold water, not the fire that her church envisioned.

"She poisoned him," I said. "Then he drowned in the bathtub. He must have passed out and slipped under the water. I think that is why she is in water. I saw her almost drowning in my nightmare I told you about."

Melissa agreed. "She definitely manufactured her own hell. I've seen this a few times. It's terrible how people punish themselves."

"My dad always came in visions, saying he forgave her. Even when I was a little boy. I don't know why she doesn't remember that. I would always tell her that and get slapped."

"That's a good idea. Let's call on your dad. Maybe he can coax her into the light, you think?"

I was hesitant. "Well, his name is Olivier. Olivier Berradi. Not sure if he will help. He said he forgave her, but he also was pointing the finger at her. Like he wanted me to get answers, closure." I was excited to see what Melissa would pick up about my father. I really missed him.

"We won't know until we try. Let's give it a shot!" She held my hands and said, "Say his name with me three times." We did it together and as I closed my eyes, I felt a jolt go through me. I heard a large mechanical sound, like a big machine turning on and off. *Boom! Boom!* It was coming from behind the house.

"Whoaaaaa, Nelly! He's a fucking powerful dude. That was my generator! The electricity just shut off and on for a minute. That doesn't happen every day. Only when I read really high-level folk."

"Wow, that's what that sound was?"

"Yep! Ohhh, he's really proud of you. Really, really proud. He's clapping. He was trying to get our attention! What a show-off." She laughed.

I heard in my ear, "That's my son!" It was as if he were right next to me. I started to smile and goose bumps formed on my scalp and all the way down my arms and legs.

"He is happy you stayed on your purpose, you are constantly rising. Everything you touch will turn to gold, he says."

I felt overwhelmed with love. I could actually feel the love in the room. I got warm all over. I began to well up and just couldn't hold it in any longer. "I miss you so much, Dad. I miss you sooooo much! Thank you for always talking to me, for believing in me, for loving me so much to show me the truth. Don't ever stop, please don't ever stop talking to me." Melissa handed me a box of tissues. "Mom is gone, please help her. I know what she did to you; you didn't deserve it," I cried.

Melissa spoke for him: "Son, it was a part of my process. I had to play a part in your mother's growth. She played a part in mine. We are souls that are always growing. Do not worry about your mother. She is going through her process." Melissa grabbed my hand and spoke as herself again. "Come 'in' with me, see if you see anything. Your mom is closer now, but her back is to me, she is terrified of your father. She doesn't want to face him."

"We have to send her to the light. Dad, please take Mom with you," I begged.

Melissa repeated, "Can you take her to the light, Olivier?" She smiled and got a tissue for herself. "He said yes and reached out his hand. She is walking toward him reluctantly."

"Mom, go with him," I pleaded. I held on to Melissa's hand, with my eyes closed, and the strangest thing happened. I started to see what she was seeing. It was like we were watching a movie together with our eyes closed. Our energies meshed together and it was as if I were in her mind. I saw a dark watery tunnel and my mom was at the end of it with her back to us. Then I saw a big bright light in the distance. It was blinding, yet beautiful. It was filled with yellows, greens, and blues; it was almost like looking through a kaleidoscope. I saw my mom walking toward the light and a hand reaching out. I couldn't see my father's face clearly, but his spirit was tall and strong like I remembered him.

Melissa said softly, encouragingly, "Keep going, Marguerite, come on. . . . You will be fine." She sounded like she was cheering on an infant who was taking her first steps. "Everyone loves you there, you are forgiven. You are safe. You will still have work to do, but you will be safe. You will be warm, out of that water." She grabbed my hand. "Can you see it, she's walking faster, she's innnn, she's innn, she's crossed over!"

We both sighed with relief. I said, "My guides just said to me that they won't be together for a while."

Melissa agreed. "Yes, she is on a lower level of spiritual development than him. The universal 'law of progress' ensures that, at some time in the future, those with lower vibrations will eventually graduate to the higher spheres. He's way up there on another plane. He's amazing, your dad. Very high-level being. I mean, if he's turning off electricity and shit! But she, on the other hand, has a lot of fear and guilt to work through."

"You are amazing. I mean *amazing*. I can't believe I saw what you saw when we held hands." I wiped my eyes, trying to pull myself together.

"Yes, I am surprised we never did that before. I do it all the time with other seers. It's pretty wild, huh? I once had a medium buddy whose baby brother died of a drug overdose twenty years ago. He was also a drug dealer and did a lot of bad things. Fighting, stealing, you name it. When I tried to cross him over, he was still in the hospital—in his mind! He was pissed off, too, like 'What the fuck, you are just asking about me now? No one has come to visit me all this time. All this time!' He was losing it and had no clue he was dead."

"Wow, that is insane," I said.

"Yeah, we finally crossed him over, but first we had to convince him that he was not in the hospital anymore."

I said, "I had one who was drugged up, but someone did it to her. It was like poison, too, but not sure what it was. It was pretty sad. It was a client's grandmother. She had been dead for more than thirty years and the story was that she was the town get-around-girl and a drunk. They claimed she wandered off to the beach drunk and drowned. The wild part is the client didn't tell me that until *after* I spoke to her dead grandma.

"First thing she said to me was, 'I was kidnapped, raped, and left to die. I was dragged here.' It was one of the most chilling readings I ever did. It was so sad. She led a dark life, too, so was on a lower level, but she was surprisingly crossed over. They never did find out who killed her, but it was at least confirmation that it wasn't her fault."

"Man, we need to work for the cops, Jacques!"

"Well, so funny that you say that. I am now very good friends with some private investigators. Some folks at the detective agency down the hall from my office. It's called Like a Fly on the Wall. They hinted they might need me in the near future. If it's some high-level medium stuff out of my scope you know I'll call on you to help out."

She said, "I'd love it! Anytime, Jacques! You know I love catching the bad guys! Shit, you know I'm still in the zone, let's stop chatting and finish. Vicky . . . let's get her next."

"Yeah, please tell me what to do! I fucked up. I won't lie. I didn't go all the way, but something happened."

"Something, what, you kissed someone?"

"Weeeeell, a little more than kissing."

"Oh God, what?"

I shrugged my shoulders and pointed to my crotch. "It's a client, too."

"No! What, she slobbed the nob?"

I wrinkled my nose. "Come on, why did you have to put it like that? A nob is an insult."

Melissa laughed. "Sorry, they just showed me. I didn't want to see it, but they showed me. You in a dark closet."

"Well, close . . . it was in the bathroom, during the black-out. I had a weak moment. I stopped it before it got worse. Well, the lights came on, to be exact. We were really saved by the lights." A guilty grin came across my face from that heart-stopping memory.

Melissa took a deep breath and began staring at her crystal grid. "Shit . . . Vicky is hurting. She is a wreck. She doesn't know what to believe now. You're gonna have to give her a minute. You can try to explain, but she won't listen. Why not write her an email and she can read it when she is ready? Explain everything and don't lie."

"Even about the bathroom incident?" I cringed at the thought. She'd never trust me with a client again.

"Well, yeah . . . but you don't have to give details, just say maybe a client crossed the line, and you are sorry but it didn't go further. Again, now is not the time to push her. In a month or two she will be missing you and will forgive you."

"A month or two? I didn't realize how much I loved her until this shit." I didn't want to wait that long to see her again.

"Well, Jacques, maybe it's time for that next step. If she is willing to work it out."

"You mean marriage?"

"Yep. There is a beautiful light around the two of you, just not fully ready to bloom. Give it time."

I felt hope and knew instantly what she meant. The light was a feeling of protection, a feeling of unconditional love.

"Okay, well, that's good news. Glad you don't see her rolling up on any of us with a gun."

"No, you know better than to pick crazy chicks like that," Melissa reassured me. "Your brother—I know you didn't ask about him, but he keeps coming up in my head. They are showing me his spirit. But it's crazy, it's like two people inside of him. Like he's fighting against himself. He's very angry. I almost hear a . . . a . . ."

"Hear a what?" I egged her on.

"A growl. Like he's possessed with something. A dark energy."

"Well, there's a few things going on with him. He just found out that my dad is not his dad. That he's all white and not part African—hence the two personalities. Not to mention his bad temper, and I think he has a problem with drugs and alcohol. He tends to go from high to low, almost bipolar, but he hasn't been diagnosed or anything. He's actually part of the reason Vicky found out about my mistakes. It's a whole long story, but he set me up for my birthday to get damn near raped."

"Raped?" She looked concerned.

"No, no, I am exaggerating. It was a massage, with these two beautiful girls."

"Wait, two girls? Wow, that's a nice birthday gift. I'm gonna have to have my girl get me that."

"I actually left midway through the whole 'massage.' It got a bit risqué, then one of the girls showed up at my birthday party because Hicham invited her and she was flirting hard with me . . . with Vicky standing right there. She knew I had a girl. Later, my brother was teasing me about her liking me. Vicky heard the tail end of the story and also went through my phone and found all the other stuff. It was a disaster!"

"No, not your phone! That's just disrespectful. Why do women keep doing that? I keep telling my clients, keep digging and you *will* find something." Melissa shook her head.

"Your brother is trouble. Seems like he doesn't even know it."

"Are you still picking him up?"

"Yes, something is definitely off."

I said, "I will bring him to you if I can, before he leaves town for New York. Maybe you can clear out his aura."

"Yes, he might need that. He could have some spirit hanging around, like a walk-in spirit, if he isn't bipolar, that is. You know how it is if you are checked out with drugs or alcohol, spirits feel like they can hang out in your body. They cling to you like Velcro. I've been working on a lot of vets who come back with PTSD. Many of them have had a walk-in. It's like nobody is home, when you look in their eyes."

"Oh, I've had the talk with him about the dangers of being on drugs and also being around the low-vibration folks he hangs around. He just thinks it's all superstitious bullshit and too 'woo-woo' for him. I'll try to sage him down when he's asleep. Maybe on his last night you can have dinner with us?"

"I wish. My girlfriend comes back from Guatemala tonight. She was seeing her family. I gotta get some things together and cook. Keep it a happy home."

"Okay, well, that's important. Don't do anything stupid like me. You know what's so sad?"

"What?"

"That you are probably the only female friend Vicky is never jealous of. She used to say, 'Oh good, she's a lesbian, she won't want *my* penis.'"

"Oh now, that's *funny*! Well, Jacques, I'll be at your office next week, same time we usually do? Friday at one P.M.?"

"Yes, I got you booked."

"I hope you enjoy the rest of your birthday week. Oh, one minute. I got a gift for you!"

She went to a bookshelf and got a blue gift bag and handed it to me with a smile. Inside a gold mesh drawstring bag was a medallion with a black tourmaline crystal wrapped in silver with a silver chain. "Wow, this is very, very nice. How did you know? I've been thinking about getting something like this!"

"Oh, I don't know. Some of my friends say I'm kinda psychic." Melissa laughed and hugged me.

"Oh, Melly, you didn't have tooooo."

"You need it, brother, it's for protecting and grounding."

Friendship like this was for a lifetime.

"You are about to do big things, Jacques. This is your power year. . . . Your guides are still here in full force. They want you to know that a lot of new avenues will unfold for you, so be open. More clients, more connections, and you will take a few risks. You have to prepare now so you don't get too overwhelmed. You will even get an assistant or intern."

"Yes, I'm so behind in emails and voice mails. It's not good."

"Okay, I'll text you some contact info. I have a virtual assistant who is amazing and affordable."

"Yes, I definitely need her. Thanks."

She paused, grabbed my hands, and looked into my eyes. "This is the good part of the movie, Jacques!"

"What? What do you mean?" I sat up straighter and leaned in.

"In your life, this is the good part of the movie!" She was smiling and squeezed my hands hard. "I'm so very happy for you. Don't let this relationship drama or family stuff take you out of focus. You've gotten some closure today, so now keep moving up. Your guides are extremely proud of you. The room is filled. You have no idea how much support you have."

I closed my eyes and took a deep breath. "I usually feel about three to five around me."

"Oh, no!" She laughed a hearty laugh. "Dude! You have no idea. There are a lot of people in here. It's packed. Fifty or more! Feel my hands, they are vibrating from the energy."

I felt them and it was catching. I felt the hairs on my arms rise. "I've never wanted to see them with my eyes open, so I guess that is why it's always been hard for me to get the number right."

She agreed. "They said, 'Yes, we understand, that's why we make it easier for you to condense down all of our voices into one or two messengers.' It's like you have a leader of the pack, of your council. Her name is wait, . . . Ena? Eddie? Ernie for Ernestine maybe? Erna?"

I leaned in more, overjoyed that she knew. "Yes, close. It's Edna! Wow! That's her. She has been my guide for years. She assists with the majority of my readings."

"She's no joke. Stern. Stands tall. Somewhat serious, but yet full of love for you. She feels like a schoolteacher, headmaster of like a boarding school and shit. Long dress. Hair pinned up. She was your teacher in a past life. She promised to come back and help you in this life."

I said, "Yes, that's what I get, too! You know, I usually just see silhouettes of them, never their full details. Never really in 3-D, I hear and feel more."

Melissa said, "Edna is saying that in your next level of development you will be able to see her more. You are growing and still in the early stages of your gift. More things will come if you release the fear. You have a big mission they choose you for." She was silent for a minute. "Wow, that's beautiful. So beautiful."

"What's that?" I asked.

"Edna said, 'You teach people how to fly when they didn't even know they had wings. You remove the veils from their eyes with your readings. You will get even better and beyond your wildest dreams. TV, newspapers, magazines, you name it.'"

"Wow, I don't know about all of that." Suddenly, I felt a heavy weight of responsibility on my shoulders. I didn't want it. I was already overwhelmed with the clients who were waiting on me. To be known worldwide frightened me.

"Everything you touch will turn to gold. That's what your father told you. Get ready, Jacques. Don't look like I just gave you bad news. I'm so excited for you!"

"It just feels like . . . a lot." My nose crinkled.

"Well, it is; get ready, you have a lot of people to teach how to fly. To embrace their higher selves. No time to live small. Use *your* wings. Use your wings, Jacques."

"I will, Melissa, I will. . . . It seems if I don't Edna is gonna come for me."

"You better know it! Spirit guides are always watching." We laughed.

Acknowledgments

First off I want to thank *you*! Yes, you . . . the amazing person holding this book. (Well, if you're old school like me . . . your tablet or cell phone for you modern folks. ☺) Thank you for reading, smiling, laughing, and maybe crying. Did you cry? Okay, okay . . . don't worry, I won't tell. I'm so happy to have you in my family and hope you are ready for plenty more adventures coming from my pen (yes, pen . . . I told you I was old school).

I want to send out a heartfelt thanks to my editor, Rachel Kahan—the first editor to inspire and mentor me. Thanks for seeing my strengths as a writer. I'm learning so much from you! You have been such a joy to work with and I look forward to writing many more books with your help! I'd like to also give a big shout-out to her lovely editorial assistant, Amber Oliver, for helping us create magic! I'm so happy to be working with such a talented crew at William Morrow/HarperCollins.

Special thanks to my new agent, Wendy Sherman. I'm looking forward to loads of exciting projects in the near future. Let's do thissss!

Thank you to all of my friends, family, and supporters!

My dad, bestie, and first playmate, Frank Kelly! You were the one who showed me the power of my imagination when we would record short stories for hours on my tape recorder. Thanks for playing with me, Daddy! Like Mommy said, you're a giant kid and I'm just like you. You created a monster. Ha! To my big brother, Mark Kelly . . . you are amazing and I love you. If you're reading this, that means you made it through without passing out. Great job! Now go get some holy water and rinse out your eyes.

Shout out to the entire Kelly and Gordon families, even though many of them will cover their eyes while reading . . . It's okay, this is a *work of fiction*, really it is! Aunt Madge aka Madge King, for the last time, I did not do *everything* in the book . . . maybe some things, but *you'll* never know. ~evil laugh~ Can't a girl have a wild imagination? Give me some credit as a writer, sheesh! Patrice Kelly-Palmer, Samara King, Danielle King, Diane Lee, and Cherisse Gardner Sexton—I loooooove you, cousins . . . thanks for always bragging about me like I'm famous and stuff!

Much love to the entire Own Your Power Communications Inc. team, who sticks by my side to keep our network going to inspire thousands worldwide with personal and business development. Sheila Hawkins, Patricia Lawrence Kolaras; Laron Henderson, Jenay Paulling, Melissa "Moon-child" Stokes, Ru McKenzie, Trent Partridge, Metris Batts, and Dyana Chapman—you guys *rock*! My incredible graphic designers, Dania Gonzalez and Adam Old. My cohost for the Own Your Power Lifestyle show and handsome "PR Brother from the Bronx," German Dubois. I love all of your hilarious stories and great one-liners. Hicham thanks you, too! Ha! My other cohost, Isaiah Martin aka Zay Live—thank you for the bellyaching laughs and support . . . but for the last time, noooooo, you can't play Jacques in the movie! Big hug to all of my loyal and loving clients across the country who keep my lights on. Make sure you do your homework!

Special thanks to my partner, Tru Town Productions: Stan Harris, who is behind making my dreams come true with Own Your Power Radio and Own Your Power TV.

My fabulous Miami attorneys, Marlon Hill and Myriam Louis, who don't miss a beat!

Dr. Antonia Martinez, who was my very first intuitive teacher to blow my mind and show me the power of intuition with some fun meditation exercises. And I couldn't do a lot of what I'm doing now if it weren't for the training and loving support from my adopted mom, Johanne Rutledge of the Johanne Rutledge School of Intuition. You two powerhouses opened up a whole new world for me and I'm so happy I can teach others as well just how much POWER they have! We're superheroes who are changing the world. . . . Shhhh, it's our little secret. ☺

Tony Leroy (the man, the myth, the legend, and the intuitive), who allowed me to pick his brain for hours for ideas—love you for life, man! Deena Collins, how I loved interviewing you about your childhood psychic experiences as well. Florence Delvaille, who I always refer to as "a living angel"—I love your gentle soul and thank you for your childhood stories of living in France to help develop Marguerite! Melissa Cancio—you are my sister, my friend, and you really helped me keep my head up and stay focused during the tough times. Thanks for your patience and inspiration. This is the "good part of the movie" for real!

To my writing buddies, for all of their enlightening feedback; Ayesha Gallion, Ophira Edut, Pittershawn Palmer, and Nikki Clifton, who were there from the very beginning of this book; E. Claudette Freeman, my amazing literary coach who pulled out deep characters I didn't even know I had in me; Aisha Altidor for her marketing magic; and Dr. William Ashanti Hobbs. Margot Lee Shetterly aka the "Mad Scientist," what I called you in our HBO days working together. You were hard-working then and I'm so proud of your achievements now. No coincidence we're working with the same editor and signed to same publishing house . . . *Who knew?* You are a trailblazer and I look forward to being in your shoes someday! Cydney Rax, one of my first author buds who offered me words of wisdom. And I am forever grateful to my first writing teacher, Nelly Rosario, and the Frederick Douglass Creative Arts Center, whose writing program truly changed my life.

Oh, I can't forget, Tesha Sylvester . . . my Realtor friend; you're no author, but I think you missed your calling as an editor!

Kim Lindstrom—my bestie for life and one of the first to encourage me to keep writing. Monica Gonzalez, my Florida partner in crime, thanks for listening to me babble about my story ideas and for your lifesaving yoga class. I hit the jackpot with you!

Hisham Elkoustaf, Dara Boudal, and Atossa Kia, who helped me learn a lot about Moroccan culture; my homie for life Michael Petaja aka Mike P; my mentor aka personal guru/sage (she hates when I call her that but it's true) Valerie Crawford; and Will Brown and Pat Mosera, for helping me with all of the fun detective information to develop Vince.

My Cultural Expressions family and the dedicated founder aka *my teachaaaa* Sofiyah, who gave me a new home and community to release tension . . . now I can belly dance to my heart's content because of you!

Alexi "Dr. Al" Martinez and Kay Taylor from Massage and Unwind, you guys are my weekly escape to heaven. After I spend hours sitting and writing, you get those kinks out every time! To my acupuncturist, Dr. Adeila Molina, you are a miracle worker. Thanks for keeping me balanced.

Giovanna Henson, for being my friend, client, and founder of Hotel GiGi, my home during my many book tour and business trips. Khadijah Karriem, Michelle Smith, Sharice Chasi, and Sakinah Karriem, for your hilarious stories and Southern hospitality when I come to Dallas.

But wait there's more . . . Hasan Brown, DeAnne Connolly Graham, Sean "Nat" Nelson, Tracy Grant, Delilah Garcia, Jasmine Pugh, Rosalie Khan, Hyacinth Henderson, Conchita Pleasant, Sky Maduro, Tamara and Errol Archer,

Robert Carter, Jennifer Morgan, Yahzarah, Thanit Fernando, Crystal Lacey Winslow, Cleaster Cotton, Ayanna Cook, Common Links and Pink Pages book clubs in Dallas, CJ Staples, Tamisa Covington, Zya Moses, Sophronia Scott, David Williams, Andrew Morrison, Anthony Ortiz, Carlos Gonzalez, Marjorie Raymore, Leilla Blackwell, Donna Hill, Kenya Spencer, Keyona Saquile Lazenby, and Miguel Munoz.

To my style team: Simone and Trudy Hylton of Natural Trendsetters, Aguy Smith, Allison McKenzie, and Greg Gibbs.

And finally a gigantic hug to my beta readers family on Facebook . . . you guys are so patient and your feedback is what keeps me going. Get ready for the next book. . . . It's coming!

Peace and blessings to you all.

About the author

About the book

Insights,
Interviews
& More . . .

Meet Simone Kelly

Gregg Gibbs

Born and raised in the Bronx, SIMONE KELLY is an author, Internet radio host and producer, life coach, and promotional entrepreneur. She successfully climbed the American corporate ladder by holding various positions in the marketing divisions of companies such as RCA Records and BMG Entertainment. Her career led her to become a director at HBO's Volume.com, where she managed their lifestyle and community programming. Eager to become a full-time entrepreneur, Simone decided to branch out of her comfort zone in corporate America and begin a journey of coaching others. She is now the CEO of Own Your Power Communications, Inc., a company that coaches entrepreneurs and executives looking to boost their networks and skill sets. She also focuses on being their guide to personal development. Simone also trains groups and individuals on how to develop their intuition to improve their lives. She lives and works in the Fort Lauderdale and Miami areas, making frequent return trips to visit clients in her hometown of New York City. ∼

Reading Group Guide

1. Do you believe that Jacques's intuitive powers are real? Did this novel change your perception of psychics and mediums?

2. "It was as if Paulette Collins never existed and 'True' is her new truth in America." True created a different persona once she got to America, eager to forget her past and start her life anew. What do you make of her decision? Does she successfully escape her past?

3. Will knowing the truth about her father change Kylie's relationship with True? Do you think that they will finally achieve the mother-daughter relationship she has always wanted?

4. What do you think about Hicham and his playboy persona? Why are he and Jacques so different?

5. Did your feelings about Jacques's mother and father change as the different pieces of their story came to light? How does Jacques feel about each parent at the end of the book, when he's finally put everything together?

6. Jacques says that he doesn't believe in coincidence; do you think the blackout was a coincidence? How did it change things for Jacques and

Kylie? What about for the other people who were there?

7. "We hugged one last time. My chest tightened as I sat in my car. He looked at me with a downturned mouth and his shoulders pulled low. I let out a heavy sigh and started the engine, feeling like I'd finally closed that chapter for good." Why has Kylie kept Breeze in her life for so long? Who do you think she will end up with?

8. Jacques's medium friend Melissa predicts: "You remove the veils from their eyes with your readings. You will get even better and beyond your wildest dreams. TV, newspapers, magazines, you name it." What do you think is in store for Jacques now that he knows how much support is behind him?

9. If you had Jacques's intuitive abilities, how would you use them? ∼

A Conversation with Simone Kelly

Q: *A lot of readers are curious about Jacques's intuitive powers. Is that a real thing? Are there a lot of folks like him in the world?*

A: Absolutely! It's a gift we *all* possess, but many are taught to be afraid of the messages they receive in dreams, of voices they may hear, or just of a feeling they can't put their finger on. Intuition is a superpower that needs to be honored more. It can be as simple as singing a song in your head and you turn on the radio and *boom*! There it is. Or you're thinking about someone and *boom*! They call you. It's not magic, you were just in tune with the universe at that moment.

Q: *What advice would you give readers who are wondering if they're intuitive or who want to seek out an intuitive to help them gain clarity in their lives?*

A: Start by meditating daily. If you are always ripping and running and never take some sacred time in the day to get grounded and be still, it will be a challenge to tap in. Know thyself. There are so many free guided meditations on YouTube you can use to help you. Start journaling daily on how you feel, and maybe even documenting any psychic occurrences or coincidences that happen, so you can be more aware and not blow things off. Start reading about developing your abilities. Some of my favorite authors on the subject are Echo Bodine, John Holland, James Van Praagh, and Doreen Virtue.

Then look into any intuitive teachers or schools that can help you with developing your abilities further. I've had amazing mentors over the years, and without their guidance, I wouldn't be teaching what I know now to help others. I currently train students all over the world with my Discover Your Intuition courses.

Q: How did you come to write this book?

A: I came up with the idea for this book many years ago—around 2004 to be exact. However, I kept procrastinating on it. It was originally going to be a spin-off from my first fiction book, *At Second Glance*. In that novel, Dee Johnson (who you know from this book) saw a psychic named Brother Miguel. I was going to write a book about a psychic who abuses his abilities to manipulate his clients and becomes obsessed with one of them. I eventually decided to change his name and not make it so dark. I turned him into an irresistible good guy instead, who you now know as Jacques Berradi.

My goal was not only to tell a story with colorful characters but also to help demystify the whole idea of being intuitive. Most of pop culture puts psychics in the box of freaks, weirdos, and con artists. I wanted to show that this world is not all about demons, ▶

ghosts, and terror—but about how you can use your gifts in your daily life. I wanted people to understand Jacques, get to know him and identify with him.

Q: Do you think of yourself primarily as a writer or a businesswoman or an intuitive counselor? Or are all three tied up with each other?

A: In 2007, I started training in many metaphysical subjects and advanced to the point where I was able to combine my intuitive gifts with my business and life coaching, so I'm a hybrid of sorts: I am a business woman, a coach, and an author, and I use my intuition in all these facets.

Q: Will you be continuing Kylie's and Jacques's adventures? What's next for them?

A: I'd say it's just the beginning of their adventures! Jacques is going to develop even more abilities and will work closely with the Like a Fly on the Wall team on many cases. Kylie's passion to learn and excel as a P.I. will be a journey in itself as she learns the ropes.

The supernatural ride I plan to take everyone on will explore everything from past lives, remote viewing, dreams, other dimensions, and much more. Oh, and of course things continue to heat up in their lives, so get ready! ∿

Living the Intuitive Life: An Essay by Simone Kelly

There is a superpower that we all need to take advantage of, but many of us are asleep and unaware of this skill that we have access to 24/7. What is this superpower you ask? It's intuition, that *feeling* you get in your gut—you know, the one that warns you or even gives you confirmation about something amazing that's about to take place. It's that voice in your head that might tell you to exit the highway now, and you discover later that you avoided a major car accident a mile ahead. It's our innate defense system that sends us little nudges of what to do next.

Think about it . . . when we were in the jungles, fields, and mountains as primitive humans we were in touch with our senses. We could smell fear. We knew where to go for food. Somewhere along the line in our "evolution" we were taught to not listen to our intuition or even to be afraid of it. Many religions call intuition or psychic abilities "witchcraft" or "evil" or ascribe it to only certain people, when in actuality we all have it. The truth is, you don't have to open up a psychic storefront with a crystal ball in order to be intuitive.

As we learned early on in *Like a Fly on the Wall*, Jacques just thought he was good with people as a teen. He was a magnet for people; they always came ▶

Living the Intuitive Life: An Essay by Simone Kelly *(continued)*

to him for advice or wanted to share their deepest secrets with him. He was fascinated with psychology and even majored in it at school. Unfortunately, like many of us, he blocked out a lot of memories of his psychic experiences. He began to interpret his dreams as just silly nightmares or wild imaginings. As children, many of us were told we were just making things up or just trying to get attention. We might have started to believe it and so we lost touch with our inner self. Or even worse, we knew we weren't crazy and that we did really see what we saw, but we kept it to ourselves because we feared disapproval or being called a freak.

In the past ten years, I've seen a new world unfold for myself when I started following my gut. *Things open up for you.* Doors that were closed fly open. I've seen it happen for not only myself but also my friends and others I've trained in intuition development. Life becomes easier, because we are listening to the messages from our spirit, God, the Universe, our higher power, whatever you want to call it.

Once you become more in tune with who you are, you'll pay attention to your patterns and live life with *eyes wide open* . . . meaning opening your third eye as well, the one that represents your intuition. Jacques is like many other intuitives out there, who finally embraced his gift and made it his life's work.

You can start to use your intuition more in your daily life by paying attention to the messages you receive. I like to call these messages intuitive triggers.

Here are a few I would like to share:

- **Goose bumps:** This is definitely one of my top triggers! Usually after I say something that is spot-on, I get goose bumps. For me it's a good trigger, a confirmation. For you it might mean something else.

- **Stomach or "gut" reaction:** Squirming, butterflies, churning, there are all types of feelings you might get in your belly. Pay attention! Your gut is trying to tell you something.

- **Voice in your head:** You might hear your own voice, you might hear your mother's voice, etc. But take note of the messages you receive. Just don't answer back out loud, or folks might look at you funny!

- **Dreams:** If you have vivid dreams, keep a notebook by your bedside and write them down the second you wake up, before you forget the key elements. You know by the time you brush your teeth—*poof!* It's gone. So write it down right away. There are loads of dream dictionaries online. Start ▶

Living the Intuitive Life: An Essay by Simone Kelly *(continued)*

looking up the meanings and get familiar with them. Before you know it, you'll be able to interpret your own dreams very easily.

- **Other people's energy:** Take notice of how you feel when speaking with someone. Their body language, eye contact, or lack thereof. Come on, we usually know when someone isn't who they say they are or when they seem kind of shifty! (Always ask yourself, "Do I like, trust, and respect this person?" If you answer no to any of those things, be careful!)

As a writer, I always use my intuition. I get hunches about what to write, and even about who to interview for certain characters. It's as if the characters come alive, they speak to me and ask to be heard. It comes very naturally for me, and it's almost as if they are real and I'm channeling them. When you write fiction, at times you zone out and the pen just begins to flow as the characters take on a life of their own. Usually when I get that hunch about a new character or a scene, I will get the trigger of goose bumps. If it's really good, I get them even on my scalp and down my legs! In the early development of this book, coincidences and my dreams were big indicators for me. When I constantly get signs, I follow them and dig deeper into why I'm getting them.

I'll share a little secret with you. A

coincidence surrounding my book that still blows me away is one having to do with who was going to be Jacques and his sidekick. First off, Jacques's character was inspired by the movie *Unfaithful*. I thought the main character, who had a French accent, was sexy, and I thought it would be cool to have a character with a mixed background who had a slight accent. That same week, I saw a billboard ad at a construction site with the name Kylie Minogue on it. I thought, *Hmmm . . . Kylie. I like that name a lot. I'll name my character that.*

The twilight-zone moment happened when I researched the actor who played the *Unfaithful* character. His name is Olivier Martinez (does that first name sound familiar to ya?) and I saw that his father was from Morocco. Then, in his biography at the time it said he was dating KYLIE MINOGUE. *I almost passed out.* I'm mean, come ooooon . . . What are the odds? When things like that happen, that is a sign you're onto something. Keep going.

As the book progressed, I would be at a party, meeting a random person, and he or she would be Moroccan and French (the exact heritage I gave Jacques). I took a Bikram yoga class and my handsome teacher had us all drooling with his sexy accent and his carved physique. When I asked him where he was from he said, "Oh, I am Moroccan and French." [Insert *Twilight Zone* music] When God winks at you, ▶

**Living the Intuitive Life: An Essay by
Simone Kelly** *(continued)*

take the hint. That's when I knew, *I had
to write this book*. It was as if I heard the
voice in my head say, "You're onto
something, Simone! Go. Go. GO!"

Something as simple as moving the
supermarket scene to the front of the
book was inspired by a hunch. Instead
of appearing a few chapters further in,
where it originally was, that frisky and
unpredictable scene inserted at the
beginning likely made many people
inclined to read further.

In my coaching career, I use my
intuition in all that I do. In business
coaching, life coaching, and for the
past ten years, my most popular service
has been my intuitive life coaching.
I promise that if you develop this
superpower you will be on your way
to an amazing life. Explore, learn, read,
study, take courses, but most of all,
honor and discover your intuition! ～